WEDDING NIGHT

"Jesse," she said, interrupting. [illegible]

"What?"

"Not now. Please. I kn[illegible]ng and all, but I can't th[illegible] First I've got to get thr[illegible]

"What the hell[illegible] anything?"

She lowered her[illegible] Somehow it was easier to stare at his [illegible] face the anger in his expression. "We're mar[illegible] and tonight . . . well . . ." She motioned to the bag in his hand. "You're taking me upstairs. I haven't done this before. Of course I haven't, I've never been married. I didn't want to lie when I took my vows, so I mean to try and keep some of them. Not the death till us part one, but the others. So if you planned to, well, Mama said it wasn't horrible and Augusta said it was wonderful, and I, well, I'm your wife. I wouldn't refuse you."

By the end of her speech, her voice was barely a whisper. She continued to stare at the center of his chest, noting the exact moment it stopped moving, then expanded suddenly as if he'd sucked in a breath. He dropped his hold on her arm as if he'd been burned.

"I'm sure as hell not going to bed you," he said curtly.

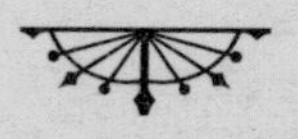

By Susan Macias

Fire in the Dark
Honeysuckle DeVine

Available from HarperPaperbacks

Honeysuckle DeVine

SUSAN MACIAS

HarperPaperbacks
A Division of HarperCollins*Publishers*

This is a work of fiction. The characters, incidents, and dialogues are products of the author's imagination and are not to be construed as real. Any resemblance to actual events or persons, living or dead, is entirely coincidental.

HarperPaperbacks *A Division of* HarperCollins*Publishers*
10 East 53rd Street, New York, N.Y. 10022

Cover illustration by Aleta Jenks

First printing: February 1996

Printed in the United States of America

HarperPaperbacks, HarperMonogram, and colophon are trademarks of HarperCollins*Publishers*

❖ 10 9 8 7 6 5 4 3 2 1

To Charlie Sheen—an incredibly sexy and talented actor. To me, you'll always be Jesse. Don't let the demons win.

Honeysuckle DeVine

Texas—1872

Every couple of months the ladies in town decided that Jesse Travers needed reforming. They sent one or two women out, usually escorted by an excited teenage boy who hoped to get a chance to ask Jesse what had really happened during the war. One time a blotchy-faced fifteen-year-old had found him in the barn and dared to ask. Jesse stared at the kid for a long time. Long enough to make the boy swallow and regret his boldness.

Finally Jesse walked over, grabbed the kid by the shirtfront and shook him like a dog. "We lost, you wet-nosed little shit. What do you think happened?"

After that incident, the ladies had stopped coming. People had stopped greeting him in town and his life had returned to the blessed sameness that was broken only by the changing seasons.

Until today.

Jesse stared at the small wagon approaching his spread. He squinted against the bright sun, then brought his hand up to shield his eyes. Sure enough. The single horse was driven by a young woman dressed in her Sunday best. He tried to see if there was someone else in the wagon, someone to provide protection against him and his ill temper. He knew what folks said when they spoke about him.

"He was such a sweet boy when he was young. So charming, and quite a success with the ladies. But now . . ." Then they sighed and shook their heads.

Jesse had heard the whispers and the sighs. He didn't remember being young or carefree. He supposed it was true. He hadn't been born old and hardened. It was the war—too much death had a way of changing a man.

Jesse turned away from the approaching wagon and urged his horse to continue toward the house. He would intercept the woman there, listen to what she had to say, then send her on her way. He didn't know why anyone gave a damn about how he spent his life. So what if he didn't go to church or attend the town socials? He had no need of a companion and no intention of marrying. He bought his supplies in town, paid in cash and never got drunk enough to be a problem. All he wanted was to be left alone.

He neared the house about the same time the wagon did. Jesse glanced at the driver. A large-brimmed hat hid most of her face. He could see her gold-blond hair and the slender length of her neck. A blue dress hugged her chest. He supposed her curves were pleasing enough. He stared at her breasts, at the way they rose and fell with each breath, and he felt nothing. While his brain acknowledged the woman's femininity, his body remained numb. All he wanted was for her to go away and leave him be.

She drew her horse to a stop and set the brake, then

secured the reins. Only then did she tilt her head slightly and glance at him. "Good afternoon, Mr. Travers." She waited a moment. "Do you know who I am?"

He narrowed his gaze. Large blue eyes stared at him, her full mouth drew up slightly at the corners. In the back of his mind something flickered. He imagined her without the hat, standing instead of sitting, a large white apron engulfing her slight form.

"You're one of the Cannon girls. Your father owns the general store."

"That's right. I'm Laura."

She smiled—brilliantly. There was no other word to describe it. Jesse blinked. Her lips parted exposing small white teeth. A dimple formed in her cheek. She was pleased that he'd remembered. For the life of him he couldn't figure out why that mattered.

"I'm not interested in the church social," he said gruffly. "Or the harvest dance, or any of those damn things."

"Good." Her smile widened. She moved to the edge of the wagon's seat and paused expectantly. "Because I'm not here about them."

Jesse stared at her. She wanted something from him. She might be all smiling and friendly, but her hands hadn't been still since the moment she arrived. Right now she was pulling off her gloves and twisting them. If she kept that up much longer, she was going to rip the leather right in two. She wanted something all right, and she was afraid of what he would do when he found out what it was.

She also expected him to help her off her wagon. Jesse dismounted slowly and tied his horse to the post in front of the house. He walked over to the woman. He had to tilt his head back some to see her face. The wide brim of her hat cast shadows on her forehead and eyes. Her skin was pale. A wide blue ribbon was tied under her chin. There were little lace ruffles around her collar and cuffs.

He became aware of his own appearance. Dusty chaps covered worn trousers, his boots were scuffed and his shirt was two days overdue for a washing. Without wanting to, he reached up and rubbed his left cheek. Beneath the beard he could feel the long ridge of his scar.

"What do you want?" he asked.

"To talk to you." She drew in a deep breath, then grabbed the back of the wagon seat with one hand and the side of the seat with the other. Half-rising, she started to turn as if she was going to step down herself.

Jesse swore and moved closer to her. "You'll break your fool neck. If you're that determined to get down, I'll help you."

He grabbed her around the waist. The warmth of her surprised him, as did the smooth wool of her dress, so different from the scratchy cloth of his trousers. He could feel the stiff boning of her corset and the faint softness underneath that could only be her feminine form.

He wanted to jerk his hands back as if he'd been burned. Instead he lifted her to the ground, then quickly stepped away. His hands still tingled. He rubbed them against his chaps. The whores he frequented required little contact. How long had it been since he'd been near a decent woman? Nine years? No, ten, if he didn't count the hug he'd given his mother six years ago when he'd healed enough to leave his family and return to Texas. Ten years. What the hell had happened to him in all that time? How had he ended up like this, living like some dried-up old rattler, wanting to bite everyone who was stupid enough to come close?

"You're not married are you, Mr. Travers?" Laura asked, smoothing her skirt in place.

"Hell, no. Why'd you want to know that?"

"No reason except I would want to pay my respects to your wife." She set her gloves on the wagon seat, then picked up her reticule and looked at him. "I have some business to discuss with you, if you have a moment."

She made him uncomfortable, this townish miss in her Sunday church dress. "I'm busy right now."

"Are you?"

She glanced around at the front of his house, which needed painting, and the weed-covered dirt that had been his mother's flower garden before the family had packed up and returned to Ohio.

"This won't take long," Laura promised. She looked at his horse, then at him. "Perhaps we could discuss this inside."

"Why?"

She bit down on her lower lip. Her hands laced together, then separated. "Mr. Travers, I have need of your services and I'm willing to pay you. However I would prefer to discuss the situation privately, if you don't mind."

"I do mind. I don't have time to help you, Miss Cannon. I've got a cattle drive starting in the next couple of weeks. Now if you'll excuse me." He took a step toward his horse.

"Mr. Travers, I want to discuss the cattle drive."

"You got steers you want driven north?"

"Not exactly."

"Then what?"

A single strand of hair drifted free of the tight bun at the back of her neck. The golden curl settled against her cheek. She brushed it back impatiently. "Can we *please* talk about this inside? I don't want anyone to see me here."

"Your reputation will be in better condition if we're seen talking in front of my house than inside it."

"Perhaps," she said, lifting her skirt and starting around the building. "But if you refuse me, I would rather no one know I was here at all. If my parents find out what I'm up to, I won't have a prayer of making it work out. And then I'll be stuck here, probably forever. I assume you use the back door?"

The question was tossed over her shoulder as she climbed the porch steps. Jesse hurried after her, taking the three stairs in one long stride and grabbing the door handle a half-second before she did. He didn't open the door.

"What are you going on about?" he asked.

"I told you. A business arrangement. Nothing more."

Jesse was willing to admit what he knew about women could fit in a coffee cup and still leave room for a mug full of brew. But he knew trouble when he saw it.

"Mr. Travers, *please*."

She didn't beg. There was too much starch in her spine for that, but her big blue eyes widened slightly and she swayed toward him a little. He'd spent a long time on his own, but his mama had trained him well while he'd been a child. A man didn't leave a lady in distress. No matter how much he wanted to.

Grudgingly he opened the door and motioned for her to precede him. She stepped past him through the mud room and on into the kitchen. Once there, she paused and looked around.

He let the door slam shut behind him, but she didn't even have the good sense to jump. She just stood there gawking. He hung his hat on the peg by the door and stepped in behind her.

"It's very nice," she said at last.

"What were you expecting?"

She turned to face him. "My brothers would starve on their own. They're fine men, but useless in a kitchen.

I was curious as to how you were getting on, what with not having a wife to take care of you."

Jesse looked around the large kitchen trying to see it as a stranger would. The home had been built for a family, so he had more space than he needed. Rather than bother with cupboards, he kept the few dishes and cooking pots he used out on the counter. A table and six chairs had been pushed up against the wall, under the wide curtainless window. Sunlight streamed into the room. Everything was clean, if not tidy. He swept the floor regularly and ate with the men as often as possible. But if he had to, he could feed himself.

"I have no use for a housekeeper," he said flatly. Better women than her had already tried that with him.

She smiled again. This time he was ready for the brilliance. "Good. I wasn't interested in being yours. Staying in Jackson Springs and taking care of a man is the last thing I want to do."

"So why are you here?"

She touched the straight-backed chair by the table. "May I?"

He didn't like the idea of her sitting. But before he could say anything, she was already settling herself on the seat and smoothing her wide skirt.

"I'm not offering you anything to eat or drink," he said. "Don't get it in your mind that this is a social call."

"Oh, never that," she agreed, pleasantly. "Purely business." She cleared her throat. "Although the trip out was a little dry. Perhaps just some water, if it's not too much trouble."

When he didn't move, she cleared her throat again, then gave a little cough. "Never mind. I'll be fine."

She was playing him the way he played the steers. Getting them to head north, all the while convincing them it was their idea to move on in the first place. He didn't know whether to admire her or to simply throw her out on her behind.

He leaned against the counter and folded his arms over his chest. "That clock behind you is two minutes away from striking the hour. When it does, I'm getting back on my horse and heading out to the range. So if you've got something to say, you'd best say it quick."

She looked over her shoulder at the clock, then up at him. "I understand you're going to be taking your herd north to Wichita." When he opened his mouth to speak, she raised her hand. "Please, Mr. Travers, you've given me a limited amount of time to say what I must. To answer your earlier question, no, I don't have any steers to be transported, but I would like to come with you myself."

He studied her, sure that he'd misunderstood. "You want to go on a cattle drive? You? A woman?" Apparently the do-gooders knew better than to show up and disturb his peace. Now they were sending the crazy ones. He pushed off the counter and started for the back door. "You found your way out here. I'm sure you can find your way back to town."

"I'm willing to pay you," she called before he'd left the kitchen. "A lot of money."

"Right." She expected him to believe her?

"Cash," she added.

Cash. He could sure use that. The cattle drive was taking everything he had. He planned to run almost twenty-four hundred head north. It was a big gamble. If he made it, he would have enough money to fix up the outbuildings, buy blooded stock, and ride out several bad years. If he lost too many steers on the way, he wouldn't even be able to pay the cowboys he'd already hired. He'd had no choice but to risk it all, so the thought of a little insurance was tempting. But a woman on a cattle drive?

He walked to the table and stared down at her. She

raised her head and met his gaze. He knew she worked in her parents' general store, but that wouldn't prepare her for a thousand-mile trip north. He grabbed one of her hands. She jumped slightly but didn't pull back. Her skin was soft and white, her fingers long and slender. Pretty hands, but not used to hard work. He released her hand.

"You'd never make it."

"I would. I can drive a wagon, I've been doing it for years. I would keep to myself, I wouldn't be any trouble."

He almost smiled. "Women are born to make trouble. You don't have to try, it just happens."

"Mr. Travers, I have to get to Wichita."

"Why?"

She tossed her head. "That's not important. I know it will be hard, but I'm not afraid."

"You should be." He motioned to the window. "It's not like this land you're used to. It's open and wild. There's renegades and Indians. Have you thought about that, Miss Cannon?" He reached forward and touched her hair at the base of her neck. "You wouldn't like being scalped. If you're lucky, that's the worst they'd do to you."

He'd touched her hair to make a point, but the feel of the soft strands against his fingers shocked him. The golden curls were silky to the touch, yet he could feel the heat of her body. He hadn't realized they were so close. He could inhale her scent—all floral and feminine. He stepped back hastily, suddenly embarrassed, as if he was a young boy who had accidentally stumbled into a room where a woman was dressing.

He shoved his hand in his pocket and retreated to the counter.

"Do you encounter many Indians?" she asked.

"Enough. If it's not them, there's the steers. Men get

killed driving cattle north. There's stampedes, storms, rains, and river crossings. You ever see a man drown?"

She twisted the strings of her reticule. "You're trying to frighten me."

"Frightened is a hell of a lot better than dead."

Laura Cannon raised her head. Determination pulled her mouth straight. "I'm going to Wichita, Mr. Travers. Either with you, or with someone else. I'm offering you cash, which I know you need."

"Where'd you hear that?"

"In town. Some men were talking in the store." She flushed and cleared her throat. "I confess I was eavesdropping. I knew about the cattle drive, so when I heard your name, I listened. They said you're risking everything you have on this. If you make it, you'll be rich. If you don't . . ." Her voice trailed off.

He didn't need reminding. He had to make it. But the money was tempting.

"How much?" he asked.

She stared at him blankly.

"How much money are you willing to pay me?" he asked, speaking slowly.

"How much do you want?"

It was going to cost him nearly five hundred dollars to outfit the cattle drive. If he could count on having at least that much. But that was a lot of money. Laura's family was well-off, but no one in Jackson Springs was rich.

Why did she need to get to Wichita? For a sweetheart who'd promised to marry her? Why did young women travel in the first place? Then he realized it didn't matter. Laura Cannon couldn't pay him enough to make up for the trouble she would cause.

"You can see yourself out," he said, heading toward the back door. He reached for his hat.

"My aunt left me an inheritance," she said quickly.

"I'm going to Wichita to collect it. I'll pay you ten percent of it if you'll let me go with you."

He paused. "Ten percent of what?"

"I'm not sure."

"What?" When he turned, she was directly behind him. "You don't know how much your aunt left you?"

She shook her head. "The letter from the attorney says that it's a sizable estate. I arranged to have the money wired to me in Wichita."

"Why not have it sent here?"

Laura took a step closer to him. The scent of her perfume surrounded him. She smelled of flowers and innocence. Her mouth straightened and her hands clutched at her reticule. "Mr. Travers, isn't it enough that I have the money? Or I'm going to as soon as I get to Wichita? Aunt Laura was quite well-off. She had a big house and servants and she left everything to me. I can pay you whatever you want if you'll just take me with you."

Jesse stared down at the woman. She hadn't answered the question. She wasn't lying, but she wasn't telling him the truth either. "You in some kind of trouble?"

She smiled. "Not yet."

A woman on a cattle trail. He swore under his breath. She would make his life hell. But the money. "Ten percent of a sizable estate or five hundred dollars, whichever is greater."

He expected her to balk, or refuse. Instead she thought for a moment. While she was quiet he noticed her blue dress was the exact color of her eyes. She had thick lashes and a slightly upturned nose. She reminded him of someone.

"Agreed. You'll let me accompany you on your cattle drive to Wichita and when we get there I'll pay you five hundred dollars or ten percent." She held out her hand, then drew it back. "You can't tell my parents about this."

"Why would I? I never see your parents."

"But if you do, you can't tell them about our agreement."

"I've already been to town. I don't plan on going back."

She swallowed. "Surely you have to go back for supplies?"

"My cook takes care of that."

"Fine. Then we have a deal?"

He shook the hand she offered. Her skin was smooth and warm against his callused palm. His fingers surrounded hers. He was careful not to squeeze too tightly. When he released her, she swallowed again, then stared up at him.

"My parents don't know about the inheritance," she said.

"I figured that."

"It's not that I don't want to tell them, or share the money. I plan to wire some as soon as we arrive. It's just that they wouldn't understand. They wouldn't exactly talk me out of leaving town, but they would interfere and make it difficult. I've been trying to get away for such a long time."

She sighed. "It's not that they don't care," she added quickly, as if afraid he would get the wrong idea. "They do. Maybe too much. I'm overwhelmed by their affection." The slight smile faded. "I don't want to hurt them, but I have to do this."

He didn't have any idea what she was talking about. Now that the deal was made, he was already having second thoughts. Still, money was money and if her aunt's estate did turn out to be sizable, he could make a lot more than five hundred dollars.

"I'm sure when you explain it all to your parents they'll understand," he said.

"I hope so."

"I'll send a man to tell you when we'll be heading out. I provide the supplies, but you'll need bedding and any extra food you might want. A cattle drive is three or four months of hell. Don't expect it to be easy."

"I don't. I'm sure it will be interesting." She looked at him, then away, as if there was something more, but she didn't know how to say it.

He waited politely, but she didn't budge. Finally he motioned to the door. "If that's all, Miss Cannon, I need to get back to my cattle."

"There is just one more thing."

He raised his eyebrows. "Yes?"

"My aunt did leave me everything. The will stated it be left to her namesake." She pointed at her chest. "Me. Her favorite niece. Her favorite married niece."

"You're not married."

"I know. To collect the money, I need to be." She stared at him, her gaze strong and direct. "If it wouldn't be too much trouble, I thought we could be married right before we leave on the cattle drive."

Laura was very pleased with herself. She thought she'd said that with just the right amount of casualness. She'd practiced the sentence for days, changing the wording, adjusting her voice. Finally she'd settled on the right phrasing and inflection. If it wouldn't be too much trouble—yes, that was exactly right. If Mr. Travers didn't agree, she wouldn't go with him and he wouldn't get any of her money. If he did agree, they would be married, travel to Wichita together, she would pay him and they would go their separate ways.

She forced herself not to look away, despite the darkness invading his eyes and the slight twitch near the corner of his mouth. She kept her hands still, her chin raised, all the while ignoring the way her legs trembled. That was one advantage of six petticoats. He couldn't know she was so nervous she was about to faint.

"What did you say?" he asked at last.

His voice was low and controlled, with just a hint of steel. She consoled herself with the thought that he wasn't yelling, he wasn't laughing, and he hadn't thrown her out. She'd hoped he would be too shocked to simply walk away from her. She drew in a deep breath and continued with the second part of her prepared speech.

"I know this is a little out of the ordinary, Mr. Travers. I'm simply suggesting a brief marriage of convenience. We'll be married here, before we leave. Once we arrive in Wichita, we'll collect my inheritance, I'll pay you what I owe you, and we'll get a divorce. I'm not coming back here, so we won't ever have to see each other again. It's a very simple plan, I'm sure you'll agree. Except for the ceremony itself, you shouldn't be bothered at all."

"Married?" he said, glaring at her. "Married?"

She retreated a step. She'd hoped he would simply agree to her plan so she didn't have anything more prepared to say to him. "If you think about it for a minute, you'll see it's not such a big thing. You said you don't have a wife and aren't interested in getting one, so it's not as if you're already sweet on someone. I'm certainly not looking for a permanent husband. The ceremony wouldn't have to be large. How long could it take? I know you're busy and all—"

"I don't give a damn about how much time it would take." He bent close and pointed his finger at her. "You're touched in the head, aren't you? You want to marry me so you can run off to Wichita and collect money that probably doesn't even exist. Lady, if you're looking for a way to hide from your family, you'll have to find another man. I'm not desperate enough to throw in with you."

"I'm not making this up." She opened her reticule and drew out a carefully folded letter. "Here. This is what the attorney sent me. The inheritance is real, Mr. Travers. I'm not crazy. All I need to do is get married and find a way to Wichita. Then I swear I'll be on my way. It's a little unconventional, I know, but—"

He took the letter and glanced at it. She held her breath. He was her only hope. She'd made a list of the single men in Jackson Springs and Jesse Travers was the only one who could help her with this. Everyone else either had no reason to leave town, or might actually want to stay married to her.

"Why?" he asked, handing her the letter.

She didn't know if he was asking why him, why arrange to have the money sent to Wichita, or why she was fool enough to come up with the plan in the first place. She decided to answer all three questions.

"I love my family very much," she said. "But I want more than just marriage to someone in town and staring at the same faces for the rest of my life. I want to get away. Travel. Really see the world." There was more to her dream, but she didn't trust him enough to share all of it with him. Perhaps she would tell him later, when they'd left Jackson Springs and there was no turning back. "I've tried to leave before, but my parents always find a way to keep me here. I was going to be a teacher, but Augusta had a baby and Mama needed me in the store." She shook her head. "I'm sure this doesn't make sense to you, but I want to leave Jackson Springs, and now I have the means. I want to go north with you, Mr. Travers. I want to travel with the cattle drive. I'm still willing to pay you. When we arrive in Kansas, I'll be on my way and you'll never have to see me again. I can't see that a temporary marriage changes things all that much."

He looked past her to the window that faced east. From there he could see out over his land to the rolling hills beyond. It was early spring. The trees were just starting to bud, the grasses still more yellow than green.

"If your parents are so determined to keep you here, heading to Wichita isn't going to make a bit of difference. What's to keep them from coming after you?"

She took back her letter and folded it, then tucked the paper into her reticule.

"If I'm married and following my husband north, they won't interfere. Once we've reached Wichita and concluded our business, you can come back without me. I'll send a note explaining everything. If they don't know where I am, how can they follow me?"

He folded his arms over his chest and leaned against the door frame between the kitchen and the mud room. "I don't like this one bit."

"I'll pay you more money."

He glared at her. "I'm not looking for anything but what we agreed on. It's the getting married that I don't like."

"It doesn't have to mean anything."

He grunted, as if he didn't believe her. Laura watched as Jesse Travers decided her fate. Bad enough that she wanted to go on the cattle drive with him, worse that she wanted to marry him. In the time he'd been back in town, he'd made it plain to everyone he wasn't interested in courting or marriage. He'd never called on a lady—not once. Laura's own sister had come visiting when he'd returned and he'd sent her away. Even though they'd been sweet on each other before.

Before. Laura sighed. Before the war. Before everything changed. Jackson Springs had lost its share of young men to the War of Northern Aggression. Her oldest brother, Washington, had gone to fight. He'd returned with only minor injuries. Unlike Jesse.

Laura stared at him. The dark beard hid the scar on his face. She could barely see the long, slim line that stretched across his left cheek. She'd heard he'd been hurt elsewhere, too, although no one was specific about the nature of his wounds. They must have been bad, though. After the surrender, when he'd been released from the northern prison camp, he'd gone to his parents' in Ohio to mend. It had been another two years before he'd returned to Jackson Springs—thin, sober, and silent. Some said he had never come back at all. That the laughing, carefree boy they remembered, was gone forever. In his place was a cold-eyed stranger.

Laura wasn't scared of Jesse. She'd seen him buying penny candy for a child when he'd come into her parents' general store. That same afternoon she'd gotten the first letter from the attorney telling her about her inheritance.

He shifted. "Anything else you've forgotten to tell me?"

Oh, there were lots of things he didn't know. If she told him everything he would refuse to help her, no matter how big the inheritance was. She smiled brightly. "Not really. Of course, you know getting married would require a wedding. Because we'd have to arrange it quickly, it would be small."

"Of course."

The corner of his mouth lifted up, but she didn't think he was smiling. She didn't remember ever seeing Jesse Travers smile. She'd only been ten when he left for the war, and since he'd been back, he hadn't been around very much. He was handsome. She would admit that. Long, dark hair hung past his collar. His brown eyes missed nothing. His nose was a trifle large, his jaw firm, his mouth well shaped.

He had hard features, as if wind had worn away stone. There was nothing gentle about his expression, but she admired the strength in him. His talk of Indians had frightened her, as he'd meant it to, yet she trusted him to keep her safe. Foolishly perhaps, because he didn't seem to like her. She consoled herself with the thought that he would want her alive long enough to claim the money.

"All right," Jesse said at last.

Laura blinked at him. "You'll do it?"

"That's what I said." He reached behind him and grabbed his hat. "Send word when and where you'll be holding the ceremony. I'll be there."

As easily as that? Oh, heavens, she was getting married!

Jesse opened the back door and stepped outside. Laura followed. "I really appreciate this," she said, trailing after him. "I know it's a bit of a bother, but you'll see. Once we get to Wichita, everything will be as it was before. You won't even remember being married."

He didn't answer. He stalked over to his horse, paused and looked at her. "I've got to finish road branding the steers. You can find your own way back to town?"

She nodded.

"Good." He started to mount his horse, then stopped as if waiting for her to leave. "You *are* heading out?"

"Yes." She walked to her wagon. He moved next to her, then placed his hands on her waist and helped her onto the seat. She smiled her thanks. Her head was positively spinning from all that had happened. She was leaving. She was actually going to leave Jackson Springs and do what she'd always dreamed of.

"There's just one more thing," she said, wondering if he would get angry.

Jesse swung up into the saddle. He turned the animal until it was facing her. "I figured there might be."

"My parents." She waited, but he didn't say anything. "They'll, um, want to meet you. This is going to be a little sudden for everyone. So I thought you might come over to see them. You know, to make sure they understand I'll be safe and everything."

"When?"

"Sunday, after church. If that's all right."

"What else?"

He was just sort of staring down at her. She didn't know what he was thinking. Actually, that was probably a good thing. She had a feeling that Jesse didn't like the idea of meeting her family. He was going to like the rest of it even less.

"My sister Augusta will be there," she said quickly. "You know she married someone else."

Jesse drew his eyebrows together. "That's who you look like. You have Gussie's smile."

Laura grinned. "I know, all the girls do. Grandma Cannon says we get it from her. I hope you don't mind . . . about Augusta being married."

"That was a long time ago, Miss Cannon. We were both children. I never wanted her to wait for me."

"You might want to call me Laura. If we're engaged and all."

He nodded. She thought he might have stiffened when she'd used the word "engaged," but it was difficult to tell.

"Anything else?" he asked.

She drew in a deep breath. "Just one more small thing." She twisted the reins around her fingers. "If it's not too much trouble, will you sort of pretend to, ah, well, like me? Not a lot," she added in a rush. "Just enough so my parents don't think we're deceiving them. I know we are. I feel badly about that. I haven't lied to them before."

"What did you have in mind?"

She felt the heat on her cheeks. She knew exactly what she wanted him to say, what she wanted any man to say. That she was beautiful, charming, unique, and the most wonderfully fascinating woman in the world.

But that wasn't likely to happen. She was just plain Laura Cannon. The middle child. Not the prettiest or the brightest or the one most like Mama.

She stared at her lap. "I'm not sure. Just something engaged people say. If it's not too much trouble."

"Anything else?"

She shook her head silently. He was going to turn her down. She could feel it. She wanted too much from him. Maybe if she offered more money or—

"What time on Sunday?" he asked.

She raised her head and stared at him. Happiness filled her, making it difficult to breathe. "You'll do it?"

"I already agreed. I don't go back on my word."

"Is two o'clock all right with you?"

He nodded. "How many people will be there? I don't like crowds."

She thought of the seven Cannon children, Washington and Augusta's respective spouses, the grandchildren, the uncles, and most likely the minister and his wife. She smiled. "No more than usual."

He tipped his hat and rode off. Laura stared after him until he was a small speck on the horizon, then she started for town. She was getting married and she was going to Wichita. At last her adventure was ready to begin.

Jesse headed east, away from the house. He focused on the trail, the steers grazing on the land, the fences that needed replacing while he was gone. He refused to think about the woman or what he'd agreed to. It was done. He needed the money.

He kneed his horse until the animal cantered over the grassy hill. In the shallow valley below, Jesse saw a small house nestled in a grove of trees. Smoke drifted from the chimney and out into the clear afternoon. He rode around back and found Hellcat Harry working on the chuck wagon.

Jesse dismounted and tied his horse to a tree. As he approached, the older man straightened and stared at him. "I don't suppose you've come to gimme a hand, here?"

Jesse grinned. "Nope. Just checking to make sure you'll be ready in time."

Harry reached up and pulled off his tattered black hat. He rubbed his forearm over his bald head, then shoved the hat back in place. "Figures. You always were a lazy son of a bitch, Travers. Makin' an old man like me take care of everything."

"If you don't think you can make the trip, Harry, just say the word. I'll find someone else to cook for the men."

Harry glared at him. His pale-blue eyes narrowed dangerously. "Someone else'd probably poison the whole lot of you before you crossed the county line." He bent over the chuck wagon and tugged on the large square of leather secured underneath. "Nope, it's up to me, same as always. This is our third trip, Travers. I know you and your boys couldn't do it without me."

"That's the first honest thing you've said, old man."

Harry muttered something under his breath. Jesse didn't bother asking what. His friend spent most of his time muttering, mostly about how much the world annoyed him, and how he was the only one who got things done right. They'd been together nearly six years, almost from the first moment Jesse had returned to Jackson Springs. He'd found the old man trying to round up a few mavericks to sell in town. Harry couldn't rope for shit, but he made the best biscuits this side of the Mississippi and could turn the toughest piece of beef into a bowlful of heaven. After tasting his coffee, Jesse had hired him on the spot and the cook had been with him ever since.

"I've been fillin' the spaces between them boards,"

Harry said, pointing at the side of the wagon. "She might float a mite better that way if we hit high water. Last thing we want on this trip is to get everything wet. Or worse."

"Yeah." The "or worse" part would be losing all their supplies. In less time than it took to sneeze, a river could wash away the chuck wagon, leaving the men with no food and no cook.

Jesse stepped around Harry and stared into the back of the empty wagon. Already bags of cornmeal, beans, and coffee had been delivered to the ranch. Jesse believed that good food kept his men alert and strong, so he was willing to buy the best he could. But the chuck wagon didn't have a lot of extra space for luxuries. If they were lucky, nesters would sell them eggs, milk, and butter along the route. A stray steer could provide fresh beef. The chuck wagon also carried the men's bedding during the day, all the cooking utensils and a barrel of water. The sheet of leather strung underneath held spare cooking fuel. A decent cook was the difference between a good trip north and three or four months of hell.

"You getting everything you need?" Jesse asked.

"Just about. I've got me one more trip into town planned before we go."

"Is that for supplies or for a woman?"

Harry rubbed his wrinkled face. Three days worth of gray stubble highlighted the stubborn set of his jaw. "Maybe some of both," he admitted, then winked. "It's gonna be a long time between ladies." He grabbed the side of the wagon and jerked it back and forth. "See. She's about as sound as she can be, boss. Just say when you want to head out and we'll be there."

"Two weeks," Jesse said. "As soon as I know the day, I'll send word."

"I figure ten extra cowboys for the first couple weeks. How many are making the whole trip? Still twelve, countin' you?"

"Not exactly." Jesse didn't want to tell his friend about the new addition to the cattle drive. Hellcat Harry might be the best chuck wagon cook in central Texas, but he wasn't known for keeping his opinions to himself. The old man was sure to give him an earful. Not that he didn't deserve it. He couldn't believe he'd agreed to Laura Cannon's foolish plan. The money be damned, he knew he was going to regret having her along. Still, he'd given his word.

"You hired someone else?"

"Not exactly."

"You fixin' to tell me what exactly, or do I have to see for myself?"

Jesse was tempted not to say anything, but he had to tell Harry. The cook would need to lay in supplies for Laura. She'd promised not to be a bother, but he doubted she would be willing to survive three months on beans and biscuits. They would have to have something extra for her. Harry would know what.

"We're going to have a passenger," he said.

Harry straightened to his full height, which was maybe two inches taller than Laura had been. His shoulders stiffened and he glared at Jesse as if he'd caught him stealing his own cows. "Passenger? On a cattle drive? You crazy, son?"

"Maybe. You know I'm risking everything on this drive. She's willing to pay me a lot of money to take her to Wichita. I can't pass up the insurance. If we make it, then I can use the money to buy another blooded bull. If we don't, her payment will cover the expenses, not to mention your salary."

Harry took off his hat and hit it against his thigh. The afternoon sunlight gleamed off his bald head. Pale-blue eyes peered up at Jesse, as thick gray eyebrows pulled together.

"You're aimin' to bring a *woman* with us?"

Jesse nodded.

Harry stepped close and hit him on the shoulder with his hat. "You're about the sorriest excuse for a trail boss I ever seen. A woman? A *woman?* Hellfire and tarnation, just go ahead and shoot me in the back now, because we're as likely to make it to Kansas with a woman along as we are to find the glories of heaven between the thighs of a whore."

"It won't be so bad," Jesse said.

"Not for you," Harry said, hitting him again, this time against his left ear. "That's 'coz you're not thinking with your head, boy."

Jesse let Harry get away with more than most, but his friend had gone too far. He grabbed the hat. "It's not like that," he said slowly. "She's not for whoring. We're getting married."

He hadn't meant for it to come out like that. Before he could explain, Harry's wizened old face split into a grin. "Well, hell, why didn't you just say so? Married, you sorry old bear. I'll be damned." Harry snatched his hat back and set it on his head. "Don't that just beat all. Married. I never thought I'd see the day. Who's the lucky girl?"

"Laura Cannon. She's one of the—"

Harry put up a hand to stop him. "I know who she is. Works in her pa's store in town. Pretty little thing about yeah high?" He held his palm level with his ear. Jesse nodded. "Nice enough girl." Harry's smile turned sly. "I didn't know you'd gone courting."

"I didn't. She came to me. She's inherited some money from an aunt. It's being sent to Wichita. To collect her inheritance, she has to be married. That's all this is, Harry. A marriage of convenience, nothing more. When we get to Kansas, we're getting the damn thing annulled."

Harry stared at him for a long time. Those pale eyes saw more than they should. It made Jesse nervous. Still he stood his ground until the old man finally turned away.

"A lot can happen on the trail," Harry said at last. He picked up a file and went to work on the corner of the wagon. "In all that time you might be able to convince her you're not so bad. Then maybe she'll stay with you."

"I'm not interested in a wife."

Harry glanced at him over his shoulder. His normal grumpy expression had been replaced with sadness. "Maybe that's because you never had one."

3

Laura hurried to the edge of the porch and stared anxiously down the road. Nothing. It was nearly two. What if Jesse had changed his mind?

Her stomach lurched at the thought. She pressed her hand against her midsection, feeling the stiff boning of the corset underneath. She'd worn her best dress that day, the rose silk. She'd taken the time to curl her hair and had even used a little of the face powder Augusta had secretly given her last Christmas, after making her promise to never tell Mama about it. She knew she looked as nice as she could. She hoped it would be enough to give her the confidence to carry through her plan and chase away any second thoughts Jesse might be having. Theirs was just going to be a marriage of convenience, but she didn't want to give him reason to regret his decision. He was going to be seeing Augusta for the first time in years, and her elder sister was by far the prettiest of the Cannon girls. Would he be heartbroken or had he forgotten the past?

Augusta wasn't the only person Laura worried about. Her parents hadn't been very happy with the news of her impending marriage. She covered her face as she remembered her mother's first question.

"Are you getting married suddenly because you're in the family's way?

Laura's shock had been genuine enough to convince the older woman that wasn't the reason for the speedy nuptials. Her parents had argued with her. They wanted to know why Jesse Travers had courted her in secret. In the end, Laura had prevailed. Her father had been convinced she was in love. Her mother had reluctantly agreed because Laura had hinted she would run off with Jesse unwed. They could, after all, be married in Kansas.

The pain in her mother's gaze had given her pause. The lies were bitter and awkward on her tongue. She hated the deception but didn't know another way to follow her dream.

The front door slammed shut behind her and she jumped.

Augusta strolled over to join her at the railing. "Laura, I haven't seen you this jumpy since the time you decided to surprise Mama by whitewashing the kitchen only to find out you'd gotten the mix all wrong. If I didn't know better, I would say you were worried about your young man not showing up to meet everyone."

"Hush. I am *not* nervous. Jesse will be here." But her straining glance toward the street belied her brave words.

Augusta squeezed her shoulder. "Don't worry. I'm just teasing. Jesse always kept his word. I doubt that's changed."

Laura turned her attention to her sister. Marriage had only added to Augusta's beauty. Her skin was clear and pale, her green eyes serene with contentment.

"You're sure you don't mind?" Laura asked. "I know you and he . . ." Her voice trailed off.

Augusta smiled. "That was a long time ago. The Jesse I knew isn't the same man who came back from the war. I didn't wait for him and when we saw each other again, we both knew it was for the best. I'm glad I'm married to Roger."

Laura had never thought of herself as a dishonest person, but the deceptions of the last few days were starting to weigh on her. She wasn't used to watching everything she said. At least she would be leaving in less than two weeks. The sooner they got on the trail, the sooner she could write and tell her family the truth.

Augusta leaned over the rail and pointed. "Here he comes."

Laura joined her sister. At the far end of the street she could see a lone man on horseback. The sun was bright overhead. She had to shield her eyes as she looked at him. He rode tall and straight in the saddle. Broad shoulders narrowed to a slim waist and hips.

As he neared the house, she felt her heart beat a little faster in her chest. She told herself it was nerves, not the sight of Jesse's handsome face. His beard had been neatly trimmed, his hat rested firmly on his head. She rushed down the stairs, then paused shyly by the hitching rail. He dismounted without saying a word.

"I appreciate this," she murmured, aware of Augusta still on the porch, no doubt watching them with interest. "We're having chicken and ham for supper. Mama's made several pies, but she's worried because the fruit was either canned or dried. It's too early for fresh. You might want to compliment her on the dessert. She's proud of her crust. It's won ribbons at the county fair."

Jesse finished tying his horse, then looked at her. The

corner of his mouth quirked up slightly. "I'll be sure to mention the pies."

Laura twisted her hands together. "I'm babbling, aren't I? I'm a little nervous about all of this." She glanced over her shoulder. Augusta *was* still on the porch. She lowered her voice. "I told them about our getting married and all. So you don't have to worry about that. The wedding's going to be next Saturday. Mama wanted to postpone it, but I knew you'd want to be leaving right away. Oh, I've got my wagon. Maybe you could look at it later and—"

"Hush." He touched her arm.

She didn't know if it was the unexpected command or the warmth of his fingers, but she was shocked into silence.

"I agreed to this and I don't go back on my word. You don't have to keep convincing me. I'll come by next week to look at your wagon and give you a list of supplies you'll need."

"Thank you."

She heard footsteps on the stairs. Augusta joined them. "Hello, Jesse," she said, moving next to him.

"Gussie." Jesse tipped his hat.

Laura stepped back. They looked perfect together. Her beautiful sister with her golden hair and moss-green eyes, Jesse with his strong, hawkish features and dark eyes. Laura felt as if she was intruding on a personal moment, but she couldn't seem to turn away.

"You picked the right sister," Augusta said.

"You think so?" Jesse's face was unreadable.

"Mama has her doubts, but I'm confident Laura will be a good wife for you. She's always longed for adventure and you're just the man to see she gets it." Augusta smiled. "Although I should warn you Laura's been known to act impulsively from time to time."

Jesse looked at Laura over her sister's head. "I've no doubt."

"I'm glad you're better," Augusta added.

Jesse returned his attention to her. The humor in his eyes faded quickly, leaving his expression shuttered.

Laura wasn't sure what her sister was talking about. Before she could ask, Augusta stepped back.

"Laura, take Jesse inside and introduce him properly." Augusta glanced up at him. "I think you'll like our father. He'll be a little gruff at first, at least he was with Roger. But he comes around."

Laura didn't want to give Jesse a chance to have second thoughts so she quickly moved next to him and took his arm. "It won't be so bad." She started up the stairs, pulling him along. "Wellington, my youngest brother, is very excited to have you here. He wants to talk about—"

"The war," Jesse said, interrupting her.

She paused on the porch. "Why would you think that? He's only fourteen. He barely remembers the war. No, he wants to talk about the cattle drive. I think he wants to be a cowboy, but I doubt Pa would approve of that."

As they neared the front door, she could feel Jesse's muscles tensing under her hand. His step didn't falter, yet she sensed he wanted to turn around and leave. She didn't blame him. The sound of conversation spilled out of the house. The uncles had arrived early and drunk. They were arguing about the finer points of horse breeding. May's latest beau was joining them, as was June's best friend.

She glanced up at Jesse. His mouth was a straight line, his jaw set. His eyes held the determination of a man going off to battle. She noticed his black jacket had been recently brushed and his trousers were clean. He'd put on his best clothes for her. Until that moment she hadn't given a moment's thought to what he would be wearing. If he'd ridden up in his dusty trousers and chaps, her parents might have sensed that all was not as it was supposed to be. But he hadn't.

She touched the handle on the front door, then smiled at him. "Thank you," she whispered.

"For what?" he asked, still looking directly in front of him as if waiting for the enemy to attack.

"All of this. I know you don't want to be here, and I appreciate what you're doing. I swear, once we leave Jackson Springs, I won't be a lick of trouble all the way to Kansas."

Jesse thought about pointing out that she would be nothing but trouble, but he couldn't. He couldn't do anything but stare at that damn door. He knew what was inside. The people, the heat, the crush, the bodies pressed too close together. He knew and it terrified him.

He couldn't go inside and he couldn't leave. Behind him he heard Augusta's soft steps on the stairs. "You two going to stand there until summer?"

Laura laughed. "We were just going inside."

He tried to focus on the sound of her laughter. There wasn't much of that in his life, certainly not the female kind. She had a sweet laugh—joyous, as if she'd never been touched by anything evil. Perhaps she hadn't been. Life in Jackson Springs was far from dangerous.

She pushed open the door and stepped inside. Her gentle hold on his arm pulled him along with her. He had a brief impression of a square open area with a staircase. To his left was a dining room. Two teenage girls were setting the table. They looked up and saw him, then leaned toward each other and giggled.

On his right was the parlor filled with people. Men in dark suits, women in bright dresses. So many bodies, he couldn't count them all. So many conversations he couldn't distinguish any one. It was warmer inside, too warm. He felt the first bead of sweat trickle down his back.

Laura said something. He saw her lips move, but he couldn't understand her. Augusta moved in and out of his vision. A teenage boy approached and shook his hand vigorously. Jesse felt as if he was in the grip of some nightmare from which he couldn't awake.

He blinked and the house was gone. In its place was the prison camp. He saw the ragged tents, the half-starved men. He felt the gnawing of his own belly as his body devoured itself to survive. He could hear the orders of the Yankee Captain, and the moans of the dying. There were too many men in too close a space. He couldn't move, couldn't breathe. There was nowhere to run.

He blinked again and the house returned. His stomach growled, but only from his noontime meal being a couple of hours late. The ragged, starved prisoners disappeared, leaving behind Laura's family.

"Jesse?" He stared into Laura's wide blue eyes. "Are you all right?"

He wasn't, but he couldn't tell her that. He thought about just making a run for it. But he'd given his word.

"Fine," he said curtly.

Before she could ask anything else, a tall man with short blond hair approached. He looked like Augusta, so Jesse figured he was one of the brothers.

"Jesse," the man said holding out his hand. "I heard you're going to take on little Laura here. You might want to run off while you still can. She's a nag about keeping clean and doesn't speak civilly until at least noon."

"I do not!" Laura swatted at her brother's arm.

Jesse searched his brain for a name. "I'm not one for

conversation before breakfast myself," he said, taking the other man's hand. "Washington."

Washington grinned. "Come on, I'll introduce you to the kinfolk." A loud burst of laughter filled the room. Washington grimaced. "We're making more than our share of noise today."

Laura didn't let go of Jesse's arm. "I can introduce him," she said.

"Don't be a goose." Her brother gave her a slight push toward the back of the house. "Mama needs you in the kitchen. Jesse wants to be with the men right now. I'm sure a glass of whiskey will go a long way to making his first meeting with Pa bearable."

Laura glanced at him anxiously. "I can stay with you."

Jesse looked at the crowd and swallowed. "Go on. I'll be fine."

"If you're sure." She hovered for a moment, then reached up and kissed his cheek.

He barely felt the soft pressure of her lips on his cheek, but her gesture shocked him. Then he reminded himself they were supposed to be engaged. She wouldn't want her brother to get suspicious.

Washington waited until Laura was gone, then leaned close. "The crowd here a problem for you, Travers? I ask because I saw the look on your face when you came in. We're overwhelming at the best of times, but I know there might be something more bothering you. Because of the war." He shrugged self-consciously. "I still jump at loud noises. Makes me feel like a fool, that's for sure, but there it is."

Jesse stared at the other man, remembering Washington had been as eager as himself to go prove his valor in service for the Confederacy. He wondered if Laura's brother had learned the same lesson he had.

"Maybe if I could meet your family one at a time," he said.

Washington slapped him on the back and grinned. "We can arrange that. Now how about that glass of whiskey to make the whole thing a little easier?"

A half hour later Jesse was back in the entry way watching Laura's relatives chat with each other. True to his word, Washington had singled out his brothers and uncles, Augusta's husband, and Laura's younger sister, May. Jesse had been polite to them, all the while fighting the urge to flee. Now he stood against the wall with his hand grasping the doorknob. He would stay as long as he could, then he would escape outside to breathe.

He hadn't felt so confined since he'd left his parent's house and returned to Texas. When he'd been released from the prison camp in early May 1865, he'd been scrawny and sick. The knife wound in his leg had festered until he'd feared losing the limb. The train ride had passed in a blur of delirium made all the stranger by his traveling north instead of south and west.

While he'd been off fighting, the family had moved from Texas back to Ohio. He'd followed because he'd been too sick to go to Texas on his own.

Even as Laura's family moved around him, he remembered his parents' house. The small rooms, the too many relatives wanting to know how he was doing, the sounds, the smells. He'd been unable to fight the fever and his mother, so he'd stayed until he was well enough to leave. It had taken him almost two years to regain his strength. Two years of nightmares and recollections of war. Not just the battles and the death, but the horror of the camp.

He shook off the memories and tried to relax. The meal was almost ready. He could tell because the women moved between the kitchen and the dining room more quickly. He watched Laura and her sisters flow around the table in some intricate dance. Their colorful skirts billowed, brushing against chairs and walls. They chatted with each other, their voices high-pitched, their laughter frequent.

Laura swept into the dining room and placed a silver tray in the center of the table. She glanced up and saw him, then smiled. He wondered if the cattle drive would be long enough for him to get used to her smile. The brilliance seemed to keep surprising him. She approached him, and he knew exactly what she was thinking. She hoped he was having a fine time with her family, but she was nervous because he hadn't talked with her father yet.

She stopped in front of him. "How is it going?"

He was about one minute from losing his fragile grip on self-control. He wanted to growl that he'd changed his mind, that he didn't care about her damn money, that nothing was worth this. Instead he opened the front door.

"I'm going outside for a bit," he said, keeping his voice calm.

Laura frowned. "Are you leaving?" She glanced over her shoulder. "Is it Augusta?"

"Augusta? What's she got to do with anything?"

"I thought—" Laura folded her arms at her waist. "I was afraid seeing her would be difficult. Roger is here, and her children. I thought you might regret that it wasn't you."

He stepped out onto the porch. Laura followed. He walked to the stairs and stared out toward town. The Cannon home was on the street behind the general store. From here he could see the back of that building, along with the small hotel and one of the saloons.

He avoided coming to town whenever he could because he didn't want to answer questions. He didn't want to have to be polite or try to fit in with a way of life that he no longer remembered. Yet here he was in Laura's house, speaking with her family, about to sit down at her table. The band around his chest was so tight, he felt as if his ribs were going to crack. And she wanted to know if he was still sweet on Augusta.

He moved to his left and perched on the railing. "I'm glad your sister is happy," he said. "I was never going to marry her when I came back from the war. We both knew that."

Laura exhaled audibly. Her arms relaxed to her sides. "I'm glad," she said simply.

He wondered why it mattered to her. Once they got to Kansas she would leave him to do whatever the hell it was that drew her to Wichita in the first place.

He stared at her, at the pretty rose dress and the lacy ruffles on her skirt. He thought about her smiles and easy laughter, at the way she touched the small children in the house and hugged her mother. Laura was as foreign to him as the open ocean. He supposed once he could have fit in with her family, but it was long past. Being with her didn't make him miss that time. Instead he viewed it with the disinterest of a stranger. As if he'd never been anyone else.

"Have my brothers been boring you to death?" she asked, moving closer.

She leaned against the railing next to him. The scent of her drifted to him. She smelled sweet and innocent. He wondered if she knew what she was getting into by going with him.

"We've mostly talked cattle, although your uncles have some peculiar ideas about horseflesh."

She sighed. "I know. Mama's brothers haven't amounted to much. Between the liquor and the women, they never have two cents to rub together. But they're family. Do you miss yours?"

"No."

He thought briefly of his mother's accusing, silent stares and his father's more vocal complaints. His parents had moved to Texas before he was born, but they'd never settled in well. At the first signs of war, they'd started making plans to return to Ohio. Jesse had refused to go with them. He'd run off at sixteen and joined the Southern army.

"I'm sure your mother misses you," she said.

"I've got three brothers. That should keep her occupied."

"But you're the oldest."

The front door opened. Laura glanced up, then paled. Her father stepped out onto the porch. "I wondered where the two of you had gotten to," the older man said.

Jesse moved toward him and held out his hand. "Good afternoon, sir."

Ambrose Cannon was tall and spare, with a shock of gray hair. His blue eyes were kindly, his manner friendly. Jesse wondered if the man would be as open if he knew the truth about what his daughter was planning.

"My wife tells me you want to run off with our Laura. This was very sudden for the both of us."

"Oh, Papa, don't make a scene." Laura stepped between the two men. She leaned against her father, then seemed to realize she should be siding with her intended. She glanced at Jesse and shuffled awkwardly toward him. He offered his arm. She shot him a grateful glance.

Her hands were small and sure as she held onto him. He could feel her individual fingers. If he shifted slightly, she would press against him. He wondered if she was as soft as she looked, if her curves would yield to his touch.

The curiosity surprised him. He avoided the good women in town as much as he could. When the urges threatened to overwhelm him, he took his ease quickly and paid in cash. He never considered doing anything else. But at that moment, with Laura looking up at him hopefully, he realized she was pretty.

"I've made inquiries about you, Travers," Mr. Cannon said gruffly. "Men speak well of you, although you're known for keeping to yourself."

He returned his attention to the older man. "Yes, sir. I don't like crowds."

Mr. Cannon glanced over his shoulder toward the house. "Can't say that I blame you. My wife's brothers would try a saint." He grinned.

Jesse saw Laura had gotten her smile from her father's side of the family, although it lacked the same brilliance on Mr. Cannon.

His humor faded slightly. "Laura's our middle one. The marker between the older children and the youngsters. My wife and I hadn't thought her old enough to think about having babies of her own, but it might be time. Laura seems determined to do this." He glanced at his daughter. "Even without our permission."

Laura flushed. "Papa, I never said that."

"It was what you meant, wasn't it?" her father asked. When she didn't answer, he turned his attention back to Jesse. "I expect you to take care of her, son. She's real special and we don't want anything to happen to her. If you want our blessing to marry, I'll need your word on that."

Laura glanced up at him, obviously horrified by the request. Jesse had told her he kept his word, and he did. No doubt she was imagining being trapped with him forever. He reached up and rubbed the scar on his cheek. Later he would tell her he didn't want her to stay any more than she wanted to. He was doing this for the money and nothing else.

"Pa, you're being silly. Jesse's a good man. He'll take care of me."

"You hush, Laura, this is between us men. If you can't be quiet, then you go on inside."

Laura clutched Jesse's arm more firmly. Jesse nodded. "If I had a daughter like Laura, I would want to know the same thing, Mr. Cannon. For as long as she is with me, I give you my word I'll keep her safe."

Beside him, Laura sighed with relief.

The older man continued to stare at him. Jesse met his gaze steadily. He'd spoken the truth. Once Laura left, she wouldn't be his problem anymore.

Finally her father nodded. "Then we'll see you at the wedding on Saturday. Although if you ask me, I think the two of you should wait." He glanced at his daughter. "You going on a cattle drive is a fool thing."

"I'm looking forward to it," she said. "I want to share in Jesse's work."

"There'll be plenty of it to share. Running a ranch isn't easy."

"I know," Laura answered. "But Mama and Augusta have trained me right. Don't worry, Pa. I'll do you proud."

Her father touched her cheek, then walked to the door. "Your ma said she'd be serving in a few minutes. I suppose the two of you can stay out here privately until then. But don't think you'll be taking her for any long buggy rides between now and Saturday, young man." He opened the front door and stepped inside.

Laura leaned her forehead against his arm. "I'm so embarrassed. Really, I have to apologize for that. I can't understand why he said all those things to you."

"He's your father. What did you think he would do when you told him you were getting married?"

She raised her head. "I guess I didn't think it through. I thought I would tell them I was marrying you, they would be happy and then we would be on our way. I didn't know it was going to be this much trouble." Her blue eyes widened. "I swear it."

"I believe you."

"Really?"

Her mouth parted as she said the word. He noticed her lips were full and only slightly darker than her dress. He caught himself thinking about leaning forward to kiss her, then pulled himself up short. She wasn't for him. No woman was. He couldn't risk caring about anyone. Besides, Laura Cannon didn't want him any more than he wanted her.

"I'll make your excuses after we eat," she said. "You won't have to stay if you don't want to."

He nodded. From behind them, he heard a faint noise. Laura turned toward the sound and grimaced.

"It's just June and her friend, and Wellington," she said. "They're spying on us."

He glanced over his shoulder and saw three pairs of eyes peering through the bushes. "What do they want?"

Laura blushed. "They're waiting to see if we do anything interesting. You know, sparking."

The word took him back to another time. When he'd been a teenager and tasting Augusta's sweet mouth had been all he'd thought of. Those memories felt as if they belonged to another man, or another lifetime.

"I don't know who's the worst of the two," Laura said. "Wellington and June are always in trouble."

"How'd your brothers and sisters get such unusual names?"

Laura leaned against the railing. "The boys are all named after famous generals. The girls are named after the months of their birth." She shrugged. "I'm the plain one in the middle. I was named after Aunt Laura because she was here and helped Mama while I was born. I would have liked a more interesting name, but not a month. I was born in February. That would have been pretty horrible to have to carry around."

"If you hadn't been named after Aunt Laura she might not have left you the money."

Her expression brightened. "You're right. That does sort of make up for being so plain."

Her mouth curved up in a smile. He wanted to tell her she could never be plain, even if she tried, but the words stuck in his throat. Once, when he was young, he'd flirted easily, likening a girl's skin to the moonlight and her lips to the ripest summer berry. Now those phrases had no meaning.

"When my sister and her intended are sparkin' they kiss *all* the time," June's friend whispered loudly.

"Who'd want to kiss dumb old Laura?" Wellington answered. "I bet Mr. Travers doesn't even really like her. He probably prefers them fancy ladies in town. I know I would."

"Brothers," Laura said weakly, as her smile became strained. "Maybe we'd better go in."

Jesse glanced at the three interested faces, then back at Laura. Her fingers twisted together.

"I bet they've never kissed," June said. "I'm gonna go tell Mama."

Jesse couldn't remember the last woman he'd kissed. He supposed it didn't matter how long ago it had been, it was unlikely to be the sort of thing a man forgot how to do. Laura stared at him. Her mouth trembled. It would be simple to tell her he wasn't playing this part anymore. There were plenty of easier ways to earn five hundred dollars. Then he saw the flash of pain in her eyes, and the shadow of her self-doubt. He'd always been a sucker for a lost cause.

"Hell." It was just a kiss. How much trouble could it be? "This'll shut the kid up," he said as he bent his head toward her.

4

Laura had a brief impression of strength and masculinity, then his mouth brushed against hers. The faint contact sent a jolt of awareness clear down to her toes. Jesse's whiskers tickled her skin, her stomach jumped, and her heart fluttered in her chest. She blinked, not quite sure she hadn't imagined the intensity of her reaction.

Jesse raised his head. "I might not have done this in a while, but I do remember the ladies I kissed closed their eyes. Is this some new fangled idea, or am I doing something wrong?"

His voice was soft, a whisper of air that caressed her cheek. She was curious about this man she was to marry. Curious about why he was so quiet and why his eyes were always sad. The children behind them wouldn't be able to hear what he was saying. She tried to remind herself this was for show, so June wouldn't run off and tell their mother that she and Jesse hadn't ever kissed before. Jesse was playing at sparking. So why was it so difficult for her to catch her breath?

"Laura?"

"You're not doing anything wrong," she told him. "I was just surprised is all. You kiss fine."

One corner of his mouth tilted up. It was almost a smile. Laura realized she hadn't seen Jesse smile yet. "Do you have the experience to make that judgment?" he asked.

"I—" Her voice faltered as a heated flush climbed her cheeks. She took a half-step back and ducked her head. "I'm not sure what you're asking. I've kissed a boy or two, but I'm not—" She laced her fingers together in front of her waist and stared at her thumbnails. She wasn't *loose*. Every girl her age had been kissed.

"Is that it?" June asked from her place in the bushes.

"I dunno," Wellington grumbled. "I swear, this is more borin' than bailin' hay. I thought when people kissed it was interestin'."

"Maybe they're not doing it right," June told her brother.

"June, Wellington, where have you two gone off to?"

Their mother's voice cut through the afternoon. Laura heard the children scrambling to their feet.

"We're comin'," Wellington called. "Ain't nothin' gonna happen here." He was still complaining as he walked around to the rear of the house. The two girls with him giggled as they trailed behind.

Laura watched them go, then turned her attention to Jesse. He was staring at her. She stared back. For the first time she noticed his eyes weren't pure brown like she'd thought. There were flecks of gold in his irises. And tiny speckles of green and a lighter brown. Thick lashes and dark eyebrows contrasted with the colors.

He was a handsome man. So handsome that even

though their audience was gone, she didn't want to move away. Her body remembered the jolt she'd felt when he'd kissed her.

"Is June right?" he asked. "Are we doing it wrong? I'm a little out of practice so I'll have to rely on your more recent experiences."

"You're teasing me," Laura said.

He straightened, obviously startled. "I suppose I am."

"Thank you for—" She waved her hand toward the bush her brother and sister had hidden in. "For . . . um . . . kissing me. I know it wasn't part of our agreement."

"It was hardly unpleasant."

"Really?"

"It was just a kiss, Laura." He moved away from her and shoved his hands into his pockets. "Barely that, even."

He turned his back on her and stared out at the town. Laura touched her fingers to her lips.

The front door opened. Her father stuck his head out.

"It's time to eat, you two. So stop your sparking and come join the family."

"Yes, sir," Jesse said. He turned toward her and held out his arm.

Her gaze drifted across his face before settling on his mouth. She wished there was an excuse for them to kiss again. She wanted to know if the tingling awareness she felt was from being nervous or if it had something to do with him. She tucked her hand into the crook of his arm, and he led her to the door, pausing to let her precede him. As they entered the dining room and everyone turned to stare, Laura had the oddest sensation that marriage to Jesse wasn't going to be quite as simple as she'd planned.

* * *

Jesse rode through town and turned left just before the general store. Recent rains had left the streets damp but not too muddy. He could see the Cannon place, and the garden beyond. As he got closer, he heard the sound of voices and laughter. Laura's family was happy and loud—so different from his own family. He thought of the politely stilted conversations that had filled his own childhood, and the silence that echoed in his house now.

June and Wellington ran in circles around a wagon which stood next to the three-story house. Laura's parents sat on the porch talking together. Laura burst through the front door and ran to her mother's side. She said something to the older woman, then grinned and started for the stairs.

Her movements were quick and lively, as if she had an excess of life welling up inside of her. She'd piled her medium blond hair on top of her head, but a few strands fluttered around her face and neck. Her calico dress clung to her chest and waist before flaring out over several petticoats. Graceful arms moved as she spoke to her brother. She didn't simply walk—she danced and skipped and swayed to music only she heard.

Jesse grimaced at his fanciful thoughts. Since leaving the Cannon place two days ago, he'd tried to put Laura out of his mind. More precisely, he'd tried to forget the brief kiss they'd shared. It hadn't been passionate or romantic. They'd had an audience for God's sake. He hadn't even been aroused. But he also hadn't been able to forget.

Even now he could see Laura staring up at him. Her big blue eyes wide with questions, as if she, too, had been ripped apart inside when their mouths touched.

He hadn't expected to feel anything so the sensation had caught him off-guard. It wasn't arousal—it was awareness. Life. A splash of color in his gray world.

He didn't want to feel again. He didn't want to leave his silence. Like a worm caught on a rock after a rainstorm, he might shrivel up and die if left too long in the sun.

His horse tossed its head and the jingling of the bit caught Laura's attention. As always, he knew what she was thinking. Her mouth started to curl up at the corners, then straightened, as if she wasn't completely sure she was glad to see him. She took a step toward him, hesitated, then glanced behind her. When she saw her parents had noticed him as well, she moved forward purposefully.

"Jesse," she said, and smiled.

He squinted at the brilliance. "Afternoon, Laura. I see you have your wagon."

"Do you like it? Roger, Augusta's husband, found it for me. He swears it's sound enough to take me to California and back."

"We're only going as far as Wichita so I'm sure you'll be fine."

She held his horse's bridle while he dismounted. He turned and found her standing closer than he'd thought. Her gaze met his, then slipped away, as if she was embarrassed. He glanced at her parents who were watching them with interest, then at the two children who were climbing in the wagon and jumping around. He had no business involving himself with this family.

"Did you bring a list of supplies?" her father asked as he came down the stairs.

"Yes." Jesse led his horse over to the porch and tied the reins to the railing. Then he reached into his inside jacket pocket and pulled out a sheet of paper. "There's a cook on the trail, but our fare is basic. Mostly beans and biscuits. She'll need some extras, maybe canned vegetables and fruit."

The older man took the list and studied it. "Bedding, blankets. Medicine?" he raised his eyebrows. "Laura, do you know what you're getting yourself into? This isn't an adventure. This is hard, dangerous work. Man's work."

"I know, Papa. I'm not afraid."

She spoke bravely, but Jesse saw the tremor in her hands as she clutched her fingers together in front of her waist. She bit down on her lower lip.

He was torn between wanting to tell her everything would be fine and exposing her plan to her family. Her father was right; a woman had no business being on a cattle drive.

Laura's blue eyes widened, as if she could read his thoughts. "I want to do this," she said, but the comment was directed at him, not her father.

"Foolishness if you ask me," the older man mumbled.

"Jesse?" She spoke his name softly, pleading with him to defend her.

He thought about the money. He thought about how kissing her had made him remember his life before the war and how much those memories hurt. He thought about the brilliance of her smile and the silence in his life. He thought about the sound of her laughter.

"I gave my word," he said to Mr. Cannon, although the statement was really for Laura. He wouldn't go back on what he'd agreed. If she was fool enough to want to go on the cattle drive, he was fool enough to take her.

"I know you did, son, and I'm not saying I doubt you." Her father moved next to her and put his arm around her shoulders. "I'm having second thoughts, Laura, but if this is what you want—"

"It is," she said quickly. "I swear it is."

"Then let's get busy," her father said.

Jesse walked over to the wagon and shook the sides. "Seems sturdy enough. Make sure the cover is a double thickness. That way the dew and rain won't drip inside. She'll need mules to pull it. Sturdy animals are best. We only go ten or twelve miles a day. This isn't a race."

He continued to list the supplies she would need while her father asked questions. Wellington and Laura trailed behind, her mother joining them.

"When are you leaving?" she asked. "The wedding is Saturday."

"Early Monday," he said as he bent down and inspected the wheels. "Just after daybreak."

"I guess you're going to have to sleep on straw," her mother said. "I can sew two sheets together to make a mattress you can stuff. The double bed should fit in the back of the wagon just fine."

Jesse rose to his feet. He looked at Laura who was staring at him, horrified. The color drained from her face. If her family hadn't been around, he might have smiled at her obvious discomfort. He'd wondered when she would start to question their sleeping arrangements. Obviously the thought hadn't occurred to her.

"A double bed will take up too much room," he said. "Besides, I'll be sleeping outside. I'm the trail boss and I have to stay near the cattle."

Her mother frowned. "This is the oddest excuse for a wedding trip I've ever seen."

He didn't have to glance at Laura to feel her relief. He could feel it from ten feet away.

"We'll be fine, Mama," she said.

"If you say so." The older woman started toward the back door. "I'm going to start setting out your canned goods, honey. When Mr. Travers leaves, you come on back and help me."

"I will."

Jesse started toward his horse. "If there isn't anything else, I should get back to my ranch."

Her father followed him. "There is one more thing, Travers."

Laura frowned at her father. She moved close as if she was afraid of what he was going to ask. June looked up curiously from her place in the wagon. Wellington crawled out from behind the wheel and stood nervously, shifting from foot to foot.

"I need to ask you a favor," Mr. Cannon said. "My youngest boy, Wellington, has been pestering me since he found out about the cattle drive. He wants to go with you."

"But he's just a child," Laura said.

"I'm not." Wellington puffed out his chest. "I'm fourteen an' I'm bigger than you."

Wellington topped Laura by an inch or two, although he was still scrawny. Too-long blond hair fell into his eyes. He brushed it away impatiently. "I can ride better than just about anybody and I work hard. I'm even a good shot so if we get set on by Injuns, I could help defend us."

His enthusiasm made Jesse feel old. Wellington saw life as an adventure. He wanted to get out and experience everything at once. Jesse had felt that way about the war. He'd been terrified it would end before he was old enough to go off and fight. He, too, had been an expert rider and a good shot. He'd expected to face the fighting bravely. Instead he'd been so scared during his first battle he'd lost his breakfast and damn near wet himself.

He'd also killed three men that day. He'd taken aim and fired, just like he'd been taught. Only no one had warned him it was different from hunting game. No one had explained most men didn't die easy and that their screams would echo in his sleep long after their souls had found rest.

"I ain't afraid," Wellington said.

"Everybody's afraid some time," Mr. Cannon said.

"Not me."

"Quiet," his father ordered. He placed his hand on Jesse's shoulder. "I know you don't want the responsibility and I don't blame you. It's your decision. Marrying Laura makes you part of the family, but that doesn't mean you have to do everything we say." He grinned. "Only our children have to do that."

Jesse started to refuse. Laura was going to be enough trouble on the cattle drive. He didn't need some kid getting in the way. Ambrose Cannon squeezed his shoulder. It was a fatherly gesture that made Jesse think about belonging. He hadn't fit in for years.

"What do you think?" he asked Laura.

She looked startled to be included in the discussion. "He's a pest."

Wellington rolled his eyes. "Am not."

"Yes, you are. But it would be a good experience for him. I wouldn't mind having someone from my family along." She looked at Jesse. "I'm sorry. This isn't what you expected when you took me on, is it?"

"Not exactly."

He stared at the boy. Wellington was all arms and legs. He would get more gangly as he reached his full height. But his gaze was sharp and intelligent, and his eagerness made Jesse remember that gnawing sense of wanting to do something exciting.

He walked over and glared at Wellington. "If you come with us you're going to be one of the men, not a guest. You get up before dawn and work your ass until it's raw. You ride a string of horses that would rather throw you than herd cattle. You'll be in back, riding drag. That means four months of eating dust. You make one mistake, you disobey one order, and you'll be dead. I don't mean punished, I mean dead. On the trail a man only gets one chance to do his job right. Is that clear, boy?"

Wellington had his sister's eyes. They were wide and blue. Excitement tightened the lines of his face. He couldn't keep from grinning, even as Jesse spoke the warning words.

"Yes, sir. I understand everything. I'm good at followin' orders. Ain't that so, Pa?"

"You always manage to forget to keep the shelves stocked," his father said.

"That's different." Wellington placed his hand over his heart. "I'll do everything you say. I swear it."

"You'll need a good saddle, a change of clothes and a bedroll," Jesse said. "Get your mother to sew leather on the seat and inner knees of your trousers or you'll wear them out before you get there."

"Whoopee!" Wellington ran to his sister and wrapped his arms around her waist. She squealed as he picked her up and spun her around. "I'm going on a cattle drive."

"Wellington Cannon, you put me down," Laura ordered.

Wellington let her go, then jumped in front of Jesse and held out his hand. "Thank you, sir," he said as they shook on the deal. "You won't regret this. I swear you won't."

He ran toward the back of the house. "I'm goin', Ma. Jesse said I could go." A door banged shut and cut him off.

Mr. Cannon nodded at Jesse. "I'm obliged to you. I know he's going to be a pest."

"I'll take care of him."

"That's why I'm letting him go." The older man tapped his daughter on the nose. "You picked a good man, young lady. I hope you know that."

"Yes, Pa."

He turned back to Jesse. "My other two boys and I will look in on your place while you're gone."

"I appreciate that, sir, but I've got a foreman taking care of the ranch."

"I expected as much, but employees aren't the same as family. We'll check around and make sure everything is right."

Jesse hadn't thought they would take him in and make him one of their own. He felt slightly guilty, as if he was taking advantage of the man's kindness. His marriage to Laura wasn't anything but a means to an end. He wanted the money. He'd expected to be treated like a stranger.

Laura stepped next to him and smiled at her father. "That's good of you, Pa. I'm sure it'll take a load off of Jesse's mind."

Her father nodded, then started for the house. "You two can say your good-byes in private." He glanced at the sun. "A half hour should be plenty. Don't even think about going into the barn." He disappeared around the back of the building.

"I am sorry," Laura said. "Our bargain sounded so simple when I first thought of it. I guess I didn't think everything through."

He had a feeling that was one of Laura's failings. She acted before she thought. As failings went, it could be worse. "Your family's real nice," he said.

"Yes." She sighed. She walked over to the porch stairs and sat down, then patted the wood next to her. "I know you have to get back to your ranch, but maybe you could sit for a minute or two. Long enough to make Pa think . . . "

She ducked her head. "What must you think of me, Jesse? My family is nice. Nicer than I deserve them to be. And I'm lying to them. I'm running off without telling them the truth." She raised her gaze to him. "Do you understand?"

He sat next to her, but was careful not to get too close. He didn't have to get back to his ranch right away. Most of the steers already had their road brands. Hellcat Harry was coming into town tomorrow for the last of the supplies. The extra cowboys had been hired. All that was left was the waiting.

Laura wanted him to grant her absolution for her sins. If she knew the blackened condition of his soul she wouldn't be so quick to trust him. If she knew what he'd done and what he'd seen . . .

Jesse closed his eyes briefly. The past swept around him, closer until the chilly fingers of death and suffering trailed up his spine.

"You've made up your mind," he said. "Seems to me if you plan on feeling guilty about going, you might as well stay home."

"I don't want to stay home."

"Then accept the consequences of what you're doing."

"You make it sound so easy."

He glanced at her. She brushed a strand of hair off her cheek. Her skin was pale. He wondered what four months on the trail would do to her. Would she blossom in the sun or would she wither away?

She straightened and squared her shoulders. "You're telling me to quit complaining. All right, I will. At least for today." She smiled, then the corners of her mouth drooped a little. "I'm sorry about Wellington. Pa shouldn't have asked."

"The boy won't be too much trouble."

"Yes, he will, but thank you for not saying so. How will he get home?"

"The same way as the rest of the cowboys. Ride. It's an easier trip without the steers."

"Roger needs the wagon back."

"Someone will drive it. Don't worry."

She nodded, but he could tell she had more questions. He supposed this was difficult for her. Leaving his family had been easy. He'd never once looked back. Even at the height of battle, when he'd longed to be anywhere but there, he hadn't thought about his parents or brothers. He'd missed the land, but by then, everyone had gone back to Ohio.

He stood up and started for his horse. "I've got chores to attend to."

She rose and followed him. "Thanks for coming by today."

He untied the reins, then walked his horse to the edge of the road. Laura trailed along. She didn't say anything, she was just there. Waiting.

She was a little thing, her head barely coming up to his chin. Her hands were soft, her gaze trusting. He had no business with a woman like her. A lady. An innocent. She stared at him with her big blue eyes and thought he was going to keep her safe. She didn't know that the Indians and the rivers were the least of it. The real danger was from inside. The darkness—the fear. The past.

She patted his horse's nose. "I'll see you Saturday."

He grunted, then swung into the saddle.

"Saturday," he said. "Two o'clock. I'll be there."

She glanced up at him. Disappointment darkened her eyes. What the hell did she want from him? For a moment he thought about their kiss, then he dismissed the image. She was a foolish girl with foolish dreams. He would do well to remember that.

She stepped back from his horse. "Thank you, Jesse. You've been very kind."

"The hell I have," he said. "I'm doing this for the money, Miss Cannon, and for no other reason. I'll marry you, I'll take you to Kansas and I'll leave you there."

"I know. It's just—"

He wheeled his horse around and squeezed his thighs. The animal started to trot away. Jesse didn't look back and he didn't try to listen. He didn't want to know what else she had to say. When he cleared the town, he gave his horse its head and they galloped back toward the ranch. Toward safety and the one place where he could forget.

Her mother's gown had been white once, but it had yellowed to an elegant, rich shade of cream. The full skirt had originally been designed to fall over boned and metal hoops. It had since been altered. Now the lace and silk draped over several petticoats and a bustle. The bodice that had been let out for Augusta's generous curves was taken in to fit Laura.

Laura stared into the looking glass and promised herself she wasn't going to cry. Not today. She would cry on the trail, or when she was in Wichita. Until then, she would be brave.

But it was hard, she thought, touching the white blossoms pinned in her hair. Mama had woken her up early and they'd taken the time to curl her hair in ringlets. Now the blond curls fell over her bare shoulders. The beautiful gown hugged her upper arms and dipped low in front. The layers of lace whispered as she moved. Laura almost didn't recognize herself in the mirror. Only the apprehension in her eyes looked familiar.

She turned from the reflection and surveyed the small room. It was the bride's alcove at the back of the church. A quiet place for last adjustments of gowns and reflections of the heart. Her heart was heavy with guilt and apprehension. Thank goodness she wore gloves. At least no one had to know her palms were damp.

The door opened and her mother stepped in. The older woman's dress was pale green and brought out the color in her hazel eyes. She'd worn the same gown for Augusta's wedding, and for her first grandchild's christening.

"You look pretty, Mama," Laura said, and tried to smile. Her face felt stiff, as if she'd been caught outside in an ice storm. Her lips didn't want to move.

Her mother dismissed the compliment with a wave of her hand. "I'm an old woman, Laura. You're the bride. Let me look at you." She took Laura's hands and held her arms out to the side. "Perfect. The dress fits wonderfully." The older woman released her hands and smiled. "I'm so pleased you wanted to wear my dress. First Augusta, and now you. It's become a tradition."

"Yes, it has." Laura swallowed hard, but the taste of guilt stayed in her mouth. She could hear the devil carving out more steps on her road to hell. She must be halfway there by now. She could almost feel the flames licking at her feet.

Her mother walked around her. Their skirts brushed together in the small room. There was a dresser in the corner, and the mirror, but no other furniture. No chairs, of course. Neither of them could sit and risk getting their gowns wrinkled before the ceremony began.

"About tonight," her mother began.

Laura swallowed again. "Tonight?"

"Yes. I've put together a cold supper so you won't have to worry about cooking."

"I can cook fine, Mama. I've been cooking supper since I was twelve."

Her mother moved to the tiny dresser and rearranged the brush and comb there. She placed them even with the edge of the lace doily, then moved them to the center. "It will be easier if you don't have to worry about anything else."

The knot in Laura's stomach, the one that had been there for days, tightened. She pressed a hand against her midsection. "What are you saying?"

"You're getting married. There are things a man expects of his wife, Laura. Intimacies."

Oh, Lord. She could feel the blush on her cheeks. The marriage bed. She'd been thirteen when she'd experienced her cycle for the first time. On a quiet evening her mother had taken her aside and talked about what it all meant. About being a woman. The vague whispers of pressing bodies and babies had alarmed her. She'd tried not to think about it since. Surely Jesse didn't expect—

The knot tightened again. She had no idea what Jesse expected.

"You told me this already," she said, hoping her mother would stop talking about it.

"I know. I'm just reminding you it's a wife's duty." Her mother finally looked at her. Her hazel eyes darkened with compassion. "It's not so bad. At least it's quick. The good Lord willing, you'll have babies soon enough. Children are a woman's joy."

Babies? She didn't want babies. At least not yet. They weren't part of her plan. Wichita was only the first stop. Her dream was much bigger than a cow town. She wanted to travel the world, to be famous, to experience all life had to offer. She didn't want to hear about duty, however quickly it might be over. Surely Jesse didn't expect her to do *that* with him.

"Tonight will be difficult," her mother said quickly. "Try to relax. Think of something else. That always helps."

Tonight? Panic tightened her throat. They would be alone. In Jesse's house. Laura twisted her hands together and stared longingly at the door. She hadn't thought this through.

A knock at the door startled her. She jumped slightly, then reached over and opened it. Augusta stood in the long hallway. "Mama, it's time for you to take your seat."

Her mother leaned over and kissed Laura. "You'll be fine," she promised. "I love you, child. I'll always be near to take care of you."

"Thank you." Laura kissed her back. She inhaled the familiar fragrance of vanilla that always seemed to surround her mother. The guilt welled up inside and threatened to suffocate her. Would her family ever understand or forgive her?

The two women squeezed hands, then her mother left the room. Augusta shook her head. "You're as pale as a sheet. Has she been telling you about a wife's duties?"

"How did you know?"

"I heard the same talk just before I married Roger." Augusta glanced down the corridor, then stepped into the room. "It's nothing like she said. In fact, it's quite wonderful."

Laura frowned. "It doesn't sound wonderful."

Augusta laughed. "It's not like that, silly. It's warm and lovely. Oh, when Jesse asks you to take your nightgown off, don't say no."

"My nightgown?" Off? "But then I'll be—"

"As bare as a babe, yes, I know. You're going to have to trust me," her sister told her. "Let him do whatever he wants. Men have more experience than women."

"But Jesse hasn't been keeping company with anyone."

Augusta raised her eyebrows and Laura remembered the fancy women on the other side of town.

"You'll be fine." Augusta reached up and adjusted the flowers in her hair. "You look very beautiful. Jesse will be proud."

"You think so?" Laura looked at her sister. Augusta was the pretty one. She had the perfect hair and skin. Her figure was fuller, her smile wider. She made Laura feel dowdy by comparison.

She wanted Jesse to be proud of her. Their marriage wasn't real, but he was going to have to live here after she was gone. Bad enough that he had to carry around the stigma of a divorce without making it worse by having her be an ugly bride.

"Father is here," Augusta said. "I think it's time to get married."

Ambrose Cannon shooed Augusta toward the chapel, then held out his arm for Laura.

They walked to the double doors that led to the chapel. The minister's wife opened them. Laura stared down the long aisle. Her heart thundered in her chest, pounding harder and faster when she realized the entire town had turned out for her wedding. There wasn't an empty seat to be had.

At the end of the aisle stood the minister. He smiled at her. A Bible lay open in his hands. She began to shake. It was one thing to lie to her parents, it was quite another to lie to God.

Guilt turned to fear. She clutched at her father's arm. He smiled down at her, whispered that she was sure pretty, then started down the aisle.

She couldn't do it, she screamed silently. She'd changed her mind. She would confess everything, then convince her family to let her go anyway. Except they wouldn't let her go. And she had to be married to claim her inheritance. She wanted just one chance at her dream, one moment of being more than just plain Laura Cannon. She wanted to be special.

As they walked slowly toward the minister, she wrestled with her emotions. The wanting was stronger than the fear and the guilt. Finally, she looked at Jesse.

He stood tall and silent, with his arms at his sides. Dark eyes held her gaze. He wore a suit and a white shirt that emphasized his beard. He'd agreed to marry her and take her to Kansas. All for five hundred dollars. She tried to read his thoughts, but it was like looking at a stone wall. He couldn't be any happier about this than she was, but he was here. He'd given his word. He wouldn't betray that. She could do no less.

When they reached the end of the aisle, her father moved aside. Jesse stepped forward and held out his hand. She placed her palm against his and forced her trembling lips into a smile. For better or worse, she would marry this man.

"Good-bye," Laura's parents called. They waved from their places on the porch.

Jesse waved back, then snapped the reins. The mules moved out slowly. Jesse had ridden his horse into town for the wedding, but he was taking Laura and her wagon back now. His mount was tied on to the rear.

"I don't see why I've got to wait here," Wellington complained loudly enough for Jesse to hear over the clip-clop of the mules. "I could just go with 'em."

"They're not going to want you with them tonight, young man," Mrs. Cannon said. "Tomorrow is soon enough."

Wellington continued to grumble, but soon they'd moved onto the road and the boy was out of earshot. Jesse drew in a breath of relief that the ceremony was over.

He'd seen the surprise in Laura's face when she'd first entered the church, as well as the guilt and fear. She'd nearly changed her mind. But somewhere about halfway down the aisle, she'd squared her shoulders and raised her head up high. She was one determined cuss.

He leaned back in the seat and rested his left boot on the top of the footboard. After pulling off his string tie, he shoved it in his suit pocket and glanced at Laura.

She was staring straight ahead. She'd changed out of her wedding gown into a simple blue calico dress, although she'd left the white flowers in her hair. He could smell their sweet fragrance.

"I'm glad that's behind us," he said, and was startled to realize he felt obligated to make her feel comfortable. He supposed it was because they were married.

He reminded himself that it was just a marriage of convenience, then knew that didn't change anything. He was responsible for Laura for as long as she was with him. Until the divorce, she was his wife.

"You looked real pretty in that white dress," he said when she was silent.

"Thank you," she said softly. "It was my mother's. Augusta wore it, too."

He glanced at her. She bit down on her lower lip. There was a slight nip in the air. She pulled her brown woolen shawl closer around her shoulders.

"You all right?" he asked.

"I'm fine." Her voice was a whisper.

But she wasn't. He could tell from the slump of her shoulders and the way she clutched her fingers so tightly together.

"Laura?"

She looked at him. He felt as if someone had punched him in the gut. Tears collected in her blue eyes. She blinked and one slipped down her cheek. She reached up and quickly brushed it away.

"I lied to everyone," she said. "My parents, my brothers and sisters. They all think we're in love, that we're going to be together forever. My mother was talking about us having babies." She sniffed. "I've never been selfish before. It's harder than I thought. I keep asking myself if it's wrong to want something so badly you'll do anything to get it. I can't imagine what you must think of me."

"You're not so bad."

"It's kind of you to say that." She wiped away another tear. "I must be the sorriest sinner in all the world today."

"You don't know what you're talking about. You're no sinner."

"But I've lied to them." Her voice shook. She clamped her lips together and swallowed. She hunched down in the seat. "I've betrayed their trust."

"You're doing what you have to do. Sometimes people get hurt."

Sometimes people died. He didn't want to think about the war today. He didn't want to think about anything but the bright blue sky and the feel of the breeze on his face. But instead of the crisp spring air, he felt the blinding sting of gunpowder. Instead of the sound of the mules' hooves on the dirt road, he heard gunfire and the screams of the dying.

Laura didn't know about sinning. She didn't know about being so frightened a body would do anything to escape. She didn't understand about bargaining with the Devil only to have the Devil laugh and turn away.

Jesse knew. He remembered the fear—the way it coiled in his belly like a snake, squeezing around his heart and loosening his bowels. He remembered when he'd prayed to die, when death had been cruelly withheld by an uncaring God, or a wily Devil. He remembered finally believing they were the same.

Jesse shuddered. The memories came faster now, catching him in the center of a whirlwind. There had been so many times he'd wanted to die, to simply end it all. But he'd never had the courage. He couldn't, like some, slowly starve himself to death. He wouldn't willfully risk escape, knowing the guards were happy to shoot men in the back. He wasn't hopeful enough to want to live or brave enough to end the suffering. In the end he had simply hung on, because there wasn't another choice. Madness had beckoned. The quiet silence of another place. Only David had kept him sane.

The thought of his friend was worse than the memories of the killing and the hunger. He couldn't bear to think of David, so he forced himself to stare at the countryside. He counted the bare trees, noting the budding branches of the cedar elm. He listened to the sound of Laura's breathing and knew by the slightly uneven cadence, she still fought her tears.

She cried for her sins. They were so minor when compared to his, she could tell a lie each hour she lived, from now until the end of time and still not come close to what he'd done in a single week of war.

"I hope they'll forgive me," she said. "Do you think they will?" She looked at him. Her lashes were spiky, her nose a little red. She clutched a damp lace-edged hanky in her hand.

He'd spent the last few years avoiding people, staying out of town and keeping to himself. In two short weeks, he'd agreed to let her accompany him on the cattle drive, had married and was now feeling uncomfortably responsible for her female worries. He should have asked for a hell of a lot more than five hundred dollars.

"They'll forgive you," he said, and he knew it was true. People like the Cannons didn't let one of their own stay long outside the circle. She would be lovingly scolded, then brought back into the fold.

"I hope you're right." She touched the hanky to her

cheek and sighed. "I was alone when I got the letter from the attorney. At first, it didn't occur to me to keep it a secret. We were busy. May had influenza, and Augusta was near her time. There was trouble in town and Papa was gone a lot dealing with the situation. I remember I read the letter so many times I nearly had it memorized. But every time I went to tell Mama, she was too busy to listen."

Laura shifted on the hard wooden seat. He wondered if she would grow tired of riding in the wagon as they traveled north. He wondered if she would change her mind and he would have to spare one of his cowboys to escort her home.

"I was supposed to leave and go teach," she continued. "Mama sat me down and told me I couldn't go. What with Augusta and the store and all." She twisted her hands together. "That's when I decided not to say anything. I realized then the inheritance was my chance to get away. I could finally make my dream come true."

She glanced at him out of the corner of her eye, then looked away. It was as if she had something else to confess, but she wasn't ready yet. He knew all about confessing and not confessing, so he didn't ask.

"Do you think I'll miss them?" she asked.

"Why would you? You're the one who wants to leave."

"Do you miss your family?"

"No." He rarely thought about them. The first summer he'd returned to the ranch, his mother's garden had struggled to survive in the hot Texas sun. What with rounding up the branded herd, then roping mavericks and hiring men, there hadn't been time to tend to the vegetables and flowers. By the fall, everything there had died. He'd felt a twinge of guilt when he'd walked past the parched stalks, but it hadn't been strong enough to make him tote water from the well. The following year, only the hardiest blossoms had tried again. By the third year, the wild grasses had claimed the garden completely. Nothing of his mother's grew there anymore. He preferred it that way.

"You don't want to go see them?" she asked.

"No. They would tell me to move to Ohio and I don't want to."

"Why not? If everyone you care about is there . . ." Her voice trailed off.

"I care about the land more," he said. The land didn't change. His luck might be bad, the weather, the bugs, the seasons might all try to destroy him, but the land was constant.

"It's like having a dream," she said. "You care about the land more than anything and I care about, well, my future away from here."

Again he had the sense she was holding something back. He almost asked. Almost. Then he caught himself in time and squashed the faint flicker of curiosity. He couldn't get close to Laura Cannon. She was simply a paying customer. Nothing more.

"While I'm baring my soul to you, I might as well apologize for the wedding," she said. "I didn't know it was going to be like that. All those people." She shuddered.

In spite of himself, he grinned. "I could tell you were shocked. You should have seen the expression on your face."

He glanced at her. She was staring at him, looking much as she had when she'd first stepped into the church.

"What's wrong?" he asked.

"You smiled."

"So?" He rubbed his scarred cheek self-consciously.

"I've never seen you smile before. You're very handsome." Laura made a slight gasping sound, then touched her fingertips to her mouth as if she couldn't believe what she'd said. She ducked her head down. "Um, anyway, I'm sorry about everyone in town showing up. I didn't think anyone would be interested in our marriage. I didn't really think the situation through."

She thought he was handsome. Jesse took that statement and turned it over in his mind. Him? But he was scarred. And his hair was too long. His eyes were empty, as if he'd lost his soul. He knew; he'd seen the haunting darkness in a reflection. So how could she think him handsome?

"I know this wedding will make it difficult when you want to marry again," Laura said sadly. "I'm sorry about that, too."

That broke through his musings. "Married again? What in hell—" He paused. Shit. He hated being married. "What the heck gives you the idea I would want to get married again? I didn't want to in the first place."

"Now that the ladies in town believe you're the marrying kind, they're going to be after you, Jesse. You are very—" Her gaze swept over his face, pausing briefly on his scarred cheek before settling on his mouth. "—attractive. You have the ranch. You're young. If you're successful on this trip, you'll be wealthy. That makes you the sort of man a woman sets her cap for."

He knew he was a lot of things, but a catch wasn't one of them. Laura said he was young. Some nights he felt as old as the land. In truth he was twenty-six.

He searched his mind for a topic that would distract her. "Wellington sure is happy about coming on the cattle drive."

"I know." Laura smiled at him, her sad thoughts apparently forgotten for the moment. "It's all he's talked about. It was very good of you to agree."

He grunted. He still wasn't sure why he was letting

the boy tag along. The kid would be trouble; all greenhorns were. Maybe Wellington could help keep Laura from being in the way.

"I'm glad he's getting this opportunity," Laura continued. "It's important for a young person to travel. Travel broadens the mind."

Jesse stared at her. "How the hell would you know? You haven't been out of the county."

She bristled. Her back got all stiff and she raised her chin. "I read. I know things."

"What kind of things?"

"I know what's important."

"It seems to me no one in your family needs his mind broadened. They're doing just fine without traveling."

Laura surprised him by grinning. "I suppose we are sort of overwhelming all together."

"Overwhelming? I felt like a cat caught in a stampede of bulls."

"I can't imagine you ever feeling that way," she said, then laughed.

Her eyes crinkled at the corners and her mouth turned up. He liked the sound of her laughter. The soft noise was easy and smooth, as if laughing was something she did often. His own throat closed at the thought. Humor was rare in life. He'd spent the last several years learning it was easier to feel nothing. No joy, no sorrow. The blessed sameness of a gray world kept the memories at bay.

Laura leaned back in her seat. "I chose well when I chose you, Jesse Travers. I'm glad you agreed to help me."

"Were there others on your list?"

"One or two. But you were my first choice. You're a nice man."

Nice? "There's not too many people here who would describe me as nice," he said. Himself included.

"Well, they're all wrong. You *are* nice." She looked around at the budding trees and the cattle grazing on either side of the road. A few minutes before, they'd crossed onto his land. The house was still a couple of miles away.

"I'm really looking forward to the cattle drive," she said, then glanced at him out of the corner of her eye. "I'm sure you'll be pleased to see the last of me in Wichita."

He would, he thought grimly. But not for the reasons she would think. He wanted to be done with her because she was dangerous to him in ways he never could have imagined.

When the wagon pulled up in front of the house, Laura was struck by the silence. No one came running from around back to welcome them home. A faint breeze rustled the grasses and made the bare tree branches click together. There were no flowers in front of the two-story house and the wide railed porch was empty of furniture. There wasn't even a swing.

She moved to the edge of the wagon and waited while Jesse walked around to help her down. He was her husband now. He was expected to do that sort of thing. They were married.

Married. She didn't want to feel any different, after all the relationship was purely for business purposes. Yet she couldn't help the pride that swept over her when her husband glanced up at her. Foolishly, she was pleased he was so handsome and kind. If she were interested in a real marriage, she would want her husband to be someone like Jesse. His brown eyes met hers as he held out his arms. She bent down, placing her hands on his shoulders.

He swept her to the ground. For a moment, before

her feet touched the dusty driveway, she pressed against him. She felt the heat of his body and inhaled his masculine scent. He didn't smell anything like her brothers. Washington smelled of bay rum and Wellington smelled like he needed a bath. But Jesse was different. His fragrance was muskier, but clean, as if he'd bathed that day. As he released her and stepped back, she noticed that he'd trimmed his beard and that while his hair was still long, almost to the bottom of his jacket collar, the neat edges showed he'd recently visited a barber.

Her stomach tightened with a feeling of anticipation. She wasn't sure why. They wouldn't be leaving until Monday and it was only Saturday afternoon. But the sensation didn't go away. If anything, thinking about what day it was only seemed to make it worse.

Jesse walked to the rear of the wagon, opened the back flap and stared inside.

"How much of this luggage are you going to need tonight?"

"Just the small carpetbag." She motioned to the one nearest the opening. "There's some covered dishes for our supper tonight and tomorrow," she said. "Mama and June cooked them so we wouldn't have to bother."

Jesse grabbed the bag with one hand. With the other, he took her elbow and led her toward the back door of the house.

His touch was polite rather than possessive. She hadn't thought he would have such good manners, then realized she'd had no reason to see them. After all, until a few months ago, when she'd first received the letter from her late aunt's attorney, she hadn't given Jesse Travers a single thought. As he opened the back door and motioned for her to step inside ahead of him, she wondered why not.

The kitchen was as clean as she remembered.

"I'll get the covered dishes," he said, putting her carpetbag by the stairs.

"I can get them," she offered.

"It's no trouble. Go ahead and look around."

He was gone before she could protest. Slowly Laura removed her bonnet and set it on the table. The large bare window allowed the late afternoon sun to flood the room. Everything was brighter here. Almost raw with exposure.

She moved into the dining room. A large bare table sat alone. There weren't any chairs or even a buffet. Again the windows were uncovered. She could see a crack in the table, where the sun had damaged the wood. She rubbed her finger over the uneven surface and frowned. Didn't the man believe in curtains?

The front parlor was also sparsely furnished. The wallpaper was a pretty gold-and-blue print, and still in excellent condition. The horsehair sofa had seen better days, as had the straight-backed chair in front of the fireplace. In her mind, she rearranged furniture, adding a small bookcase, and a bigger sofa. She imagined thick drapes pulled tight against a stormy night and a fire blazing brightly. A rug would warm up the room and protect the wooden floors.

She turned to find a piece of paper so she could make a list of what she would need, then stopped herself. She wasn't really Jesse's wife and this wasn't really her house. She had no right to make changes.

Behind the parlor, she found Jesse's office. It was the first room that showed signs of being lived in. Papers were stacked on the large desk. A pile of old newspapers stood in one corner. There was a chair by the stone fireplace, with a table pulled up next to it. A single mug sat on the table.

She walked toward the chair and paused behind it. Her fingertips rested on the cool leather. As it had when they'd first arrived, the silence surprised her. She hadn't known the absence of sound could be so very loud.

Her gaze swept over the neatly stacked logs, then settled on the single mug. She didn't recall ever having tea alone. Someone was always around. If not her mother, then one of the girls. In the store, there was always a customer to chat with, or her brothers, or her father.

This was how Jesse lived. Alone. With a single mug, a solitary plate. Was he lonely? Or was she an intrusion on his otherwise perfect life?

She heard him walk into the kitchen and hurried to meet him. He had already set the covered dishes down on the counter.

"Looks like we have enough here to last a week," he said as he shrugged out of his coat.

"Mama didn't want us going hungry. She mentioned something about—" Laura cleared her throat. Her mother had said something about not having time to cook. Until they left on the cattle drive, she wasn't going to have anything to do. Unless Jesse had some chores for her.

"Is there anything—"

"You're probably tired—"

They spoke at the same time. Jesse dropped his coat over the back of one of the chairs. "You're probably tired," he said. "Why don't you go upstairs and rest? I'll see to my horse and the mules."

"I'm not really tired," she said. "Is there something you would like me to do around here?"

"No."

On the journey from town she thought she was learning how to read his expression. Now, staring into his dark eyes, she knew that she was wrong. She didn't know anything about him, and if he had his way, she never would.

Without waiting for her to offer again, he picked up her carpetbag and headed for the stairs. "You'll sleep up here," he told her.

Laura sucked in a breath. Her muscles tensed up as she watched him start to climb toward the second story. Her mother's words filled her mind. She had a duty to her husband. The marriage might not be real in their minds, but in the eyes of God . . . She wasn't sure what God thought about what they were doing. She had a feeling He wasn't pleased.

In truth their marriage was real today and every day until they divorced. She had promised to love, honor and obey. She had sworn to worship him with her body. Augusta had said it was wonderful.

Jesse paused halfway up the stairs. He glanced back at her. "Don't you want to see where you'll be sleeping?"

"I—" She nodded, then started after him. What was she supposed to say? Perhaps he wouldn't expect conversation. She tried not to think about it, but she couldn't stop. She bit her lower lip. Oh, why hadn't she thought this part through? Why did she jump in without looking first? This is exactly what her father had always warned her about. In fact, if he knew the mess she was in he would tell her that—

"Ooof!"

She collided into something hard and warm. Her head came up and she reached for the railing to keep from tumbling. She stared at Jesse's broad back. He'd stopped again on the stairs and she hadn't noticed.

He spun around and grabbed her arm. "Are you all right?"

"I wasn't looking where I was going."

He frowned. His eyebrows drew together and his mouth pulled into a straight line. "You'd better start looking if you expect to last a day on the cattle drive.

There are snakes and all kinds of critters, holes in the ground and—"

"Jesse," she said, interrupting.

"What?"

"Not now. Please. I know you're right about looking and all, but I can't think about the cattle drive. First I've got to get through tonight."

"What the hell does that have to do with anything?"

She lowered her gaze to his chest. Somehow it was easier to stare at his buttons than face the anger in his expression. "We're married. And tonight . . . well . . ." She motioned to the bag in his hand. "You're taking me upstairs. I haven't done this before. Of course I haven't, I've never been married. I didn't want to lie when I took my vows, so I mean to try and keep some of them. Not the death till us part one, but the others. So if you planned to, well, Mama said it wasn't horrible and Augusta said it was wonderful, and I, well, I'm your wife. I wouldn't refuse you."

By the end of her speech, her voice was barely a whisper. She continued to stare at the center of his chest, noting the exact moment it stopped moving, then expanded suddenly as if he'd sucked in a breath. He dropped his hold on her arm as if he'd been burned.

"I'm sure as hell not going to bed you," he said curtly.

"You're not?"

Without thinking, she raised her gaze. Then wished she hadn't. He was glaring at her as if she had some disfiguring disease.

"What's wrong?" she asked.

"Nothing's wrong."

"Then why are you looking at me like that?"

"Like what?"

"Like—" She squeezed the railing for support. "Like you're sorry you ever agreed to this."

He muttered something that sounded like "damn woman," but she wasn't sure. Before she could ask, he continued up the stairs to the second floor, then walked through the first door on the right. When he came out a few seconds later, he wasn't carrying her carpetbag.

"You'll be in there," he said, pointing back the way he'd come. "Alone. Is that clear?"

"Yes, but—"

"But what?"

"Why are you mad at me? Is it because I offered to, well, you know? I figured it was the least I could do after all you've agreed to help me with. I thought you'd want to."

He opened his mouth, then closed it. "How am I supposed to answer that?" He shook his head. "I'll be in the barn." He started down the stairs.

She turned sideways so he wouldn't have to brush past her. "Supper's at five," she called after him.

"Fine."

The word sounded as if it had been growled from between clenched teeth. Laura didn't know what Jesse was so upset about. After all, she *had* offered.

She entered the room he'd given her. A narrow single bed had been pushed up against a papered wall. There were curtains up here. Pink ones that matched the flowers on the wall. Her carpetbag sat on the dresser next to a pitcher and basin. She glanced inside and saw the pitcher was filled with water. Jesse had planned for her to sleep here. Alone.

She washed up quickly. When she felt as if she'd removed the worst of the travel dust, she hurried downstairs and back into the kitchen.

She found the flour and other supplies easily enough. In a few minutes she had a stew heating on the stove and biscuits baking in the oven. A quick search of the drawers allowed her to find a tablecloth. The starched linen was yellowed and dull, as if it hadn't been used in years. She took it out back and shook it briskly. The fabric snapped in the still afternoon.

Laura paused before returning to the kitchen. She looked out over the neatly staggered corrals, the wide barn and the grazing land beyond. In a hollow, slightly west of the house, she could see the roof of a large building. It was probably the bunkhouse. She was the only woman around for miles.

The sun slipped low toward the bare trees. The temperature dropped and she rubbed her arms. She could hear her own breathing. In the distance, night creatures rustled in the long grass. A chill swept through her, more from the solitude than the coming night and she turned back to the bright light and warmth of the kitchen.

Once inside she smoothed the tablecloth over the table, then found napkins. They, too, were stiff and dull as if they hadn't been used. She checked the coffee, then the biscuits. By the time the stew was bubbling, she could hear the scrape of Jesse's boots on the back porch.

"Supper's ready," she said as he came inside.

He paused by the mud room and stared at her. His gaze swept over her body, then moved to the table and finally to the stove. He inhaled deeply.

"Smells good," he said gruffly. After placing his hat on its peg, he started for the table. He glanced at the tablecloth, then at his hands. "I'd better wash up." He crossed the room and reached for the pump.

She picked up a thick towel and used it to wrap around the metal bucket's handle. While Jesse watched, she poured the heated water into the basin she'd put out. When she was done, he moved in front of the sink and reached for the soap. She returned the towel to the counter next to him.

Their movements were awkward and strained. Laura thought about the way she and her sisters swept around each other so easily, familiarity giving the chores grace. She wished for the silly conversations and the laughter, then pushed the wish away. She was on her way—if this was the path necessary to achieve her dream, then she would survive.

Jesse plunged his hands into the basin. He drew them back so quickly, Laura was afraid he'd been scalded. She rushed to his side.

"Are you hurt?" She grabbed his wrist and turned his hand palm up. She couldn't see any red marks.

"I'm fine," he muttered.

She touched the water. It was pleasant, but not hot. "What's wrong? I thought you'd been burned."

"I didn't think the water would be warm." He pulled his hand free and picked up the bar of soap he'd dropped. His gaze focused on his task.

"You saw me pour it from a bucket on the stove."

He shrugged in response.

She moved away, not sure what to say. Her usual quick wit deserted her and she was left feeling awkward and tongue-tied. She pulled the pan of biscuits from the oven and set them on top of the stove. Working quickly, she tossed them into a cloth-lined bowl. When she was done, she blew on her fingers. She looked up and saw Jesse watching her.

She'd never been so alone with a man before. Young men had come calling, but they'd taken her on walks or escorted her to socials. They'd had the illusion of being alone, but her family and the townspeople had always been within earshot. Here there was no one.

The sun had finally disappeared behind the trees. Lantern-light from the kitchen reflected on the bare glass, allowing her to see what was going on in the room. Jesse finished rinsing his hands, then dried them on the towel. His movements were slow and studied, as if he, too, felt awkward.

She reminded herself that Jesse was a kind man. He'd agreed to take her to Wichita, he'd married her, he'd even kissed her to keep her brother and sister from tattling. She wasn't afraid of him. She was afraid of the unknown. She needed a distraction, something to take her mind off the silence.

"I could make curtains," she blurted out, then moved to the window. "I could measure the windows and get the fabric tomorrow. By the time we reached Wichita, they'd be done and you could bring them back and hang them up." She touched the bare pane. "Something cheerful and bright. Maybe red or yellow. What do you think?"

She turned and looked at him. His gaze narrowed. "No."

"But—"

"No. No curtains. I want to be able to see out."

"But in the winter, curtains help keep in the heat."

"I'd rather be cold." His shoulders hunched forward. "Damn it, woman, leave it be."

She flinched. "I'm sorry. I was only trying to help."

"I don't want your help."

"I see." She could feel the burning start behind her eyes. She clenched her hands into fists and vowed she wouldn't cry. If the stubborn fool of a man didn't want curtains, that was fine with her.

The smell of something scorching caught her attention. She spun toward the stove. "The stew." She flew across the room and reached for the pot without thinking. Before she could touch the hot metal, Jesse clamped his hand on her wrist.

"Don't," he said loudly. "You'll burn yourself." He thrust the towel at her.

She stared at it and just wanted to disappear.

Nothing was going right. "I'm sorry," she whispered. "I'm sorry about the stew and the curtains and the wedding and everything. I'm so sorry."

He cursed under his breath and took the towel from her. When he'd pulled the pot off the heat, he stepped in front of her. "Look at me, Laura."

She shook her head.

"Stubborn female."

That made her smile, just a little. She sniffed and raised her head. "Don't be mad at me," she said.

His expression was resigned, as if he'd expected her to be nothing but trouble and she hadn't let him down. "The supper's fine. Just don't scrape too near the bottom of the pot. I know. I've eaten a lot of burned food."

"If you're sure."

She reached for the bowls, but he stopped her with a quick shake of his head. "About the curtains." He reached up and rubbed his left cheek, the one with the scar. "I want the windows left bare. When I was in the prison camp, they used to lock us up, sometimes for weeks. We couldn't see out. When I got out I swore I'd always be able to see the sky."

She could feel his pain and discomfort. He didn't want to confess his weaknesses to her, but he had. To help her understand. Rather than embarrass him with pity, she served their supper.

Not another word was spoken. They ate in silence, and when they were done, Jesse left. She saw him head toward the barn, then he disappeared into the night. Laura leaned against the counter and thought about the stranger she'd married. Her brother Washington had come home from the war a very different man. It had taken him months to stop having nightmares. The family had gathered around to give him support. They'd talked when he'd wanted to talk and respected his quiet days. Eventually, he'd healed.

Jesse had no one to help him. Laura picked up their dirty plates and carried them to the sink. She might just be plain Laura Cannon, but she knew how to be a friend. Jesse needed her to help him heal. They were going to spend the next few months together on the cattle drive. She would be with him, offering friendship and comfort. She owed him. It was the least she could do.

The predawn sky was pale gray without a hint of clouds. Jesse reined in his horse and paused to watch the two men knock down the north pasture fence. The few cowboys staying behind would have it replaced long before the cattle reached Kansas.

The sound was deafening. Cattle snorted and bellowed. The men called to each other. Hammers rang out as the men pounded on the wooden fence and finally pushed it to the ground.

The point riders moved into place at the front of the herd, but well behind the lead cattle. One of the steers, Skunk, had made the trip before. He was steady and followed the belled ox regardless of the weather or distractions around him. Rather than sell him for slaughter, Jesse had herded Skunk back so he could lead the herd again.

Mike, one of the point riders, slapped the belled ox on its rump. The animal snorted, then started north. Skunk moved into place behind him and the other steers followed. As the animals moved out, the cowboys slowly took their places around the herd. Once on the move, the herd would stretch out for nearly half a mile. For the first week or so, they would all ride hard to get the steers trail broke. A dozen extra men kept the cattle in place. After a week, those men would return to the ranch and the herd would continue on to Kansas.

Despite the rain last week, dust floated toward the sky. Soon the air would be thick and gritty. It would be like that for the next three months. Only a pouring rain would ease the drag rider's throats. Of course then they had to worry about the mud. It was always something, Jesse thought as he tightened his thighs. His horse trotted faster, then broke into a canter. They cleared the herd and turned north.

Up ahead, Jesse could see two wagons. Hellcat Harry led the way with Laura not far behind. Soon the bellowing of the steers and the calls of the cowboys faded. Spring was coming quickly; already the grass was thickening and turning green. In a few days wildflowers would sprout up all over. If the weather was decent, if there weren't a lot of storms and hail, if the grass held and the water was plentiful, then maybe, just maybe they would all make it.

As he neared the wagons, he drew back on the reins and his horse slowed. Laura had been up and packed before he'd ever knocked on her door. She'd made coffee cheerfully and had even heated up some muffins for his breakfast. Her tangible excitement and ready smile had left him feeling old and empty inside. He'd been a fool to agree to bring her along. There were a hundred different ways she could die on the trail. If only she hadn't offered him so much money. If only her damn blue eyes weren't so trusting. He hated the way she gazed up at him, as if she really believed he could keep her safe.

So far all he'd managed to do was avoid her. Since he'd left the house Saturday night, he'd kept himself busy outside. He'd counted supplies, much to Harry's annoyance, mended his tack, and checked out the string of horses. He'd gotten in everyone else's way and had growled at the men brave enough to complain.

He knew he was a fool. He didn't know if not bedding her when she'd offered made him more or less stupid.

He shook his head, then adjusted his black beaver-felt hat. It didn't matter. The chance was gone. But without closing his eyes, he could see her standing on the stairs forcing out her words and trying not to show how scared she was. She wouldn't mind if they did "that." If Laura had any thoughts about bedding a man, they would be the romantic dreams of a young girl. What would she say if she knew about his cash-up-front quick couplings with strangers?

What had surprised him more than her offer—and her offer had surprised the hell out of him—was his body's reaction to her invitation. Her words had evoked an image in his mind, of Laura dressed in little more than lace and a smile. He'd almost felt the touch of her small hands on his suddenly heated body.

In the past, when he'd had a restless stirring he'd visited town and had taken care of his needs with as little thought as drinking a glass of water to ease his thirst. The wanting hadn't been about any one woman, the desire had been manageable.

Saturday night his arousal had awakened him more than once. He hadn't been able to forget the determined set of her head as she'd offered herself for the sake of her vows. Another man would have bedded her on the spot.

His horse caught up with her wagon. Laura glanced up and smiled at him.

"We're really going," she said.

"Looks that way."

He studied her control of the mules. The four animals walked forward purposefully. Laura held the reins easily, with a practiced air. Her gloves were new and would protect her hands.

She'd placed a wide cushion under her behind. He bit back a grin, wondering if it would be enough. Sitting all day in a wagon was going to leave her stiff and sore. Instantly he saw her lying on her belly, his hands massaging away her aches. He could feel the soft curve of her buttocks and hear her sigh of contentment. Her pale skin, long smooth legs, and delicate bare back taunted him. He moved higher and—

His horse tossed his head. Jesse realized he'd tightened his hold on the reins and immediately loosened his grip. Where the hell had that thought come from? Jesus!

He shifted on the saddle. It took him a moment to realize why he was uncomfortable, then shifted again. He was hard. Just like that.

Laura had dressed in a sensible wool dress. He'd given her one of his coats so she wouldn't have to fight with a shawl for the next few weeks. The oversized garment hung past her knuckles, but she'd rolled up the sleeves to her wrists. A wide-brimmed hat protected her face from the rising sun.

She tilted her head. "Do I pass inspection or does your fierce expression mean I've done something wrong?"

Once again her smile took his breath away. The openness and joy left him feeling as if he'd stumbled out of the dark into an unexpected light. She made him want to smile back. He resisted. Not because he didn't like her—he did. He liked her smiles and that she acted without thinking things through. He liked her giving spirit and the fact that lying to her family about her inheritance was the worst thing she would ever do in her life.

He resisted her smiles and her laughter because he was afraid for her. Afraid that if she got to know him too well, if she started to understand, some of the blackness might leak out and stain her. He didn't want her to change because of him.

"You haven't done anything wrong," he said gruffly. He motioned to the wagon. "How does it feel?"

"Fine for now." She took the reins in one hand and shook the other. "Although I suspect I'm about to learn that driving a wagon ten miles to a customer's spread for delivery isn't exactly the same as driving all the way to Kansas. When I step off the wagon I might hobble a bit, but I'll straighten up eventually."

Her grin was contagious. He felt his mouth tugging upward in response. Her eyes widened slightly and he remembered her surprise the last time she'd seen him smile. She'd said he was handsome.

"Did Wellington get everything packed?" he asked.

"Yes." She wrinkled her nose. "I can't believe my mother sent all those supplies. Didn't you tell her I would be eating with the men and that I didn't need my own food?"

"I've never been on a cattle drive where people complained there was too much for dinner."

"I suppose." She glanced over her shoulder toward the covered portion of the wagon. "I've got several cases of vegetables, as well as enough dried apples to make a pie every day."

"The men will like that."

She tugged on the end of the ribbons tied under her chin, then removed her hat. She brushed a few loose strands of hair off her forehead. "Now I can see you. I don't think I'll be making many pies on this trip. I couldn't even heat stew without burning it." She sighed. "I *am* a fine cook, though. Really."

"I believe you."

Her mobile mouth straightened. "Harry said he would show me how to make coffee on the trail. He said it wasn't as easy as I thought."

"That's a good skill." Jesse glanced ahead of them to the chuck wagon leading the way. "If you have any problems and I'm not around, go to Harry. He'll take care of you."

She ducked her head. "I don't want to be a bother to anyone."

The faint rays of sunlight seemed to find their way to her hair. They reflected off the blond strands and made him wonder how long her hair really was. The whores in town kept their hair short, probably because it was convenient. He hadn't seen a woman with her hair down since he was a boy and his mother had brushed hers out every night.

Would Laura's curls tumble to the middle of her back, or clear down to her waist? He thought about touching her hair and the weight of it in his hands.

"What are you thinking?" she asked.

"That if I don't keep my mind on the cattle, none of us are going to make it past the county line." He shook his head. "We'll be going about fifteen miles today, if we can. The same tomorrow and for the rest of the week."

She nodded. "George told me you push the cattle harder at the beginning." She raised her eyebrows as if flaunting her knowledge.

"George?"

"He's one of the cowboys." She leaned over the side of her wagon and looked back, but they were too far ahead to be able to make out individual riders.

"I know who George is. Why were you talking to him?"

"Shouldn't I?" She bit down on her lower lip. "Oh, Jesse, I'm sorry. Was it inappropriate? I didn't know I wasn't supposed to speak to the cowboys. It won't happen again."

He clamped his teeth together. It was the first goddamn morning.

"You can speak to anyone you like," he said at last. "It doesn't matter. I was just surprised is all."

"You're sure?" Worry crept into her eyes. "I'm your wife for this trip. I don't want to do anything to make you ashamed of me."

"You couldn't if you tried."

She straightened in her seat. "I don't know about that. My pa said I'm more than a handful of trouble."

"That I'm willing to believe."

She smiled. "How's Wellington?"

Jesse pointed behind them. "See that cloud of dust?"

She leaned over the side again and nodded. "It's getting bigger, isn't it?"

"Your brother is going to be eating it for the next three months. But he'll learn a lot. If he really wants to work a cattle drive, next time he'll be able to hire on as a swing and flank rider."

"I'm glad he's with us."

Jesse didn't answer. He stared to the west. As the sun rose higher in the sky he could make out the distant wall of clouds. "There might be rain later," he said.

"At least it's not cold enough to snow."

"Snow would be safe. We can always build a fire to get warm, but if there's lightning, the cattle will stampede."

"Is there anything I can do to help?"

He almost laughed. She meant it. He wanted to tell her that she was more trouble than all twenty-four hundred steers combined.

Before he could say that, he heard a faint sound from

the back of her wagon. It was muffled, but he could have sworn it was a yap. He glanced at Laura. She was staring straight ahead as if she hadn't heard anything.

The yap came again. This time she jerked in her seat.

"Laura?"

"What?" She glanced up at him, her eyes wide and innocent.

"What's in the back of your wagon?"

She transferred her reins to her left hand and ticked off items with her right. "My clothes, bedding, extra sheets, food, a couple of—"

"Laura." Her name came out as a growl.

She hunched forward. "It's King. He's small, Jesse. Really small. He can eat from my plate. I don't mind. I wouldn't have brought him at all, but he's so young and he's Wellington's puppy. My brother was heartbroken at the thought of leaving his dog behind, so when he asked me, well, what could I say except yes? I didn't think it would be a problem. He's a little dog and the wagon is big. . . ." Her voice trailed off into a whisper.

He'd learned that when she rambled on, she was trying to convince herself as much as him.

"A dog," he said coldly.

She nodded. "A little one." She held her hand about eight inches above the seat.

"A dog?"

She flinched as if he'd hit her, then reached behind her and untied the flap. "King, come here, boy."

There was a happy bark, then something small and brown bounded out of the back of the wagon and onto the seat. The puppy was all fur and big brown eyes. Its coat was long, sort of a dirty white with beige splotches on its back and legs. It was small enough to get stepped on the first time it touched ground, and loud enough to start a stampede.

The animal raced to the edge of the seat and barked

at Jesse's horse, then ran back and hid behind Laura. She petted the pup. It curled up next to her and gave a contented sigh.

"It can't stay," he said.

She nodded. "I know. I told Wellington, but he wanted King with him. He was afraid the dog would forget him while he was gone and I didn't really mind sharing my wagon."

She looked up at him. For a moment, he thought she was going to cry. But Laura was made of sterner stuff than that. She raised her chin slightly. "Do you want to shoot him here?"

Now it was Jesse's turn to be surprised. "He doesn't have to be killed, he'll go back with one of the cowboys."

"When?"

It was an excellent question. He couldn't afford to spare one of his men on the first day. Of course if they took the pup now, he would only be short for half a day, if that. He eyed the little dog. It had already gone to sleep, its small head on Laura's lap.

A dog would be some protection for her. At least Jesse wouldn't have to worry about one of the men sneaking into her wagon at night.

As if she sensed his hesitation, she cleared her throat. "I don't mind being responsible for King. I'll keep him out of trouble."

Who was going to keep Laura under control? It was just a matter of time until the mutt started a stampede. He thought about how lonely he'd been when he'd gone off to war. A dog would have helped.

"It's a damn stupid name for a dog that small," he said.

"I know." One corner of her mouth curved up. "You won't even know he's here."

"If he makes trouble he'll be that night's stew."

Laura paled slightly, but nodded. "That's fair."

He glanced back at her wagon. "Are there any other surprises? Stowaway brothers or sisters? A pregnant barn cat?"

She laughed. The sweet sound carried on the faint morning breeze and made his chest tighten.

"No more surprises. I promise." She raised her gloved hand to her chest and made an X above her left breast. The action drew his attention to her feminine curves.

Before his imagination could make trouble, he wheeled his horse away. "I'll keep you to that promise," he called as he rode back toward the herd.

They made their evening camp at sundown. Laura stood next to her wagon, trying not to think about how sore her derriere was and wishing for a hot bath. She looked around at the vastness of the land, so different from life in town. Oh, she'd visited ranches before. Augusta was married to a rancher. Laura had ridden to the edge of town and stared at the open land before. But until this moment, she'd never been out of the county. As twilight swept over the sky, bringing with it the promise of night, she stared toward the horizon and saw only empty land.

There were no people, no buildings, no gardens. Only the trees, most still bare, a few budding with leaves, the grasses and some bushes. In the distance, to the west, clouds scurried across the darkening sky. The wind turned chilly and she briskly rubbed her arms. Her coat, the one Jesse had given her, was still in her wagon, on the seat where she'd put it that afternoon. With the sun warming her back, the temperature had been pleasant.

She inhaled as if she could still smell the scents that

had woven themselves into the wool. The faint mustiness of disuse, the sharp woodsmoke smell of an open fire, and something else. Something that made her think of Jesse.

Without wanting to, she turned and looked south. The cattle milled around, finding places to graze and settle for the night. She'd known the herd was large, but no description had prepared her for the sheer number of steers that slowly walked behind the wagons. Even now, they spread out farther than the eye could see. The dull colors blurred together. Black and brown, dun, pale red, dusty cream with brown blotches. Their horns made her shiver, their rhythmic steps made the trees tremble.

"You gonna stand there gawkin' or you gonna try to make yerself useful?"

Laura smiled as she glanced at the man who approached her. He was old, older than her father, with a gray beard and a fringe of white hair that stuck out below his hat. Pale-blue eyes squinted permanently, as if the man had spent too many days staring at the sun.

"I'd love to help," she said, trying not to smile at his obviously false ill temper. "But you implied women were useless on a trail drive. I believe your exact phrase was as useless as a priest in a whor—"

Harry held up his hand. "I know what I said. I also recall I was gonna teach you how to make coffee. That's somethin' even a woman can learn."

"I'd be much obliged." This time she allowed her lips to curve up.

His gaze narrowed. "How come you ain't scared o' me? I got them greenhorn cowboys cowerin' at the sight of me, but you don't even have the good sense to pretend."

Laura made a show of glancing over her shoulder, to make sure they were alone. "I had a grandfather just like you," she said. "He was gruff and colorful. He nearly drove my mother crazy with his demands. But he didn't frighten me because I knew deep inside, he had the biggest heart in the world. You're just like him. You act mean, but deep in here—" She touched her chest. "You're as tender as—"

Again Harry stopped her in midsentence. "Tarnation, girl, where'd you get those silly ideas of yours?" He drew himself up to his full height. It was only a couple of inches taller than her. "Get over here and make yerself useful. I can't imagine what Jesse was thinkin' of, bringin' a woman on a trail drive. You're gonna be the death of us, I swear."

She followed him to the chuck wagon. Already Harry had a big fire burning and a pot of beans simmering over the flames. He handed her a pot and pointed her in the general direction of the small stream to the east of camp.

"Get on down there before the steers muddy up the water. Clean this out good, then bring it back full. You think you can manage that?"

"Yes, Mr. Hellcat."

The old man sighed. "It's Harry. Just plain Harry."

She took the lid off the pot and stared at the grounds inside. "I'm going to try not to be any trouble," she said quietly. "I don't want to be a bother to you or to Jesse. I'm going to try to fit in."

Harry placed his hands on his hips. "Women can't help bein' trouble. It's just the way you was born."

"Is that so awful?"

A sharp bark interrupted their conversation. King stood on the wagon seat. His skinny tail wagged back and forth.

"Come on, King," Laura called.

The puppy jumped down and scampered over to them. He sniffed her shoes, then promptly moved over to Harry's feet.

The cook glared at the dog. "Damn nuisance. Can't believe Jesse's so touched in the head that he's lettin' a *dog* on the trail with us. The critter's gonna start a stampede for sure."

"No, he's not." Laura leaned over and scooped up the pup in her free arm. King wiggled closer and licked her chin. She giggled. "You'll be a good boy, won't you?"

King woofed in response.

She glanced up quickly and could have sworn she saw Harry smiling, but decided not to say anything just yet. "I'm going to get the water for coffee," she said.

"You do that." Harry headed for the fire and stirred the pot of beans.

Laura let the dog down and walked toward the stream. The ground was damp from a recent rain, but not muddy. She wondered how bad the storm would be tonight. The clouds seemed darker now, and the air was definitely cooler. She hurried to the bank and carefully dumped out the grounds.

While King sniffed around and chased shadows, she cleaned the pot, then refilled it. Before she could return to the welcome light of the fire, a rider approached.

For a moment Laura was startled. She stared at the man sitting tall in his saddle, then she recognized the proud set of his head.

"What are you doing out here?" Jesse asked as he dismounted.

King yapped loudly and raced toward him. Jesse's horse reared slightly. Jesse swore and grabbed the reins more tightly, steadying the animal with a low voice. As King circled them, Jesse ordered the dog away. Laura set the pot down and ducked close. She picked up King and held him.

"Don't cause trouble," she ordered.

"It's a little late for that." Jesse made sure his horse

was calm, then glared at the dog. "I bet Harry could use you in a stew."

"You wouldn't." She kissed the puppy on the forehead. "He doesn't mean that, sweetie."

"The hell I don't," Jesse said, although his grim expression relaxed a little. In the twilight, his eyes were dark, like the sky itself. His beard shadowed his face. Only his teeth flashed white as he spoke. Or if he smiled, but she didn't think he would be smiling anytime soon.

"What are you doing out here?" Jesse repeated the question. "You shouldn't be alone."

"I'm not." She set King on the ground and picked up the coffeepot. "Harry sent me for water."

He kept a hold of his mount's reins and placed his hand on the small of her back. "Don't go anywhere by yourself," he said. "Especially not at night. Harry shouldn't have sent you for water. I'll talk to him. It won't happen again."

"But I just want to help."

"And I want you to make it all the way to Kansas without being hurt."

The pressure on her back increased. She took a small step. Jesse kept pace with her. She could feel his fingers through her skirt and petticoats. His hand was warm and strong. A ribbon of heat seem to coil from his touch clear through to her belly. She wanted to step closer to him and feel more of that heat. She wanted to keep walking slow enough for him to need to push her along.

How odd. Being with Jesse made her think all kinds of things. Things like remembering their brief kiss. She couldn't forget the jolt she'd felt, or the brush of his heated skin against her own. She couldn't stop her gaze from resting on his broad chest or the way his muscles moved as he walked.

He was a handsome man. Why hadn't some woman

taken the time to heal him? He would be a worthy husband. If she was interested in that sort of thing, she would want to marry someone like Jesse. Someone she could trust.

King danced around in front of her, almost making her stumble. She scolded the dog.

"Stew," Jesse muttered.

Laura laughed up at him. "You stop that this minute. Do you hear me, Jesse Travers?"

He stared at her. They were close enough to the campfire that she could see his face clearly. Something flickered to life in his eyes. Maybe amusement.

"Yes, ma'am." He removed his hand from the small of her back and touched the tip of her nose. "Any other instructions?"

Her breath caught in her throat. She almost lost her grip on the coffeepot. In a second Jesse would smile. She could feel it. She had the most overwhelming urge to lean close to him, to be held and maybe kiss him again.

One of the cowboys rode close to camp. "Nice night, eh, boss?"

Laura looked up and saw that it was George. When she glanced back at Jesse, his expression was distant again, and he'd stepped away from her. When no one addressed him, George rode on. Jesse continued to keep his distance.

The sharp jab of disappointment surprised her. Why should it matter if Jesse didn't smile? She wasn't sweet on him. She was simply accompanying him on his trip north. When they reached their destination, they would part company as if they'd never been together.

Harry wasn't around, so she set the pot near the fire. King trotted after her, then found a warm space and curled up next to a log.

Jesse fingered his mount's reins. "Stay away from the

men," he said abruptly.

"What?"

"They're not used to having a woman on the trail. It's amusing now, but in a few weeks, they'll get restless. Better for everyone if you keep your distance now."

She didn't understand, but she wasn't going to argue with him. "All right. If you think that's best."

He turned to leave. She didn't want to be alone. More than that, she wanted to talk to him a little longer. "Jesse?"

"What?"

She bit her lower lip. "Um, there sure are a lot of steers out there."

"Yeah. Everyone one of 'em is money on the hoof."

She eyed the grazing cattle. "They just look like cows to me."

"When we get north, you'll see them transformed."

"I look forward to that." She glanced at the sky. "You think there's going to be a storm?"

"It's hard to tell. In spring they move fast. The clouds might continue this way, or they might circle north. We're hoping they avoid us. A stampede on the first night is deadly."

"I thought you said the cattle would be tired."

"Not tired enough. If something sets them off—" He didn't finish the sentence. Instead he moved close to her. His brown eyes flashed with questions. "Why are you doing this, Laura? You know it's dangerous. What's so damn important that you're going to risk your life to leave Jackson Springs?"

She flushed. It was getting darker by the minute and she was sure he couldn't see her blush, but she ducked her head all the same. "I can't tell you," she whispered. She wasn't ashamed of her reasons, but she didn't want anyone to make fun of her. Especially not Jesse.

"Are you running off to meet a man?"

Her head snapped up. "No! How could you ask that? We're married."

He raised his eyebrows. "It's a marriage of convenience. We're going to get a divorce."

"There's no man. I—" She twisted her hands together. She'd never told a living soul. She'd carried the secret with her since she'd been seven years old and vowed she would do whatever she had to in order to make her dream come true. "Can I trust you?"

"I don't know," he said. "That's for you to decide."

"You won't laugh?"

Firelight danced on his features. One moment his eyes were in shadow, the next she could see them clearly. His mouth curved up slightly. "I won't laugh."

She drew in a deep breath. "I want to be a famous singer. I've been planning this for a long time. The worst part about being born in the middle is that there was nothing special for me to be. I'm not the prettiest, or the youngest, or the smartest, or anything. I hated not being special. Then, one day, I realized what I wanted. I'm going to go to Wichita and sing, then get a ticket and go on to New York. I want to travel the world, see places. Meet interesting people. Oh, I know what you're thinking, I'm just plain Laura Cannon. What right do I have to those dreams?"

"You have every right," he said. "You can do anything."

"Really?" She held her hands out in front of her. "Are you just saying that?" She didn't wait for an answer. "I want—" She drew in a breath. "I want so much." She spun around and stared at the sky. "Look at how beautiful it is, Jesse. There's a big world under that sky and I want to see it. All of it. But not as myself. Not as plain Laura Cannon. I want to be more. I want to be—" She paused and looked at him. He was staring at her. Waiting. Not laughing. "I want to be Honeysuckle DeVine."

"Who?"

She giggled. "She's me. I'm going to be Honeysuckle DeVine. When we get to Wichita. I've got everything planned. I'm going to get a beautiful dress made. Red satin with lots of black lace." She slipped her hands over her waist and hips. "It will be sinfully low cut and tight, with ruffles. I'll have a hat and a wig."

He frowned. "A wig? Why? What's wrong with your hair?"

"The color. It needs to be red. Honeysuckle has red hair with lots of curls."

"I like your hair just fine the way it is."

The compliment surprised her. "Really?"

"I said it, didn't I?"

"But it's just plain."

"It's pretty."

He thought her hair was pretty. She touched a hand to the nape of her neck and felt the neat coil resting there. No one had ever said her hair was pretty before.

"Thank you," she said.

"So you're going to get this fancy dress and wig and leave for New York?"

"Yes. I'm going to be somebody wonderful."

"Seems to me a dress isn't going to make that much difference."

He didn't understand. That was fine. Most people wouldn't. It was enough that he hadn't laughed. Jesse couldn't know how she'd spent her nights imagining her life as Honeysuckle DeVine. All the years growing up, she'd planned every part of her life.

"Aunt Laura's inheritance has finally given me the means to my dream," she said. "I've got a way out of Jackson Springs."

A restless lowing caught her attention. She turned toward the sound. Jesse pulled his horse closer. "The storm's coming."

"Are they going to run?" she asked.

"Maybe."

Mike, one of the point riders, trotted by. When he saw Jesse, he drew his horse to a halt. "We've got trouble, boss."

"I can hear it. Tell the men to get ready."

Mike grinned. "First night out and we're already missing supper."

"Wouldn't have it any other way."

Laura stared at the dark mass of moving steers. She could feel their turmoil. It wouldn't take much to set them off. In the distance, the clouds flashed with lightning.

"What happens if they stampede?" she asked.

"We chase 'em down." Jesse pulled his hat low. "Hell of a way to start the cattle drive."

Maybe she could help. "Would you like me to sing for them?" she offered. "It might calm them down."

"I hadn't thought of that. It couldn't hurt."

"I'll try. I know a couple of lullabies." She walked closer to the herd.

"That's near enough," Jesse said, from beside her. She was about thirty feet from the closest steers.

Laura cleared her throat. Her first audience. Cattle. Funny how nervous she felt. She wiped her damp palms on her skirt and cleared her throat again.

"I know a place—"

The steers nearest to her rolled their eyes. She could see the white part, bright against their dark faces. She glanced at Jesse. He was staring at her as if her hair was on fire. She frowned, but continued with her song.

"Where all things beautiful—"

A mighty wail rose up from the cattle. The ground seemed to quiver beneath her feet. From the distance came a single cry.

"STAMPEDE!"

"Shit!" Jesse watched in disbelief as the cattle ran east and south. "Harry," he yelled, grabbing his horse.

"Right here." Harry came running toward the campfire.

Jesse swung into his saddle. "Take care of Laura and that damn dog. Don't let her get into any more trouble."

"She'll be safe with me."

"What's happening?" Laura asked. "Why are they stampeding?"

Jesse spared her a quick glance. She was staring up at him, her cheeks pale, her eyes wide. From the look on her face, she really didn't know. She didn't have any idea that her off-key, hair-raising singing had set the animals off.

"Git goin'," Harry ordered. The old man took off his hat and slapped it against Jesse's horse's rump. "I'll take care of the girl."

The gelding leapt forward. Jesse spurred the animal, then bent low over his neck. He didn't have time to think about anything but the steers. If they weren't brought under control soon, they could run all the way back to the ranch. Worse, a couple hundred head could scatter and precious time would be lost finding them.

He saw one of the cowboys up ahead and rode toward his man. Twenty feet away a river of steers thundered past. The ground shook from their pounding hooves. Waves of heat rolled out across the land. If they kept this up much longer, they'd lose more weight than they would gain in a week. He swore loudly.

The cowboy Lefty heard him and pulled up his horse. "They're heading somewhere in a hurry, boss. Mike's gone up ahead. He's hoping to find old Skunk. If we can get the herd turned—"

If they could get the herd to pinwheel in on itself, then they had a chance of stopping the stampede quickly. Jesse squinted in the darkness. The sun had long since faded and he couldn't see a damn thing except for brief patches of white on a passing steer.

"We couldn't even get through the first night," he muttered.

"You know what started it?" Lefty asked.

Jesse didn't answer. He gave his horse its head and took off after the cattle. He thought the herd might be slowing.

Up ahead he spotted several men on horseback. He slowed his mount to a canter and joined them. The herd was tiring, still running, but more slowly. The animals veered right, as they always did. After a quick consultation, the men formed a line and slowly began to force the herd more to the right, turning it back on itself. The halfhearted run became a trot, then a walk. Finally the cattle began to mill around. As the moon rose over the horizon, the herd settled down.

A tall rider came through the middle of the herd. Jesse waited until Mike joined him. Mike was experienced and had traveled with Jesse twice before. He trusted his judgment and his cow sense.

"I got to Skunk," Mike said, then drew in a deep breath. He wiped the back of his hand over his forehead. "I always forget how hot the herd gets when they run."

Jesse's horse tried to jump back from the milling cattle, but he kept the animal in place. "You get Skunk to turn?"

"Yup." Mike grinned. "I don't think his heart was in it tonight. He was running slow from the start. Otherwise I wouldn't have been able to catch him at all. What set 'em off? I didn't see any lightning."

Jesse stared down at his reins. "I'm not sure."

He grimaced. Why was he lying? He knew exactly what had set the cattle off. He just couldn't believe it. When Laura had opened her mouth to sing, he hadn't known what to expect. A pleasant voice, or maybe even a great one. He hadn't expected screeching. She sounded like a chicken being plucked alive. He shuddered at the thought. Maybe she needed to practice a little more.

"George said he heard something strange, like a coyote with a broken leg."

Jesse swung his horse around and started back for the camp. "Leave extra men on the herd tonight. I don't want them running again." He squinted into the darkness toward the clouds. "I can't see a damn thing, but I don't smell rain, do you?"

Mike sniffed loudly. "Nope. We might just get through the rest of the night."

"If we're lucky." He started to ride off, then stopped. "Check on the two boys, will you?"

"Sure thing, boss."

Laura would want to know if Wellington was safe. He wasn't the only greenhorn they had. The other cowboy riding drag was Bobby Jones. He was a year or two older than Wellington, although just as inexperienced. Their place was behind the herd. With a little luck, they'd been left behind and wouldn't have been able to catch up. Of course, the way his luck was running these days, the boys were probably in the thick of it.

He headed for the main camp. When he saw another of his cowboys, he reined in. But the approaching rider wasn't either of the boys.

"What are you doing back here?" Jesse asked.

George shifted on his saddle. "I thought I'd better check on Mrs. Travers. I didn't want her to get hurt in the stampede. You know how curious women are. I was afraid she'd ride out to investigate."

"Harry's with her."

George nodded once, the brim of his black hat dipping down to cover his face. "I didn't know that."

"Now you do." Jesse didn't like that one of his men had thought of Laura instead of the steers. He didn't much like George, either, although the man had come highly recommended. There was something about him. "Stay away from my wife," Jesse said.

"Is that an order?"

Moonlight illuminated the other man's face. He was about Jesse's age, with permanently tanned skin—a legacy of a life spent outdoors. Jesse's gut tightened at the thought of George near Laura. He wasn't sure why.

"Yeah, it's an order." Jesse leaned close to the cowboy. He pushed his hat back so George had a clear view of his eyes. His expression hardened. "Stay away from Laura or you'll be walking back to the ranch."

George turned and rode off without saying a word. Jesse watched him go, then made his way to camp.

As he approached, several people stood up and

watched. He searched the small crowd until he found Laura. She was standing next to Harry. Her coat dwarfed her small frame. Firelight reflected off the few strands of hair floating around her face, making her curls glow like liquid gold. The knot in his gut tightened more. He told himself it was because she was safe and for no other reason. He wasn't glad to see her.

Wellington broke free of the group. "Jesse, we saw the stampede." The boy raced toward Jesse's horse and stared up at him. "Bobby 'n' me wanted to go after the steers, but Harry wouldn't let us. Would you tell that old man we're cowboys, same as the rest of you?"

"Yeah." Bobby came running over and joined his newfound friend. "I'm big enough to wrestle a steer." The lanky adolescent had shaggy red hair and nearly as many pimples as freckles. He looked too skinny to wrestle more than a day-old lamb.

Watching them made Jesse feel old. He swung down from his saddle and handed Bobby the reins. "See to my horse, son."

Bobby started to grumble, but Jesse shot him a quelling look. "You help him, Wellington."

"Yes, sir," the boy said, but his tone was sullen. The two boys walked slowly away.

"Harry?"

"I got coffee going, boss. And biscuits. In fact the whole damn, ah, darn supper's waitin' on you boys to come back."

"The men will be here shortly."

Jesse glanced over his shoulder. When the two boys were out of earshot, he smiled wearily at the old man. "You did a good job, Harry. Thanks for keeping those two here. They'll have to learn how to handle a stampede soon enough, but not their first night out."

"Are you all right?" Laura asked. She moved close to

him and studied his face. "I've never seen a stampede before. It was frightening. Is everyone all right?"

"Last I heard, everyone's fine."

"Good." She touched his arm. He could feel the light pressure of her fingers through his coat. He liked that she'd been worried about him, fool that he was. "What got them stampeding?"

Before he could say anything, Harry thrust himself between them. "Here," he said, pushing a mug of coffee at Jesse. "Drink this." The older man glared at him. "There's no tellin' what set them steers off. Coulda been a flash of lightning, a tree branch. On the first night, they don't even need a reason."

He was answering Laura's question, but he kept looking at Jesse. As if warning him.

"Laura, could I have a spoonful of sugar in this," Jesse said, handing her his mug.

"Of course." She gave him a quick smile, then moved to the chuck wagon.

"Don't you say nothin' to her," Harry ordered as soon as she was out of earshot.

"I wasn't going to," Jesse answered, irritated that the old man thought he would be that mean-spirited. "I don't know for sure that her singing set them off anyway." He rubbed his left ear. "Was it just me or did she sound like—"

"A badger in heat?" Harry grinned. "Never heard noise like that comin' from a livin' creature before in my life. But we can't say nothin' to her." He sidled closer, then glanced at Laura to make sure she was still at the chuck wagon. "She confessed her secret to me, too."

"What do you think about her wanting to run off and be a famous singer?"

Harry's mouth straightened. "Hell if I know. She could tan leather with her voice, that's for sure. But I ain't gonna tell her and neither are you. That little girl's sweet as the sugar she's spoonin' in your coffee and you've got no right to hurt her."

"What do you take me for?" Jesse asked. "I wasn't going to say anything. Laura's business is her own. We'll just have to keep her from singing around the cattle. We can tell the men not to say anything to her, either."

"Or get her to do it so much, them steers get used to the caterwallin'."

Before Jesse could respond, Laura returned with his coffee. He thanked her and took a sip of the steaming liquid.

"Will the men be coming in for their supper?" she asked.

"Any minute. You already eat?"

She nodded. "Once Harry said it was safe, he suggested we dine first so as not to take up space by the fire. He said the men eat in shifts."

"That's right."

"Would you like me to fix your plate now?"

"You don't have to serve me, Laura. You're not working for me."

"But I'm your wife."

He kept trying to forget that part. "That doesn't mean you're expected to serve me."

"I want to help."

Firelight flickered on her face. Her cheeks looked soft and he wondered if she would let him touch her. The fierce need overwhelmed him. He fought it down, then grimaced at the pain that followed. He'd always known the danger of returning to life. He'd been cold and empty for so long, any emotion, even desire, was painful, like blood seeping back into a frozen limb. Now splinters of sensation pierced him. Better to feel nothing.

He opened his mouth to order her away, then found himself asking for an extra biscuit with his beans. She flashed him a smile, then hurried away to do his bidding.

Before he could chase after her and tell her he wasn't worth her effort, Wellington and Bobby reappeared.

"Your horse is bedded for the night, sir," Bobby said.

"Fine. Help yourself to some supper." He motioned to where Harry was hunched over the cookfire. "Wellington, I'd like a word with you."

The two boys exchanged worried glances, then Bobby slowly shuffled away. Wellington shifted his weight from foot to foot.

"If it's about King, sir, well, I can explain."

"King?" Jesse stared at him blankly. Oh, the damn dog. "You can't bring an animal like that on a cattle drive," he said.

Wellington hung his head. "I know. It's just him and me are buddies and I was afraid . . ." His voice trailed off.

In the firelight, he reminded Jesse of himself when he was young. Worse, Wellington reminded him of Laura. Their hair color was similar, as was their inability to hide their emotions. Through a marriage he neither wanted nor intended to continue, he was kin to this boy. That was the main reason he wasn't sending the boy walking home with his dog.

"Did Laura tell you my rules about King?" he asked.

"Yes, sir. If he gives you any trouble, you'll—" He swallowed. "—serve him up for the evening meal."

"That's right. Just so you know. But that's not what I wanted to talk about."

Wellington straightened. "It's not?"

"No. It's about your sister. Laura." How was he supposed to ask this? "Does she sing much?"

"Sing?" Wellington laughed loudly. "Our Laura? Sure she sings. All the time." He grinned. "If she gets too loud by the henhouse it's three days before the hens start laying again. Pa says Laura's voice can peel paint."

Jesse had been afraid of that. "She doesn't know, does she?"

Her youngest brother sobered instantly. "No, sir, and I'd be obliged if you wouldn't tell her. Laura's always thought she had a real pretty voice. I guess she can't hear herself the way we hear her."

"I won't say a word. Go on and get something to eat."

Wellington dashed off toward the fire. Jesse watched him run, then saw Laura approaching. She held a large tin plate in her hands. He couldn't see her individual features, but her silhouette was all feminine curves.

"I brought you an extra biscuit," she said shyly as she handed him his plate.

He took it from her and sat on a tree stump. Laura pulled up a camp chair next to him and chatted about her afternoon. He heard about which of the cowboys had dragged wood over for the cookfire and how Harry was going to let her help with the beans tomorrow. He thought about pointing out the fact that Harry "letting" her help simply meant the old man was having her do his work, but he didn't want her to stop smiling.

He watched her hands move as she told him about the stampede and how close the steers had come to their wagons.

"Harry says maybe distant lightning set them off," she said.

"Could be."

"Is the storm coming in this direction?"

Jesse stared up at the dark sky. He could make out a few stars, and the moon was brighter. "Looks clear. We got lucky this time." He shoved a forkful of beans in his mouth and chewed. After he swallowed, he spoke. "Why don't you try to get some sleep."

She glanced down at her hands. "All right."

He took his plate over to the wash area and set it down. After picking up a lantern, he lit a match and touched it to the wick. Soon the lantern was glowing brightly. He paused to give Mike instructions.

Laura was waiting where he'd left her. As he approached, she stood up. "I am a little tired," she said. "It's been a long day. Very exciting, though."

"We prefer things to be boring when we're on the trail." He held out his free arm.

"That makes sense." She placed her hand in the crook of his elbow and moved close to him. She barely came to his chin. If he turned his head just a little, he could brush against her hair and find out if it was as soft as it looked. He didn't. Not just because he knew his men were watching him, but because it implied a weakness he couldn't afford.

As they neared the wagon, Laura slowed. "What did you think of my singing?" she asked.

Jesse was glad it was dark. For the first time in ten years, he was sure his thoughts would have been plain to read on his face. "You didn't get a chance to finish your song," he said, then knew that wasn't right. Hell. "But it sounded pretty enough." He winced, waiting for her to accuse him of lying.

"Did you really think so?" she asked shyly. They stopped in front of the wagon. She turned to face him.

"You have a lot of power in your voice." He remembered how the sound had carried in the night. "People will be able to hear you all the way in the back of the room. I'm sure that's good. Who would want to pay money for a ticket, then not be able to hear?"

He hadn't believed in God in a long time, but he

half-expected a bolt of lightning to strike him dead on the spot.

Laura leaned close and placed her hands on his chest. His coat had come open, so her palms pressed against his shirt. The heat of her burned him. "Thank you, Jesse. Your opinion means a lot to me. You're not family so you don't have to be nice." She wrinkled her nose. "Not that my family's nice all the time."

"You really mean to do this? You're going on the stage?"

She nodded. "In Wichita there's plenty of saloons that provide entertainment. I had my lawyer investigate that for me."

He set the lamp on the edge of her wagon. "You ever been in a saloon?"

"No, but I'm sure I'll be fine. I'm only there for a little while. I want to get some experience before I take the train to New York." Her eyes widened with excitement. "I've read about famous lady singers. They live magical lives. Why, I might meet a crown head of Europe. Sometimes, when I run off to the far end of the orchard and practice, I close my eyes and I can see myself there. The dress I've planned is so beautiful. I'll look like a princess myself. The best part is, it won't be me at all. Honeysuckle DeVine is going to be famous." She lowered her gaze. "I made up her name myself, when I was seven. The 'DeVine' part is French."

"I sort of figured that. They're never going to forget being entertained by you." Jesse couldn't bear to think about what would happen when she did appear on stage for the first time, fancy costume or not. He pulled open the covering at the back of her wagon and drew out the step stool. "It's late."

She stepped up. Before she could start to climb inside, he placed his hands at her waist and lifted her up. He'd helped her up and down from wagons before.

Except this time, instead of encountering the protective barrier of her corset, he felt only layers of clothing and the yielding softness of a woman.

As soon as she was settled on the lip of the wagon, he dropped his arms to his sides. It made sense. There wasn't another woman on the cattle drive to lace her up every morning. She couldn't stay in her corset for three or four months. He wasn't shocked, just—

He swore silently. It wasn't the sort of information that was going to help him sleep better. He didn't want to think about what she was wearing under her dresses, let alone what she *wasn't* wearing.

"I've had fun today," she said. There was a rustling noise from the front of the wagon, then King poked his head out. "Harry put him in here when the stampede started."

"Good. He wouldn't survive long in the herd."

She grabbed the little dog and pulled him onto her lap. "At least he wasn't responsible for the steers running like that. I told you I'd keep him out of harm's way."

There was nothing he could say to that, so he changed the subject. "If you can't sleep, stay in your wagon. Don't go wandering around at night. The men won't bother you, but there's no reason to invite trouble." He waited until she nodded, then continued. "I'll be sleeping under your wagon."

"On the ground?" She sounded horrified.

He grinned. "Where do you think all the men will be sleeping?"

"I hadn't thought about it. What if it rains?"

"Then we get wet."

"I wouldn't like that at all."

"That's why you have a wagon."

"I wonder if Wellington knows."

"If he doesn't, he's going to pretty soon."

She set King back in the wagon, then leaned close to Jesse. "Thank you for everything. I know I'm in the way. You're trying not to let me know, but I can see it. You're a good man, Jesse Travers." She brushed her lips against his cheek.

The brief contact seared him down to his groin. He couldn't decide whether to run away or join her in the wagon. The thought of easing himself down next to her, of touching her bare body, of . . . He gritted his teeth against the longing that swept over him.

So much for being a good man.

"Go to sleep," he ordered and walked away.

He went directly to the campfire and poured himself a cup of coffee. He drained the mug in three swallows. The hot liquid scorched his mouth and throat. He welcomed the burning. It gave him something else to think about.

He'd known having a woman along would be a pain in the ass. He hadn't thought he would like her, or want her. He hadn't thought he might feel the first stirring of life. Life meant remembering. It meant what had happened to David could happen to him. David hadn't been able to shut down his feelings in the prison camp. He'd chosen to remain attached to the world around them. At the time, Jesse had envied the other man's ability to still feel something. But in the end, those feelings had killed David as surely as the bullet that shattered his brain.

Mike stood up and approached him. "Everything's quiet now," his second in command told him. "The steers are settled for the night. The storm's gone north of us."

"Good news, unless it floods the rivers."

"Hell, boss, you can't have it both ways. It's always something on the trail."

"I know. Have you assigned the night watch?"

Mike removed his black hat and smoothed down his light hair. "Yup. I'm giving the extra dozen men the most duty. They'll head back to the ranch in a week. They can sleep there. I figured it would be better if the men staying for the whole drive started out rested."

"Good thinking," Jesse said, then reached for the coffeepot. He was going to keep an eye on his point man. If Mike continued to do as well as he had on the previous trip north, Jesse would hire him to be the trail boss next year. His spread was getting so big, he couldn't afford to be gone nearly half a year.

"Lookee here," George said, straightening on his seat and pointing toward the wagon. "Nice of your wife to provide us with a little entertainment."

Jesse turned in the direction the man was pointing. Laura had hung the lantern from a hook inside. She was in the process of undressing. The light cast a perfect shadow on the canvas walls, outlining every inch of her torso. As she finished unbuttoning her blouse, she thrust her chest forward. In a few seconds she would pull it off and every man here would see her breasts.

"Don't you look at my sister," Wellington said from somewhere behind him. Jesse didn't know the boy was still up.

"Everybody turn their backs," Jesse roared. "Mike, keep the boy out of trouble." He didn't bother to wait and see if his orders were obeyed, he just took off running.

"Laura!" he called when he was close enough.

The wagon shifted as she jumped slightly, then crawled to the back. She stuck her head out, but was careful to keep the bottom of the cotton cover closed. All he could see was her face and a bit of her hair.

"What's wrong?" she asked.

He stopped in front of her and caught his breath.

"You can't—" How could he tell her? He glanced back at the camp. The men had stretched out on their bedrolls. Apparently Mike had calmed Wellington down. No one was watching, but that didn't mean she would be any less embarrassed.

"I can't what?"

He drew in a deep breath, then looked her square in the face. "Don't keep the lantern on while you undress. It makes a shadow on the side of the wagon cover."

Her mouth opened but she didn't speak. She raised her hands to her face and moaned softly. The covering gaped open slightly, exposing her unbuttoned blouse and the lacy chemise below.

Jesse told himself a gentleman wouldn't take advantage of her inattention and look. But he hadn't considered himself a gentleman in years. He stared at her bare neck and chest, then lowered his gaze to her breasts. They were full enough to make his palms itch. He closed his eyes and tried to think about something else, but her shape had been engraved on his memory.

"I just want to die," she murmured.

"It doesn't work that way," he said. "I've never seen anyone perish from embarrassment."

"I'll never be able to show my face again."

"Unfortunately it wasn't your face they were looking at," he said without thinking.

Laura dropped her hands to her thighs and stared at him. Her eyes widened. He thought she might slap him. Instead she giggled. Jesse found himself smiling in return. Her giggle turned into laughter. He joined in.

"And I promised not to be any trouble," she said in a few moments. She shook her head. "Thank you for telling me. I'm still embarrassed, but I suppose I'll get over it." At that moment, she became aware of the fact that her blouse was hanging open. She pulled it closed.

It took every ounce of self-control Jesse had, but he kept his gaze fixed firmly on her face. "Turn off the lantern before you undress."

He waited until she'd extinguished the lantern before walking back to the fire. All the men were stretched out in their bedrolls. Those with night duty had tethered their mounts nearby. Jesse collected his bedroll and carried it back to Laura's wagon. He unrolled the oilcloth and blankets, then lay down between the wheels. This far away from the fire, he would freeze for the first month or so, until the nights warmed up. However, if it rained, he wouldn't get as wet. He'd survived worse.

Above him, the wagon shifted. He heard a soft yap from King, then Laura urging the dog to be quiet. The straw mattress rustled as she settled down.

He wondered what she wore to bed at night. Was it a pale gown edged in lace? He never spent much time concerned about a woman's clothing. Whores dressed to be accessible. Their chemises pulled down over corsets to expose their breasts, while their pantaloons were slit from thigh to thigh. He'd never asked one to undress more. Why take the time? But when he'd seen Laura's open blouse, he'd thought about removing it slowly. Of kissing her bare arms and shoulders, of tracing her delicate neck before pulling off her chemise. He didn't want her partially clothed like the whores. He wanted her naked and willing, hungry for him alone.

His thoughts produced an uncomfortable if expected reaction. He shifted on the hard ground, but it did nothing to alleviate his condition. He forced himself to think of something else. If the first day was anything to go by, this wasn't going to be an easy cattle drive. Laura was more responsibility than any one man should have, especially him.

Yet she was his wife, and he'd given his word to keep her safe. No matter what, he would get them to Kansas. He would protect her—even from himself.

Something cold brushed against Laura's face. She huddled deeper under her blankets and batted it away. The cold thing returned, and this time it was damp, too. She didn't want to open her eyes. She'd had a hard time falling asleep and she was tired. But the cold, damp, *whimpering* interruption wouldn't be dissuaded.

"Can't it wait, King?" she mumbled.

Ecstatic that she'd said his name, the little dog licked her face and quivered.

"I guess it can't," she said, and rose up on one elbow.

It was still dark outside. She thought about opening the laced canvas at the back of the wagon, but Jesse had told her to stay inside. She was determined to obey his instructions and not give him any trouble.

King wiggled closer. She held up the blankets so he could duck underneath. The little pup curled up next to her and rested his head on her belly.

Laura closed her eyes and started to drift back to sleep. From outside she could hear the sounds of the cattle and the rhythmic chirping of some night creature. There were also footsteps close to the wagon. For a moment she tensed, then she relaxed. It didn't matter who was out there, she reminded herself. Jesse would keep her safe.

Before she could do more than doze, there was a faint scratching at the canvas cover.

"Laura," Jesse said softly. "It's time to get up. Are you awake?"

She scrambled into a sitting position, then pulled the covers up over her shoulders. As she moved to the rear of the wagon, King scampered ahead of her. She opened the lacing and stared out.

The night sky was clear. There were more stars than she'd ever seen before. The moon was gone and there wasn't a hint of the sun yet. In the distance the campfire burned cheerfully. She could smell the burning wood and the fresh coffee. Something was baking as well and her stomach growled.

Jesse was a tall, broad silhouette in the early morning darkness. She smiled at him.

"What time is it?"

"You don't want to know."

She giggled. "It's early, though. I wonder if I've ever been up this early before." Her yawn surprised her. She covered her mouth.

"Did you sleep?" he asked.

"I was so excited about the trip starting, I had trouble relaxing, but after that I was fine."

She felt King trying to get around her. She opened the back wider. The little dog rushed forward and jumped. Jesse caught him.

"I'll take this menace for a walk while you get dressed," he said. "We'll be moving out in half an hour.

Don't worry about your mules. Frank takes care of the horses. He'll see to the hitching and unhitching of your mules, as well as feeding them."

"I could do it." She leaned toward him. "I don't want to be a burden."

He shook his head. "You're a paying passenger. I don't expect you to do chores."

She tilted her head and stared at him. "If I didn't know better, I would say you don't want me to touch anything, because if I don't, I have less chance of messing things up."

"You're pretty smart." He set King on the ground. The little dog immediately began sniffing the grass.

"Did you sleep?" she asked. For some reason she didn't want Jesse to just walk off and leave her.

"The first few nights are difficult. The ground's harder than I remember."

She opened her mouth to offer her wagon to him, then closed it tight. She'd already offered herself once and been turned down. Not that she was offering *that*. Surely people couldn't act that way out in the open, or in a wagon where everyone around them would know. She shuddered at the thought.

"Does it get easier?" she asked.

"It gets familiar."

"Not exactly the same thing." She smiled.

Jesse took a step toward her. The air was cold with a stillness that can't be found during the day. She felt a sense of expectation, of promise, as if the dawn would make all things possible. Her stomach jumped a little, but she knew it wasn't from hunger. Something else was making her nervous.

She felt his gaze on her face and self-consciously touched her braid to make sure it was smooth. With her other hand, she pulled her blankets tighter around her shoulders.

"Jesse?" she whispered.

"Get dressed," he told her, then walked away toward the campfire.

When she was alone, she had the oddest sensation of being abandoned. She shook it off and retreated inside the wagon.

Ten minutes later she decided that saying one was going dress and actually performing the act were not the same thing. After what had happened the previous night, she didn't dare light the lantern. She thought she'd carefully left out her clothing for the day. But sometime in the night it had become tangled with her blankets. The cold air and chill bumps on her arms and legs urged her to hurry while the darkness made her clumsy. Thank goodness she wasn't bothered with a corset.

She fastened the first petticoat around her waist and pulled the second one over her head. When it settled on the first and was fastened, she reached for the third. And paused. She'd been comfortable enough riding in the wagon, but it had been difficult to walk around camp with all her petticoats. Perhaps she could consider wearing less.

At the thought, a blush swept up her neck and cheeks. She pressed her hands to the heat. No one was going to know, she told herself. Modesty wrestled with practicality. In the end, she wore one less petticoat and hoped it would help.

She pulled on her blouse and did up the small buttons. In the dark, she had to feel if she'd matched the ends, or if there was one extra hole at the collar and one undone button at the bottom. Her shoes were impossible. She pulled them on, but couldn't begin to tie them in the dark. No problem, she told herself. Surely she could fasten her shoes by the fire. She could sit on a log and not even show a hint of ankle. After pulling the ribbon from her braid, she quickly brushed her hair, then pinned it up.

When the last pin was secure, Laura quickly tidied her bedding, then drew open the back covering and jumped to the ground. Her skirt and petticoats were all bunched up. She rotated her hips back and forth several times until all the layers fell neatly to the ground. She straightened her cuffs and made sure that her blouse was buttoned correctly. Except for her unlaced shoes, she was dressed and ready for the day.

"All set?" Jesse asked, materializing from the darkness.

"Yes, I think so."

He handed her King and they headed for the fire.

Several cowboys were still there eating breakfast. They stood up as she approached and mumbled greetings. Laura kept her head high, even though she just wanted to curl up and die. Had they all seen her last night? Did they remember watching her undress? Embarrassment crashed over her in hot waves. One of the men, George, winked at her. She turned away and sank onto the nearest camp stool.

King jumped from her lap and trotted over to Harry. The old man glared at the pup. "I suppose yer expectin' me to feed you."

King barked.

"Hmph." Harry ladled something onto a plate and set it on the ground.

Laura smiled. Jesse handed her some coffee. "There's biscuits and bacon," he said. "This being the first morning out, there's even eggs. If you're not hungry now, take biscuits with you because our next stop isn't until midday."

"Thank you." She sipped the hot coffee and tried not to gag at the strong, bitter flavor. The previous night she'd avoided the brew. How did the men drink this day after day? She had some tea in her wagon. She was going to have to get up earlier so she could make it before they left.

Wellington came up and crouched next to her. "Isn't it great?" he asked. "I was up almost all night with the cattle."

"You were on patrol your first night?"

"Nah. Bobby and I just watched 'em."

His too-long hair hung past his eyebrows. Laura reached up and brushed it out of his eyes.

Wellington shot to his feet. "Laura, you can't do stuff like that." He glanced around, then lowered his voice. "I'm one of the cowboys, here. Not your little brother."

He was growing up fast. "I won't do it again. But you need a haircut."

Wellington groaned.

Jesse came over with a plate of biscuits, bacon, and eggs. "Your sister is right," he told the boy. "You're no use to me if you can't see the cattle. Talk to Harry. He'll take care of it tonight when we stop."

Wellington's shoulders slumped down. "Yes, sir," he mumbled, then turned and shuffled away.

"I wish I could get him to listen to me like that," Laura said.

"You're just his sister." He glanced over his shoulder. "Your mules are already hitched up. Move out when Harry does. Later I'll ride out and check on you."

He sounded worried. She smiled up at him. "I'll be fine, Jesse."

In the campfire light she couldn't see the flecks of gold in his eyes, but she knew they were there. Wellington wasn't the only one with shaggy hair. Despite his recent haircut for the wedding, Jesse's hair hung almost as low on his forehead. In the back it went clear down to the bottom of his collar.

"Maybe you should have a visit with Harry yourself," she said.

Jesse put his hat on. "I just might do that." He looked at the cook. "Harry, I'm saddling up. Watch out for Laura."

The old man glared at him. "You already told me that once today. If you're gonna remind me every time you leave the campfire, I'm gonna have to put somethin' nasty in your supper."

"I thought you already had."

The few men still around the fire laughed. Laura bit back a smile. Harry narrowed his gaze. "It ain't too late for me to head back to the ranch."

"Sure it is. You love the trail."

Jesse mounted his horse and rode off toward the herd. Harry walked away, mumbling under his breath.

George finished his breakfast and tossed his plate into the large wooden basin next to the fire. He poured more coffee, then moved closer to her seat.

"Morning, Miss Laura," he said and smiled.

She smiled back. "Morning. Isn't this exciting? It's our first real day on the trail."

"I've done this before, so I don't have your enthusiasm. Although having a pretty lady like yourself along will surely help pass the time."

His lines were smooth and practiced. Her sister Augusta had often repeated the more outlandish phrases young men had used when they courted her.

"I would think being as busy as you men seem to be would pass the time fast enough," she said.

He took the camp stool next to hers. "How long have you and the boss been married?"

The question made her uncomfortable, as did his gray eyes. They seemed to focus on her bosom instead of her face. She hunched forward so her thick coat hid her shape from him and wished it wouldn't be too obvious for her to fasten the buttons.

"A while." She didn't want to tell him it had only been a few days.

"You don't wear a wedding ring."

It was true. Jesse hadn't given her one. She'd told her family she would have a ring when she got home. One more lie in a long list.

"That doesn't make us any less married," she said and stuffed a forkful of eggs into her mouth. She stared at her plate and wished the man would go away.

"Interesting that your husband sleeps *under* your wagon instead of in it."

"Why? Jesse wants to keep me safe."

George leaned toward her and smiled. "I would be more interested in keeping you warm."

"That's silly," she said. "I am warm." She had enough blankets to weather a blizzard. Her mother had made sure of that.

George touched her hand. "You misunderstand me."

She didn't misunderstand him touching her. She rose to her feet. "Sir, I must ask you—"

But she didn't get to finish. Harry returned to the fire. "You gonna eat standin' up?" he asked.

"No, I—" When she turned, George was gone.

It was all very strange, she thought as she finished the last of her breakfast.

"Last call for bedrolls," the cowboy named Frank said loudly. The rangy man stood next to the cook wagon.

"See to them mules when you're done," Harry said.

Frank touched the brim of his hat and grinned. "Yes, sir."

Harry grumbled. Laura smiled. Frank was in charge of the extra horses, as well as hers and Harry's mules. He led the horses north, roped the animals for the cowboys when they needed a new mount and generally saw to their well-being. Her team was already in place.

Laura took her plate over to the basin where Harry was washing. She grabbed a towel and helped him dry. Frank loaded up the Dutch oven, then tossed the unburned wood into a leather shelf that was slung under the chuck wagon. By the time everything was put away, the cattle were already moving north.

"They just start walking?" Laura asked.

"For a bit. They'll spread out and graze, then cover about five miles or so until noon. They'll water and eat again, then push on till supper." Harry took off his apron and shook it. "You ready?"

"Yes." She called for King. The little dog came running. She placed him in the back of her wagon, then drew on her gloves and climbed up to the seat.

Harry pulled out and she followed. To the east, the sun was just drifting over the horizon. Between her and the sunrise, cattle stretched out. She stared at the large animals. They had wide, curved horns and broad faces. They were a moving blur of color. Dull coats, reds and duns, black, brown, and everything in between. She wasn't sure if the muted colors came from the dust or if they didn't have the vivid hues of domestic animals. She must remember to ask Jesse when she saw him.

She shivered a little in the early morning chill. Her coat was already buttoned so she pulled up her collar. To distract herself, she started to hum, then sing.

She sang softly, at first, then a little louder. The four mules pulling her wagon flicked their ears toward her. They tossed their heads and shuddered as if shaking off flies.

"Don't you like my song?" she asked. They broke into a trot.

Laura continued to sing and hum. As they passed the

walking steers, the animals seemed to shy away a little. She wondered if the wagon frightened them.

After a couple of hours, she was able to unbutton her coat. She and Harry had passed the cattle and were making their way toward the noon camp. She kept a watch out for Jesse, but once the herd was moving, she couldn't see one end from the other, or even the edges from side to side. The ever-present dust cloud rose up and hovered above the steers.

"How you doing?"

She started at the unexpected voice, then smiled when she recognized her husband. "Morning, Jesse."

He'd taken off his coat and tied it in front of his saddle. His pale-blue shirt contrasted with his dark hair. A black vest hugged his chest. She could see the pistol strapped to his thigh and wondered if he ever had cause to use it.

"Everything going well?" he asked.

"Just fine. King's been asleep since we left camp. I think sniffing all the time tires him out."

Jesse didn't answer. She was afraid he would just ride off now that he knew she was safe.

"How long have you wanted to be a singer?" he asked before she could think up an excuse to keep him at her side.

"Since I was little." She smiled, remembering how she'd given performances in the barn. "I used to make sketches of what my dress would look like. I have them with me now. Not the original designs, of course. Those are pretty silly. But I've been looking over fashion books and I've come up with something I think will be perfect for the stage."

He nodded. "Lefty said you were singing earlier."

"I like to keep my voice in tune. I hope you don't mind."

Jesse tugged on the brim of his hat. "The cattle aren't

used to anyone singing, but he said it didn't bother them too much, so I don't mind." He glanced at her warily, as if afraid she might take offense.

"I understand. They're easily startled by anything unfamiliar."

"Exactly. We'll be making camp in a couple of hours."

"I'll be glad to stand up and stretch."

"You can stop if you want, but make sure you let Harry know."

She glanced up ahead at his wagon. "I've been wondering. How did Hellcat Harry get his name?"

Jesse chuckled. She loved the sound of his laughter. It was a little rusty from disuse, but she didn't mind that.

"I probably shouldn't tell you."

"But you will."

He grinned. "Harry bedded down in the barn one night. He was as drunk as a—" Jesse paused and looked at her. "He was very drunk."

She grinned. "I understand."

"About midnight, we heard this screaming coming from the barn. Next thing we knew, Harry comes running outside. He wasn't wearing a stitch of clothing except for his hat. He went on about a hellcat being loose in the barn."

As he told the story, his posture relaxed a little and he urged his horse closer to her wagon. Laura watched him, the way his eyes brightened with the telling, his mobile mouth. She wondered what he would look like if he ever shaved off his beard. Her gaze settled on the scar. It hadn't been there before the war.

"What did you do?" she asked.

"We collected our pistols and went to investigate. Turns out one of the barn cat's kittens had gotten tangled up in Harry's bedroll. He must have woken the critter up and startled it. His legs were scratched some." Jesse laughed at the memory. "I doubt that cat weighed all of four pounds. The next morning one of the men started calling him Hellcat Harry. It's been about five years, but the name stuck."

"I like it," she said and chuckled. "But I don't think I'll call him that to his face."

"I wouldn't."

Jesse continued to ride next to her. She thought about asking him if he wanted to sit with her on the wagon, but she didn't. It wasn't right, somehow. He might be her husband, but they were still strangers. He was only being kind because she was paying him.

Funny, when she'd been planning her escape from her family, she'd only thought of Jesse as the man who would help her get what she wanted. She hadn't really thought about what it would mean being with him for the length of the cattle drive.

"You're looking serious about something," he said.

"I was just remembering my family," she said. "In all the excitement yesterday I forgot to feel guilty."

"Why don't you wait until you get to Kansas and feel guilty there? It will make the trip a lot more enjoyable."

"Can I do that? Put off guilt?"

He shrugged. "Why not?"

It was a novel idea. She liked it. She started to tell him so, but became distracted when he removed his hat and ran his fingers through his hair. The long, shiny strands looked clean, as if he bathed often. His profile was strong and handsome. Suddenly her palms felt damp inside her gloves. Her stomach got all emptylike, although she'd eaten breakfast. Her gaze lowered to his mouth and she remembered their brief kiss.

Had she really felt that jolt when his lips had touched

hers? Was it a one-time oddity or could she feel it again, if he kissed her? Did he think about it, too?

"Laura?"

"Hmm?" What if he kissed her like other boys had? What if he held her close and pressed his mouth against hers for a long time? The funny feeling in her stomach sharpened. She shifted on the seat.

"Laura, are you listening to me?"

"What?" She blinked and found Jesse staring at her. He'd put his hat back on and was waiting patiently for her to answer him. "I'm listening."

"We're going to cross a small river this afternoon."

"All right."

"Harry will fill up his water barrel first. Then you fill up yours. Your mules will drink, then the remuda—the horses. The steers are last. When we cross the river, the remuda goes first. You follow Harry. The water won't be deep and I'll be with you."

She listened intently, then nodded. "My wagon has been caulked, so it should float just fine."

"There's not going to be any floating. The water isn't that deep. Still, it's the first crossing and everyone's a little nervous."

"I'm not afraid."

"How'd you get so brave?" he asked.

His compliment pleased her. "I don't feel brave. But I'm not afraid of much. I've always been pretty fearless." She smiled. "I've done some silly things because of that, too."

"Like going on a cattle drive to get to Wichita?"

"That's one of them." She glanced at her lap, then at him. "I don't think I've changed at all since I was little, but you have. I know Washington came home different after the war, too. Washington used to get angry. I'm not sure at who. Himself, maybe the war. Do you get angry, too?"

He didn't answer for a long time. Laura feared she'd insulted him by the question, or pried where she wasn't welcome. "You don't have to answer that," she said quickly. "I shouldn't have asked." She stared at Harry's wagon fifty or so feet in front of them.

"I'm not angry about the changes," he said at last. "They exist. I can't go back. I'm not sure I'd want to."

"Do you stay away from town because you think people won't like the changes?"

"Do they?" he asked and raised his eyebrows.

She shook her head. "No. I've heard the talk. I'm sure you have, too. They say you used to be . . . different." A charmer. That's what the women said. Jesse Travers could charm a saint into sinning. Many had been disappointed when he'd returned to Jackson Springs a silent, haunted man.

"My family didn't like the changes either," he said. "That's one of the reasons I came back to Texas. They wanted to talk about the war. They wanted to keep my medals out for the neighbors to admire." His mouth twisted with derision. "As if medals won in battle are an honor."

"Aren't they?"

"They're a prize for death. I always expect the ribbons to be red, from the bloodstains." He drew in a deep breath. "There's no glory in war. No victory. I didn't do anything a thousand other men couldn't have done better. I never felt courageous or brave. Being alive in the prison camp meant living like a starving dog. I've seen things, done things no man should do. If you knew the truth about me—"

He stopped and stared at her. Laura wanted to touch him, to comfort him and help him heal. "There's nothing you can say to frighten me away," she whispered and reached her hand toward him.

He stared at her face. His was expressionless; there was a cold emptiness in his eyes.

"You're wrong," he told her and wheeled his horse toward the herd.

Jesse spent the afternoon riding hard. He crossed the shallow river himself, then went back. He checked banks for two miles in each direction. He circled the herd and spoke with each of the cowboys. Everything was going well, but he couldn't shake the coldness at the back of his neck.

It was Laura. From the moment she'd ridden into his life, she'd made him do things and say things that he had no business doing. She made him feel. Worse, she made him remember and that was the most dangerous act of all.

Without wanting to, he recalled the first time he'd seen David Beaumont. The man had been leaning casually against a fence post as if he were attending a spring ball and not up to his knees in mud and garbage. He'd smiled and bowed slightly, introducing himself as, if not the senior officer of the camp, then the one with the most seniority. He had the slow Southern drawl of a man born and bred in the Carolinas, the educated speech of a man who had spent time abroad, and the manner of a gentleman. He and Jesse had little in common. Perhaps that was why they'd become friends.

The first weeks in the prison camp were horrifying. The overcrowded rooms, the stink, the rats, the death. It was worse than a battlefield. Worse than the death he'd always feared. David had stayed with him, protected him from those who preyed on the new prisoners, had taught him how to hoard his food, how to avoid the worst of the illnesses. Jesse had taught himself to ignore the memories. Anger, disappointment, hatred, despair. All emotions were enemies, as much as the Yankees. A man could go mad from the remembering. Jesse had learned to forget.

Now, all these years later, he was a master at forgetting, at ignoring the ugly, the painful, the past. But sometimes the memories won. The memories had killed David. Jesse shook his head. He didn't want to think about that. Only he couldn't not. Nothing in Laura's world had prepared her for a man like him. If she kept prying, she would find out how black and hideous his soul really was.

"Every moment you're in pain, the Yankees are winning," David had told him. "Enjoy prison life, such as it is. Remember better times. Laugh at the bastards."

Jesse smiled sadly. David would have liked Laura. He would have enjoyed her easy humor and her dream. The fact that she couldn't sing a note wouldn't have mattered. If anything, it would have encouraged him to make sure her dream came true.

Laura, no doubt, would have been charmed by David. With his blond good looks, he would have set her female heart fluttering. David was everything Jesse was not—a hero. Until the end. Until he'd turned his back on everything he believed in.

Jesse looked at the herd of cattle slowly heading

north. Despite the past and pain, he'd made something of his life. He got through the days. Better, he got through the nights.

Voices broke through his musings.

"Hell, Frank, if you want me to do your job for you, just say so. Don't be makin' such a mess of things that I've got to work twice as hard to clean it up." Harry's tirade drifted to him over the afternoon breeze.

Jesse urged his horse down the embankment to the edge of the river. Frank, their wrangler for the trip, had filled the chuck wagon's water barrel and was wrestling it up the embankment. Harry stood several feet away, offering advice but no practical assistance.

"Don't get in my way, old man, or you'll be hitching your mules yourself."

"And you'll be eatin' cold gravel for breakfast," Harry shot back.

Jesse urged his horse closer. Frank and Harry fought the entire trip to and from Kansas. They'd been at it as long as Jesse had known both of them. Neither would say why. He suspected they were both just ornery. No doubt either would protect the other at the risk of his own life, although they'd rather be hog-tied and flogged than admit it.

"I'd like to get everyone across the river this afternoon," he said, when he was close enough to be heard. "If we wait too long, the cattle will have to cross into the sun. We can't afford to have them milling and drown."

Harry put his hands on his hips. "Don't be jawin' at me about that. I ain't the one holding us up."

Frank wrapped his arms around the full barrel and heaved it into place on the side of the wagon. "Done," he said, glaring at Harry. "With no help from you, old man."

"I can burn your supper as easy as not," Harry grumbled.

Jesse coughed to hide a smile. He surveyed the river. The flowing water stretched about twenty-five feet from bank to bank. The current was slow. Bare trees and bushes lined both sides for as far as he could see. There were tracks of small animals in the damp soil.

He kicked his horse and the gelding stepped into the river. His mount crossed easily, finding his footing on the slick bottom. The water barely touched his belly. When Jesse was on the other side, he took off his hat and waved it. "Let's start across," he called.

Harry climbed up into his wagon and flicked the reins. His mules started forward. Jesse looked for Laura's wagon. It was off to one side, but he didn't see her. He frowned and he scanned the area. Finally he saw her down by the river. She had a small barrel she'd filled with water and was trying to carry it back. It was obviously too heavy for her. She walked stiff-legged, her blue calico dress flapping around her legs. A few strands of hair had escaped the neat coil at the base of her neck.

He shook his head. Just like her to want to take care of it herself instead of asking for help. He started his gelding across the river to assist her.

But before he arrived, one of the cowboys rode up and dismounted. George said something to Laura, then took the barrel from her arms. Jesse glared as he saw how close the other man's hand came to her bosom. Something hot and ugly flared in his belly. He leaned forward and kneed the gelding. His mount shot out of the river and up the embankment. Laura and George turned to look at him.

His wife smiled. Her innocent eyes told him she'd had no hand in this. She probably didn't even realize what George wanted. The cowboy was a different matter. He didn't meet Jesse's gaze. Instead he busied himself with the water barrel.

"Get back to the herd," Jesse said.
George glared at him. The two men faced each other down. George blinked first. Swinging into his saddle, he kicked his horse into a canter.
Jesse stared after him. He thought about sending the man back to the ranch. But aside from Mike, George was the most experienced cowboy he had. With Laura, Wellington, and Bobby all being greenhorns, he needed George around. But he was going to have to talk to the man again and make sure he left Laura alone.
"What's wrong?" she asked.
The afternoon had grown warm and she'd removed her coat. He could see the outline of her bosom and the narrowness of her waist. He alone knew she wasn't wearing a corset under her clothing, so the contrast in curves was due to her perfect form and not some dictate of fashion.
"Jesse, want me to go next?" Frank asked.
The question allowed him to ignore the wanting inside of him. His wrangler had the remuda poised by the river. Jesse nodded. "Laura will go after you."
The small herd of horses plunged into the river. In less than five minutes, they'd crossed and were safely on the other side.
"You're next," Jesse said.
Laura climbed into her wagon. He moved next to her. "Are you afraid?"
"No." She took up the reins and smiled at him. "This is an adventure. The river's not deep and I can swim."
"Then let's go."
Her mules stepped into the water and started across. They were large animals, so the water wouldn't come much higher than their shoulders. They weren't going to have to swim. Jesse kept upstream of Laura, his left hand poised to reach for her if there was a problem. He didn't feel the water splashing against his boots, or his

horse's pull as the gelding tried to stay farther away from the wagon. He didn't see the men waiting on the bank ahead or hear the cattle coming up behind. All his attention was focused on Laura.

She held the reins loosely but firmly. Her gloved fingers didn't tremble. She stared straight ahead, her teeth biting down on her lower lip. In the center of the river, the current caught the wagon for a second and it started to float. The wagon jerked slightly. She gasped and struggled to stay in place.

"Hang onto the reins," Jesse called.

Her grip tightened. The wagon settled back on the ground and continued to roll forward.

When they reached the other side, he rode ahead and urged the mules up the embankment. Harry and Frank took the mules' bridles and pulled them clear of the stream.

Laura grinned. Her white teeth flashed as she gave him her most brilliant smile. "I did it! Did you see me, Jesse? I did it."

He didn't bother pointing out he'd been next to her the whole time. He understood her excitement. "You did a fine job."

"Thank you." Her smile faded as her gaze locked with his. "Thank you for everything."

She meant more than getting her across the river. He swallowed uncomfortably. Frank and Harry had moved off, leaving the two of them alone. Jesse shifted in his saddle. "Laura—"

She transferred the reins to her left hand and slid across the seat, closer to him. "No, you don't have to say anything if you don't want to. I just want you to know that I'm grateful for everything. And . . ." She drew in a deep breath. Emotions drifted across her face. He read sorrow, compassion, and guilt. "And I'm sorry if I made you uncomfortable. Before." She motioned with her free hand. "I didn't mean to make you relive your past. I understand if you're mad at me. You have every right to be."

"I'm not mad," he said.

"Really? You promise?"

Hell. What did the woman want from him? "I said it, didn't I?" Even he could tell his tone was harsh.

He expected Laura to shrink from him, or pout. Instead she leaned closer and placed her gloved fingertips on his arm. "I'd never do anything to cause you distress," she said quietly.

Concern radiated from her, like heat from a fire. With her soft pale skin and pretty ways, she didn't fit in his world. He should tell her that and be done with it. Except she was too sweet to destroy. The world was a better place for having her around.

Without stopping to consider his actions, he took her hand in his and squeezed gently. "Follow Harry. He knows where we're going to make camp." He released her.

She stared at him for a moment, as if trying to figure out exactly who he was. He wanted to tell her not to bother. He wasn't worth the puzzle. Before he could, she slid back to the center of the wagon and flicked the reins. As the wagon moved forward, King popped out of the back and ran to the side of the seat. The little dog looked out and barked once. Laura hushed him.

Jesse heard the steers start through the water. Skunk came in front, and with him, the other leaders. Skunk made it across first and followed after Laura. King barked again. Mike started across the river. Everything was going smoothly. Jesse had no warning, no sense of danger.

King yapped, louder this time. Skunk raised his head toward the sound. The large steer bellowed. The little dog jumped down from the wagon and charged the animal. Laura screamed and leapt after him.

Her skirt got tangled and for a horrifying second, Jesse thought she was going to be dragged to her death. He kicked his mount sharply and bent over the saddle, urging the animal faster. King got closer to the steer. Laura jerked her skirt free and started after the dog. Her wagon shot forward as if the mules realized there was no one at the reins. Skunk changed directions. Instead of trotting toward King, he headed for Laura.

Jesse angled between them. He could hear the confusion of the steer behind them. Mike cried out something, but all Jesse could see was Laura running directly toward King and the now charging steer.

"Laura, no!" he yelled.

She looked up at him, then at Skunk and realized the danger she was in. She froze. He thundered closer. Holding the saddle with one hand, he bent low.

"Grab onto me," he told her.

She reached out toward him. He wrapped his arm around her waist and hauled her up against him. The muscles in his shoulder and back screamed in protest. He hung on. He could feel her hands clutching at him. She was draped across the saddle in front of him, her skirt and lower body dangling over his left leg.

From the corner of his eye he saw Mike bend low in his saddle and grab King by the scruff of his neck. The little dog yelped once, then was quiet in Mike's arms. Skunk circled around twice, looking for his target. The big steer pawed the ground, snuffled, then bellowed. The other steers behind him paused uncertainly. They moved in the same direction as their leader.

Lefty came riding up, pulling the belled oxen behind him. Skunk heard the familiar noise. The dun-colored steer fell into step behind the ox and order was restored.

Jesse rode until he was clear of the cattle, then he slowed his horse and grabbed Laura by the arms. He pulled her into a sitting position. Her face was inches from his. He could see the different shades of blue that made up her irises and the faint quiver at the corner of her mouth. Her chest rose and fell with her labored breathing. Most of her hair had come loose and lay tangled around her shoulders and back.

"You hurt?" he asked. When she didn't answer, he shook her slightly. "Damn it, Laura, are you hurt?"

"What?" She blinked several times. "No. I don't think so." She stared at him, then collapsed against him. "I was so scared. I thought that steer was going to hurt King."

"Do you know what Skunk could have done to you?" But his voice was more gruff than angry and he couldn't help wrapping his arms around her.

He held her close. Her warm breath heated a spot on his chest. He could feel her soft breasts, and her hands where they clutched his waist. Slowly, so as not to draw attention to what he was doing, he moved his fingers and touched a lock of her hair.

Pain seared his gut. Silk. Pure silk. He'd touched the cloth once before. A whore he'd bedded had worn a silk robe when they were done. He'd felt the fine fabric, but it hadn't meant anything to him until this moment.

He twisted the lock around his finger, fighting the urge to run his hands through her smooth, soft hair. He inhaled the scent of it, of her. She smelled sweet and feminine. How the hell did she manage that after all she'd been through?

It was only then that he realized she was shaking and trying to muffle her sobs in his shoulder. Tears. Oh, Lord, how was he supposed to handle tears? He touched her back, patting it awkwardly.

"Don't cry," he said. "You're all right, now. There's nothing to be scared of."

Her slender body shook harder. She raised her head. But instead of tears, he saw she was laughing. "I'm not crying," she said between breaths. "Do you mean to tell me I was almost trampled by a steer named Skunk? Skunk? What kind of name is that?"

Relief coursed through him, chasing away the fear. He managed a smile of his own. "He's got that stripe down his back. What else were we supposed to call him?"

"Skunk the Steer?" She shook her head. "Oh, Jesse, there's hope for you yet."

He didn't ask what that meant. Instead he did what he'd wanted to do from the moment he'd seen her. He touched her face.

Her skin was softer than her hair, and warm. Faint color stained her cheeks. Her wide eyes widened even more. Her mouth parted and he had the oddest sensation that she wanted him to kiss her. He would have, too, if he hadn't heard the calls of the cowboys and the sounds of the cattle. They weren't alone. This wasn't the place. She wasn't for him.

He swung down, then held out his arms and helped her slide to the ground. When she was standing, he took hold of her chin.

"Never do that again," he said. "Never approach one of the steers. You could have been killed."

"But I—"

"No. Never leave your wagon like that. Anything could have happened. You were nearly trampled by the wheels. You can't act without thinking. Not out here. Not if you want to stay alive." He dropped his hand to his side.

"I understand."

Just talking about it brought back his fear. Before he

could say anymore, Frank came riding up. "We got her wagon, boss," the wrangler said. "The steers are crossing. Don't look like there's going to be any more trouble. Oh, and Mike got the little dog. He's safe, too."

Jesse nodded his thanks. As Frank was leaving, another rider cantered up, then jerked his horse to a stop. He nearly fell out of his saddle in his haste to dismount.

Wellington pulled off his hat as he approached. The boy was covered in dust, except for the clean band of skin on his forehead, where his hat rested, and the area of his nose and mouth that his kerchief covered. Wellington stared at him for a long time. At first Jesse thought he didn't know what he wanted to say, but then he realized the boy was fighting tears.

"I heard," Wellington managed at last. His voice cracked on the last word. He glanced at his sister. "Laura, you shouldn't have gone after King. You could have been hurt."

"I've been told," she said. "I'm fine. What are you doing here?"

"I came—" Wellington swallowed hard. His blue eyes shone with unshed tears. "I wanted to say good-bye to King. Before . . . Before . . ." He couldn't finish the sentence.

"Before what?" Laura asked, then gasped. "Oh, no. He caused trouble. Oh, Jesse, I—"

"Don't," Wellington said. He squared his narrow shoulders. "You're right, sir. He's just a bother. It's my fault for bringing him along. If you don't mind, I'll just say good-bye to him. I won't be a minute."

Jesse felt Laura pleading with him. She didn't say a word. She didn't have to. He could read her emotions as clearly as if they were his own. She wanted him to spare the dog, but she wouldn't ask. That would violate her sense of fairness. He'd given them all warnings.

They'd understood. Lives had been at risk because of King. She knew that. She accepted the animal's sentence. And still she silently pleaded.

Jesse swung up in his saddle. For those few seconds he hadn't thought about the dog or his men or the cattle. All he cared about was getting Laura to safety. All he'd wanted was her alive. He couldn't bear to have her life end.

He told himself it was because he'd been too intimate with death. So many were gone. Friends, strangers, enemies. In the end it didn't matter. In the face of death, all men were equal.

This is what he'd spent the last six years trying to avoid. The feelings. The pain. The caring. Laura had ripped open the protective cover and now his wound lay bare. His life's blood seeped away slowly, each drop agony.

Mike trotted up, King in his arms. "What do you want me to do with him, boss?"

The puppy sat happily on the saddle. A tear trickled down Wellington's cheek. Laura twisted her fingers together.

"Keep him tied up when we're on the trail," he told Laura. "He can run loose when we camp."

The happiness in her eyes nearly blinded him. Before she could say something to make the pain worse, he kicked his horse and rode off toward the herd.

The sun beat down all morning, heating the air and making Laura long for a brief rain shower. But the skies above them were blue and clear for as far as she could see. She leaned back in her seat and watched the wagon in front of her. Harry led the way as he had since they'd first left Jackson Springs. She'd become intimately familiar with the shape of his wagon. She'd counted the number of planks that made up the back, she'd studied the shape of the water barrel and watched the wheels turning round and round until she could have picked them out from a row of a hundred.

Jesse had warned her about the danger, but he hadn't said anything about the sameness of the days. She drew in a deep breath and let it out slowly, then eyed the bright sun. It was nearly noon. They would be stopping soon.

She hummed to herself. The mules' ears flickered toward her, as if they were listening. She glanced around at the trees and rich green grasses. Wildflowers sprang up everywhere, turning the countryside into a riot of color. The trees had budded and the first leaves stretched toward the bright sun.

Laura pulled her dress away from her chest and wished the weather had waited a couple more weeks before becoming so unseasonably warm. She was hot, sweaty, and dusty. Not to mention thirsty. She could stop and get a drink from her barrel, but she didn't want to cause any trouble. So far she'd managed to go a whole week without upsetting Jesse. Of course he'd been avoiding her, so that made staying out of trouble a lot easier.

She still remembered the look on his face when he'd decided King's fate. She'd believed he would let the little dog live. Wellington had been very grateful, but Jesse hadn't stayed around to hear the boy's thanks. He'd ridden off to tend the herd. Since then, that's all he'd done. She'd gone entire days without seeing him, except from a distance. Jesse had warned her about the danger, but he hadn't told her she would be lonely.

Laura didn't want to think about that, so she started a game she'd invented to pass the time. She imagined that Harry would stop his wagon in a hundred steps, then she began counting. When she reached thirty, she saw Jesse riding up toward the chuck wagon. He came in at an angle, so he didn't pass near her at all. She watched him sitting so tall and sure in his saddle. His beard wasn't as neatly trimmed anymore and his hair needed cutting. They were all getting a little scruffy. The extra cowboys had been sent home three days before and the herd was considered trail broke. They weren't being pushed so far each day. She'd hoped that meant more time to spend with Jesse, but he'd still managed to avoid her. She wouldn't mind so much, if only she knew why.

As Jesse spoke with Harry, she stared at her husband. He might be tired, she thought. He worked long hours. A thunderstorm a few nights before had caused the herd to stampede, but they'd been slowed in less than an hour and only three head had been lost. The cowboys had them rounded up in the first hour past dawn.

Maybe he stayed away from her because she was a woman. She caused him extra work, even though she was getting pretty good with her team.

Maybe it was because he'd told her about the war. She suspected the past still had the power to hurt him. The talking might have brought all the pain to the surface. If only she knew how to ease his suffering. Should she make him talk more, or leave him be? Not that he'd given her much choice. He was polite when they were together. He still slept under her wagon, although he retired long after she did and was up before the sun each morning.

The other cowboys picked up Jesse's mood. They weren't speaking to her much either, except for George and Harry.

The sound of a cantering horse broke through her thoughts. She glanced up and saw Jesse riding toward her. She straightened in her seat and smiled.

"Morning," she said as he approached.

He reined in his horse. "We're going to be crossing a wide river in the next half mile or so. We'll make noon camp on the other side."

"That's fine," she said. "King is tied up in the back."

"You up to crossing on your own? The water's shallow."

"I can do it," she said. "Don't you worry about me."

One corner of his mouth turned up slightly. "Wish that were possible." His dark eyes flickered over her face and seemed to want to linger at her mouth. She felt a tingling start low in her belly. She liked it when Jesse stared at her like that. She felt all nervous inside and welcomed the sensation, just like she welcomed the man's company.

Before she could say anything else, he tugged on his horse's reins and rode away. Laura stared after him. She had the feeling she could live to be a hundred and she would never understand Jesse Travers.

The river crossing went smoothly. Laura pulled her wagon up next to Harry's on the other side of the stream. The old man went right to work, cooking the main meal. She tied off the mules, then checked on King. The pup was sound asleep. Jesse let him run loose in camp, but Laura decided to leave the dog sleeping for now. She walked around the mules. Frank would be by shortly to feed and water the animals.

At the campfire, Harry was busy mixing up dough.

"Can I help?" she asked.

"Nope. I've been fixin' vittles since afore you were born. I expect I'll keep doin' it after you're gone."

"I was just offering."

Harry looked up and chuckled. "I know, girly. Why don't you take yourself for a walk? Just stay inside of the camp. Leastways you can't get in trouble doin' that."

"I can cook," she told him.

"Never doubted that you could."

He went back to his batter. Laura wrinkled her nose. She hadn't realized she wasn't going to have anything to do on the cattle drive. She glanced at the herd still crossing the river. She and Harry had pulled upstream of the steers. Where they sedately strolled through the shallow water, mud churned up to the surface. As she stared without blinking, the colors blended together into a blur of dull, moving shapes. They didn't move like she'd thought. In her mind, she had a picture of a herd neatly stretched out in the shape of a piece of pie.

Instead the animals spread out into a nearly unmanageable shape almost as wide as it was long.

She started walking away from the herd. Several black willows lined the bank of the river. Already the long blade-like leaves were forming. In another week or so, the tree would be bright with yellow flowers. Behind her she could hear the calls of the men as the steers continued to cross.

Laura drew in a deep breath and began singing. The song had no words, but was simply designed to warm up her voice. She started with low notes and slowly worked her way up higher. From the corner of her eye, she spotted a flash of color as a small rabbit darted away. She looked around, wondering what had frightened the creature.

One good thing about being on the trail was that she had plenty of time to practice her singing. For a time she'd thought the cattle might not like her voice. They seemed to shy away whenever she was around. But they'd grown used to her. Or maybe she was getting better.

She smiled at the thought. Laura knew she'd been blessed with a special talent. Her family had told her so when she was very young. All she needed was the opportunity—the chance to try. Soon she would get that.

She rounded a slight bend in the river. More trees crowded together here. There was an outcropping of rocks. A small lizard sat on the top one, basking in the sun. She tugged at her bodice, wishing she shared the creature's love of the heat. She was sticky and dusty. She hadn't had a bath since they'd left home.

Past the rocks, green grass stretched invitingly to the edge of the water, where a section of the river swept out to form a shallow pool. Laura walked close and stared down into the water. The current was gentle. She could see clear to the bottom. The pebbles looked smooth and cool. Her mouth watered. The pool was about six feet wide and maybe three feet deep. Perfect for wading.

She glanced behind her. She couldn't see the herd anymore, although she could hear them and feel the ground shaking with their steps. She turned back to the water and bit her lip. Just one sip was fine, she told herself.

She squatted down and scooped up a handful of the clear liquid. It was cold and tasted delicious on her dry tongue. She swallowed quickly, then scooped up more. A few drops fell on her skirt. She touched the spot. Her whole body was parched and dusty. Maybe she could just take off her stockings and wade in the water.

After making sure no one was around, Laura sat on the grass and pulled up her skirts. She removed her shoes, then her stockings. She hiked her petticoats up to her knees and stepped into the water.

It was so cold, she jumped a little, then laughed out loud. Chills raced up her legs, cooling her instantly. She stepped in farther, so the water lapped at her ankles. Heaven, she thought, then sighed. Pure heaven.

The stones on the river bottom were as smooth as they looked. Her feet brushed against them. She shook her head and felt a single strand of hair brush against her neck. Hair that she hadn't had a chance to wash. She hadn't brought soap on her walk, but maybe she could rinse it. That would be something.

Laura eyed the sun high in the sky. She glanced around again, just to be safe. There were the trees, a few birds in the branches, and the hum of an insect or two.

She stepped out of the river and let her skirts fall to the ground. Working quickly, and trying not to think about what she was doing, Laura unbuttoned the bodice of her calico dress and pushed it to her waist. She knelt at the edge of the river and began scooping the cold water onto her hair. A drop ran down her back and she shivered, then giggled. It felt wonderful.

As she scooped and rubbed, she closed her eyes. She wished she had some of her mother's special hair soap with her. Laura bent closer to the river and admitted the real truth. She wished her mother was here. She'd spent most of her life trying to get away from her family. Now that she had, she found that she missed them. She certainly hadn't planned on that. It was lonely on the trail. The cowboys didn't talk much to her. Even if they were willing, they were often busy. Wellington chatted when he was in camp, but if he wasn't riding at the rear of the herd, he was usually trying to sleep. Harry never had much to say about anything, and Jesse avoided her.

She shifted on the grassy embankment and began wringing her hair dry. At that moment she realized she hadn't brought anything to use as a towel. Just one more thing she hadn't thought through. She rung out her wet hair as best she could, then crossed the rocks and leaned against them. Water dripped down her chest, making her chemise transparent. She smoothed her hair out on the rock and waited for the sun to dry it, then held the thin fabric away from her body. Chill bumps puckered her arms and chest. She felt foolish and exposed sitting here like this, but she couldn't pull on her bodice, not while she was so wet. It would just be a few minutes, she told herself.

Her mother would scold her for sure, she thought. "Laura Cannon, your impulsiveness is going to be the death of you." Laura closed her eyes and smiled. It was almost as if her mother was here with her.

"Well, well, aren't you exactly what a man would wish for."

Laura jumped and stared up at the tall man standing in front of her. The sun was directly in her face. She had to shade her eyes to see him. Her breath caught in her throat and she tried to jerk her bodice up to cover her. "George."

"You weren't expecting anyone else, were you?" he asked, then laughed.

"I wasn't expecting anyone at all. Please leave right this minute."

She continued to tug on her bodice, but without putting her arms in the sleeves, it didn't offer much protection. George didn't act like he was going anywhere. She told herself not to be afraid; he wouldn't hurt her. But a voice inside her head didn't want to listen. She didn't know whether to shrink back against the rock, or scramble to her feet and try to run. Her heart pounded hard in her chest and her mouth was dry.

"I saw you walking away from the herd and I knew what you were going to do," he said, dropping to his knees and reaching for her. "It was as if I knew what you were thinking."

He grabbed her bare arms. She shrieked. "What are you doing?"

"What we've both wanted from the beginning. That husband of yours doesn't seem to be keeping you satisfied."

Laura squirmed to get away. This couldn't be happening. She stared at George and wondered what had gone wrong. He'd always made her a little uncomfortable, but she hadn't let him know. Had he taken that as encouragement?

She tried to twist free of him, but his fingers bit into her skin. His face loomed closer. He was going to kiss her!

She was so stunned, she stopped moving. "I don't want this," she said.

George's smile faded. "You think I care what you want, bitch?"

Her mouth dropped open. He took advantage of her shock and plunged his tongue inside.

Laura tried to scream, but the sound was muffled. His tongue made her gag. He tasted sour and disgusting. He was too close. She hated his touch. She kicked out but her bare feet couldn't do any damage. She shoved him, then raked her nails down his chest. He yelped and backed away. Instantly she screamed as loudly as she could.

"Jesse, Jesse, help!"

George slapped her across the face. "Shut your damned mouth."

The impact of his blow forced her head into the rock. The world faded into swirling darkness punctuated by flashes of light. She struggled to stay conscious and felt his hands on her breasts. Outrage gave her strength.

"Stop it," she screamed. "Get away from me. Get away."

A rider plunged through the trees. Laura felt the hoofbeats in the ground below her. The man jumped from the saddle and pulled a pistol. George moved away from her and held up his hands in a gesture of surrender.

"You all right?" the man asked. "Laura?"

It was only when she tried to sit up that she realized she'd been pushed to the ground. Every part of her hurt, her face most of all.

"Jesse?" She tried to stand, but couldn't. She sagged heavily against the rock and felt as if she were in a dream.

"The bitch asked for it," George said, rising to his feet. "She's been after me from the first day we left the ranch. You can't blame a man for finally saying yes."

Laura opened her mouth to speak, but no sound came. She could only stare.

She turned to Jesse, ready to defend herself, but he wasn't even looking at her. A cold feeling swept over her body and she drew her knees close to her chest. She hadn't thought about whether or not her husband had killed a man before, but now she knew. She read it in his eyes as he stared at George.

"I'd shoot you here," he said at last, "but it would start a stampede and your sorry hide's not worth that."

"I told you—," George started. "It was her."

"Laura wouldn't know the first thing about seducing a man," Jesse said. "She's innocent and we both know it. So take a horse and get the hell out of here. If I see your ugly face again, I'll shoot it off, stampede or not."

George paled. As he brushed a strand of blond hair off his forehead, Laura saw he was shaking. "You can't send me off in the middle of nowhere."

Jesse cocked the gun. "Then die right here, you bastard."

George glanced at her. She saw the hatred in his eyes, and the fear. A shiver of apprehension raced through her. George would make her pay. She could feel it.

Then he walked away without saying a word. Jesse watched him as he mounted his horse and rode off, east, away from the herd. Laura stared after him, too. When the man was little more than a speck on the horizon, Jesse holstered his gun and turned toward her.

She was shaking, as much from fear as the cold. Her wet hair molded itself to her back. She could feel her chemise clinging to her breasts. She couldn't meet Jesse's gaze.

"I know what you're thinking," she said, pulling her knees closer to her chest and grasping them. Her throat hurt. She wasn't sure why. "It's really my fault. I know

I'm not supposed to go off by myself. Harry said to go for a walk, but he told me to keep the camp in sight. I should have. But I was hot and dusty." She picked at a loose thread on her dress. "I saw this little pool and I just wanted to wash my hair. But I didn't have any soap, or even a towel. I didn't think it through. I'm s—sorry."

The burning in her throat got worse as she fought back the tears and wished the ground would just swallow her up. She heard Jesse's footsteps as he walked to his horse. For one horrifying second, she thought he was going to ride off and leave her.

"I didn't encourage him," she whispered. "I swear, I didn't. I tried to be nice, but I didn't like him. He was always there, watching me. It made me nervous."

She raised her gaze and saw him standing in front of her. He knelt at her side and wrapped her in the blanket he kept strapped behind his saddle. When she was covered, he pressed a knuckle to her chin, then touched the aching side of her face.

"He hit you," he said.

She nodded.

He grimaced. "If I'd realized that, I would have killed him."

She caught her breath, but his dark eyes told her he didn't lie. "I'm sorry," she said.

"It's not your fault," he said, then pulled her firmly against him. She went willingly, resting her head on his broad chest. Only when she heard the steady beating of his heart and felt the gentle touch of his hands on her wet hair did she at last give in to the tears.

The campfire burned bright and hot in the evening's coolness. Jesse squatted at the edge of camp and nursed a cup of coffee. He didn't want to have to think. He didn't want to have to feel. But he couldn't stop. The anger filled him, starting low in his belly before spreading to his chest and limbs. Cowboys sat around the fire and talked. He told himself to join them, to try to forget, to at least be distracted.

Instead he turned his head slightly and saw Laura sitting on a camp stool, next to her wagon. She'd pulled on her coat and buttoned it to the collar. Her hair was dry now, and neatly coiled at the base of her neck. King trotted around, investigating smells on the bushes and grass. But he didn't stray far away. Every few minutes, he returned to Laura as if to reassure himself she was all right. Jesse knew how the little dog felt.

He stared back at the fire, but the brightly colored flames couldn't burn away the pictures in his mind. He didn't have to close his eyes to see her lying there, on the ground, George on top of her.

He'd barely heard her first scream, but the sound had cut through him like the sharpened blade of a bayonet. He'd known instantly what was happening and had steeled himself to face the worst. Thank God he'd arrived in time. George had done little more than frighten her.

His hands curled around his now-cold coffee. He wished he'd killed the bastard while he'd had the chance. Jesse remembered the red mark on her cheek, the haunting fear in her blue eyes. Jesse hated that George had seen her when she was so vulnerable. Her chemise hadn't provided any protection. He hated that the other man had touched her. Jesse was an expert at facing the cruelties life had to offer. He knew how she would relive the moments of the attack over and over again. He understood about the dreams and the frantic prayers that something, anything would take the place of the memories. Would Laura ever be able to forget?

With a flick of his wrist, he tossed the remains of his coffee onto the ground, then rose to his feet. After tossing his dirty cup into the wreck pan, he headed toward her wagon.

Laura watched him approach. It was too dark for him to be able to read her expression, but he could feel her fear. It wasn't that cold out, but she was shivering.

"How you doing?" he asked.

She shrugged. "All right. I've been thinking and I want to apologize for this afternoon."

"What?" The word came out sharper than he'd intended and she flinched. He cleared his throat, then lowered his voice. "Laura, you don't have anything to apologize for."

"Yes, I do. Ever since we left home, I've been nothing but trouble for you. I promised not to be, but it keeps happening. It's not that I want to be a bother." She drew in a deep breath. "I knew I shouldn't have washed my hair. It was foolish. But . . . "

"You didn't think it through," he said quietly.

The corner of her mouth lifted slightly. "Exactly."

Jesse crouched down in front of her and gathered her hands in his. Her fingers were cold in his grasp. He rubbed them gently. "You shouldn't have walked so far from camp, but that doesn't give any man the right to do what George did. I'm partly to blame. I knew what he was thinking. I warned him off, but I should have thrown him out of camp."

She leaned toward him. "You don't believe him, then? You don't think that I wanted him to—" She faltered. Her gaze slipped down his face to his chest. She blinked several times and he knew she fought against her tears.

"Never," he said quickly. "You wouldn't encourage a man like him. You've got too much sense. Hell, you wouldn't encourage any man. Your dream is too important to you right now."

"You're very good to me."

"You're—" He almost said "my wife." The words lodged in his throat. Where had that thought come from? Laura might be his wife in the eyes of the world, but the two of them knew better. "You're my responsibility."

"A bigger one than you thought, I would guess."

He smiled. "You're not so bad."

In the firelight, her eyes darkened to the color of the sky. He could see the flames reflected in her pupils. Shadows danced across her smooth skin, making it hard for him to see the bruise. But he knew it was there.

Her fingers clutched his firmly. She was warmer now, and had stopped shaking. He had the strongest urge to bring her hands to his mouth and kiss them. He resisted, not knowing if the action would make her feel better, or frighten her.

"I should have thought you might want to take a bath," he said, trying to distract himself. "Next time it's convenient, I'll let you know. I'll stand guard so you'll be safe."

She nodded. Her implicit trust stunned him. For whatever reason, Laura believed he would keep her safe from everything, even himself. He wondered if that was possible.

Here, in the night, with the darkness around them and sounds of the herd not far off, he wrestled with the demon of desire. He hated that he wanted her. Not only because the need weakened him and left him vulnerable to the pain of his past, but because to want her this day, after all that had happened, made him little more than the animal her attacker had been.

So even as she swayed closer to him and her mouth parted invitingly, he held back. His iron will kept his wanting firmly under control.

King stopped his endless snuffling and raised his head. As the dog raced into the night, Jesse heard approaching footsteps. He rose and turned in one fluid movement, dropping Laura's hands and reaching for his gun.

King barked out a greeting and Jesse released his hold on his pistol. Wellington stepped out of the shadows and gathered the dog up in his arms. After greeting the animal, the boy looked at Jesse.

"Is everything all right?" he asked. His voice was low and concerned.

Jesse grimaced. There were few secrets on the trail. Although he hadn't told anyone but Harry about the attack, Lefty had seen him riding into camp with Laura in his arms. Mike had probably noticed him standing guard outside her wagon while she'd changed clothes and dried her hair.

"I'm fine," Laura said as she stood up. She walked over to her brother and hugged him. "Nothing happened."

"That's not what I heard." The boy swallowed hard. "Did he hurt you?"

"No. Jesse rescued me."

The smile she gave Jesse nearly blinded him. A cold knot settled low in his chest. She imagined him to be a hero.

"Is he really gone?" Wellington asked.

Jesse nodded. "If he comes back, I'll kill him."

Wellington continued to pet King. "Dumb ol' dog," he muttered. "You probably slept through the whole thing. You're supposed to be protectin' Laura. What am I going to tell Pa when I get home?"

"You don't tell him anything, you hear me, Wellington Arthur Cannon?" Laura said briskly. "I was foolish, going off by myself, but I've learned my lesson. It won't happen again. I should have listened to Jesse. So you learn from my mistake and listen to what you're told."

"Yes'm," Wellington said. He drew in a deep breath and stared at the stars. "Bobby says we can tell where we are by the lights in the sky. You reckon that's true?"

Laura looked at Jesse. He nodded.

"I suppose so," she said, glancing up. "I never thought about it before."

"You reckon Ma and Pa are looking at the stars and thinking about us?"

Laura moved close to her brother. She took King and set the pup on the ground, then held Wellington close. The boy was already taller than her, but he went willingly into her embrace. "They miss us," she said. "They're thinking about us all the time, and they want us to come back."

"I like being on the trail," her brother said, his voice muffled against her shoulder. "But sometimes I want to see them somethin' fierce."

"I know."

Jesse watched the two of them. He'd missed his family when he'd first gone off to war, but the desire to return had been tempered by the memory of how he'd left. His parents hadn't wanted him to fight on the side of the Southern cause.

After prison he'd been sent to them. His mother had fussed over his wounds; his father had offered him whiskey when the nightmares got bad. But he didn't remember ever being just held, like Laura held her brother. They'd only wanted to hear about the glories of war, not the reality of it. They'd wanted victories, not the sound of death. They hadn't wanted to know about his months in the prison camp and how staying alive had been an hourly struggle, how decency and dignity were lost when a man was forced to fight off a rat for a crumb of bread. They wouldn't understand how a friendship born through those trials would bring men closer than brothers and that when one was betrayed, the wound went clear to the soul.

Laura brushed Wellington's hair off his forehead. "What is it with you cowboys? Even after a haircut you still look shaggy." She kissed his cheek. "Go on to bed. Morning comes earlier out here on the trail."

The boy smiled at her, then saluted Jesse and strolled off toward his bedroll. Most of the men had already bedded down.

"You should get some sleep, too," he told her when they were alone.

Laura shoved her hands in her coat pocket. "I'm afraid," she admitted. "Every time I close my eyes, I see George standing above me. I can't see his face, but I know it's him. Then I feel him next to me, touching me." She wiped her hand across her mouth, as if she could brush away the memory. "I don't think I'll sleep much tonight."

She paced to the edge of the wagon, then turned and stared out over the land. He moved close to her, wanting to help her, but not knowing how.

"I can still feel it," she said and shuddered. "Him. I can't scrub his touch away."

"You'll forget," he said. "It takes time, but eventually it will fade."

She spun toward him. They were in shadow, hidden from the rest of the camp by her wagon. He couldn't see her individual features, just the faint outline of her face. He could hear her, though. The uneven breathing, the whisper of fabric as she brushed her hands against her coat.

"Jesse, help me forget," she whispered. "Kiss me so I can think of you instead of him."

Her request startled him. The desire that immediately swept through him nearly brought him to his knees. He had to refuse, otherwise he would lose control.

"Jesse." His name was a prayer.

He took a step closer to her, then bent his head and brushed his lips against hers. The heat burned away his control, leaving him raw and hungry. He clenched his hands into fists, determined not to betray her trust. This was about Laura and what she needed, not him. Only her.

She was soft. Tempting. When he lifted his head, she raised her chin toward him, inviting him to kiss her again.

This time he lingered. He pressed his mouth more firmly against hers. This time he noticed the sweetness of her breath and the scent of her body. This time he felt the softness of her lips and the way she yielded to him.

The need inside him was hot and heavy. He wanted to plunder her mouth, to taste her and touch her, to satisfy the hunger. He fought against the long forgotten desires, wondering when exactly he'd begun the return to life.

He opened his eyes and looked at her. She was smiling.

"Just as tingly as I remember," she murmured, then glanced at him. "Do you feel it, too? That jolt? Like being hit by lightning. Isn't it amazing?"

His mouth grew dry. The desire wasn't all his? He cursed silently. Why the hell did she have to tell him that? Hard enough to keep his needs to himself. Worse, when he knew she shared the passion.

But she was an innocent, he reminded himself. They weren't kissing because she cared about him or wanted him, but simply to counteract the horrible memories of George's attack.

She sighed and unbuttoned her coat. "I'm not so cold now. Even my hands are warm." She tilted her head to one side. "You kiss much better than Andrew Bartholomew. He's a mortician in the next town. Do you think it's because he's around dead people so much?"

"Maybe." Jesse chuckled, pleased that she thought he kissed well. He wondered what she would say if she knew how out of practice he was.

"Jesse?"

"Yes?"

She touched her index finger to his chest. He was wearing a vest over his shirt, and long underwear under that, but he still felt the contact clear to his bones.

"Can you kiss me again? Like George did?" Her head dipped as if she was embarrassed. "Or is it disgusting with everyone? I mean, if you don't want to, if it's an awful thing to ask, then never mind. I suppose it might be considered rude, like slapping someone. After all, George did hit me."

"What in God's name are you talking about?"

She flinched. "Please don't be angry."

"I'm not angry," he said quietly, then gently touched the unbruised side of her face. "I'm just confused. I don't mind kissing you. Just tell me what you want?"

"He stuck his tongue in my mouth," she blurted out, then covered her face with her hands.

Blood surged to his groin. The hardness there tightened painfully. But not by a breath did he let her know. Instead he placed his hands on her wrists and drew her fingers to his shoulders.

"Look at me," he said. Slowly, she raised her head. "There's nothing you can say to me or ask me to do that's bad. You wouldn't know how to do anything disgusting." Before she could speak, he brought his mouth back to hers.

Her lips trembled. He wanted to think it was from desire, but he knew it was fear. Of the unknown, of him, of the memories. They were the most dangerous of all.

Her hands gripped his shoulders. He slipped his fingers under her coat and touched her waist. She jumped slightly, then leaned toward him.

Perhaps she expected him to plunge inside her mouth, assaulting her as George had done. He didn't. Instead he moved his hands to her back and traced ever-widening circles against her dress. He nibbled at the corner of her lips, then kissed her jaw and behind her ear. She giggled when he drew her lobe into his mouth and suckled. She sighed when he trailed damp kisses down her neck. She leaned into him when he returned to her lips and gently moved back and forth.

How small she felt in his arms. He could span her back with his hands. He felt he could crush her spine if he wasn't careful, so he held her as gently as he knew how. Her fingers slipped down from his shoulders to his chest. The tips of her thumbs swept perilously close to his nipples and he held back a groan.

His breathing increased, as did hers. He had trouble remembering why he was kissing her. Need pooled between his thighs, reminding him his body hadn't found release in a long time. Nor would it tonight, he thought, trying to ignore the insistent pressure.

He swept his tongue across the seam of her mouth. She stiffened. He retreated, moving to kiss her neck. Her pulse fluttered there. The rapid beats matched the pounding in his chest. He returned to her mouth and touched her lips with the tip of his tongue. She drew in a breath, then parted slightly.

He didn't enter right away. Instead, he traced the dampness of her lower lip. He felt the beckoning moistness and heat. Her hands clutched at him. Tension stiffened her back. He circled her lips over and over until the tingling nearly drove him mad. His hips thrust forward involuntarily. Fortunately, Laura's petticoats kept her from feeling his hardness.

Only when her hands flattened against his chest and the muscles in her back relaxed did he slip inside her mouth. He savored the sweetness of her, knowing he could taste her forever. He touched the tip of his tongue to hers. She jumped again. He stopped, ready to retreat. But she didn't pull back. Instead she leaned closer, until her breasts brushed against his chest. She moved her tongue slightly, until it slipped against his.

Fire swept through him. He groaned low in his throat. It took every ounce of strength he had not to haul her against him. Instead, he circled his tongue around hers in a delicate dance of desire. She followed. Her hands moved down his chest to his waist, then back. The movement grew more frantic.

He angled his head and plunged in deeper. Her mouth widened. She sagged against him in surrender. He wanted to touch her everywhere. Instead, he traced a line from the nape of her neck to her waist. His fingers ached to feel her breasts, her soft, bare skin. He contented himself with her impassioned responses to his kiss.

When he withdrew slightly, she moaned a protest. When he tried to pull away to regain control, she clung to him. She kissed him back, following him into his mouth, touching him as he had touched her. At last, when he felt himself slipping over the edge, he took her hands in his and gently pushed her away.

The night was silent except for their rapid breathing. Jesse grabbed hold of the wagon and fought against the need to find release. Thank God she didn't know to touch him there. If she did, he would explode instantly.

"I don't understand," she said, her voice trembling. "When George did that, it was horrible. When you do that, I want to be closer."

"Do you think you can sleep now?" he asked, his voice thick.

She looked up at him. He caught the faint outline of her face and thought she might be smiling. "Oh, yes. I'm sure of it."

At least someone would be getting some sleep, he thought grimly. In his condition, he would lie awake for hours.

He helped her into the wagon, then watched as she started to lace the covering closed.

"I'll be right here," he promised. "I'll keep you safe."

She looked down at him and nodded. "I know you will, Jesse. I trust you with my life."

Laura rooted through the back of her wagon, searching for the canned peaches. The small space was crowded and it was difficult to move boxes and find things. Her straw-filled mattress sat up front, on top of several trunks she didn't plan to open until she reached Kansas. There was a narrow walkway from the rear of the wagon to the bed, with crates piled on either side. Overhead were three hooks for lanterns, although after the first night, she'd never bothered bringing one inside. She shuddered at the thought of the men watching her undress. With the exception of Jesse's wonderful kisses, she had no intention of ever letting a man touch her again.

Laura lifted the lid on the top crate and saw that it was nearly full. Her mother had sent along plenty of food for her, even though Jesse had said Laura would only need extras. She'd tried to offer it to Harry to use for the men, but the old man had told her to keep it. If the chuck wagon was lost, they could survive on her supplies. So while the men had beans and bacon for the first three weeks, and then just beans when the bacon ran out, Laura was surrounded by tins of vegetables, including tomatoes, and canned fruit. She was getting tired of opening a can and eating it in guilty solitude.

She pulled the top crate onto the bed and opened the next one down.

"Finally," she said, pulling out a can of peaches. She removed three more and tossed them next to her, then fitted the crates back in place. After climbing over the mattress and onto the wagon seat, she slipped a can in each skirt pocket and took one in each hand, then jumped to the ground.

Harry crouched by the fire starting dinner. To the south, Frank was settling the remuda for the night. The horses had been trained to respect a rope corral. He strung it carefully, using the trees in the area to form posts. Her mules stayed with the horses, grazing comfortably and resting after their day on the trail. The steers hadn't made camp yet. In the distance, a dust cloud rose in the clear afternoon and marked their passage.

"I brought these," she said, walking to the fire and handing the cans to Harry. Before he could protest, she pulled the other two from her pockets and set them on the lowered back end of the chuck wagon. "Don't say you can't take them because they're mine. I thought we could make a cobbler for dessert."

Harry stared at her. "Boss don't want us usin' your supplies."

"They're mine to do with as I please," she said. "Besides, we'll be in Fort Worth in a couple of days and I can buy more there. Please, Harry, we haven't had anything but beans and biscuits for nearly a week. Everybody's tired of that."

The old man shook the can and listened as the

peaches sloshed around inside. "Tarnation, if you don't know how to tempt a man. All right, I'll make you a cobbler, but you explain it to Jesse if he gets a burr up his—" He stopped talking. "You know what I'm gettin' at."

"Yes, I do." She pointed to the cans. "May I help?"

Harry stepped back and glared. "Girly, you know how I feel about someone helpin' me with the cookin'. If you got a mind to interfere, then go ahead and open these tins. But that's as much as I'm willin' to let you do."

"Thank you," she said solemnly, then grinned. Harry grinned back.

He actually let her do more than just open the cans. By the time the cobbler was ready for baking, she'd even measured out the flour and sugar. While Harry secured the cover on the Dutch oven, she stirred the beans.

She leaned over the large pot and sniffed. "Harry, there isn't even any meat in here."

"We're outta meat. There ain't none to be had until we get to Fort Worth."

She stared at him. He was crouched over a hole in the ground, settling the Dutch oven in place. "But we're driving twenty-four hundred head of steer north. We're surrounded by meat."

"A cowboy gets sick if he eats his own herd."

"That's ridiculous."

He straightened. "Maybe, but it's true. There ain't a man worth his salt who'll slaughter his own steers. Best we can hope for is supplies in town, or finding a cow belonging to someone else. You can ask Jesse if you don't believe me." He pushed his hat off his face and stared south. "If you're gonna walk that mutt of yours before the steers get here, you'd better do it right quick."

She followed his gaze and saw the dust cloud was closer. "You're right." She returned to the wagon and woke King from his nap. The little dog licked her hand as she untied him, then jumped down after her. He took off after some creature, real or imaginary, then jumped in the air to snap at a fly.

It was warm in the late afternoon, although the clouds in the distance promised a cool night and rain. Below her feet the rich spring grasses were soft and springy. Bushes of mountain laurel reached out to the sun. She could smell the blue-violet flowers. Mama had never cared for the scent, but Laura didn't mind it.

This was the part of the cattle drive she liked best. The quiet times. She liked being outdoors and not having to worry about milking cows or taking care of customers in the store. She liked the sounds of the insects and birds and the way the sun felt on her back. Sometimes she got lonely, missing her family. She wished they were with her and sharing the adventure. In their place, she longed for someone to talk to, someone like Jesse.

Just thinking about him set her heart to pounding in her chest. If she dwelt on the memory of his kiss, her insides would get a squishy feeling and her mouth would start to tremble. Did he remember what had happened between them? Sometimes she was embarrassed about what she'd asked him to do, but other times, she was just grateful. Now, whenever she recalled what George had tried to do to her, she shook those thoughts away and remembered the feel of Jesse's mouth instead.

He hadn't tried to kiss her again, not since that night. But he'd watched over her. When she was ready to return to her wagon, he walked her there. She hadn't had a chance to take a bath, but he often brought her a bucket of tepid water just before the sun went down, so she could tidy up without having to use a lantern.

"*I know a place,*" she sang loudly. King stopped and stared at her. The little dog shook once, then barked. She ignored him. What did she care if he didn't like her voice? Everyone else did and that was enough. "*Where all things beautiful. Wait for me . . . wait for me.*" She continued to hum. King whined as if he was in pain.

"Don't be so critical," she told the dog. "I won't invite you to my premiere performance."

He whined once more, then took off after a rabbit. Laura laughed as he tore through the bushes. She looked around and found an open area of grass, then sank down and raised her face to the sun. They would be in Fort Worth in a couple of days. Soon they would enter Indian Territory, then, finally, Kansas. She was on her way to reaching her dream.

As she closed her eyes, she pictured herself standing on stage. Every detail was clear in her mind. The stunning dress she would wear, her wig, the black lace on her hat. She sighed and leaned back. She could see everything. The candlelight in the saloon, the crowd of people applauding.

Her dress was layers of red satin. At first she'd thought to wear velvet, but that would be too heavy. The bodice was low and fitted, with tiny sleeves that barely covered her shoulders. She wanted glass beads sewn on everywhere. And long lacy gloves. Also red. There were to be tiny black bows on her gloves and maybe a wisp or two of black lace on the deep flounces of her dress.

She could see herself singing to the adoring crowd and hear the cheers. She bowed—make that curtseyed, the dress was very low cut. Besides, she had to remember to keep her head straight. After all, she would be wearing a wig. Auburn. A little darker than her dress, not quite as bright, with curls that cascaded down her back. Laura smiled. It would be perfect.

A distant mooing interrupted her fantasy. Beneath her, the ground shook as the steers entered camp. She sat up and stared at the milling herd, then called for King. When he came bounding up, she took him in her arms. It was time to return.

Laura made her way back slowly. As she neared the vast expanse of milling cattle, King struggled to jump down and start chasing them.

"Stop causing trouble," she murmured in the dog's right ear. "You wouldn't like being stew and Wellington would miss you terribly." She didn't bother mentioning that she would miss the little dog as well. King was her faithful companion, keeping her company during the day and sleeping on her straw mattress beside her at night.

She hummed to calm him, then broke into song. The dog stirred in her arms, whimpered once, then was silent. The steers closest to her rolled their eyes, but didn't start away as they had at the beginning. She'd been surprised by how jumpy the cattle were. They'd stampeded a couple times, despite her efforts to calm them through song. Lately, though, her singing seemed to be working. That or they were simply ignoring her.

A rider circled around the herd and came to a stop in front of her. She glanced up and smiled. From the top of his hat to the tips of his boots, Wellington was covered with dust. It formed a thick layer on his face and clothing, collecting on his eyes, shoulders, and thighs.

"Once we get to Kansas, it's going to take you a week to wash off the trail dust," she teased her brother.

Wellington didn't respond. Instead he jumped off his horse, then opened his arms. Before she could stop him, King leapt toward his master. The boy hugged the dog close, as if they'd been parted a month instead of just since morning.

"What's wrong?" she asked as a knot of worry formed in her chest. "Did something happen?"

Wellington looked at her and shook his head. "Nothin's wrong. I just wanted to see King. Jesse told me to come by and visit with him early, before he could cause trouble."

"That was very thoughtful of him," she said, and wondered if that was all there was to it. She knew her brother pretty well and sensed he was holding something back. "Are you feeling all right?"

"I'm fine." The boy set the dog on the ground, then pulled a worn stick from his saddlebag. He tossed it and King went chasing after it. "Jesse says we're makin' good time. That there ain't been too many lame steers."

"Wellington." She drew in a deep breath. If her youngest son came back talking like Hellcat Harry, Mama was going to be furious. "The correct word is 'haven't.' You know that."

"I'm gonna be a cowboy, why can't I talk like one?"

Blue eyes, so like her own, stared mutinously at her. She didn't remember him growing, but she realized he was almost half a head taller than her and he was only fourteen. "You can talk like one when you're grown up and on your own. Until then, you have to do what your parents say and you know Mama would wash your mouth out for sure if she heard you swearing and saying things like ain't."

King returned with the stick. Wellington mumbled something as he took it from the pup and tossed it again. It went sailing high in the blue sky. King barked excitedly as he chased it through the grass and around a cedar tree.

"Anyway," the boy said, "we *haven't* had many lame steers so we've made good time."

"Why does it make a difference if there are lame steers?"

Wellington looked at her as if she'd just asked him the difference between a milk cow and a bull. "The herd travels at the speed of the slowest steer," he said with barely concealed impatience. "If the trail boss sets the right pace, all the animals can gain weight on the trip north. If he allows the lead steers to walk too fast, the ones behind will run to catch up. Running steers lose weight. That's one of the reasons stampedes are so dangerous."

Laura stared at her brother. He wasn't just taller, he was growing up. "Where'd you learn all this?" she asked.

"From the cowboys. Mostly Mike and Jesse." He puffed his chest out with pride. "I might be a greenhorn, but I learn fast and I'm a hard worker."

Foolishly, she was pleased that Jesse took so much time with Wellington. He would be good for the boy, and in an odd way, her brother would be good for Jesse. Wellington wouldn't understand Jesse's dark side, his pain and his memories, but he would remind him about the simple fun of being young and alive.

"It's my job to watch after the lame steers," Wellington continued.

"I thought you rode drag."

"I do. When a steer goes lame, he drops from his place in the herd. When he's fit, he goes back there. I make sure they're gettin' better and if they're not, I let Jesse know. Jesse says I'll be a first-rate cowboy by the time I'm seventeen. He says—"

But Laura didn't listen to her brother's story about Jesse. She was too busy watching the boy smile and gesture. His pleasure was tangible and his excitement pleased her. Who would have thought that the simple act of Jesse buying penny candy for some poor children in town could have changed all their lives so much.

As Wellington chattered on about cattle and the proper way to water them, she watched the steers stroll into camp. These untamed animals were Jesse's dream of success and fortune, much as her singing was her dream. He was doing what he could to help her along, but she was only getting in his way.

She grimaced. It wasn't supposed to be like that, she thought. She'd never wanted to hurt anyone. First her family, although they still didn't know that she'd lied to them, and now Jesse.

"Jesse says I can come next year if I want, and even ride swing and flank."

"I'm sure he was just being kind," Laura said. "We've both disrupted the cattle drive enough. Jesse will probably be pleased to see the last of us."

Wellington stared at her, his mouth pulled straight, his eyes cloudy and unreadable. In that moment, as their gazes locked and he stiffened, she realized he wasn't really a boy anymore. Sometime in the last few weeks on the trail, Wellington had taken an irreversible step toward manhood.

"The last of us? You're talking like you're not coming back to Jackson Springs."

"Wellington . . ." She paused, not sure what to say.

"I've heard talk." He shifted his weight from foot to foot, then turned toward his horse and adjusted the saddle. "Why, Laura? Don't you like us anymore?"

"I like you just fine." She drew in a breath, then released it slowly. "I want to be a singer. I want a life on the stage. When we get to Wichita, I'm going to get a job entertaining in a saloon. Once I'm comfortable performing, I want to go to New York. Maybe even Europe."

"You're gonna be a singer?" He sounded incredulous.

"What's wrong with that?"

He shrugged. "Nothing, I suppose. If that's what you want. But what's wrong with doing it in Jackson Springs?" he asked, still not looking at her.

"I've always wanted more. From the time I was little, I've dreamed about a different kind of life. Travel. Adventures."

"I know you have, but I thought when you married Jesse—" He turned quickly. "Does he know?"

"Of course. I told him at the beginning."

"So why'd he marry you if you're just gonna up and leave him?"

She winced. Put that way, her actions sounded even worse. "Jesse did me a favor by marrying me. He was helping me get away. You know how Mama and Pa are."

Confusion darkened his eyes. "I thought if you got married you stayed together. I've never known married folks who were apart."

She didn't know how to explain it. Somehow this didn't seem to be the time to discuss the divorce. When King returned with the stick, she crouched down so she could take it from him. Instead of throwing it right away, she petted the little dog. She knew she was being selfish. She knew it was wrong of her to deceive her family, but she didn't know another way to make her dream come true. Did the wanting justify her actions? She didn't have an answer for that. She only knew she'd chosen her path and she had no choice but to see it through.

"Everyone's gonna miss you," he said.

"I know. I'm going to miss them, too." She straightened and tossed the stick. It didn't go very far and King gave her a disgusted look before running after it. "I'm going to write them a letter when I get to Kansas and explain what I'm doing. I think they'll understand."

"They won't," Wellington said loudly. "They won't and I don't. You're not supposed to leave forever." He swung into his saddle and kicked his horse. The gelding took off for the herd. The boy never looked back at her.

King trotted up, the stick in his mouth. He stared at his retreating master, then dropped the stick and whined low in his throat.

"That's how I feel, too," she said. "He doesn't understand and I don't know how to make him. I can't find the words." As Wellington circled around the back of the herd and then disappeared from sight, she felt a slight pain in her chest. She supposed it was a bit of her heart breaking off.

Wellington would return home with Jesse and his men, but she would stay in Wichita. The last link with her family would be broken. She would miss the boy, she thought sadly, just as she missed her parents and her other brothers and sisters. She hadn't thought she would. Being separated from them was all she'd ever dreamed about. But now that it had happened, she was finding out that freedom had a high price—loneliness.

It wasn't supposed to be like this, she thought. It was supposed to be easy and wonderful and fun. She'd only ever wanted a chance to be Honeysuckle DeVine. Being the famous singer would allow her to do things and experience life in a way plain Laura Cannon never could.

Only she wasn't still Laura Cannon, she thought suddenly. She was Laura Travers. She picked up King's stick. She started to throw it, but he'd flopped down on his belly. Apparently now that Wellington was gone, he wasn't interested in the game.

She scanned the herd, searching for a familiar rider. At last she spotted him, sitting tall in his saddle. He moved easily around the steers, guiding his horse with invisible signals. Man and animal worked well together. At first Laura had thought Jesse had trained his horse well, but then she realized he changed mounts several times a day. So it was as much his skill as the horse's.

He worked with the other cowboys, bringing the stragglers up from the rear so they stayed with the main herd. There was more work now for everyone since George was gone. That was her fault, too. If she hadn't been there, Jesse wouldn't have had to send him away.

As she watched her husband, she realized she would miss him when their time was up. In the beginning she'd thought of Jesse as a way to get what she wanted. Now he was someone she cared about. He was a kind man, honest and decent. He deserved more than a pretend wife who was using him to achieve her own selfish dream. He deserved someone who could love him and help him fight his demons as he had helped her fight hers.

As if her thoughts of him called him to her, Jesse looked up and glanced around. At last his gaze settled on her. He nudged his horse forward. She stood her ground, waiting for him to approach her. King took one look at the large horse trotting in his direction and made a dash for the wagon. He hopped up onto the wagon seat, then disappeared inside.

"Everything all right?" Jesse asked as he reined in his horse.

She walked close and petted the black gelding's soft nose. "We're fine. Harry's making peach cobbler for desert tonight. I'll be sure to save some for you."

"Much obliged."

She looked up at him. He tilted his hat back, exposing his face. Sometime in the last day or so, he'd trimmed his beard. The dark hair clung to the firm, square line of his jaw. She wondered what he would look like without the beard. Was the scar on his cheek still red and angry or had it faded? She knew she wouldn't mind seeing his scar. It was a part of him and it didn't frighten her.

"I saw your brother a couple of minutes ago," Jesse said. "He seemed upset. You know what that's about?"

She nodded. "He knows that I'm staying in Wichita instead of coming home with you. He's angry and hurt."

"He'll miss you."

"I know. He also said—" She hesitated.

"What?"

"That . . ." She moved closer to him, close enough to rest her hand on his boot. "He said you're the one I'm treating the worst. That married people are supposed to stay together. But I told him you'd be pleased to leave me behind. After I've been such a bother and all."

It didn't matter that he'd pushed back his hat. In less time than it took to blink, his brown eyes turned expressionless. Jesse stared down at her. She felt as if he could see into her soul. She hoped not. The lying and deceiving she'd done recently had left it in sorry condition.

At last he tugged on the reins and turned his horse, then rode away.

She stared after him, not sure what his silence meant. He couldn't mind that she was leaving. He'd always known that. It had to be something else. But what?

Before she could wrestle with the question, she forced it from her mind. As much as she cared about Jesse, she couldn't think about him right now. She had to remember what was important. All the women she'd ever known had spent their lives living in one place.

Seeing the same faces year after year, growing old and dying without once leaving the county. She wanted more. She wanted an adventure.

She didn't want her last breath to be drawn through the bitter fragrance of regret.

Black clouds threw themselves against the sky in a billowing battle of darkness and sunlight. Jesse narrowed his gaze and knew the darkness would win. The question was, would it just bring rain or did the ominous skies promise lightning as well?

He strained to see in the distance, but there were no telltale flashes of light reaching for the ground. Skunk and the other leaders were calm, as was his mount. Maybe it would just be rain.

As the clouds drew closer, the temperature dropped. Jesse reached behind himself and untied his coat, then pulled it on. Freezing rain wouldn't make the afternoon pleasant, but it also wouldn't cause a stampede. Better cold than hot, he thought as he turned his horse toward camp.

When Jesse rode up, Harry already had the noon meal ready. Laura was helping him. Despite the old man's insistence that only he knew the right way to cook on the trail, Harry was allowing Laura to assist him more and more. Even as Jesse watched, she stirred the beans, then moved the coffee away from the hottest part of the fire.

Her skirts swayed as she moved. Despite the hardship of the trail, she managed to look fresh and clean. Her hair was always neatly coiled at the base of her neck, her face and hands were free of dirt. Even her dress had been brushed vigorously that morning. He knew; he'd heard the sound in the quiet moments before dawn.

"We're just about ready," Harry said as he approached.

"Good." Jesse drew his horse to a stop, then swung down from the saddle. He handed the animal to Frank and approached the fire.

Laura glanced up at him. As always, her smile caught him by surprise. After all this time he would have thought he would get used to it, and to her. But every time he saw her, he was surprised. By her beauty and easy, graceful acceptance of her circumstance.

Trail life had to be difficult for her. She had little privacy, no other women to talk to. Her quarters were small and cramped; she couldn't use a lantern at night. The days were long, dusty, and boring—or wet, clammy, and cold. She risked her life at river crossings, with the potential of tornadoes, Indian attacks, and floods. He understood that she was the one who had wanted to come on the cattle drive, but so did a lot of cowboys. That didn't mean they had any trouble spending the entire time bellyaching about the conditions. Yet Laura was always cheerful. She always had a good word for the men, and a ready smile for him. She had backbone and a kind heart. They were an irresistible combination.

"Morning, Jesse," she said, reaching for a mug and pouring him coffee.

"Feels like it should be night already," he said, taking

the steaming liquid from her. He blew on the mug, then gulped down a mouthful. It burned all the way to his stomach.

She stepped closer. The dark blue calico dress she wore hugged her torso. He could see the shape of her breasts and the narrowness of her waist. The full skirt fell gently to the ground, although it didn't seem as full as he remembered. If he didn't know better, he would think she was wearing fewer petticoats than when they started.

"Are you tired?" she asked, her blue eyes wide with concern.

"Driving cattle is hard work."

"You do more than your share. Maybe too much." She bit her lower lip. "It's my fault, isn't it?"

"How the hell could it be yours?"

"You had to send George away because of me. You're one cowboy short. As the trail boss, you have to make up the difference."

Harry had drifted over to the chuck wagon and Frank was taking care of the horses. Until the men arrived, they were alone. After transferring the coffee to his left hand, he reached out his right and touched the tip of his index finger to her nose.

"You're getting freckles," he said. "Why aren't you wearing a hat?"

"Sometimes I forget."

He raised one corner of his mouth. "If you get as brown as an Indian, how are we going to tell you apart if they attack? I won't know who to rescue."

She smiled and pointed to her hair. "I think I'm blond enough, don't you?"

"Maybe. But wear a hat anyway."

She nodded.

Because she was so close and smiling, because being around her made him ache inside, and because the pain made him weak, he risked placing his hand on her shoulder. She was slightly built, with delicate bones. Yet he knew she would survive. In her own quiet way, Laura was tough.

"I'm not mad at you," he said. "It's not your fault that George is gone. What he did was wrong."

Her good humor faded. "But if I hadn't been here, he wouldn't have . . . done that."

"Don't take on trouble," he told her. "It'll find you soon enough. Saying what happened with George is your fault is like saying an outlaw wouldn't have robbed a bank if the town hadn't been fool enough to build one."

"A town needs a bank," she said slowly.

"And you need to be able to take a walk without worrying about one of my men hurting you." He squeezed her shoulder. She brought up her hand and rested it on top of his. The gesture caught him unawares, like an unseen blow to the chest. Most of his air rushed out. Jesus, why did she trust him so? Did she know—

But she didn't. Laura assumed everyone was her friend, just like she assumed all she had to do was show up in Kansas and her dream would come true. She hadn't planned on heartbreaks or disappointments. There was no secondary plan. She "hadn't thought it through." Not just the singing, but her life. One day she was going to fall on her pretty little ass and it was going to hurt like hell. Only it wasn't going to happen while he was there to prevent it.

At least he didn't have to worry about her being attacked again. Since the incident with George, the other cowboys had become protective rather than interested. She was their sister, not a potential lover.

She reached for his mug. "Would you like some more coffee?"

"Sure."

He handed the half-full cup to her, simply to watch her walk to the fire, fill his mug, then smile at him. One of the cowboys, Lefty, rode up and distracted her. In the few minutes she spent talking to the other man, Jesse studied her.

He'd come to know her these last few weeks. At night he lay under her wagon and listened to her sleep. He could hear the rustling of the straw as she turned over and the dog's whimpering wheeze as it dreamed. He heard her horrible off-key humming and the way she talked to herself when she forgot he was near.

Sometimes, when the past threatened, or the night grew too long to bear, he closed his eyes and imagined he was in a bed. Laura was in the room next to him—preparing to join him. He pretended their marriage was real, that soon he would feel the soft weight of her body next to him and the sweet caress of her long hair against his bare chest. Sometimes he ached for wanting her.

In those hours, when the night sky began to lighten and the new day was only a breath away, the pain of living was worst. He felt himself thawing, feeling. He fought against it, against the inevitable suffering, the memories that would ultimately destroy him as they'd destroyed so many other men. He fought against the madness that had taken his friend. Yet he couldn't elude it. Caring about Laura, having even a single spark of emotion, meant the door had been cracked. Soon the pressure of what was inside would overwhelm him. The door would burst open and everything would rush out, flooding him, sweeping him up in a current he couldn't control or contain. He didn't know the outcome. Would he float along the top and find his way safely to shore, or would he be pulled under and drown?

He had no answer. Only the prayer that the floodgates

would remain closed for as long as Laura was with him. He wanted to face his demons in private. Where it was safer, not only for him, but her.

She laughed at something Lefty said. The sound of her amusement carried to him on the rapidly cooling late-morning breeze. How was it she accomplished what no one else had? How had she brought him back to life?

Perhaps it was because the others—his family, the townspeople—simply wanted the old Jesse back. They couldn't understand that the man he had been was gone for good. Instead, Laura accepted him as he was. Her spirit was strong—strong enough to touch him and draw him back from the brink. She was laughter and life, all things bright.

"You promise you'll be there?" he heard her ask Lefty.

The old cowboy stared at her a moment, then touched the dusty brim of his hat. "Ma'am, wild steers won't keep me away."

"Good." She smiled and petted his horse's neck, then moved back. She turned around and saw Jesse, then shook her head as if to say she was forgetful.

"At least you don't have to worry about it being too hot," she said, walking over and handing him the cup. "I'm sorry, I got carried away. Lefty's promised to come to my singing debut in Wichita." She glanced down at the ground, then back up at him. "I hope you'll be there, too."

"It means a lot to you."

"Everything. I've waited my whole life for this."

Pink stained her cheeks. The flush of life. He'd often thought of telling her the truth: that her voice was so off-key, so imperfect, she made his hair stand on end. But he didn't. The cattle had grown used to the sound and he . . . well, he'd grown used to her.

"Of course I'll be there," he promised. Somehow he would find a way to make her dream come true.

"Thank you. I was hoping you would. It means a lot to me. More than having the other cowboys there."

Everything about this marriage was a mockery. But whenever he tried to remind himself of that, Laura said or did something to give him pause. Even now, he wanted to believe her. It was easier not to, though. Because as much as he pretended it was real, as much as she made him want to believe, he knew the truth. That when she was gone, if he was able, he would firmly shut the door on his feelings. He wouldn't risk the flood. It wasn't being pulled under that frightened him—it was surviving.

She clapped her hands together. "So, when do we leave for Fort Worth?" she asked, obviously trying to change the subject. "I have a list of supplies I need."

"Harry and Lefty should be leaving right away."

"Aren't you going?"

"I want to stay with the cattle." He pointed to the west. The black clouds were thicker, although they didn't seem to be moving that quickly. "I said *should* be leaving. They won't be. That storm could get dangerous. We're going to have to wait it out, then the men can head into town. You're welcome to join them then, but I don't think you'd like the ride." Not to mention having to spend the time alone in a hotel room while Harry and Lefty sampled the delights of gambling and whores. "Fort Worth isn't going to be much fun after the rain."

She was staring at the clouds. "If you're not going, I don't mind staying here."

She spoke thoughtlessly—innocently. Without knowing what her words would mean to him. She couldn't feel the fire that raced through him, the wanting that grew difficult to control. She would never understand the pain that followed desire, the rawness, the bleeding from his soul.

She trusted him. As a newborn calf trusts its mother. She trusted him without reason, without conscious planning. Her trust was as much a part of her as the brilliance of her smile and the sweet scent of her skin.

He swallowed a mouthful of coffee and realized that Laura's blind devotion would be her salvation. He would cut out his heart before betraying her.

But he was drawn to her. His grip on the mug tightened as he thought about touching her, being close to her. He recalled her offer to be his wife in every sense of the word and knew if he requested she join him in his bedroll, she would. Her eyes would get wide and she'd swallow her fear, but she wouldn't refuse him.

To distract himself from the vision of them together, and to distract her from whatever she might read in his expression, he pointed at her hands.

"You been wearing your gloves?"

"Every day." She held out her hands, palms up. "I would be afraid not to. Those reins would rub my skin raw. As it is, I'm still getting a couple of calluses." She pointed to the raised, reddened skin at the base of her fingers.

"Road brands," he said.

"What's that?"

He jerked his head toward the herd. "We brand the cattle before they leave the ranch. It's a road brand so they're easy to round up if they get lost or in with another herd. Cowboys get 'em, too, from all the hard work. Sometimes it's a broken leg or arm that doesn't set right, or a scar. You've got your calluses."

"Really?" She glanced down at her hands, obviously delighted. "So I'm like one of the cowboys?"

"Something like that."

"I want to show Harry." She hurried toward the fire and splayed her fingers for the old man.

As Jesse finished the last of his coffee, he stared at the herd. Several of the cowboys were watching the dark clouds roll closer. The temperature continued to drop. He began to button his coat. The clouds raced over the sun, turning the late morning dark.

As the first raindrops fell, one of the men came riding up. It was Lefty. He glared at the sky. "Damn it all to hell. We ain't goin' nowhere today."

"Looks like it," Jesse agreed.

"I had my heart set on gettin' to town."

Jesse grinned. "It wasn't your heart."

The cowboy returned the smile. "It wasn't at that. Still, the girls'll be waiting when we finally get there." He sniffed the air. "Smells like snow."

"I know. It's going to get a lot worse. Tell the men to pull on their blankets. If we don't have lightning, the herd won't stampede, but everybody's going to freeze. I'm going to check on Wellington and Bobby."

Lefty nodded and rode off. Jesse walked over to the fire. Harry was putting on another pot of coffee. His slicker hung loosely around him. He'd set four poles around the fire and hooked a piece of oi cloth on the poles. The covering would protect the flames from the worst of the rains.

The drops came faster. Jesse tugged up his collar and prepared to get drenched. "You gonna be all right, old man?" he asked.

Harry glared at him. "I've been through more storms than you'll ever see."

"I know." Jesse pulled his hat lower, to keep the rain out of his eyes. "It's going to get colder. Get your sorry ass into the chuck wagon and keep dry. The men are going to have to ride out the storm. Let's pray we don't have lightning."

Harry sniffed. "More likely snow."

Jesse didn't want to think about that. An unseasonably late blizzard could be deadly. "Where's Laura?"

"Back in her wagon. I sent her there when it started raining."

"Good. I'm going to check on the greenhorns."

"They're just boys," Harry said. "They ain't gonna be much help. You might as well send 'em to me."

"Good idea." At least the kids would stay warm and dry. If the storm got worse, he didn't want to have to worry about them, too. "I'll go get them right now."

He collected his horse and mounted, then urged the animal forward. The rain was freezing. It was going to be a long afternoon.

He checked on the men. Mike rode up and gave him a report. The skies darkened and still the temperature dropped lower. But the rain didn't turn to snow.

He found Wellington and Bobby guarding the rear of the herd. Both boys were soaked and freezing.

"We're at our p-post," Wellington said proudly, through chattering teeth. His face, so like Laura's, was pale with cold. Bobby's coat only came to his hips, so his woolen trousers were drenched.

"You're a sorry lookin' couple of cowboys," Jesse said. "Get your asses back to camp. Hole up with Harry until the storm passes."

Wellington drew himself up to his full height in the saddle. "I want to stay at my post."

"This isn't the army, son. While I appreciate your courage, you're no good to anyone if you freeze to death. We might have snow. Neither of you would know what to do, then. Harry's got hot coffee waiting for you. Next time we have a storm, you can stay out the entire night, all right?"

The boys looked at each other, then at him. He could read their warring emotions. Relief at the thought of getting warm and irritation at being treated like the greenhorns they were. Pride was a powerful motivator in a man.

"That wasn't a request," Jesse said when the boys continued to hesitate.

"Yes, sir," Wellington said, and kicked his horse. Bobby took off after him.

Jesse followed more slowly. The bite in the air warned him the freezing rains weren't far off.

Pea-size hail started about a half mile from camp. It pelted him and the cattle. The steers huddled together and showed no signs of stampeding. Thank God.

He circled closer to the herd. Their warm breath formed steam clouds that quickly disappeared. Hail bounced off the animals backs and settled on the ground. A few of the cattle let out low moans of distress, but otherwise, they were silent.

When Jesse returned to camp, the ground was littered with hail. He left his horse with Frank, then made his way to the fire. His boots crunched as he walked. After pouring himself a mug of coffee, he sipped the hot liquid and shuddered as the heat warmed his belly.

Jesse's looked at Laura's wagon. He wondered how she was faring. The double-layer cover would keep her dry, but he wasn't sure she was warm enough. He filled a second cup with coffee and started toward her.

"Laura," he called when he was a few feet away.

"Jesse?" She stuck her head out the back. "It's hailing."

"I know."

Her face was pale and her teeth chattering. "I can't believe it's so cold."

"I brought you coffee."

She looked at the cup and sighed. "Thank you. I'm freezing in here. King is curled up next to me on the bed, but he doesn't warm a very big space."

He told himself she would be fine. It wasn't as if she was going to freeze to death. So she might be a little chilly for an hour or two. People had survived worse. But the sensible thoughts didn't keep him from handing her his cup, too, then motioning her back so he could climb into her wagon.

Her eyes widened, but she didn't say anything. Not even when he brushed past her in the narrow aisle to get to her bed. He stripped off the blanket, then placed his hands on her shoulders and urged her to sit down. Her big eyes widened.

"Jesse?"

"You want to get warm?" he asked, taking the cups from her and setting them down.

"Of course, but . . . "

"Then trust me."

It was as if someone had lit a candle in a dark room. All questions and concerns fled her expression, leaving only contentment. "I do," she murmured.

I do. The phrase from their wedding. He didn't want to think about that now. Especially not now.

He sat next to her and pulled off his boots, then slipped off his coat. The cold air hit him like a slap. He stood up and put his hat on one of the crates stacked beside the bed. Scooping up King with one hand, he motioned to the bed with the other.

"Lay down and scoot over," he said.

She swallowed, then raised her feet onto the mattress. She was still wearing her boots, but he figured that didn't much matter. Hers weren't wet and muddy like his. When she was settled, he slipped in next to her. After drawing the blanket over them, he placed King next to his knees. He grabbed his coat and settled it over their lower legs, then fluffed her pillow and laid back.

The softness of the straw mattress and feather pillow was unfamiliar to him after several weeks of sleeping on the ground. He wondered how long it would take him to get used to a real bed again. After the previous year's cattle drive, he'd had a week of sleepless nights before his body had adjusted to a mattress.

Laura lay beside him, her arms stiffly at her sides. She was wearing her coat and gloves. He could feel her fear, along with the shivers that rippled through her. He thought about trying to explain he wasn't interested in bedding her right now.

Except he was interested. He had trouble thinking about anything else. But he wasn't going to act on his thoughts. Could she understand that a man could want something without taking it, or would trying to explain it only make things worse? He wasn't sure, so in the end, he didn't say anything at all. He simply drew her into his arms and held her close.

Gradually the shivers quieted, although she continued to hold herself stiffly.

"You're going to get a crick in your neck if you keep your head up like that," he said after a few minutes. Although her body pressed against his side, her head didn't rest on his chest.

"I don't want to be a bother," she said.

"You warmer?" he asked.

"Yes." She sounded surprised. "Much."

"I'm warmer, too." How could he not be? Her body lay against his. Her legs and the layers of her skirt touched his. "So relax." He rested his hand on her head and urged it down to his chest. She resisted slightly, then sighed her agreement.

The slight weight, the feel of her breath, the slow beating of her heart stirred him in ways he hadn't thought possible. A thick, hot emotion filled him. Not desire, although that lurked just under the surface, ready to spring to life. No, what he felt was something more dangerous.

"Tell me more about your dream," he said.

She shifted against him and rested her hand on his chest. After a moment, she realized what she'd done, gasped faintly, and started to slide her arm down to her side. He grabbed her fingers and held her in place.

"Tell me about the dress," he prompted.

Her fingers were cool to the touch. He rubbed them gently between his. She might be getting calluses from driving the wagon, but her skin was soft. He rubbed his thumbs against each pad and traced the shape of her trimmed nails. Low in his belly, need heated and grew. He ignored it, much as he ignored the hardness tightening in his groin.

"It's red," she said. "With flounces and ribbons. I want it to be satin, with black lace."

With his other hand, he touched her hair. "That will be beautiful."

She sat up a little and smiled at him. Color had returned to her cheeks. Her eyes were wide and dark in the dusty light of the wagon. Her mouth parted slightly. He thought about the last time they'd kissed. The taste of her, the sound she'd made, and the untutored response that had left him aching for days.

"Honeysuckle DeVine is beautiful," she said. "At least I hope she will be."

"You talk about her as if she's not you."

"She's not, in a way." Her nose wrinkled. "That sounds silly. Of course I'm her, but she's nothing like me. When I'm Honeysuckle, I'll be able to do all the things I'm afraid of."

"You're not afraid of anything."

"I wish that were true." She rolled toward him a little and placed her free hand on his chest, then rested her chin on her fist. "I'm afraid of lots of things. If I was really brave I wouldn't have lied to my family."

"You'll be telling them the truth soon."

"I know, but not to their faces." She grimaced. "Honeysuckle is a lot of things I'm not. When I'm her, I can leave plain Laura Cannon behind."

A single strand of hair drifted across her cheek and caught at the corner of her mouth. He brushed it back and tucked it behind her ear. He wished he could pull the pins out of her hair and see it hanging loose around her shoulders. He wished he could forget his promises to himself and to her, and simply draw her close enough to kiss.

"I happen to like plain Laura Cannon," he said.

"Really?" She smiled. "Thank you, Jesse. I like you, too. You've been good to me."

Her confession slammed into him like a steer running into a wall. He felt himself crumpling into dust. As Laura chattered on about her hopes and dreams, he clung to the simple words. "I like you, too."

How long had it been since someone had liked him? His men respected him, but he kept his distance from them. He didn't want to make friends. He was too afraid of the consequences. He'd been David's friend and in the end, the loss of that relationship had nearly destroyed him.

He focused on Laura. Her clear skin, marked only by faint freckles, seemed to glow from a hidden light. Her lips were full, changing shape to fit her mood—one minute smiling, then next pulled straight with concentration.

Perhaps Augusta was prettier, but he didn't care. Laura made him believe. For all he knew, that belief would be the death of him, but for today, he stared into the doorway of hope and chose to live.

"I've been thinking," she said thoughtfully.

He hadn't been paying attention to her conversation. She'd been saying something about what she was going to do when she got to Kansas.

"About what?"

"Well, do you think it's wrong for a woman to take lovers?"

14

"Lovers?"

Laura had never been able to know what Jesse was thinking—until this moment. His mouth hung open and he stared at her with all the shock of a minister facing a naked woman.

"Lovers?" he repeated.

She felt the blush rising on her cheeks. "I didn't exactly mean lovers," she said quickly.

"What the hell *did* you mean?"

She started to sit up, but he wrapped an arm around her back and held her in place. "Well, I haven't exactly thought it through yet. That's why I was asking." She couldn't bring herself to stare at his face. Instead she kept her gaze firmly fixed on his throat.

Despite being on the trail, Jesse washed regularly and kept his beard trimmed. She stared at the line where dark hair gave way to tanned skin. She'd often looked at that place and wondered what it would feel like to touch that line. Was the skin especially soft there, or the hair especially smooth?

The question made her chest feel funny. She drew in a deep breath and tried to make it go away. Instead, the action brought her body in contact with his as her breasts rested briefly against him. Her chest tightened even more until she wondered if she would be able to keep breathing.

"What do you want to know?" He'd managed to control his voice some, although she still heard an edge to his tone.

"I've read several books on famous singers," she said. "They all live very exciting lives. However, the books mentioned that these women had men in their lives." She cleared her throat. "Lovers, really. Dukes, sometimes, even princes. Rich men. It confused me and I didn't know who else to ask. I mean, I suppose I could have said something to Augusta or my mother, but neither of them know about my dream to be a singer, so they would ask why I wanted to know. Besides," she went on quickly, afraid he was going to stop her before she got it all out, "There's no one else I can trust. I don't really understand about being lovers. Does everyone take a lover? What do lovers do?" She thought about George and grimaced. "I wouldn't want anyone to do that with me if it was liking kissing with Andrew, or when George stuck his tongue in my mouth. But when we did it, I—"

She clamped her lips together and dropped her forehead to his chest. The fire in her cheeks burned. She could taste her embarrassment.

"I'm sorry for asking," she mumbled against his shirt.

The wagon was silent except for King's snores and the tapping of the hail on the covering. She thought about how cold she'd been before Jesse arrived and how warm she felt now. Lying next to him was like being near a nice big stove. He radiated heat. Long legs stretched out next to hers. She liked how large he was and how he made her feel safe. The arm around her back was a pleasant weight. His shirt smelled nice, a mingling of horses and the unique masculine fragrance she'd come to associate with him.

"Are you mad?" she asked, keeping her eyes closed and breathing in the scent of him.

"No. Startled. Look at me."

She drew in a deep breath and raised her head. Once again Jesse's face was unreadable. Without thinking, she stretched out her arm and touched her finger to his beard. The hair on his face was smooth and soft. She could feel the faint outline of the scar and wanted to weep for the pain he'd suffered.

"I really meant it when I promised not to be any trouble," she whispered. "You don't have to tell me about lovers if you don't want to. I don't want to embarrass you."

He raised his eyebrows. "Do I look embarrassed?"

He looked incredibly handsome. She stared into his brown eyes flecked with gold and watched his pupils get bigger. She drew her hand back and rested her chin on her fist. "No. I suppose not. Still, it was rude of me to ask. I'll find out another way."

"How? By taking a lover?"

Involuntarily she squeaked. "Why not?"

He chuckled. She felt the vibration in his chest as well as hearing the sound.

"So you've never had a lover?"

"People do not have lovers in Jackson Springs," she said. "Mama wouldn't have approved. What do you know about it?"

"Damn little."

"Oh." She tried not to sound disappointed, but she

was. She'd expected Jesse would have had a little more experience than she had. "If you haven't had a lover, have you ever been to a—" She cleared her throat again. "A fancy lady?"

His gaze narrowed. "What do you know about them?"

"Nothing," she said quickly, wondering how it was possible for her to be blushing *again*. Hadn't she used up all her blood yet? "I've heard my brothers talking about them. I tried to ask questions, but they wouldn't answer. Is that like taking a lover? Doing that? You know, what married people do?" She grimaced. "I was hoping it would be better than that."

"We shouldn't be having this conversation."

"Why not? We're married." As soon as she said the words, she wanted to call them back. They weren't really married and thinking about it made her feel guilty. She plunged on before Jesse figured out what she was thinking. Somehow the man always seemed to know. "Besides, no one ever tells me anything. I won't know what to do. Goodness, I probably won't even know when it's happening. What if I don't pay attention and then I miss the whole thing?"

"I promise you'll know when it's happening."

"How?"

He swore under his breath. "Where do you come up with these questions?" He shifted on the mattress and brushed his dark hair off his forehead. "Don't answer that. I suppose you might as well know what most men want so you can protect yourself from them. Did you know George was dangerous?"

That was the last question she'd expected. She shivered slightly, despite being toasty and dry. "I'm not sure," she said slowly. "I didn't much like him, but I thought I should be polite."

"Don't do that again," he said. "If you have a bad

feeling about a man, trust that feeling. Better to be rude and safe than polite and—" He shook his head. "He wanted to have his way with you and he didn't care if you wanted to or not."

She was shocked. "That's horrible."

"If you're forced, yes. But if you want to, and it's with the right person, it's not so bad." One corner of his mouth tilted up. "It can be pleasant."

"Pleasant?" She thought about the way George had stuck his tongue in her mouth and squeezed her breasts.

"My point is men sometimes use women for their own pleasure. You need to remember that."

"What pleasure?"

Jesse's gaze narrowed. "How much do you know about what happens between a man and a woman?"

She was getting used to blushing now and didn't even bother ducking her head. "I know that when a man and wife bed each other, he touches her in a certain way and she has a baby. Mama told me that it wasn't too horrible all the time. Augusta said it was wonderful and that I was to do whatever you—" She coughed. "If men do that when they visit fancy ladies, why don't the fancy ladies have lots of babies?"

"They use something to keep them from having babies."

"What?"

"Laura, that isn't the point of this conversation. I want you to trust your feelings about a man. If you don't want to be around him, you have to protect yourself. A lot of men don't care about women, and they simply take what they want. If that were to happen, you would be badly hurt."

She nodded solemnly. "What if it was someone I trusted and liked. Would he be a good lover?"

"Possibly," he growled, as if the thought upset him. "But you can't make every man you like your lover. You have to pick and choose carefully."

"Why?"

He opened his mouth, then closed it. "You just do."

"Do married men visit fancy ladies?"

"Some of them."

"They don't want babies."

"No. They want—"

She could see him struggling for the right word. "Pleasure?" she offered helpfully.

"Yes."

"Do men want pleasure more than women?"

"Sometimes. Some men don't know how to do it so the woman enjoys herself. A woman has to be taught about pleasure. Once she has, she won't suffer a man foolish enough to only think of himself. But if she doesn't know any better, she doesn't know to complain."

"That's not fair."

He touched the back of his fingers to her cheek. "I know, but that's the way it is."

Could you teach me?

She wanted to ask the question, but didn't. It wouldn't be right. Yet she thought it and risked looking at him, knowing he would see it in her eyes. Jesse always knew what she was thinking. Sometimes it bothered her, but other times, like now, it was very convenient.

She knew the exact moment he figured out what she was thinking. His body stiffened beneath hers and his hand dropped to the mattress.

She felt as if he'd slapped her. "I'm sorry," she said quickly, pushing away from him. Humiliation swept through her, leaving a bitter taste in her mouth. He wasn't interested in her *that* way. In fact, the only time he'd ever kissed her had been when she'd asked him to.

She hadn't thought her face could burn hotter, but it did. Tears sprang to her eyes. She wanted to run away and never face Jesse again. But she couldn't. She could hear the storm howling outside. Hail still beat against the cover of her wagon and the temperature was close to freezing.

She sat up and felt the chilly air seep through her coat. She clutched her arms to her chest.

"Laura?"

"No, I'm fine," she said softly. "I forgot myself. It doesn't matter, of course. I'm just a paying passenger on the cattle drive. You must forgive me if I sometimes can't remember that. You've been kind to me. I understand. You feel sorry for me. I've been nothing but trouble to you and you're—"

"Damn you, woman," he growled.

Before she could get frightened and slide away, he placed his hands on her shoulders and drew her close. Her legs got tangled in her skirts and she tumbled awkwardly over his lap. One of her hands pressed into the mattress next to him, the other splayed across his broad chest. His shirt was soft beneath her fingers, his body warm and muscled.

"Look at me," he ordered.

She continued to stare at the second button below his collar. It was easier than facing the pity in his face.

"Laura."

Slowly she raised her gaze. Past the dark beard, past his unsmiling mouth and the straight line of his nose, to his eyes. Something odd flared there. Something hot. It wasn't pity, or even anger. She wasn't sure she'd seen that particular expression before, but it compelled her to stay close to him, to keep her hand on his chest and let her breathing slow to match his.

"There are times when a man wants things he can't have," he told her.

"You mean like wanting all your steers to arrive safely in Kansas?"

He smiled slightly. "Not exactly. When a man finds a woman attractive, hell, sometimes if he doesn't, he wants to be with her. Touch her. Bed her. But it's not right. So he doesn't act on his urges. He fights them."

"Why?"

"Because you can't go around fu—" He glared at her. "You can't do what you want all the time. Ladies need to stay ladies. Society has rules about these things and everyone follows them."

"What if the lady wants to be touched? Then is it all right?"

He drew in a deep breath and let it out slowly. "You are the most curious woman I've ever met."

She smiled. "I'm sure I am. Mama always said I had a thousand questions for every one my brothers and sisters asked. Did you—" She paused, not sure how to ask. Her gaze dropped to his chest and she noticed how small her hand looked against him. "Did you like kissing me, Jesse?"

"Yes." The single word was clipped, but she didn't mind.

"Really?" She risked looking at him again. The fire still burned in his eyes. If anything, it was hotter now. She felt herself growing quite warm. "I liked it, too."

"Oh, God." He raised his gaze to heaven and groaned. "Laura Cannon, you're going to be the death of me."

"It's Laura Travers, and I'm just trying to understand. So if you won't teach me how to be a lover, I'll just wait until I get to Kansas. I don't mind. Really."

She was trying to be helpful, but Jesse didn't seem to notice. He lowered his hands to the mattress, but his mouth was still twisted up and he wouldn't open his eyes.

"I can just see you walking up to the first decent man you see and asking him to bed you," he muttered. "You don't have the sense the good Lord gave a steer. You win. What do you want to know?"

At last. Real information. She scooted closer to him and smoothed her skirt over her knees. "What really happens when a man beds a woman?"

He reached next to him and pulled her second pillow from under the sheet. After fluffing it, he shoved it behind his head. He was half-sitting, stretched out against the mattress. The hail still pounded on the covering, while King wheezed from the foot of the bed.

Jesse grabbed her right hand and slowly pulled off her glove. She watched him, liking the way his strong fingers worked so easily. He was a powerful man. Around him she felt content, as if she'd found her place.

"A man and a woman lie down together," he began.

"Do they have to be lying?"

"Not at first, but it helps." He glanced at her. "Why don't you save your questions to the end, otherwise, we'll never get through this."

She nodded, then offered her other hand to him so he could remove that glove.

"A man and a woman lie down together. They touch each other."

"Where?"

He raised his eyebrows.

"Oops. Sorry. Go on."

He'd removed her gloves, but he didn't let go of her hand. His fingers stroked her palm. Tiny shivers rippled up her arm and fanned out in her chest. She tried to ignore the feelings and concentrate on what he was saying.

"They touch each other all over. Arms, chest, belly. They kiss. Then they take their clothes off."

"What?" She sat up straighter. "They do it *naked?"* Naked?

"It helps."

She almost asked how, then clamped her lips shut. Augusta had told her but she'd assumed her sister had been teasing. Her gaze drifted from Jesse's hand still holding hers to his chest. Under the soft wool shirt was a layer of long underwear. But under that was bare skin. She thought she might not mind seeing his chest, perhaps even touching it. She could feel his heat through his clothes.

She shifted. Her hip pressed against his. Her hand lay on his belly. She could feel the waistband of his trousers. She didn't want to think about that part of him naked. She'd seen her brothers undressed several times. It wasn't very attractive.

"They touch each other again until both of them feel a strong need."

"To what?"

"To . . . do more. It's a powerful urge. Like being hungry and wanting something to eat."

"If you say so." It sounded silly to her. Hungry for what? "Then what happens?"

Jesse cleared his throat. If she didn't know better, she might think he was embarrassed. "The man touches the woman between her legs. If she's ready, he enters her."

"How does he know?"

He groaned. "She gets wet."

"Wet? You mean she pees?" Laura jerked away from him. "That's disgusting. I'm never doing this. Ever. I don't care if it means I can't have babies."

"It's not like that. When a woman likes what a man's doing, her body changes. It gets ready for him. To make the mating easier. Just like a man's body changes."

She frowned. Changes?

He caught her confusion. "You've seen animals, right? The male gets larger."

The blush returned, but she ignored it. She rested her hands on her thighs and thought about it. "Yes, I know what you're talking about. That happens with men, too?"

He nodded. "A woman's body has to get ready to receive a man, so she gets softer and damp. It's not disgusting, it's just the way it is."

"Then what?"

"Then he enters her and—" He cleared his throat. "Hell, that's enough to get you where you want to be. You'll have to figure the rest of it out as you go."

Laura tried to imagine what he was telling her. It didn't make sense. Where did their legs all go? Did their bellies touch, too? And they were supposed to do this naked? She shuddered. It was all too horrible to consider.

"People like this?" she asked doubtfully.

"Could we talk about something else?" he asked. His voice sounded strangled, as if it was difficult to speak.

"Why?"

"Because talking about it . . ." He threw his hands up in the air, then sagged back against the pillows. "I just don't want to think about it anymore."

"It *is* pretty awful," she agreed.

He swore under his breath.

Laura wanted to know who had thought this whole thing up. Amazing that people actually did that. It would have to be pretty powerful pleasure to get her to take her clothes off and let some man stick anything anywhere near her nether region.

"Did you ever want to do that with me?" she asked.

"Go away," he muttered.

"Where do you want me to go?"

"Never mind, I'll leave."

She was confused. She leaned closer to him. "Jesse, did you?"

"What do you think?" He turned his head so he was staring directly into her eyes. Fire flared so brightly, she half expected to get burned.

She opened her mouth, then closed it. "Do you want to right now?"

"Let's just say talking about it has put me in a mind to, but don't worry. I'll get over it."

Something funny was happening in her chest. Something tingly and nervous. Her gaze dropped to his mouth. The thought of the act was frightening, but the beginning part—the touching—didn't sound so bad.

"Maybe I could practice the first part and then worry about the rest of it later."

"I don't know if I have that kind of self-control," he told her.

She smiled. "Oh, Jesse, I trust you."

"Then you're a fool."

But she didn't want to hear that. She didn't want to hear anything. She leaned closer still, until her mouth brushed against his.

It was as if the heat from his eyes radiated out from him. She gasped when she touched him, but not because the burning hurt her. If anything, it drew her closer. She placed one hand on his shoulder, then delicately brushed her tongue against his bottom lip. His skin was firm and slightly salty. She licked it.

He groaned, and with one strong movement, swept her over him and down onto his other side. As she settled onto her back, she stared up at him.

"You're going to be the death of me," he said, his body looming over hers.

"Are we going to do that?" she asked, only a little afraid.

"No. But we're going to come damn close."

With that, he pressed his mouth against hers. She arched up to meet him, savoring the warmth. His chest pressed against her breasts. She felt toasty and content. Without thinking, she brought her arms around him and touched his back. She could feel the strength of him, the muscles, the way they moved as he shifted against her. She slipped her fingers up to his head and felt the silkiness of his too-long hair.

A sigh slipped past her lips. He took advantage of that and touched his tongue to hers. She parted for him, remembering how wonderful it had felt before.

Instantly, the shivering began. It started at her toes, which were both hot and cold, then rippled up her legs, before settling between her thighs. Her whole body hummed, especially her breasts. As he moved in her mouth, she could taste him and feel him. It was as if each place he touched had a ribbon of connection somewhere else in her body. When he touched the tip of her tongue, her breasts seemed to enlarge and grow hot. When he stroked slowly in and out of her mouth, her legs pressed together. When he angled his head and plunged in faster and harder, her fingers couldn't do anything but grasp at air and curl slowly toward her palms.

He moved his mouth away and she was able to breathe again. He propped his head up on one hand and stared down at her. His lips were damp from their kisses. She could see the faint line of his scar. She touched him there, feeling the ridge of marred skin through his beard.

"Don't," he said, pulling her hand away and kissing her palm.

"Why? I like your scar. It reminds me that while you're strong on the outside, inside you're just like everyone else. It reminds me to be kind to you because you have pain I'll never understand. Sometimes I think your scar is the most beautiful part of you."

His eyes darkened until she couldn't read his expression. A flicker of fear started low in her belly. "Jesse, I'm sorry. I didn't mean anything bad by that."

"Don't apologize," he said harshly. "Never apologize for having a pure heart."

Then he rolled on his back and pulled her with him. She stretched out atop him, her upper body resting on his chest. As she stared at his handsome face, he reached up and started to remove the pins from her hair. She felt the tugging, but didn't offer to help. When he was done, her hair tumbled over her shoulders. He smoothed it out, then brushed the long strands away from her face.

"I've dreamed about this," he murmured.

He had? Dreamed about her hair? She wanted to ask why, but she didn't dare spoil the mood. Jesse was staring at her the way the boys had always looked at Augusta. As if she was pretty. Fierce gladness swept through her. She raised herself up and moved higher, until she could kiss him. As her lips brushed his, he finger-combed her hair.

She opened her mouth against him. He followed suit. She kissed him as he'd kissed her, touching tip to tip, tasting him, learning the shape and texture of his mouth. The achy feeling inside her grew. Her breasts were tender and full, yet she wanted to rub them against Jesse's chest. Her legs trembled as if she'd run across town and back. Her dress was too tight, her coat too heavy.

She sat back on her knees and shrugged out of her jacket. It fell to the floor of the wagon. Still lying on his back, Jesse placed his hand on her stomach. Her muscles jumped at the contact. His hand moved up slowly, toward her breasts. She knew he was going to touch her there. She also knew she was going to let him.

She glanced at his face. He was watching the ascent of his hand. Anticipation curled through her. Her fingers caught at her skirt and pleated the fabric nervously. Fire flared between them. She waited, her breath catching in her throat.

He cupped his hand against the underside of her right breast. She arched into the exquisitely delicate embrace. She'd never felt anything like that before. It was better than kissing. He brushed his thumb against her nipple. She jumped and gasped. A jolt of pure pleasure shot down to her woman's place, then clear to her feet where her toes curled inside her boots.

"Jesse," she breathed. Her eyes widened as she stared at him. "Do that again."

He grinned. He'd smiled before, but not like this. Never with pure male satisfaction. She wanted him to always be like this, proud and strong and—

He moved his thumb again and she couldn't think of anything.

"I can't breathe," she gasped.

"Sure you can."

He sat up and drew her close to him, then stretched her out so she lay across his lap. One arm supported her back. She rested her head on his shoulder and listened to the quick pounding of his heart.

"I'm not going to hurt you," he whispered into her ear.

"I know."

"You're too trusting."

"Only of you. Touch me like that again."

He chuckled. She felt the vibration against her cheek. "Greedy little kitten, aren't you?"

"Yes."

She closed her eyes and gave herself up to the sensation. He cupped her breasts, one at a time, then circled them over and over again. He brushed against her nipples, teasing the sensitized tips until she was in a frenzy. She arched into his torturous assault and knew nothing would ever be sweeter than this.

He kissed her forehead. She raised her face to his, and their lips met. As she opened her mouth, his finger and thumb took her right nipple and squeezed gently. She gasped. He touched his tongue to hers, tip to tip, and squeezed again. The combination of sensations was unbearable. She wanted to scream her pleasure, she wanted to sob. She wanted someone to tell her what to do about the throbbing ache between her legs.

Over and over he kissed her, touching her breasts, teasing her into a frantic state. Her breathing grew rapid. She clutched at him. "Jesse, help me."

"What's wrong?"

"I don't know. I've never felt like this before."

Instead of telling her what to do, he lowered her to the bed and reached for the first button of her bodice. She vaguely recalled her thought that she would be embarrassed to take her clothes off and would want to protest. But as Jesse drew the sides of her bodice apart and exposed her chemise, she didn't feel embarrassed at all. She felt alive.

"You are so beautiful," he whispered. His gaze had darkened to the color of night, highlighted only by the fire. His hands were large and tanned against her white undergarments. She felt him tug on the ribbon of her chemise and knew he meant to loosen it. She waited, breath held, body quivering.

The cool air shocked her slightly. She glanced down and saw her breast lay bare to him. The fabric of her dress had been tucked down by her arms, her chemise was pulled almost to her waist. Her pale skin tightened as he looked at her. Her nipples were already hard and pointed.

He moved his hand up her ribs toward her exposed curves. Silently she screamed at him to touch her there, to ease the ache, to work his magic again. His fingers reached her and stroked her. She moaned her pleasure and slowly closed her eyes.

It was so much better this way, she thought mindlessly. Rough fingertips delicately touched her. She arched her back and sighed. "More," she murmured. She wanted him to touch her nipples, to tease them as he had before. She wanted to feel the tightness, as if a string were being drawn taut from her chest to her woman's place.

But instead of a tweaking from his fingers, she felt something warm and damp. Her eyelids flew open. He'd taken her in his mouth. She was so shocked, she couldn't speak, couldn't move. Then he suckled her, drawing more of her into his mouth, and she didn't want to speak or move. She wanted this moment to go on forever.

He touched his tongue to her nipple. She did scream, then. Softly. Involuntarily. Jesse looked at her. She could feel the blush climbing from her chest to her hairline.

"You like it." He wasn't asking a question.

She answered anyway. "Yes. I never thought it could be like this."

"Enjoy," he said, then lowered his mouth to her other breast.

Back and forth he moved, over and over until she became lost in the feelings. She touched his back, his hair, his arms. Once, she even placed her hand over his, and felt the warmth of him and the soft skin of her curves. Her legs moved restlessly, as if not all of her was enjoying his ministrations. As if there were parts being neglected. Parts that needed more.

At last he raised his head and smiled at her. "Now do you believe me about the pleasure?"

"Oh, yes." He began pulling up her chemise. "What are you doing?"

"Remembering that we're in your wagon in the middle of camp. There are a dozen or so cowboys outside, not to mention twenty-four hundred head of cattle. I don't think you want everyone to know what we're doing."

"They wouldn't have to." She wasn't ready for it to stop.

His smile faded. "Not like this. Not your first time."

And not with me. He didn't say the words, but she heard them. She wasn't sure why he was stopping or holding back. She was still too foggy from the wonderful feelings flowing through her. She wanted to ask for more, but she didn't dare. He was right. It was the middle of the day. She'd forgotten about the cowboys around them. Just the thought of them out there while she and Jesse were— She shuddered, not even able to picture it in her mind.

He fumbled with the buttons, so she pushed his hands away and finished them herself. "Thank you," she said. "For everything. For explaining what happens and for—" She motioned to her chest. "It was lovely."

"I'm glad."

She glanced at him. His expression was pained. "Did you like it?"

"Of course."

"But you look as if you've eaten a lemon."

"I'm fighting the urge."

To what? Oh, she remembered what he'd told her about a man wanting to do that with a woman. Apparently Jesse wanted to do it with her, now. Only he couldn't.

"Can I do anything to help?"

He shook his head, then moved to the edge of the bed. His movements were awkward, as if he was in agony. Her gaze slipped down his body to his groin. She saw the outline of his maleness there. Her mouth dropped open. He looked very different from her naked brothers. He was bigger and it was long and stiff, pressing out against his trousers. As she stared, it jerked and she jumped. He turned toward her and she hastily looked away.

"I just need a little time," he said through gritted teeth. "I'd best be getting back to the herd."

"But it's cold out."

"That's the point."

Nothing he was saying made sense to her, but she didn't stop him as he pulled on his coat and moved to the rear of the wagon. She followed him.

He paused before going outside and looked at her. "Thank you," he said, then kissed her cheek.

Thank her? She was the one who was thankful. Before she could tell him, he was gone. Laura touched her fingers to the lingering warmth of his kiss.

By the time the hailstorm had passed, Jesse was able to breathe again without wincing. His body had returned to normal, although his mind hadn't forgotten. Even as he rode around the herd, he could feel Laura's body against his. He could taste her mouth and her breasts, inhale the scent of her and hear her soft sounds of surprise as he caressed her.

Holding her in his arms, touching her soft skin and knowing no man had seen or done what he was doing had made him feel possessive. As if he wanted to claim this woman as his. He ignored the impulse. She wasn't his. Not only because he couldn't have her, but because she didn't want him. Laura had a purpose in life and it wasn't to be his wife.

As he neared the camp, he saw Harry swinging into the saddle of one of the more docile geldings. Mike was with him. Both men had hold of a mule to bring back supplies. Jesse kicked his horse and trotted over to his two men.

"We're ready," Harry said, adjusting his seat. "There's plenty of stew for today and tomorrow. Laura's gonna take care of the biscuits and coffee. Make sure the cowboys don't give her no trouble."

"I'll take care of it, old man." He grinned. "I thought she was just a woman and not good for anything but getting in the way."

Harry adjusted his battered black hat. Wisps of gray hair floated out from underneath. Pale-blue eyes glared at Jesse. "Don't be throwin' my own words at me, or I won't come back from Fort Worth."

"You'll be back," Jesse told his friend. "You know we can't go on without you."

Harry didn't answer. Mike gave Jesse a last minute report on the effects of the storm. The cattle survived without injury or stampeding.

"Then get going," Jesse said, slapping the rump of the nearest mule. "The sooner you get your sorry hides out of here, the sooner you'll be back."

The two men rode northeast, away from the camp. When they were almost out of earshot, Harry turned.

"Take care of that little girl, you hear me?"

Jesse waved and sat watching until the cowboys disappeared. Then he returned to his patrol of the camp.

Hail had flattened the grass, but not destroyed it. Most of the budding leaves had been knocked from the trees. His horse's hooves still crunched as the animal walked, but the damage was minimal. It could have been a lot worse.

They would make camp here until Mike and Harry returned with supplies, probably some time late tomorrow. Then they would continue north. He turned in that direction and wondered what awaited them there. So far the trip had been calm, but they still had to pass through Indian Territory.

As he urged his horse forward, he saw Laura step out of her wagon. Wellington was nearby and stopped to chat with her. The boy dreamed of being a cowboy much as Jesse had dreamed of the glories of war. At least Wellington's dreams had a chance at coming true.

What about Laura? She wanted a different life than the one she'd known. He watched her, so small against the backdrop of the herd. Fragile. His hands tightened on the reins as he realized he would do anything to protect her. He wanted her to survive and flourish, even though granting her dreams meant he would never see her again.

He closed his eyes and recalled the feel of her next to him. In that moment he knew he would never forget her. Laura was as much a part of him as the pain he lived with. She was a beacon of light and for that he would always be grateful.

For the next two hours, he rode the herd and kept his eye on camp. When the sun had nearly set, he heard men approaching. He whistled a warning to the cowboys on patrol and pulled out his pistol. Then he recognized Mike and Harry.

"What's wrong?" he called when they were close enough to hear.

Harry didn't say anything. The old man rode until he was next to Jesse, then reined in his horse. His normally ruddy face was ashen.

"What happened?" Jesse asked. "Was there trouble in town?"

Mike rode up and shook his head. "We found something on the way to town. George, that cowboy you fired."

"He jump you?"

"We found him on the side of the trail," Harry said. "George is dead."

15

"What do you mean he's dead?" Laura asked.

Jesse took off his hat and turned it in his hands. She stared at his face, hoping he would tell her he'd made a mistake.

"We think his horse got startled by something. Maybe a rattler. He was probably thrown. His neck's broken."

"No," she said, shaking her head and backing away from him. "No, that's not possible. He was just here. In camp. He was fine. He can't be dead. He can't."

She heard the rising tone of her voice and tried to stay calm. But she didn't feel calm. Her chest was tight and there was a sick feeling low in her stomach. She pressed her hands there, trying to make the sensation go away. Jesse continued to watch her. His dark eyes missed nothing, yet she didn't know what he was thinking.

She turned away and started for the fire. Halfway across camp, she veered toward her wagon, then stopped in front of it. "I can't believe it. I can't."

Cold wind snapped at the hem of her skirt. The storm had passed, leaving the temperature close to freezing. Hail littered the ground and crunched underfoot when she walked. Her hands were nearly frozen, but she didn't bother to pull on her gloves. She couldn't imagine gathering the strength to complete the task.

"I'm sorry," Jesse said, coming up behind her. "I didn't want to tell you, but it's hard to keep secrets in camp. I figured you'd want to know anyway."

She raised her head and looked at him. The breeze blew his hair into his eyes, but he didn't bother to brush it away. He looked strong and safe standing in front of her. She wanted to throw herself at him and let him hold her until the sick feeling passed. She wanted him to tell her it was all right. But it wasn't. Because of her a man was dead.

"It's my fault," she said.

"Bullshit. You had nothing to do with it."

"You're wrong. If it hadn't been for me, he wouldn't have been sent from the cattle drive. He would still be alive."

"Men die on cattle drives, same as anywhere else. It's dangerous out here. George knew that when he signed on."

"But he wasn't killed on the cattle drive, was he?" She stared at him. "He was alone out there. If I'd stayed where I belonged, none of this would have happened. Everything would be fine." She grabbed onto the side of the wagon. She could feel the bite of the breeze and the solid wood of her wagon, yet none of that felt real. The shock was too great.

"It's not your fault," Jesse said.

"Then whose fault is it?" she asked. "George's? Yours? I know it was just an accident, but that accident occurred because of me." She dropped her gaze to the ground. "You know the worst part? I've known from the beginning something would happen. I knew I would be punished for lying to my family. I was prepared for that, and I was willing to pay the price. I just didn't know—" Her throat closed and she couldn't talk anymore. She paused, waiting until the tightness eased a little. "I didn't know someone else would pay, too."

"It's not like that," he told her.

"You don't know that for sure. We'll never know for sure."

With that, she turned away and started walking. Jesse called after her, but she ignored him. She heard Wellington's voice and kept walking.

There were bare trees around her with piles of new leaves on the ground. She walked and walked until her legs ached. When she came to a group of large boulders, she sat on a smooth one and stared at the southern horizon.

The sky was clear now, after the storm. A bright blue that hurt her eyes. She stared up until tears ran down her cheeks, then she brushed them away impatiently. Tears were useless. A man was dead because of her.

She drew her legs up toward her chest and hugged them close. As she rested her forehead on her knees, she wondered what the body had looked like. How long had he lain there? Had he died right away, or had it been slow? She forced herself to imagine what George must have thought as he lay there alone on the trail. She hoped he died quickly and easily, if men ever did.

Her stomach heaved and she thought she might be sick. She took slow deep breaths until the feeling passed. She didn't know what to do now.

"I just wanted to be more," she whispered and closed her eyes tight. "Is that so bad?"

The wind didn't answer, nor did the birds or the bright, clear sky. The silence pressed on her, and she knew there would be no divine solution to her problem.

She had always thought she would do anything to make her dream come true. Everything had a price and George had paid in blood.

She squeezed her eyes tightly together and fought against the tears. She didn't deserve to cry. She deserved to be punished. She was a horrible, selfish liar who was responsible for a man's death.

Her teeth began to chatter. The sun dropped toward the horizon. She was cold, but she wasn't ready to go back to camp. How was she supposed to face everyone, knowing they must blame her?

She raised her face toward the sky. There were no clouds. Around her, the land was forbidding and unfamiliar. She was alone. She wanted her mother to hold her and promise it would be all right, but her mother wasn't here and she couldn't fix the problem.

She wasn't sure how long she sat there. Finally her legs cramped and her back got stiff. She straightened slowly, then slid off the rock. She couldn't stay away from camp forever. Jesse would worry, then send men after her. She didn't want to be any more trouble than she was.

She straightened her dress, then glanced around to get her bearings. Jesse was already there, waiting for her. She hadn't heard him approach. He leaned against a bare tree, his arms folded over his chest. He'd pulled his hat low so she couldn't read his expression.

He started walking toward her. She wanted to run away, but she forced herself to stand still. She deserved whatever he had to say to her.

When he was less than a foot in front of her, he reached forward and took her chin in his hands. He studied her face.

"Damn it, Laura, it's not your fault."

"Yes, it is."

His mouth twisted with impatience. "Life isn't that

tidy. Death isn't convenient. It doesn't pick and choose based on a moral code. George's death was an accident. You aren't being punished."

She jerked her head back and stared at him. "How did you know what I was thinking?"

"You haven't learned to hide your feelings. Your eyes give you away. You can't lie and you'll never be a poker player."

"I managed to lie to my family well enough."

"They didn't know what to look for. I do."

She turned away from him. "Maybe you're right. Maybe it isn't punishment, but that's how it feels to me. If I hadn't been on the cattle drive, George wouldn't be dead now."

"Maybe he would have died another way. Maybe you being here has saved someone else's life. Maybe if you'd stayed in town, Wellington would have been run over by a wagon."

"Stop trying to make me feel better."

He grabbed her arm and tugged until she faced him again. "There's no retribution," he told her. "There's only luck, or fate, or whatever you want to call it. I know. I was there during the war. Some men lived and some men died. There was no reason, no sense to it. If you were lucky, you were standing next to a tree that protected you, or between two men who got their faces blown off. If you were unlucky, you died."

She stared up at him. She could see the starkness in his eyes and feel his pain. She wanted to stop him from saying the words; they obviously hurt him. Yet she let him talk. As much for himself as for her. She sensed the words were cleansing.

"Better men than me got shot. Better men died slowly, badly. Braver men screamed in pain."

"You were brave." She placed her hand on his arm and squeezed. "They gave you all those medals."

He stepped back and glared at her. "They don't prove anything. They're meaningless pieces of junk given out by men who don't know what it's like to be a foot soldier. I was never brave. Not for a minute. I went to war looking for glory, but the only thing I found was death. There's no glory, no victory. Nothing but trying to survive. Trying not to die today."

The darkness in his eyes deepened until she thought he might disappear into it. Jesse's pain was a tangible beast between them. She wanted to comfort him, to hold him close and heal him, but she couldn't. What he described was so far removed from anything she'd experienced, she couldn't begin to find the words.

"No one can say why one person dies and another survives," he said. "It just happens. It was George's time. That's all. It had nothing to do with you." He glanced at the sun drifting toward the western horizon. "We need to return to camp."

He pulled his hat low and started walking. She followed after him. The pain in her belly worsened. She ached for herself and for Jesse. For all he'd endured. For what he put himself through trying to help her. She wanted to tell him that his words had made her feel better, but they hadn't. They'd only pointed out the truth.

Jesse had been afraid during the war, but he'd forced himself to do the right thing. He'd forced himself to fight. That was true bravery. She was nothing like him. Her new life was built on lies and deceptions. She was a liar and a fool—a fool for believing her dreams wouldn't have a price.

The night was cold as hell, but that wasn't the reason Jesse couldn't sleep. He lay under Laura's wagon and listened to her muffled sobs. She was trying to be quiet, but she wasn't doing a good job of it.

He didn't know what to do about her tears. His mother had cried often, usually to get her way, but Laura didn't seem to be that kind of woman. She hadn't cried since George had attacked her and even that outburst had been brief. Tonight the same man caused her pain, but this time because she blamed herself for his death.

She hadn't eaten a scrap of food at supper, or spoken with anyone. She'd sat by herself on the edge of camp. None of the men had known what to say to make her feel better. Even Wellington had been at a loss. Only King had braved her silence to settle next to her.

Now she cried as if her heart was broken. Jesse threw back his blankets and pulled on his boots. He grabbed his hat and started to walk away from the wagon. He got about ten feet, then paused. Faint moonlight illuminated the camp. The men were sleeping close to the fire. His breath came out in foggy puffs. He couldn't hear her sobs, but he could feel them. He knew the sounds and he could picture her trembling body.

"Damn it all to hell," he muttered, and returned to the wagon.

He tossed his hat on his bedroll, then pulled open the cover in back and climbed in. Laura sat up and stared at him. There was just enough light for him to see she wore her hair in a braid. It draped over one shoulder and across her pale nightgown. Her eyes were wide and dark with tears, her mouth swollen from crying.

"J—Jesse?"

He bent over so he wouldn't bump his head on the supports and moved toward her. When he reached the straw mattress, he sat down and held open his arms. She flung herself against him. Sobs racked her slender body. Hot tears spilled onto his neck and shoulder, quickly dampening his shirt. He pulled his jacket around her.

"Hush," he murmured, stroking her back and resting his chin on her hair. "Hush, sweet Laura."

She continued to cry. His hardened heart cracked a little. He tried to ignore the painful sensation, instead concentrating on the softness of her nightgown against his fingers and the warmth of her skin.

She was curvy and sweet-smelling. Earlier that day, he'd been with her on this very mattress. He'd touched her and loved her into a mindless frenzy. He'd heard her moans of passion as she was caressed by a man for the first time. Now she lay broken in his arms, shattered by events she couldn't understand.

He shifted on the mattress, sliding up until he lay propped against the pillows. She draped across him. He tried not to think about the fact that she wore very little under her delicate white gown. He ignored the way their legs tangled together and her breasts pressed into his chest. He fought against the need burning between his legs and the fire heating his blood. None of that mattered. Nothing mattered except finding the right words to heal her. He could survive anything if only Laura would smile at him again.

Her hands curled against his chest, clutching his shirt tightly. He kept one arm around her. With his free hand, he stroked one of her tight fists, moving back and forth until she released her grip. Then he slipped his palm under hers and laced their fingers together.

"It's not your fault," he told her.

"I want to believe you but I can't." Her voice was muffled against his shoulder. He felt as well as heard the words.

"I was a prisoner during the war."

"I know that."

"I always wondered why I survived long enough to

be captured. Most of the men I was with died. At first I thought I was lucky. When I arrived at the prison camp, I realized the dead were the lucky ones."

The memories pushed hard against the door holding them in place. He fought to only let a few out. Just enough to show her she was wrong. Perhaps one or two extra to remind him of the danger of caring. But no more than that. Certainly not all of them. He would never survive the onslaught.

"I was healthy enough when I arrived, but that didn't last long. Everyone was starving. Disease moved through the camp as quickly as the rats. Those weren't the only dangers. Men formed groups to protect themselves and prey on others."

He felt her stirring against him. He stared over the top of her head toward the small opening at the rear of the wagon. He could see the faint flickering light of the campfire.

"I made a friend in camp. David. We kept each other company and protected each other's backs. People died there. We couldn't stop it or make it go away. It just happened. We never knew if we were going to be the ones to wake up sick, or not wake up at all."

"That's different," Laura whispered. "You didn't have a choice about being there. I chose to come with you."

"I chose to go to war. I believed in the glory, I wanted the excitement. I didn't know how hard it would be to watch men die. Things happen. You can't control them. You can only do your best and move on."

"But I didn't do my best. I lied to my family about everything. I lied to God. I promised to be your wife and I'm not. Everything's a lie."

He glanced down at her. She was staring up at him. It was too dark to see her features, but he knew the shape of her face. He could imagine the pain darkening her eyes, and the faint twist to her mouth.

"You're the best wife I've ever had."

She snorted. "You don't have anything to compare it to, so how would you know?"

"I know. When you make your choices, they're done. Regrets are meaningless. I didn't want to get sick, but I did. Sometimes it was bad, sometimes it wasn't. Usually David and I weren't sick together, so we took care of each other. No one can say why it happened that way. Or why it happened at all."

"Where's David now?"

"He's dead." The short, clipped sentence didn't do his pain justice, he thought grimly.

"I'm sorry. Did he die in camp?"

"After we got out." Those were the memories Jesse feared most. He didn't want to think about that day or what had happened to his friend.

"Oh, Jesse." She curled up closer to him and wrapped her arms around his neck. "I understand," she murmured. "That's so unfair. You went through so much together, and then he was taken from you. I'm so sorry."

Her compassion was as tangible as her body. It swept through him and around him, stirring old wounds back to life. He didn't want to think about that anymore.

"Was he sick?" she asked.

"No." Suddenly her embrace was too confining, the wagon too small. He removed her hold on his neck and slipped away from her. "Go to sleep," he said, as he moved to the rear of the wagon. "Don't think about it tonight. Just go to sleep."

He stepped out into the night air and took a deep breath. It wasn't enough to chase away the stink of the prison. The smell invaded his dreams. He walked away from the wagon, away from the herd, stopping only when he was out of sight of the fire.

The night sky stretched out endlessly. Stars shone down on the land. He remembered being locked up in a barnlike structure with hundreds of other men. How he'd longed for the sky. He wanted to lose himself in the stars and never return to earth. He wanted to forget.

He wanted to ignore Laura's guilt, because it reminded him of his own. She blamed herself for George's death. He blamed himself for David's.

He should have known, he told himself. He should have seen what his friend was going through. He should have understood.

The door in his mind flew open. The memories rushed out, a thick, dangerous flood of darkness and pain. He stood alone, surrounded by the hell of still being alive.

"No," he screamed, clutching his head and falling to his knees. But it was too late.

He was back. Back in the prison, fighting to stay alive, wanting to die, but not wanting to die slow. Like David was dying.

David's fine-boned, aristocratic features were pale, the skin pulled tight. The unhealthy flush on his cheeks was from the fever. Jesse drew back the makeshift bandage. The wound on his leg was worse. Dark-red and black streaks shot up toward his knee and down to his ankle. Pus oozed from the torn skin.

"Stupid, really," David said, studying it. "If only I'd been wounded in battle."

The injury was an accident. David had slipped on the ice during a brief exercise period. He'd fallen on a broken piece of wooden fence. A large splinter had pierced the skin—almost all the way to the bone. Then the infection had set in.

Jesse stared at his friend. He'd grown weaker in the last few days, and feverish. He needed a doctor. The problem was they both knew what the doctor would do.

"If we had a pillow, you could hold it over my face and be done with it," David joked. "I'm too weak to put up much of a struggle."

"And leave me to face this alone," Jesse said, motioning to the room overrun with men, rats, and lice.

They shared a look of understanding.

Jesse carried David to the medical tent and watched as the doctor examined the wound, then wearily shook his head. It was his hand David clutched as he realized what they were going to do.

"I'll fight you like a son of a bitch," David said, grabbing the table.

Jesse placed the piece of wood in his friend's mouth. His eyes burned. "I'm sorry," he whispered as he took hold of David's arms and held on.

For as long as he lived, he would never forget the sound of the saw, or David's screams, or the silence that had followed both. The next few weeks were a blur. He remembered the constant weariness as he'd stayed by his friend, nursing him back to health. He remembered fighting to keep possession of their meager rations. He remembered cooking beans for days, boiling them to a gruel, then adding cornmeal and forcing David to swallow it a spoonful at a time.

It had been two weeks before David had opened his eyes long enough to know where he was. Even now, kneeling alone in the cold night, Jesse smiled as he remembered his friend's first words.

"Shit. I dreamed I was fucking the goddamn French ladies' charity league."

"Welcome back," Jesse told him.

David's weak smile had faded. "They cut off my leg."

Jesse nodded.

"What am I supposed to do with all my left shoes?"

Jesse had felt then that his friend would survive. Through some miracle, or a twist of fate, it was going to be all right.

From that moment, David had healed quickly. Soon word had come that the war was nearly over and they would be going home. Rations got better, as did their treatment.

Then David was gone. Try as he might, Jesse couldn't figure out what had happened, and that's what scared him the most. At times he raged against David, hating him for what he'd done. Occasionally he understood. Mostly he was afraid. The blackness that took his friend could come for him at any moment. That's why he didn't want to care. He would have to face the horror and survive. David hadn't survived, and David was the strong one. Jesse knew if he tried, like his friend, he would be destroyed.

16

Laura stirred the beans for the noon meal. Harry was frying thick steaks for the men. Two days before they'd found a maverick steer and slaughtered it. They were eating the choice bits quickly, before it all went bad. Laura didn't have much appetite lately, but she was pleased the cowboys were happy. She had to admit the steaks smelled a lot better than the beans.

"You about done there, girly?" Harry asked.

"Yes. I'll start serving just as soon as the first cowboys ride up." She motioned to the collection of bent tin plates next to her.

"Check on them biscuits, for me, will you?" Harry asked. "I've got to turn the meat."

She grabbed a singed towel and lifted the lid of the Dutch oven placed near the fire. The biscuits closest to the flames were brown and fluffy. The ones farthest away were still pale. She replaced the cover, then expertly turned the pot. "'Bout five more minutes."

She turned her attention to the coffee. It was done. She poured herself a mug of the brew, then blew on it until it had cooled enough to sip. She hadn't been able to teach herself to swallow it while it was still burning hot.

In the distance, to the south, she could see the inevitable cloud of dust raised up by the steers. Soon they would stop at the spot Jesse had chosen for their midday grazing. The men would eat in shifts, and when the cattle had finished, they would move on to their stop for the night.

The days had begun to blur together. One much like the next, broken only by the change in scenery and the crossing of the rivers. Spring had arrived and everything was in bloom. The grasses were thick and green, the wildflowers abundant. Everything around her was alive, but Laura felt as if she were sleepwalking. Her eyes were gritty, her movements slow. Maybe it was because she wasn't sleeping. She hadn't slept much . . . not since she'd found out about George.

"Pour me some coffee, too," Harry told her.

She reached for a second mug. When she handed it to him, she tried to smile, but it was too much effort. His bushy eyebrows drew together as he looked at her. "How long you gonna act like a horse's ass?" he asked.

Laura stared at the man, sure she couldn't have heard him correctly. Her mouth opened, but no words came out.

"Don't be givin' me that hurt look, girly. You've been sulkin' around here for near two weeks now. If somethin's botherin' you, then spit it out. If not, quit lookin' like someone just shot your best huntin' dog."

Tears filled her eyes. She blinked to hold them back. She was tired of crying.

"Just as I thought," the old man said. "You're sulkin'

for no reason. Probably 'coz we ain't payin' you enough mind. Just like a woman. I told Jesse you were going to be trouble on this cattle drive, and you are."

She stood up and stared at him, stung by his words. "How can you say that?" she asked. "You especially. I've helped out with every single meal since we left home. I've cooked, dragged in firewood, washed dishes, anything you've asked me to do." She placed her hands on her hips. "Don't you dare tell me I'm trouble, at least not for you. I've made your job easier."

Harry swallowed a gulp of his coffee. "That's better," he said. "I finally see some life in your eyes. I'm askin' you again. What's got you so down in the mouth?"

"I've got a whole list of troubles."

"Like what? What kind of troubles could a lady like you have? You're gettin' your wish. We're nearly halfway to Kansas. Soon you'll be a famous singer, just like you planned."

Laura sat on a fallen log by the fire. "It's not that simple."

"Why not?"

She leaned forward and stirred the beans. "I miss my family. I didn't think I would, but I do." She sighed. "It's not like I thought, Harry. None of it is. I want to talk to my sisters and hear my mother tell me to get my elbows off the table. I want my brothers to come over and argue with my pa about the right mare to breed next. I thought I'd miss living in a house and having my own room, but I don't. I miss the people."

"Go on," he urged, settling next to her.

"I've lied to them all," she said softly, staring down at the ground. "They think I married Jesse because I love him. They don't know that I'm paying him to get me to Wichita. He's going to have to go back to town and face everyone. I hadn't really thought that part through. Besides, I've been nothing but trouble to him since the moment I came on this cattle drive. Between me, King, and Wellington—" She sniffed, then stared up at the sky, determined not to cry again. "Well, I'm sure he's regretted his decision a thousand times."

"Is that all?"

She shook her head. "George is dead because of me."

Harry took a drink from his mug, then set it on the ground. His pale-blue eyes seemed to stare into her soul.

"I was married once," he said. "Jesse ever tell you that?"

"No. Did your wife die?"

"A long time ago. I still remember when I first met her. She was the prettiest gal I'd ever seen. Bright yellow hair, sorta like yours. Green eyes and a mouth that would make a man think he'd died and gone to heaven." He smiled sadly. "I sure thought I had. I never did figure out what a gal like her saw in a sorry old coot like me. But she married me when I asked her, and followed me out west."

He stared into the fire. "I never planned on settlin' down 'till I met her. I got us some land, built a little house. I was fixin' to be a farmer. But tillin' virgin soil ain't the easiest job in the world and I wasn't much good with crops. We had two little ones, but not enough to eat. I went out huntin' to get us some meat."

He took a long sip from his mug. Laura watched him. Pain moved slowly across his face, deepening the wrinkles and making his mouth tilt down at the corners.

"It was a Sunday," he continued. "The Lord's day. She said it weren't right to go huntin' on the Sabbath, but I was determined." He glanced at her. "I'm a might stubborn, not that you could tell."

"Of course not," she agreed. But his joke wasn't enough to make her smile. "What happened?"

"When I got back, she was dead. Her and our babies. Killed by Injuns."

He downed the last of his coffee and set the mug on the ground. "I blamed myself. God punished me for huntin' on the Sabbath. For a time, I went crazy. Nearly killed myself with liquor. But I couldn't forget her. Or the babies. For a while I took up with some folks fixin' to get rid of all the Injuns around. But I couldn't stomach the killin'. I knew she wouldn't have wanted that. All the dead in the world wouldn't bring my family back. In the end I figured out it was my fault, but it was also bad luck and a bad season. If I'd gone a different day, if the buffalo hadn't been so far away, if the crops had been better. But none of that made any difference once she was gone."

"I'm sorry," Laura whispered.

"It was a long time ago. My point was this. She wouldn't have wanted me to spend my life dyin' just 'coz she was dead, too. I wasn't ready to get me another wife then, and hell, now I'm too damn old, but I'm here. I still think about her. But I won't tarnish my memories by punishin' myself forever. I had to let the hatred go and remember the good times."

She stared at him. "What are you telling me?"

"If you're feelin' guilty about lying to your family, you'd best be tellin' them the truth. Seems to me, there's two ways to do that. You can go back and tell 'em in person, or you can write 'em a letter."

She bit her lower lip. "They'll be so disappointed."

"Will they want you to give up your dream?"

She frowned. "I don't know. I was always afraid to say anything. I didn't want them to discourage me. No, that's not right. I didn't want them to know because I like having something for my own. My secret was my prize. The only thing I didn't have to share."

"From what I know of your family, they seem like they care about everyone, especially their children. You think they'd want you to come back to Jackson Springs and give up the one thing you've always wanted? You think your ma and pa are that mean-spirited?"

"No, of course not," she said quickly. "I know they care about me. That's why they always want to keep me with them." She mulled his words over in her mind. Harry was right. Her family wouldn't have wanted to let her go, but now that she was gone, they wouldn't expect her to give up what she'd always wanted.

"I have to tell them what I've done," she said slowly. "I need to apologize for lying and make it right with them." She raised her head and nodded. "As soon as we get to Kansas, I'm going to send them a long letter telling them the truth. After they know everything, if they want me to come back, I will."

She drew in a deep breath. It was as if a great weight had been lifted off her shoulders. She smiled. "Oh, Harry, I feel so much better."

He leaned close and bumped her shoulder with his. "I'm glad you do, girly. And I'll tell you a little secret. I suspect your parents are going to want you to be the best singer you can be. Now, as for missin' your family, hell, there's a dozen cowboys on this cattle drive who are just as lonely for their families as you are for yours. Instead of moanin' about your problems, think on theirs. Maybe they'd like a little conversation with someone pretty. Maybe they'd like to hear a song they remember from their growin' up times. Sometimes a smile is enough to lighten a heart."

"Harry, you're making me feel very foolish. I hadn't

thought of that. They must be just as lonely as I am. Why didn't I realize they were lonely, too?"

The old man grinned. "Maybe you ain't as smart as you look. Now what else was on your list. George. Is that right?"

Her feeling of elation faded as quickly as it had come. She'd almost forgotten about George. Tears burned in her eyes, but she blinked them away. "Oh, I feel so badly about that. If I hadn't come on the cattle drive . . ." She clamped her mouth shut in an effort to stop the trembling that swept through her.

Harry leaned forward and rested his elbows on his knees. His trousers were worn and dirty. His shirt had been darned so many times, it was more patch than shirt.

"I know for a fact Jesse's told you it ain't your fault."

"But—"

He shook his head. "Listen to me, girly. I agree with Jesse. If George had been where he was supposed to be instead of bothering you, he might be around now. But none of us can say that for sure. I believe if it's a body's time, there ain't nothing any of us here can do to stop that." He turned his head toward her. "Seems to me you're not talking to the one person who knows exactly what happened that day. Maybe it's time you took your problem and all your guilt to the Lord. Seems to me He's the one to be passin' out forgiveness on this matter."

She sniffed. That made sense. She would, that very night, pray and ask for forgiveness. If it wasn't to be, then she would suffer her guilt gladly.

"Hmm, that about does it," he said. He put his hands on his thighs and started to stand up, then he relaxed back on the log. "Wait. There was one more thing, wasn't there?"

"It doesn't matter," Laura mumbled, remembering

that she'd complained about her relationship with Jesse and what a trial she was to him.

"If you want my opinion, and you must, else you wouldn't have bothered to ask it in the first place—if you want to stop being trouble to Jesse, then get on with the business of helping him. We've got us a lot of miles between here and Kansas. Ain't nobody stoppin' you but maybe yerself."

"You make it sound so simple."

"No need to make it hard."

"You could be right," she said, wondering if it really was that easy.

"I usually am." Harry rose and moved to the fire. He slipped the pan back over the flames and turned the meat.

"I get in trouble when I don't think things through," she said.

"Jesse's mentioned that."

"He's talked about me?" She wasn't sure why, but the thought pleased her.

"He's brought up your name a time or two."

Before she could ask him anything else, Mike and Lefty rode into camp.

"I could smell that cookin' back a mile. I'm starved enough to eat a whole steer," Lefty said as he swung down from his saddle.

"I only fixed you half a steer, so you'll have to go hungry," Harry answered.

Laura smiled as she turned from the men. She used her hand to shield her eyes and stared out toward the herd. A tall man on horseback caught her attention. She moved toward him.

A blur of brown and white flew by on her right. King! She'd forgotten all about him. "King," she called. "Get back here. King!" The little dog ignored her and headed straight for the herd.

"Not again," she said, pulling up her skirts slightly and racing after him. She'd learned her lesson from the last time, so she watched the large steers as she got closer. King wasn't as aware. He dashed up to Skunk and started barking at the lead animal.

Laura stopped and held her breath. She flinched in anticipation of the herd stampeding and the small dog getting trampled.

"King," she called softly, so as not to upset the cattle. "Come here."

The dog ignored her. He planted his feet in the ground and barked at Skunk.

The dun-colored steer lowered his head and stared at the dog. Skunk took a step closer. Laura called King again, then waited for the yelp of pain as the dog was impaled on the steer's wide horns. Instead, Skunk nosed the mutt out of the way and calmly began eating grass.

King continued to bark. The other steers moved around him, ignoring the yapping animal. At last the little dog gave up and trotted to her side. Laura gathered him in her arms.

"Are you trying to get yourself killed?" she asked as she cuddled him close. "I should take a switch to you." Instead she kissed the top of his fuzzy head, then tied him to her wagon. When the dog was secure, she went in search of Jesse.

He was still heading toward camp. She walked in his direction. When he saw her, he urged his horse forward.

"What's wrong?" he asked, when he got close enough to call out.

She shook her head and waited until he stopped next to her. As she patted his gelding's smooth nose, he slid to the ground.

"Nothing's wrong," she said, then was sorry she'd

been moping for so long. She tilted her head back and studied his handsome face. A wave of longing moved through her. She wanted to be more than a concern. Fierce need blossomed in her chest. She wanted to be much more.

But she didn't know how to say that. The words swirled around in her throat, getting caught and tangled by confusing emotions.

"Where is your blue shirt?" she asked, when he continued to stare at her. He wasn't wearing a coat anymore. The weather had turned warm. She admired the strength of him, barely concealed by the tightly woven cloth.

"Why?"

"I noticed a tear in the sleeve and I want to mend it tonight."

Jesse pushed his hat back, then folded his arms over his chest. "Why?"

His obvious confusion at her offer embarrassed her. She stomped her foot. "You'd better get it and give it to me before I change my mind."

"All right." He handed her the gelding's reins, then went to the chuck wagon, where he stored his small bag of clothing. After rooting through it, he took her the blue shirt.

"Thank you," she said, looking at his face. No matter how busy he was on the trail, he always kept his beard trimmed. She remembered how soft it had felt when she'd touched his cheek. A funny sort of lightness started low in her midsection and floated up into her chest. Jesse's gaze locked with hers. She tried to read what he was thinking, but he was far too gifted at keeping his feelings concealed. She had to content herself with admiring the gold-flecked brown of his eyes and remembering how they'd brightened with fire when he'd kissed her.

The silence stretched between them. She felt the

urge to say something, but couldn't think of any words. Finally, Jesse glanced away self-consciously, then reached up and touched his scar. Impulsively she took a step close to him. She reached up on her tiptoes and kissed his marked cheek.

He frowned. "What was that for?"

"Just because," she said, then smiled and returned to the fire.

They reached the banks of the Red River four days ahead of schedule. Jesse rode up and down, two miles in each direction, searching for the right place to cross. It was early in the day, so there was time.

The Red River was the largest body of water they'd crossed so far. At Jesse's nod, Harry started the chuck wagon across the rapidly flowing water. The current was strong, the river deep and wide. Mike and Lefty kept the herd back, although Skunk and a few of the other leaders were already pushing forward.

Frank brought up the remuda. The horses tossed their heads, smelling the water. They'd finished drinking upstream of where Harry was crossing, then stepped into the swirling depths. Jesse watched them. When they were halfway across, he rode down to Laura's wagon.

"Ready?" he said, pulling up next to her.

Her blue eyes widened as she looked at him. "What's wrong?" she asked. "You seem worried."

He frowned. "This river has a bad reputation. It can rise in less time than it takes to cross. The currents are rough." He stared out at the rapidly flowing water. Men had died here, but he didn't want Laura to know that. "I want to get the cattle across early, before the sun sinks too low in the west."

She glanced up at the sky. "That won't be for hours."

"You've seen how long it takes all the cattle to cross."

She nodded. "Sometimes it takes nearly the entire afternoon."

"See how the river bends here." He pointed at the gentle curve in the bank. "The steers will be looking right into the sun if we cross too late. They don't like that. They'll mill around. Once that starts, they panic and drown. I haven't lost but two steers and I'd like to keep it that way."

He didn't tell her his other concern. Once they crossed the Red River, they entered Indian Territory. The thought had kept him up for the last three nights. Pray God they got through without encountering Indians. Bad enough that the herd was in danger, but he couldn't bear to think about something happening to Laura.

She leaned toward him in the seat of her wagon. Her broad, straw hat kept the sun off her face, although she was still getting more and more freckles each day. He liked the pattern they made on her nose and cheeks.

"I'm glad the cattle drive is going well for you," she said and smiled. He was starting to get used to the brilliance and no longer had to blink to recover. But his chest got a little tight when she looked at him that way.

"We're not there yet," he said.

"But we'll get there. You work hard, Jesse. You deserve your success. I wish—" She glanced down at her hands gripping the reins. "I hope I haven't been too much of a bother."

She hadn't been anything but trouble from the first moment she'd ridden onto his ranch. But he couldn't tell her that. Besides, he liked having her around. He knew he was going to regret it for the rest of his days, but for now, he allowed himself to stand inside the circle of her light and bask in the glow. In time he would return to the safety of darkness. In time, but not today.

"It's your turn," he said, motioning to the river.

Laura flicked the reins and the mules started forward. The sturdy animals didn't hesitate as they entered the water. The strong current pulled them downstream as they crossed. Jesse grimaced and quickly rode in after Laura. His horse jerked its head and went upstream of the wagon. By the time Jesse realized he was on the wrong side of Laura, it was too late to go around.

He urged the gelding closer to the wagon, then grabbed hold of the side. Laura glanced at him. Water lapped at her feet. She shrieked, then laughed and raised her feet to the top of the footboard.

As they neared the center of the river, the sound of the rushing water drowned out all other noise. He tried to call her name, but she didn't respond. At the moment his horse began to swim, the wagon jerked forward and began to float. The mules continued to swim forward, but the wagon pulled them. It was tugged downstream by the strong current. Jesse hung on and used his horse to try and keep the wagon stable. They drifted down one foot for every two they made across.

He glanced over his shoulder and saw Skunk and the other leaders in the river. Up ahead, Harry and Frank waited on the bank, ready to jump to Laura's assistance. But she was calm and capable, handling the mules with an expertise he admired.

She was a hell of a woman.

The water rose to his calves, soaking his boots. It was cold as hell, and dark. The wagon lurched as it bumped into a rock on the bottom. Jesse reached for Laura. She swayed in her seat, but remained upright.

She glanced at him. A single strand of gold-blond hair drifted across her face. She shook her head.

"I'm fine," she called. The breeze caught her words, but he read her lips.

King came out from the rear of the wagon. He braced himself on the far side of the seat and yapped at the river. The wagon hit another rock and jerked to the left. Jesse hung on despite the shaft of pain that shot through his arm. King tumbled off the side into the swirling water.

"No!" Laura screeched and reached for the animal.

Jesse let go of the wagon and grabbed her arm. He cursed as she tried to pull free. The mutt had gone under on the far side of the wagon, so he couldn't help him, but he sure as hell wasn't going to let her jump in.

"Keep control of the mules," he called. "The dog can swim."

Sure enough King popped out of the water. He paddled furiously for the shore, but the current was too strong for him. He was quickly swept downstream. Ten feet away from the wagon, he went under the water again.

Laura glanced at him, her eyes dark with pain. "Jesse, help him."

He looked for the animal, but there was no way to reach him. Frank raced along the shore, calling the dog's name. King didn't resurface. Then Skunk changed course in the river. He ducked his massive head and came up with the wet pup on his snout. King lay limp for a few seconds, then he coughed and promptly fell back in the water. Skunk dipped his head and nosed the animal in front of him. King swam valiantly with the steer keeping him on course. The unlikely pair continued until King could touch the bottom and run up the embankment.

As soon as Laura's mules reached the far side, Harry and Frank took hold of their bridles and led them to safety. Jesse urged his horse out of the river. He rode close to the little dog, then dismounted and grabbed the animal by the scruff of the neck.

"I ought to have you served up for supper," he said, shaking King. The wet dog simply stared at him, his big brown eyes bright with excitement. King squirmed closer, then swiped a lick at Jesse's nose. Behind him he heard Laura laughing. He turned just in time to have her throw herself at him. Her arms came around him, crushing the wet dog against his chest.

"You saved him," she murmured, burying her head in his shoulder.

"Skunk did."

"But you would have if you'd been on the other side of my wagon."

He wanted to tell her that he would have let King drown, only he knew he would be lying. Even though he knew better, he probably would have risked his hide for the sorry critter. Jesus, when had he gotten so soft?

He stepped back and handed her the dog. "Get your wagon out of the way of the steers," he said gruffly.

He expected her to turn away hurt, but instead she gave him one of her smiles, then climbed up and flicked the reins. For some reason he would never be able to explain, instead of staying to make sure the cattle crossed safely, he found himself riding next to her as they made their way to camp. He was as tame as an ox, he thought with disgust.

"Jesse?"

"What?"

Laura looked up at him. "I was wondering. If there was a little cove or something, could I go upstream and take a bath?"

He didn't want to think about her wet and naked, so of course that was the first image that appeared in his mind. His body reacted instantly and painfully.

He bit back a moan of both pleasure and pain. A fitting punishment, he thought grimly, for a man who dared to long after an innocent.

Jesse thought he'd imagined the worst. While they'd collected her soap and towels, he'd told himself he would stay as far away from her as was safe. Even as they'd ridden upstream and looked for a secluded area for her to bathe, he'd told himself it wasn't going to be a problem. He'd been wrong.

He leaned back against the black willow and tried not to glance at the river. His need was stronger than his sense of self-preservation. Like the fool he was, he peeked through the screen of bushes.

He could see parts of her. A bare elbow, a flash of hair loosened from its customary knot at the base of her neck, a shoulder. The sight of creamy skin hit him hard and low, leaving him gasping for air. She was beautiful. He'd thought that from the first time he'd seen her. Not with the obvious beauty of her sister Augusta, but with a freshness as foreign to him as her laughter.

"Harry's hoping we find another maverick steer in the next day or so," she said, continuing a conversation they'd been having for the last several minutes. At least, she'd been having it. He'd been struggling to respond without giving anything away. The last thing he wanted was for Laura to be frightened of him.

"The meat from the last one is about gone," she continued. "I think there's going to be stew tonight."

"Good," he said, trying not to be brusque. His throat tightened with each wave of desire. He told himself to think of other things, but it was an impossible task. Even now, Laura reached up and loosely pinned her hair on top of her head. A single strand slipped down her back. The erotic image burned into his brain as fire coursed through his blood.

She stepped into the river. Her laughter carried to him over the rushing of the water. "It's freezing," she said.

"Spring runoff," he told her. "What did you expect?"

"Bathwater."

She half-turned toward him. The screen of bushes between them was incomplete. He saw the curve of her jaw, her shoulder and bare arm and a bit of her hip. She wore a chemise and pantaloons, but as soon as they were wet, they became transparent. She might as well have been naked. Her awkward movements, perhaps brought on by bathing in the open, only made her more dear to him. He told himself if he was any kind of a gentleman, he would look away. But if he was any kind of a gentleman, he wouldn't have looked in the first place. He hungered for her, yet with his last breath he would deny himself.

It didn't matter that he'd come to care for her. When they reached Kansas, she would leave him. Even if he wanted her to stay, he didn't have the right to ask.

"I thought I would have a long soak," she called, "but I won't be a minute. This water is freezing."

She bent back in the river and wet her hair, then reached for her soap. As she raised her arms to lather her head, she lost her balance in the rapidly flowing water. She staggered a couple of steps and found her footing again. Unfortunately, he now had a clearer view of her.

Water clung to her breasts. The moisture collected and ran down her ribs to her waist. Her rosy nipples were tight and pointing toward the sky. He remembered the feel of them against his tongue and between his fingers. His hands curled into fists as the sensations came back to him.

She turned toward him. If he didn't know better, he would think she was exposing herself deliberately. Except her eyes were closed as she continued to lather her hair. He stared at her nearly naked body, his hungry gaze tracing her narrow waist and the flare of her hips. Between her legs a small triangle of blond curls protected her woman's place. The wet undergarments she wore only added to the erotic nature of the moment. As if even the protection she sought had betrayed her.

He wanted to remove his clothing and join her. He could take her tenderly. She'd responded passionately before, and she was the one trying to find out about taking lovers. He could teach her and in the teaching, ease his own pain. Sweat broke out on his back. The need grew more intense, as did the pressure from his arousal. He had to find release.

He took a step toward her. Laura took a step back into deeper water, then bent and began to rinse her hair. Every part of him urged him to go to her. She wouldn't refuse him. Instinctively he knew she would never refuse him anything.

"I know a place . . . where all things beautiful," she sang.

Jesse flinched. Laura hadn't sung in a few days. When he didn't hear her for a while, he forgot how terrible her voice was. Around them birds took flight and the insects were silent.

She continued her song. The harsh discord of her tune made him shudder, yet not for the world would he tell her the truth.

She reached for the bar of soap she'd placed on a rock by the river, then turned her back and peeled down her wet chemise. He didn't have to see her to know what she was doing, what she was touching. Her voice softened to a hum.

She bent over and splashed water on her chest. He could see her bare breasts. They swayed with her movements, the nipples tightening as the cold water chilled her. He wished she would splash him with the water. Perhaps it would help ease his discomfort. He was so hard, he feared he might explode. When he'd needed a woman before, he'd taken his pleasure quickly, impersonally. But the desire hadn't been insistent. More like a nagging hunger, while this was as intense as the urge to breathe while drowning.

Still he forced himself to stay back where he was. She trusted him.

She pulled her chemise up, then knelt in the water. He didn't dare think about her washing herself below the waist. He didn't want to imagine her small, sure hands touching herself with the soap. He didn't want to know that—

He swore under his breath and turned to grip the tree behind him. He squeezed the bark, daring the hardwood to yield to him. It bit into his skin and still he hung on, concentrating on the tension in his hands.

"Jesse, the water's quite lovely. You should take a bath, too. I don't mind waiting."

Her sweet voice snapped his patience. "Damn it, Laura, you've wasted enough of my time today. Get out of the river and get dressed now."

His words hovered in the silence. The birds and insects hadn't returned. He could hear the sound of his strained breathing, and something else. A faint catch, as if Laura had, for a moment, forgotten to breathe.

Calling himself a bastard, and worse, he released his dead-grip on the tree and turned slowly. She stood in the shallows of the river, with one foot on the embankment. There were no bushes or trees to screen her and she made no effort to cover herself. The damp undergarments clung to her, baring her to his gaze. But his attention wasn't drawn to her breasts, nor even her hair hanging over her shoulders. Instead he looked at her face, and the hurt stealing into her eyes.

"I'm sorry," he said and looked away. He wished she would learn to conceal her feelings from him. Sometimes he didn't want to know what she was thinking.

"It's all right," she murmured. "I've taken too long. I didn't mean to keep you from the herd. I'll dress quickly. You can go on back, if you would like. I'm sure I'll be fine."

He cursed long and low, then moved toward her. She was standing on the bank and reaching for a towel. He took the thick cloth from her hands and wrapped it around her shoulders.

"You trust me to take care of you, but I'm the one who's going to hurt you the most," he said. "Why can't you see that?"

Her face turned toward his. Her eyebrows drew together. Her skin was pale, the freckles standing out across her nose and cheeks. He touched the dots, tracing the pattern they made. Her damp hair was a dark blond. He picked up a strand and squeezed it between his fingers. Water ran down his hand. He tugged until she stepped closer, until they touched.

Without warning, without asking or offering an explanation, he lowered his mouth to hers. He thought she might protest or pull away, but after an initial start of surprise, she simply leaned against him and sighed. He caught her breath in his mouth and made it his own. He traced her lips with his tongue. When she parted to admit him, he hesitated, teasing them both by continuing to circle around.

The need that drove him grew, the pounding in his ears increased. She yielded to him, wrapping her arms around his waist and pressing her breasts against his chest. She was cold and wet from the river, but that did nothing to decrease his desire.

At last, when she strained toward him, he swept his tongue inside her mouth. Slowly, lovingly, he stroked her over and over, heightening her pleasure. An insistent voice told him it would be easy to take her now. She was practically naked and obviously willing. And a virgin.

Jesse pulled back and stared at her. Her mouth was damp from his kisses, her eyes unfocused. "I'm sorry," he told her again. "You didn't take too long. I was frustrated and I took it out on you."

"I don't understand."

He took her hand in his and pressed it to his groin. Her palm cupped his hardness as her fingers explored the base of his desire. He gritted his teeth to keep from embarrassing himself.

When she continued to stroke him, he pulled her hand away. "I want you," he said bluntly. "The need makes it difficult to think about anything else."

Laura frowned. She returned her hand to his waist. "You make it sound so complicated. All this wanting and not taking. We're married. I don't mind. I'm sorry that you're so unhappy on my account." She motioned to the soft grass around them. "We could just—"

"No," he said quickly, before she could expand on what they "could just" do. "You don't make me unhappy. That's not what I was trying to explain. I watched you while you were bathing. That got me aroused. I don't have to do anything about it. In time, it goes away."

"I still don't understand." Her gaze searched his. "Of all the men I've known, you're the only one I would want to do . . ." She hesitated and blushed, but didn't look away. "Um, do that with. Why do you keep saying no?"

"Because it's not right. Because a woman's first time shouldn't be on some damn riverbank in the middle of God knows where."

And because he was afraid. The thought startled him, but he recognized the truth. He was afraid of her. Of what she had come to mean to him, and mostly of what she could be in his world. He didn't want to care about her more. Because he knew he would lose her eventually. If not to her dreams, then to the darkness inside of him.

He grimaced. "Hell, Laura, I'm trying to act like a gentleman. The least you could do is help me."

"Maybe I don't want to," she whispered.

Despite the throbbing of his groin, he grinned. "You're one stubborn woman." He looked over her head at the river. "Is that water really cold?"

"Freezing."

"Good." He moved around her and started unbuttoning his shirt.

"What are doing?"

"Getting some relief."

After pulling off his shirt, he started on his boots. Laura turned to watch him. Next Jesse unbuttoned his trousers. They fell to the ground, leaving him only in his long underwear. She told herself she should turn away to give him privacy. However, he made no attempt to cover himself or hide behind bushes. As he began to lower his underwear, she felt herself blush. She reminded herself she'd seen her brothers naked once or twice. Jesse couldn't be all that different.

He kicked off his long johns, then headed for the river. On the embankment, he paused, then jumped in. He ducked below the surface, then stood up and yelled.

"Damn it, woman, you didn't tell me it was icy."

She giggled. "Yes, I did. It's spring runoff. What did you expect?"

He turned and glared at her. "Don't mock me with my own words."

She saw the hint of a smile, nearly hidden by his beard. "I'm not scared of you, Jesse Travers."

"You should be. Now where's the damn soap?"

"On the rock, and stop swearing so much."

"Women."

He grabbed the soap and started rubbing his chest. Her gaze dropped to his chest, then quickly dipped below. Her eyes widened as she swallowed. He didn't look at all like her brothers.

Oh, the shape was somewhat similar, but he was much larger and his. . . maleness thrust out toward her. She closed her eyes. Questions darted through her mind as she remembered Jesse telling her that it got bigger when a man was aroused. He was supposed to place it inside of a woman. She opened her eyes and tilted her head as she studied him. No, it couldn't possibly fit anywhere in her. He must have made a mistake.

She watched as Jesse washed his hair, then lathered his body. His chest was broad and well muscled. Dark hair arrowed down in a fine line, drawing her eyes to his groin. She tried to look away, then couldn't when she realized it was smaller and somehow less intimidating.

He drew the soap over his arms. She cleared her throat and glanced at the bushes on the edge of the river.

"Why didn't you marry?" she asked.

"Never saw the point."

"But you were sweet on Augusta before. You must have had thoughts of getting married once."

"Maybe," he said slowly. "The war changed me. When I was young, I figured I would be like everyone else. Work the ranch, find a wife, have children. After the war, I couldn't see myself doing that anymore."

She looked back at him. He was standing in thigh-deep water completely naked. He looked up and saw her. Either he didn't care that she saw him, or he'd forgotten he wasn't wearing any clothes, because he didn't cover himself.

"I don't think I'd make much of a husband or father," he said.

"I think you're a fine husband. And you work well with Wellington and Bobby."

He shrugged. "That's different."

He ducked down and rinsed his hair. When he came back up, his body had changed even more. He was just like she remembered her brothers being. She still thought the whole man and woman thing was very poorly thought out. It sounded so uncomfortable and awkward. Jesse hadn't explained where all the arms and legs went, although she was starting to see the being naked part wouldn't be so bad. Jesse was quite handsome without his clothes. She had the most peculiar urge to touch his chest.

She turned away and went over to the small cloth bag she'd brought with her. While Jesse was gathering up his clothes, she took hers and stepped behind a bush. Perhaps it wasn't fair, but she couldn't bring herself to dress in front of him. What if he didn't think she was as attractive as she thought he was?

She drew off her wet chemise and pantaloons, and pulled on clean undergarments. After putting on her petticoat—she was only wearing two these days—she dropped her dress over her head and began fastening the buttons. When she was done, she returned to the clearing. Jesse was dressed and leaning against a tree. She settled on a rock and began brushing out her hair.

"Washington says the hardest part about the war is the remembering," she said. "He told me he could have easily lived through it once, but he has to go over it again and again when he sleeps. He says it never goes away. Sometimes it's better, sometimes he thinks he's going to go mad from remembering." She hesitated, not wanting to pry, yet longing to know. "Is it like that with you?"

Jesse closed his eyes. "Yes."

She wondered what he saw when he closed his eyes. What did he try not to remember? She knew whatever she pictured in her mind, what he saw would be a hundred times worse. One night, when Washington couldn't sleep, she'd sat up with him. He'd spoken haltingly about his experience. The half-formed phrases hadn't made sense to her, but she understood the horror and the ugliness he lived with everyday.

"Is that why you didn't want to marry?" she asked. "Are you afraid your wife will pry too much?"

He shook his head.

"But don't you get lonely, being by yourself all the time?" She bit her lower lip and continued to brush her hair. "I get lonely and I'm part of a big family. But sometimes, when everyone is talking about something and I'm just sitting there, I feel like I could disappear and no one would notice. I suppose that's why I want to be Honeysuckle DeVine. She'll never be lonely or afraid. She'll always know what to say and how to act."

"I'll miss Laura Cannon."

"Really? Why? She isn't anything special."

"I think she is."

His compliment made her glow. She wanted to ask why he thought that, then wondered if he was just being kind.

"What about you?" he asked. "Why haven't you married?"

"First of all, the only person who asked is Andrew." She shuddered.

"The mortician?"

"Yes. Can you imagine anything worse? His hands are so white. He says it's from the embalming. I never wanted him to touch me."

"That would make the marriage difficult."

She glanced at him out of the corner of her eye. "You're teasing me, Jesse. I know you are. Anyway, the other reason I didn't marry is I didn't want to be like everyone else. I didn't want to live in the same house, seeing the same faces all the time. I'd done that my whole life. I wanted an adventure."

She drew the brush through her hair. Jesse followed the movement with his gaze. The intensity of his expression made her feel warm inside, and just a little tingly. Almost the way she had when she'd seen him naked in the river. She liked the way he watched her. It made her feel special, and almost pretty. She wondered if Augusta felt this way all the time.

She shook off her thoughts and returned her attention to the conversation. "Do you realize this cattle drive is the very first adventure I've ever had?"

"How do you like it so far?"

She stared at him. His dark eyes met her own. He hadn't pulled on his hat yet, so his hair tumbled onto his forehead. It was damp, but looked soft. She wanted to touch it, to touch him. She wanted him to kiss her again, and hold her. She'd been chilled from the river, but next to him she'd felt warm.

"I like it very much."

He turned away and picked up his hat from where he'd tossed it on the ground. "Do up your hair, Laura. It's time to get back."

She wanted to refuse his request. She liked spending time with him alone. She wanted to learn more about him. She wanted to understand this stranger who was her husband. But she didn't. Instead of protesting or asking more questions, she did as he asked. She coiled her hair neatly, then accompanied him without saying a word. After all, she didn't have the right to pry. She wasn't really his wife. As soon as they reached Wichita, they would be going their separate ways. He would return to Jackson Springs and she would begin her career on the stage.

As they rode back to camp she was surprised by the feeling of disappointment that swept over her. For the first time ever, the thought of being Honeysuckle DeVine didn't make her smile.

"We have to be careful," Jesse said.

"I know that," Harry snapped. "Why do you think I'm totin' this with me everywhere?" He picked up his rifle and shook it. "It ain't easy havin' this thing around and tryin' to keep Laura from seein' it. I think you should tell her the truth."

Jesse poured himself another mug of coffee and glanced around the camp. They'd just settled in for the night. After three days in Indian Territory he was as jumpy as a barncat facing a herd of coyotes. So far everything had been quiet, but that didn't mean it was going to stay that way. The Indians could leave them alone for the entire journey, or they could attack that night. He'd warned the men to be careful, to stay close to the herd and not go riding off alone. But he hadn't told Laura. He didn't want her to worry.

"She doesn't need to know," he said.

"Damn fool," Harry muttered. "She's got more sense than most men I know. She's not gonna panic. 'Sides, how you gonna keep her from figurin' it out when a whole mess of them come ridin' into camp?"

"That might not happen."

He rose to his feet and walked over to her wagon. Laura was darning another of his shirts. She'd taken a sudden interest in his clothing. He liked having her do small tasks for him. He usually just paid a seamstress when he got to town, but it wasn't the savings that pleased him. It was the knowledge that she'd labored over something for him.

He grimaced. He was going soft in the head to be thinking things like that.

She glanced up as he approached. "Is it time for me to help Harry with the meal?"

"Not yet." He took another gulp, then tossed away the rest of his coffee. King poked his head out of the back, took a look at Jesse, then jumped onto the seat, walked over Laura and leaned his head out to be petted. Jesse scratched the dog's ears. King moaned with pleasure.

"He sure likes you," Laura said. "I think he knows you're responsible for him being alive."

"I doubt that. King's too stupid to figure out he should be afraid of the steers." He cleared his throat. "Laura, I want you to be sure and stay close to camp for the next few days. The cattle are restless and I don't want you hurt if they stampede."

She glanced around them at the quietly eating herd. "They seem calm enough."

For the first time since he'd met her, he resented the fact that she was intelligent. "What they seem and what they might be is two different things. I've had more experience than you running steers, so I'm asking you to accept my word on this."

"Fine." She glanced down at her darning and jabbed the needle through the dark fabric. "I'll stay close to camp. Any other instructions?"

"No. I didn't mean to be sharp. I just want you to stay safe."

"Oh, don't worry about me. I can take care of myself."

She smiled. He prayed she was right. He didn't want anything to happen to her.

Before he could say anything further, he felt a crawling sensation on the back of his neck. He turned quickly and glanced around the camp. Everything was quiet. There were bluffs to the west of them. He shaded his eyes against the setting sun. Nothing. But the feeling persisted.

He didn't want Laura to sit here alone. "Why don't you come help Harry now," he said. "You can finish my shirt later."

She placed her darning away, then started to step down from the wagon. He held out his arms. She placed her hands on his shoulders and let him lift her down. When her feet were on the ground, he didn't immediately release her. He studied her face, the shape, the curve of her mouth, the straight line of her nose.

"What's wrong?" she asked. "You're staring at me as if you'll never see me again."

The sensation at the back of his neck worsened. "Nothing's wrong. Sometimes I forget how pretty you are."

She blushed. "Augusta's the pretty one. I'm just—"

"No." He touched his finger to her mouth. "Don't say that. I happen to like you as Laura Cannon."

"Except it's Laura Travers."

She was his wife. Sometimes he forgot. When he remembered, it was always with a spurt of pleasure. He glanced around the still-empty bluffs and wondered if she would die his wife, killed by Indians in the middle of the wilderness.

He held out his arm. She slipped her hand into the crook of his elbow and allowed him to lead her to camp.

Most of the cowboys had collected around the fire. Harry was finished with the biscuits. Usually the men ate in shifts, but apparently they sensed it, too—the scent of danger in the air. Death was near.

As Laura stepped close to the fire, Jesse glanced once more to the bluffs. This time he saw Indians on horseback silhouetted against the setting sun. His heart clenched tight as a coldness swept over him. He watched as the first dozen or so Indians were joined by more and more, until they stretched out for as far as he could see.

Mike glanced at him, then turned and followed his gaze. The cowboy paled. Jesse knew what he was thinking. They were out-manned and out-gunned. If Jesse couldn't trade a few steers for safe passage, they were all going to die.

He turned to Laura. She still hadn't noticed the Indians. She was stirring the stew. She looked up at him, then frowned at the other men.

"I swear, I've never seen such a solemn collection outside of church. Why is everyone so quiet?" The setting sun caught her hair and made it gleam. In the weeks she'd been with him on the cattle trail, she'd become the most important part of his life. Did he have the strength to kill her before the Indians took her?

He drew in a deep breath and knew he would do what he had to. He owed Laura that. It was time to warn her.

But before he could speak, she opened her mouth and started to sing. The off-key sound echoed from the bluff and surrounded them. A few of the cattle started, shuddered, then returned to grazing. King trotted over and joined Laura. His howl was almost the same pitch, as if they were searching for the right harmony.

As last sounds went, Jesse thought she sounded a hell of a lot more comforting than the whistle of a bullet. Casually he glanced up at the bluff. His mouth opened, then he grinned.

The Indians' horses were rearing as the sound reached them. One of the Indians fell off and had to chase after his mount. Others galloped away, as if chased by demons from hell. By the time Laura was halfway through her song, the bluff was empty except for one man. He tilted his head, as if listening, then kicked his horse and disappeared over the far side of the bluff.

Jesse glanced at Mike. The cowboy stared back at him, disbelief clear in his expression. Jesse didn't know if the Indians had been scared off by her voice, or if they thought she had powerful magic. Lefty glanced worriedly at the bluff, then did a double take. He winked at Jesse and turned back to Laura. The cowboy joined in her song. Mike did, too.

One by one, the men noticed the Indians were gone. They sang with Laura. Even Jesse joined in. His voice was gravelly from disuse.

"I know a place," he sang.

Laura glanced up in surprise. She came around the fire and stood next to him. When she took his hand, he squeezed her fingers. The tightness in his chest eased, only to be replaced by a different kind of pain. The ache that came from knowing how soon she would leave him.

"You need to roll the piecrust even," Harry said, pointing to a thick spot in the crust.

"I'm trying." Laura stepped back and eyed the crust. "I'm rolling it out on a piece of cloth over a wooden plank, Harry. I swear, I'd do much better in a kitchen."

The old man grinned at her. "Girly, I don't suspect you've noticed 'till now, but we ain't got no kitchen."

She glanced around at the wide open spaces. For as far as the eye could see, prairie stretched forever. They'd left the trees behind a couple of weeks before, and the familiar plants. Now they were in the land of sod.

She smoothed the rolling pin over the crust, trying to make it even, then she set the pin down and picked up the cloth.

"Turn it easylike," Harry instructed. "Gently, so it falls nice and smooth into the pie pan."

She did as he instructed. The crust peeled off perfectly, settling into the pan. She pinched the edges, then spooned in the dried apples they'd been soaking. Harry finished his pie, then took hers.

"Are we celebrating?" she asked, wiping her hands on a clean flour sack.

"Yup. We're about into Kansas, so the worst of the trail ride is behind us. Now all we have to worry about is nesters." He glanced at her. "That's farmers to you."

"I didn't know we'd come that far," she said. The days had all blurred together. "How long until we reach Wichita?"

"'Bout two weeks. Maybe a day or so longer."

"That soon." At least she'd had a chance to perfect her stage performance. For the last three weeks, the men had encouraged her to sing to them every night. The practice had allowed her to choose her songs and make sure she had the tunes right. They'd never complained if she'd sang a song more than once, to make sure she knew the words. She couldn't wait to sing accompanied by a piano. She was never sure if she was exactly in tune, and the men were too nice to mention the occasional flat note.

Two of the cowboys rode up. Laura stood and collected mugs, then poured coffee. She'd learned it didn't matter why the men came into camp, they always wanted a fresh cup of coffee while they were there. The sky was bright blue, a perfect spring afternoon. She shielded her eyes as the men dismounted. The taller of the two was Mike; the gawky, skinny one trailing a few feet behind was Wellington.

She added sugar to her brother's cup. He drank as much as the men, but she'd seen him flinching at the taste. He was doing it because he wanted to fit in, not because he enjoyed the brew.

"Laura," Mike said, touching the brim of his hat. She smiled and handed him his mug. "Thank you." He blew on the surface for a moment, then swallowed a mouthful.

"Have you finished the letter to that gal of yours?" she asked. Mike was sweet on the minister's daughter back in Jackson Springs. He'd been working on a letter since they'd left home. When Laura found out about it, she'd tried to help him, but Mike wouldn't be rushed. He'd told her he'd "mail it when it was ready to be mailed, and not a day before." Privately Laura suspected Mike would already be back home before the letter was finished. Maybe that was his plan all along. He would deliver it in person and save the postage.

"Nearly," Mike said. "It needs another sentence or two. I'll think on it a while longer before deciding."

"I'm sure she'd be happy to get any correspondence from you. It's the thought that counts, not how pretty the letters are."

Mike shook his head. "The letter's got to be just right."

There was no arguing with him. Mike might be the best cowboy on the trail, but he was darned stubborn. She turned her attention to her brother.

As always, he was covered in dust. Riding drag left him dirty, but he didn't mind. For him, every day was a new adventure. She admired how Wellington had grown up on the trail ride. He wasn't the same boy who'd left home nearly three months before. But then, they'd all changed.

As Laura listened to Harry and the two cowboys chat, she glanced around the camp. It was no longer strange to her. She knew the comings and goings of the men and what their duties were. She'd taken Harry's advice and had tried to turn them into a family. Lefty could be counted on to tell the best stories. Mike couldn't be rushed. Bobby wanted to be considered a man. Frank preferred the company of his horses to people. Laura still thought about her family, but she'd found a measure of contentment here. She would miss them when they reached Kansas and parted ways.

"We're nearly there," Mike said.

Wellington nodded eagerly. "And we got through Indian Territory without any trouble."

Laura stared at him. "Indian Territory? When did we go through that?"

Harry muttered something under his breath, then took off his worn, tattered hat and slapped Wellington on the side of the head. The boy hunched down on his camp stool.

"Mike?" Laura turned to the cowboy. "We were in Indian Territory? No one told me. Were we in danger?"

Mike tossed back the rest of his coffee. "I'd best be getting to the herd." He walked away.

"Harry?" she said.

The old man drew in a breath, then looked at the ground.

"None of you are going to talk to me?"

Harry set his hat back on his bald head and sniffed. "Orders," he muttered.

"Orders? Whose?" She grimaced. That was a silly question. There was only one man in this camp who gave orders. She untied her apron and tossed it on a camp stool, then she walked purposefully toward the last place she'd seen Jesse.

She found him by the remuda, talking with Frank. He took one look at her and dismissed the other man. As Jesse moved over to her, he drew his eyebrows together.

"What's wrong?" he asked.

She stopped two feet in front of him and placed her hands on her hips. "Is it true? Were we in Indian Territory and you didn't see fit to tell me?"

"I didn't want you to worry."

"I had the right to know."

"Why? Except for one night, we didn't see any Indians." He got the most peculiar look on his face, as if he was going to tell her something, then decided she wouldn't believe him.

"I still would have liked to have known. I could have taken precautions."

"It wasn't necessary. You were never alone. If you'd known you would have been frightened and nervous."

"But I've never seen an Indian before. I've heard so many stories, I would have liked to have seen them for myself."

He bent at the waist, bringing his face close to hers. His dark eyes snapped with anger. "If they'd decided to attack, you would have seen them plenty close. I don't think you would have liked it much." He reached out and grabbed the coil of hair at the nape of her neck. "They don't kill their victims before they scalp them."

She tried not to react, but she couldn't help the shudder that rippled through her. "Jesse, I—"

He released her hair and stepped back. "I'm trying to keep you safe and all you care about is your damn adventure."

His tone was harsh. She blinked at him, then lowered her arms to her sides. "You care about me," she said softly. "You were worried."

"We were in goddamn Indian Territory. Of course I was worried. Only a fool wouldn't be worried."

He started to turn away. She didn't let him. She placed her hand on his forearm and, with the lightest of touches, held him in place.

"I'm sorry," she said.

"I know." The tension in him eased a little. "I didn't want you to know because you would have spent the last three weeks scared. That would have meant not sleeping, jumping at every noise. It's a hell of a way to live. I just did what I thought was best. If they'd come after you . . ." He reached out and fingered her hair, gently this time. His mouth twisted. "I know the right thing to do would have been to kill you before they could hurt you, but I wasn't sure I could do it."

She'd heard of such things, of course, but she'd never thought of them being applied to her. Jesse had wrestled with the possibility. She couldn't imagine making that kind of decision.

"I'm glad you didn't kill me," she said, trying to tease him into smiling. It almost worked. The corner of his mouth raised slightly. She continued to study his face and realized she was fighting the urge to give in to tears. It was silly. She had no reason to cry, but her eyes were burning and her throat felt thick.

His fingers trailed from her hair to her shoulders. He didn't pull away and she didn't step back. She liked it when Jesse touched her. He made her feel safe and tingly at the same time. For a man who held himself apart, he touched her a lot. She often wondered what he would have been like if the war hadn't changed him so. If she could spend more time with him, she might be able to find out. But that wasn't to be.

"Harry says we'll reach Wichita in a few weeks. Is that true?"

Jesse dropped his hand to his side and looked north. "We're nearly there. Another couple hundred miles is all. Two, maybe three weeks."

"Then what happens?"

"I sell the cattle."

"No, I meant . . ." She wasn't sure how to ask. She grasped her fingers together in front of her waist. "Will you leave right away? After I pay you."

He didn't say anything for a long time. At last she risked glancing up at him. A faint longing tinged his features, making him look sad. She wanted to go to him and hold him until the feeling passed.

"I'll stay for a few days," he said. "The horses need rest, and the men have to have time to get drunk a few times."

And visit fancy ladies, she thought, then flushed as she remembered her time with Jesse down by the river. Would he visit a fancy lady and do with that woman what he'd refused to do with her?

"Will I still see you there?" she asked, her voice low and shaky.

"Do you want to?"

"Oh, yes. Please. I like being with you." *I like being married to you*. Except she couldn't say that. It wasn't part of their arrangement. When they got to Wichita, they would visit the lawyer and collect her inheritance. Then she and Jesse would be divorced.

She'd always known the marriage would end, but suddenly it didn't seem like a good idea.

"Jesse, maybe we could—" She opened her mouth, then closed it. Maybe they could what? Stay married? She wanted a life on the stage and he would be returning to his ranch. She didn't have the right to remain his wife. She sighed. "Maybe we could go to dinner someplace fancy."

He nodded. "Sure. I've got to get back to work."

She watched him walk away and wondered how many more times he would do that before it would be the last.

19

It had been too easy. Jesse knew that. He could feel it in his bones. The cattle drive had been quiet and uneventful. Hell, they hadn't even been attacked by Indians. He smiled to himself. According to Harry, Laura's singing hadn't only kept away the Indians, there hadn't been nearly as many mosquitoes, either. The journey had been his best so far, but things were about to change.

He eyed the storm brewing in the west. It was as if God had drawn a line on the prairie. On one side was sunlight, on the other darkness. The thick black clouds raced across the heavens toward them. They couldn't outrun them so they would have to endure. It was going to be bad. He could smell the coming destruction.

He kicked his horse and headed for camp. As he passed Wellington and Bobby, he motioned for the boys to come close. "The storm's going to come in hard and fast," he told them. "Take off anything metal you have, including your belts. Put them in the chuck wagon."

Wellington's eyes widened. "What's going to happen, Jesse?"

"The cattle are going to stampede. You boys remember what I told you?"

Bobby nodded. "Ride on the left, stay with 'em, but stay clear."

"That's right. Are your mounts fresh?" Both young men shook their heads. "Then get new ones. It's going to be a long night."

He left them and headed for camp. Harry would know what to do, but he wanted to reassure Laura. So far they'd been lucky. The thunderstorms had only lasted for a short time. They'd blown through quickly. Jesse had a feeling this was going to be a long one. The herd could scatter for miles by the time it was done. If it rained hard enough, the lightning wouldn't start a prairie fire, but there were other dangers.

He met Mike on the edge of camp. The cowboy looked grim. "I'm going to get Lefty and move the white steers to the rear of the herd," Mike said. "If they get hit, fewer animals will be injured."

"Good idea," Jesse said. The first gust of wind swirled around them. It wasn't cold, just heavy with the strength of the coming storm. He could taste the dampness. "You put away your pistol?"

"First thing. You think I want to fry?"

Mike rode away, toward the herd. Jesse dismounted and secured his horse, then walked into camp.

Harry had already tied down the chuck wagon. The mules were with the horses, rope-corralled out in the open. The lone white horse had been hobbled away from the others. He saw Laura carrying a box. He loped over and caught up with her.

"What's in here?" he asked, taking it from her. It was heavier than it looked.

"Everything I have that's metal. My eating utensils and cooking pots are already in the chuck wagon." The wind tugged at her hair, pulling strands loose. Her skirts flapped around her legs. Dark clouds moved closer. "The storm's big, isn't it?"

"Yeah." He placed the box in the chuck wagon, then put his arm around her. "I want you to stay in your wagon. Whatever happens, don't come out. Harry will stay with you. You'll be safe. The chuck wagon is on higher ground, see." He pointed to the slight rise in the prairie. "All the metal is there. It will attract the lightning."

"I'm not afraid," she said, but he could feel her trembling next to him.

"I know you're not." He wanted to pull her close and make her forget her fears, but there wasn't time. Already the air had grown moist. He could see the rain and lightning on the horizon. Soon they would hear the rumble of thunder. He contented himself with dropping a quick kiss on the top of her head. He didn't want something to happen to her, but he couldn't afford to think about anything but the herd.

"Why is that horse all by itself?" she asked, pointing to the white gelding.

"Pale animals are hit by lightning more often than dark ones," he said. "If the horse gets hit, we don't want the others around it killed, too. We do the same thing with the herd. The white steers are moved to the back of the herd."

"You mean it's going to die?" she asked, staring at the gelding.

"No. You never know where the lightning is going to strike."

This time she didn't try to conceal her shiver of fear.

"Laura," he said.

"No." She pushed him away and stared at him. "You go take care of the cattle, Jesse. Harry's here and I'll be fine." Her expression was determined. Funny, all those weeks ago when she'd first approached him about coming on the cattle drive, he'd thought that a woman would be nothing but trouble. Now, with the danger swirling around them, he knew Laura was the best part of the cattle drive. All his sorry life, he would be grateful to have known her.

"You're very brave," he said.

"No, I'm terrified, but I'm going to try to be brave."

He gave into the impulse and pressed his mouth against hers. "That's what courage is."

The first drops of rain hit him in the face. He swore under his breath. Harry stuck his head out of Laura's wagon.

"Ain't no point in goin' to all this trouble, if you're just gonna stand out there and git wet, girly."

She bit her lower lip. "Jesse."

"Go." He pushed her toward the wagon.

"Keep Wellington safe," she called as she ran for safety. Once she was inside, Harry secured the cover.

As Jesse mounted his horse, he thought he might have heard her call "Keep yourself safe, too," but the wind tugged at the words and he wasn't sure.

Then there was no time to wonder. The storm descended with the fury of the devil himself. Rain poured down on the earth and a bolt of lightning cut through the sky.

"Here we go," he muttered.

The steers lowed in fear. When the explosion of thunder shook the night, the cattle raced into the darkness.

"Stampede," came the call.

Jesse bent low over his horse and gave the animal its

head. Between bolts of lightning, the afternoon was dark, almost like night. He couldn't see much through the driving rain, but he could hear the herd and feel the heat rising from them as they ran. With each flash of light, there was a moment of eerie silence. The cattle jumped as one. When they landed, often in time with the thunder, the very earth shook.

He hung onto his gelding, trusting the animal to carry him safely. The herd was on their right. All the cowboys had been positioned on the left of the herd because the steers eventually turned to the right. That was the opportunity they waited for. As soon as the herd started to turn, the cowboys pressed the leaders back into main group. Once that happened, the cattle milled around, then stopped running.

But it could be hours before the herd began to turn. For each mile they ran, there would be between twenty and fifty strays to be rounded up.

Jesse didn't know how long he raced with the cattle and the storm. The rain soaked him to the skin. Wind tugged at his hat and his clothing. He didn't see any other men, but he trusted them to be there when it was time. He tried not to think about Laura, about how frightened she must be. The gelding's stride shortened and his pace slowed. Not only from exhaustion, but from the ground turning to mud, churned raw by the pounding of the herd. On and on through the after-noon—until the sky began to darken even more with the promise of nightfall.

Up ahead he caught sight of Lefty and one of the swing riders. Mike was probably farther ahead, trying to keep up with the leaders. He thought he caught sight of Wellington and Bobby. He had time for the brief hope that they stayed the hell out of trouble.

At first Jesse thought he'd willed it to happen, that it was just the water pouring into his eyes. He wiped his face with his hand and stared hard. They were turning to the right.

The tightness in his chest eased some as the pace of the steers slowed. For the first time he noticed the lightning had passed, although the rain still poured down. He was exhausted, as was his mount. He slowed the animal to a trot. He could feel its hooves sticking in the mud.

The cattle continued to move next to him, but they'd slowed, too. The soft, thick ground sucked their strength away. Even if the late afternoon had been cold, he wouldn't have felt it. The heat generated by the stampeding herd surrounded him, like the warmth from a blazing fire. He tried not to think about how much weight each of them was losing. There was still time to make it up before they reached Wichita.

Up ahead, the herd turned. Jesse caught up with Wellington and Bobby. They looked like drowned rats. Their clothes were soaked, the brims of their hats hung down over their faces. Jesse figured he didn't look any better.

"You boys all right?" he called when he was close enough to be heard.

"Yes, sir," Bobby said. "We stayed with the herd, just like you said. When they started to turn, we were ready."

The cattle slowed to a walk. Wellington rode closer to them.

"Stay clear," Jesse called. "They're still skittish."

Wellington twisted in his saddle. "I'll be fine."

But he spoke too soon. One of the steers turned his massive head and saw Wellington's horse. The cow lunged forward. The boy's gelding tried to back up and turn at the same time. Its left rear leg gave out and the horse started to go down.

Jesse knew what was going to happen. He kicked his

horse forward and called out to the boy. As the words left his mouth, Wellington fell off the saddle. He grabbed for the sturdy leather, but his soaked gloves slipped and he couldn't get a firm hold. He tumbled head first toward the mud. The steer saw the movement and started toward him. Jesse urged his horse faster. He bent low toward Wellington, stretched out his arm for the boy to grab hold. The steer jerked around and kicked out.

"Duck," Jesse called.

The boy obeyed and the sharp hoof landed squarely on Jesse's upper arm.

The pain exploded up his shoulder and down his back. He saw Wellington reach out his hand, but Jesse couldn't make his fingers work. He couldn't bend them. He also couldn't feel the boy's grip. He kicked his foot free of the stirrup.

"Use this," he said and glanced up to see the steer turning to charge them. His horse started to slide away from the oncoming cow. Still not able to feel anything except for blinding pain, Jesse forced his fingers to close on Wellington's shirt and help haul him up.

Blood dripped down his arm, soaking his sleeve. He couldn't work the reins with his left hand. He transferred them to his right, then kicked his mount and they trotted away from the steer.

"Did you see that?" Wellington asked from behind him. The boy bounced behind the saddle. "I thought that old steer was gonna get me for sure. You saved me."

Jesse's only response was a grunt. He pulled a handkerchief out of his pocket and used it to bind the wound. The pain had settled into a dull throb that intensified with each beat of his heart. He ignored the sensation, shutting off the feelings so they didn't interfere with his job.

"Here's your horse," Bobby said, riding up, pulling Wellington's mount behind him.

The boy pushed off the back of Jesse's horse and climbed back into his saddle. "Now what?" he asked brightly.

Jesse felt old and tired by comparison. He wanted to crawl into his bedroll and sleep for three days straight. That wasn't to be. For one thing, it was still raining, so it was going to be a long uncomfortable night. For another, there was still the matter of the herd.

He saw Mike and waved him over.

"It could have been a lot worse," Mike said when he was close enough to be heard. "All the cowboys are fine." The point rider glanced at Jesse's arm, but didn't say anything. "It happened so fast, I don't think many steers had the time to stray."

"Start rounding them up," Jesse said. "I'll look for a new bed." He scanned the wet countryside, trying to remember what the landscape had been when he'd scouted the area that morning.

"But they didn't eat all the grass where they were," Bobby said. "Why can't they just go back there?"

"Never take a herd back to the same place where they stampeded," Jesse said, not bothering to glance at the boy. "You're asking for trouble. There." He pointed east. "See those two rocks?"

Mike nodded.

"On the other side, there's a shallow depression with a creek. It was dry this morning, but it should have water in it now. There's enough grass. Get Skunk out in front and take them there. I'll go ahead to the new campsite."

"Boss, you ought to get Harry to take a look at your arm. The way it's bleeding, you're going to need sewing up."

For the first time, Wellington noticed his injury. His eyes, so like his sister's, widened. "What happened?"

"A steer kicked me." He flexed his arm, refusing to wince at the flash of pain that shot through him.

"I'm sorry, Jesse."

He shrugged off the apology. "It was an accident. It's fine now."

"It doesn't look fine," Mike said. "You aren't going to be much use to us if that doesn't heal right. Besides, do you know how mad Laura's going to be when she finds out you didn't get that tended to?"

"Yeah," Wellington said. "She'll blame me."

Bobby nodded silently.

Hell. Jesse felt a trickle of blood run down his arm and collect in his glove. He'd already had to empty it twice. "Once the herd is settled, take half the men and start looking for strays. I'll be back as soon as Harry sews me up."

He rode for the campground. Once he was out of sight of the herd, he gave in to the dizziness sweeping over him. He slumped forward in his saddle and closed his eyes. The world stopped spinning, but he didn't like the beckoning darkness, so he forced himself to sit up and pay attention to where he was going.

It took about two hours to walk back to the original campsite. Once there, he dismounted and tied up his horse. The simple act took far longer than it should have. His good hand didn't want to work either. He wondered if it was from loss of blood or exhaustion.

The rain had lightened to a steady downpour. At least he could see now. It was nearly sunset. The sky stayed dark. Once the sun went down completely, the men wouldn't be able to see anything. The clouds would block the moon and stars. They wouldn't be able to find strays until morning. He had to tell Mike.

But his legs refused to obey the command to return to his horse. He felt his knees buckle. In the distance, or maybe it wasn't that far at all, he saw someone bending over a flickering flame.

"Harry?" he called. Except his voice came out all scratchy and soft. As if he'd lost all his air.

The shadowy figure straightened. "What the hell? Jesse, is that you?"

"What's left of me." His arm throbbed. He'd forgotten about physical pain, forgotten how it could sap a man and leave him weak and defenseless. He had the thought that David would protect him as he'd protected his friend, then he remembered David was dead. The war was over.

"It'll never be over," he muttered.

A strong arm grasped him around the waist. "Lean on me," Harry ordered and grabbed Jesse's left hand to drape it over his shoulder. Jesse winced at the hot, sharp jab that raced up his arm. The old man glanced at the wound and swore.

"Dang fool. I've always said you don't have the sense God gave a rock. Laura," he called loudly. "Jesse's been hurt."

Jesse's eyelids felt heavy, but he forced them to stay open. He wanted to see her when she appeared at the back of the wagon. He wanted to know if she was worried about him.

The covering was thrust back and Laura jumped down. She rushed toward him. The rain fell on her, but she didn't seem to notice. She simply picked up her skirt and ran across the wet prairie.

"What happened?"

Harry jerked his head toward Jesse's arm. She peered at the wound, then raised her gaze to his.

"I got kicked by a cow," he said and tried to smile. His lips weren't working well. He thought his words might be slurring. "Bleeding like a son of a bitch. Hurts, too." His knees buckled. If Harry hadn't been holding onto him, he would have crumpled to the ground.

Laura moved closer. She touched the bandage. Even the gentle brush of her fingers caused him to suck in a breath. He'd thought she might panic at the sight of the blood. Especially when she pulled off his glove and held it upside down over the ground. Blood poured out and splattered onto her skirt.

But as always, Laura surprised him. She didn't faint or back away. She nodded at Harry. "Can you get him into the wagon? We've got to get the wound cleaned and sewn up." She looked back at Jesse and rested her palm on his cheek. "If you had any sense, you'd go ahead and pass out, so we could take care of you more easily."

It sounded like a damn fine idea. He meant to tell her, too, but the whole world went black.

Jesse came awake to the thought that someone was holding his arm up to a fire. He could feel the flesh burning away, clear to the bone. He was cold, as cold as he could remember being in years. He didn't want to breathe in; he didn't want to know he was back.

But in the end, his body betrayed him. He was forced to draw in a breath, to smell the air, and he braced himself for the stench. Instead he inhaled something wonderfully familiar. The scent of flowers and femininity. He opened his eyes.

Laura sat next to him on the straw mattress in her wagon. She was bent over his arm, which had been propped up by a folded blanket. The burning sensation had been her rubbing a cloth against the wound.

At the same moment she realized he was awake, he

realized he was naked under the blanket. He wondered if Laura had stayed while Harry'd undressed him.

"You're awake," she said, and sighed. A single lock of damp hair fluttered by her cheek. She pushed it away wearily. "I hoped you'd stay out longer. I have to sew you up, Jesse, and I don't think I can. I mean I've tended wounds before, but nothing this big. I don't think I can stand to hurt you."

Her lower lip trembled as she spoke. He wanted to reassure her, but he was surprised to find out he barely had the energy to raise his good arm. He'd lost more blood than he'd thought.

"I'll be fine," he said. His voice was low and faint.

"I asked Harry if he had any whiskey, but he said you don't allow it on the cattle drive."

"Drunk cowboys are more trouble than no cowboys at all. Go ahead and sew me. I won't move."

She hesitated.

"If you don't, Harry will," he told her. "I suspect your stitches are a damn sight neater than his. I don't need the liquor, Laura, I've been sewn up sober before."

"In the war?"

He nodded. "A friend of mine had his leg amputated without anesthesia. I figure I can take a little needle like that one."

He'd spoken without thinking, then wished he could have called the words back. Laura paled. "Are you talking about David? Did he lose a leg?"

He nodded to both.

She picked up the threaded needle. "I don't mind if you swear at me, but please try not to move."

He forced himself to smile. "I won't swear."

There were three lanterns hanging above them on hooks. The inside of the wagon was as bright as day. Her shadow danced on the cloth covering, but the graceful pattern couldn't disguise her trembling. She drew in a deep breath and bent over his wound.

"Did the operation kill your friend?"

"No, he survived that. He even got good at walking with a crutch." He closed his eyes and felt a smile tugging at his lips. "David used to say when he got back home, he finally had an excuse not to dance with the neighborhood ladies. If he'd known how easy it would be, he would have had his leg cut off sooner."

He winced. Not from the prick of her needle, or the tugging of the thread through his flesh, but from the threats of the past.

"David sounds like an interesting man."

He opened his eyes and stared at her. She bent over his wound, working intently. The lamplight caught that single strand of gold-blond hair and made it glow. He could see the shadows under her eyes and the perfect smoothness of her skin. She was beautiful. The shape of her small nose, the curve of her mouth, now pulled straight as she concentrated.

"The war never seemed to touch David. He talked about the future. About what he was going to do when it was over. I couldn't imagine that. It hurt too much to plan. But not for him." He closed his eyes. "He was the brave one. I was afraid of dying and not dying. Not David. He should have been a coward, or at least a fool. He was the youngest son of a plantation owner from South Carolina. If we'd met in a bar, we probably would have gotten in a fight. But in the camp, we were like brothers."

In truth, closer than he'd ever been to his brothers. With David he didn't have to explain the fear. They understood each other without words.

The pain in his arm deepened so he couldn't feel the individual holes made by the needle. Instead he felt the constant burning. Long practice allowed him to disconnect from the heat that made him want to scream. Unfortunately, the act of disconnecting with the present left him vulnerable to the past.

"My brother told me facing death with another man was something no one else can understand." Laura touched his brow. Her fingers were cool. "I'm glad David was there with you. Did he survive the war?"

He nodded. "At the end, there were signs. We were afraid to hope. We'd come so far, but men around us continued to die. Someone was always ill. Then one day they gave us a clean set of clothes, a decent meal, and told us we could go. Just like that."

The end, when it came, had been unexpected. Shocking. A part of him hadn't wanted to leave the prison camp. He'd never understood that and was ashamed of the memory.

He heard something tearing. He opened his eyes and saw Laura ripping apart one of her petticoats. He glanced at his arm. Neat stitches held the edges of the wound together. It was long, almost three inches, in a nearly perfect half-circle. The bruise from the impact of the hoof was clearly visible.

She looked up. "You're going to have a scar."

"You do good work."

"Thanks." She wrapped a length of petticoat around his arm and secured it with a knot. "So you and David both left the prison camp?"

"Yes." He didn't want to think about that day. He stared at her face and willed himself to think of nothing but her. Nothing but the perfection of her features and the sweet taste of her mouth against his. He pulled the blanket up his chest and tightly clutched the rough wool.

"Jesse? What's wrong? Why are you looking at me like that?"

He couldn't answer. He could only stare. She grasped his hands in hers and bent toward him. That single strand of loose hair brushed against his chin.

"Jesse, you're frightening me. What's wrong? Are you in pain?"

He wanted to laugh at her question. He wanted to destroy his demons, but as always, they defeated him.

"Is it about David? About what happened to him?" she asked.

He continued to stare at her, as if she could save him. Perhaps she could salvage some small part of his soul and make sure it survived the coming storm.

She bit down on her lower lip. He saw her fear, read her questions. He couldn't answer. The truth was too ugly. Even after all this time, he didn't understand.

She rested her cheek against his. "Tell me," she whispered in his ear. "It's like a festering wound. We have to drain the poison. Speak the words and the past won't have power over you anymore. Tell me everything about that day. Tell me about David."

He didn't want to. Laura was all things good and pure. She was his only hope.

"Tell me," she demanded again, squeezing his hands tightly in hers. Her breasts pressed against his chest, her mouth hovered above his. Her gaze met his unquestioningly.

"It was the last day," he said. "The day we were released. Everyone was laughing and talking. David didn't say much. We'd agreed to stay in touch. He'd said something about coming to Texas. We'd heard about the destruction of the South. He didn't think he'd have much to go home to. I knew I had to go to my parents for a while. I was weak and sick, but alive."

Her eyes were so blue it almost hurt to look at them. "Then what happened?" she asked.

"I was on a cart. I couldn't walk. David joked about him being the one with the missing leg and me being driven away. We shook hands."

He continued to stare at Laura, but he no longer saw her. He remembered that day. It had been clear and sunny, as if the weather rejoiced at their freedom. He remembered how weak he'd been. Malnutrition, a stomach ailment, a list of troubles that had dogged him through his time in prison.

"We shook hands, then he limped away. I leaned back in the cart. There was a gunshot." He focused on her again. She'd raised her head slightly and he could see her confused expression. "David killed himself. He put a pistol to his head and pulled the trigger."

She gasped and sat upright. She slipped one hand free of his grasp and covered her mouth.

"I didn't want to go home after that," he said, not really seeing her. "I didn't want to go on. David had been the strong one. If he couldn't survive, how could I?" He squeezed his eyes shut. "You want to know the hell of it? I can't forgive him for what he did. I can't understand it. Was he lying to me all those days he encouraged me to go on? Was he playing at some game? Did he know what he was going to do? Jesus, that bastard son of a bitch."

"Jesse." She bent over him and held him close. "Jesse, don't. Don't torment yourself this way. You're a good man. You're strong and brave. Everything David was and more."

"You don't know that."

"I do." She raised her head so she could look at his face. Tears dampened her cheeks. "I know better than anyone. You're a kind, brave man. It took a lot of courage to tell me about your past. It took even more to go on living. Maybe David's the weak one, not you." She sniffed. "The more you talk about it, the less power it will have over you. We should talk about this again. But not now. You're tired and you need to sleep."

He couldn't believe what had happened. He'd confessed his darkest secret—his greatest fear—and she wasn't repulsed. She was holding him and telling him he was brave. He didn't know if she was crazy or if he was. He wanted to ask her if she'd really heard what he was saying. But he knew the truth. Laura had heard every word and she didn't care. She'd made up her mind about him and nothing would change that. In her eyes, he was her rescuer and that was all that mattered.

As her tears continued to fall, she straightened and smoothed the blanket over him. "Are you warm enough?"

He nodded. He wanted to tell her that he wasn't tired, if only to keep her with him a little longer. She was right. In the telling, he'd released some of the burden. His chest wasn't as tight, his heart not so heavy.

She moved off the bed and went toward the rear of the wagon. "I'll be outside for a bit," she said. "Try to sleep."

Before he could protest her leaving, the blackness began to descend. He fought it as long as he could, but in the end, he had no choice but to succumb. His last conscious thought was that he might have survived the war, he might even survive the memories, but he would never survive losing Laura.

The second her feet touched wet ground, she ran toward a clump of bushes. It was night and she could barely see, but she didn't care. Once she reached the bushes, she fell to her knees. Her stomach heaved once, then a second time. She threw up her noon meal and the coffee she'd had with Harry while waiting out the storm.

The dampness soaked through her dress and petticoats, but she didn't move. When her belly was empty, she began to sob. Harsh angry sounds filled the darkness. She hunched over and clutched her midsection. She cried for Jesse, for his pain, and for a man she'd never met. She cried for David.

How horrible to have lived through the camp only to have his best friend kill himself after being released. She didn't understand the act any more than Jesse did. None of what he told her made sense. She couldn't imagine what it must have been like to live under those conditions. To be cold and starving all the time. She didn't dare think about David's amputation. A shudder raced through her. She thought she might vomit again, but she took several deep breaths and her stomach calmed.

Jesse's life and experiences were so different from hers. She didn't understand him. Who was this man she married? After all this time together, she should feel that she knew at least part of him, but that wasn't true.

She squeezed her eyes shut. What must he think of her with her foolish dreams of being a singer on the stage? With all the pain he carried inside, it was no wonder he didn't want a wife. If he hated what was inside of himself, how could he possibly share his heart with a woman? Especially one like her. She might be able to hold him and tell him that she understood, but the truth was very different. She didn't understand, and he knew that.

He'd shared parts with her, had told her about David, but she knew there was more. The real ugliness would forever be locked inside of him. It was in her brother and probably every man who had experienced the war. She wanted to be with him and heal him. That had been her plan. How naive of her. As if she had the power to heal anyone. She was selfish and manipulating. She'd invaded his life for her own reasons. She'd used Jesse as a means to an end.

With her head bowed, she prayed for forgiveness. Despite her sincerity, she felt no divine absolution. If anything, her guilt increased.

As the mist surrounded her, chilling her to the bone—and to the heart—she wondered if she had the right to forgiveness, either from Jesse or herself.

Wichita was as dusty as the drag riders after a long, hot day. Laura stared in amazement. She wasn't sure what she'd expected, but loose livestock, packs of dogs, and trash piled up on corners hadn't been part of her dream. She shook her head, as if it would clear her vision, but the picture remained the same. As did the stench from the trash.

She wrinkled her nose, then giggled. Honeysuckle DeVine was going to have her debut in this dusty cow town. It wasn't the elegant start she'd hoped for, but it would do.

There were people everywhere. The sheer numbers startled her. It shouldn't have, then she realized that during the time on the cattle drive, she'd grown used to the silence of the prairie. She wasn't used to all the sights and sounds of being in town.

"What's so funny?" Jesse asked, as he steered the mules around a dozen or so pigs rooting in the middle of the street.

"It's the people," she said. "I wasn't expecting so many. I guess I forgot what it's like in town. Now I sound like Harry."

The old cook had spent the last three days complaining about coming to town. He didn't like the noise. It was too expensive. If Harry had his way, he would spend a single night, then head back to Texas. Laura wondered if the old man would spend that night in the company of a fancy lady. She had a hard time imagining Harry kissing anyone, although he'd spoken lovingly of a wife.

"The first couple of hours in town are always loud," Jesse said. They turned right onto the next street.

A saloon or dance hall sat on every corner. Farther down were other kinds of businesses, but saloons dominated. There were several hotels. She watched people pick their way along the edge of the road. Most of the sidewalk was missing. The few parts she could see were warped and splintered. The street looked safer. She eyed the dusty earth and wondered how deep the mud went when it rained.

There weren't many women on the street but the few who braved the conditions were treated politely. Local citizens mingled with cowboys. Laura twisted in her seat, trying to see everything at once. She spotted a man calmly riding his horse on a small tidy section of sidewalk. They rolled past. She hung over the side to get a better view. Jesse grabbed her arm and hauled her back.

"If you're not careful, you're going to fall over the side," he said. "Sit still."

She grinned at him. She could tell by his voice he wasn't really angry. He tried to hide what he was thinking with his blank expression and his hat pulled low over his eyes, but she was learning. She glanced down at his hands. He held the reins easily. In the last couple of weeks, his arm had healed. She hadn't seen the wound since the night he'd been injured, but Harry told her it was doing well. Jesse had slept for twenty-four hours straight, then he'd gotten back on his horse like nothing had happened. Laura had hoped to maintain their closeness, but he'd never given her the chance. It was as if his confession had never happened.

"Are you sure Mike will take care of the steers?" she asked.

He nodded. "They're being penned now. I'll go by when we're done and make sure everything's set. Then I get paid."

"You made it after all," she said slowly. "You didn't need my money." Of course, she hadn't wanted Jesse to fail at bringing the cattle north; it was just that she'd hoped her small contribution would have some significance. Five hundred dollars or ten percent of her inheritance, whichever was greater. That's what she would pay him today when they arrived at her lawyer's office. But he'd already made a fortune with his steers. He didn't need her or her money.

She decided she didn't want to think about that right now. She was here, in Wichita. After they talked to the lawyer, she would get settled, then get a job. Soon, she would shed Laura Cannon and be only Honeysuckle DeVine. But instead of gladness, a whisper of sorrow hovered around her. She already wasn't Laura Cannon. She was Laura Travers. She wasn't sure she was ready to give up her husband so soon.

"What's this guy's name?" Jesse asked.

"Ackerman. Jefferson Ackerman."

"There's his office." He pointed to a two-story wooden structure. It was better kept than the buildings around it. The glass windows were bigger, the flower garden in front better tended. Jesse stopped the wagon in front of the railing, then jumped out and secured the mules.

Before Laura could step down, he moved to her side and held out his arms. She leaned forward and placed her hands on his shoulders. He picked her up and lowered her to the ground. A slight tension on his left side was the only lingering sign of his injury.

A young woman walked past them. She paused, then glanced at Jesse and smiled. Laura was startled enough to stare after the woman. It was only then she noticed Jesse had put on a fine black coat and a string tie. His trousers were brushed and his boots shined. When had he done all that?

"You're all dressed up," she said.

He shrugged and offered his arm. She placed her fingers in the crook of his elbow. "We're going to see your lawyer. I thought it was important."

A rush of pleasure swept over her. He was so good to her. She cuddled close, pleased she, too, had taken the time to put on one of her better dresses. It was a little wrinkled from being folded in a trunk and it would have fit better if she'd been able to lace up a corset, but it wasn't smoke stained or tattered around the hem.

"We make a fine couple," she said, as they started up the stairs.

Once inside Mr. Ackerman's office, they were quickly shown in to the lawyer. He was an older man, perhaps fifty, with graying hair and a kind smile. He rose from his chair and came around his wide desk to greet them.

"Miss Cannon, what a pleasure to meet you at last," he said, motioning to one of the two tapestry wing chairs in front of his desk.

She frowned slightly. "It's Mrs. Travers, Mr. Ackerman. This is my husband." She nodded at Jesse.

The two men shook hands. When Jesse was seated next to her, Mr. Ackerman returned to his chair and reached for some papers in a drawer to his left. Laura nibbled on her bottom lip. Mr. Ackerman had been sending the letters to her as Laura Cannon, and she'd signed them with that name. Perhaps she should have sent him a note explaining she'd been married. Would there be a problem?

"Mr. Travers is my husband," she said.

Mr. Ackerman smiled. "You said that."

"I know, but I want to make sure you understand that we're married."

Mr. Ackerman drew his graying eyebrows together. "I don't understand. Why would it matter?"

She pulled his letter from her reticule and smoothed it flat on his desk. She turned the paper toward him and pointed to the second paragraph. "You quote from Aunt Laura's will here. It says the money was left to me, her namesake. 'To my married niece, Laura.'" She glanced at the older man. "I had to be married to inherit, and I am."

Mr. Ackerman stared at her for a moment, then threw his head back and laughed. "Mrs. Travers, you didn't have to be married to inherit. Your aunt simply assumed you would have married by the time she passed on." His smile faded as he looked from her to Jesse. "I hope you didn't go to any trouble for this. You were already married, weren't you?"

Didn't have to be married? Didn't have to be married! Her mouth opened, but no sound came out. He couldn't mean that. She felt the heat of a blush climbing up her cheeks. Oh, no. What had she done?

She picked up the paper and folded it carefully. After tucking it back into her reticule, she cleared her throat and *still* didn't know what to say. "I—" She cleared her throat again, then glanced at Jesse.

He didn't look too angry. His face was expressionless as usual, but his shoulders were relaxed and arms weren't folded. She released the breath she'd been holding. No doubt when they left the lawyer's office he would tell her exactly what he thought of her mistake, but he wasn't going to embarrass her here.

Before she could think of something to say, her husband, the man she'd inconvenienced and married simply to inherit her aunt's money, smiled at her. He took her hand in his and squeezed.

"We've been married for some time, Mr. Ackerman. Why don't we get on with the business we have here?"

"Certainly." The attorney reached for a pair of spectacles and set them on the bridge of his nose. "I have the will right here. Your aunt left . . . "

But Laura wasn't listening to him anymore. She was gazing at Jesse. Inside her chest, her heart swelled with an emotion she'd never felt before. It was stronger than any affection she'd had for friends, and different from her feelings for her family. It left her filled with joy and wanting to cry all at the same time. As she blinked back the tears, she knew she would never feel about anyone the way she felt about Jesse. No matter how far she traveled, or how many other men she met, no one would touch her in the same way.

For a moment, just that single heartbeat, she wished she didn't have a dream. She wished she was like Augusta or May and simply wanted to be someone's wife. She wished she was special enough on her own and didn't have to be Honeysuckle DeVine. Because if she were like that, she would stay with Jesse always.

If he wanted her.

The thought was as disconcerting as it was unwelcome. He'd never talked about their marriage as if it were anything other than temporary. She'd long suspected she wasn't the sort of woman he would want if he chose to take a wife. But he had been stuck with her up to now. She swore he wouldn't regret it.

"Twenty-two thousand dollars."

Laura stared at the lawyer. "Excuse me. What did you say?"

Mr. Ackerman smiled. "Your aunt left you twenty-two thousand dollars."

It was a fortune. More than she'd ever imagined. She could send some to the family, give Jesse his share, and still have more than enough to travel the world.

"Oh, Jesse!"

She flung herself at him. He caught her against him and hugged her. Somehow she settled on his lap and his arms wrapped around her waist. Her position put her head slightly above his, so she tilted his hat back on his head. His dark gaze met hers.

"We're rich," she said.

"You're rich."

"You're rich, too. From the cattle drive."

"Now you can do everything you want."

She studied his familiar, handsome face. The mouth that had kissed hers, the scar that reminded her of all the pain he carried around inside. He was what she'd wanted. But she couldn't say the words. Jesse had never hinted that he wanted to change the terms of their agreement. It would be wrong of her to say anything. He was such a gentleman, he might agree to keep her around simply to be kind, and she couldn't stand to be with him because he pitied her.

Mr. Ackerman cleared his throat. She realized she was still on Jesse's lap. She slid off and returned to her seat. In a few minutes, the lawyer had explained the details and given her the information she needed to get her money from the bank.

When she and Jesse left the man's office, she still didn't know what to think.

"Will I be able to wire money to my family?" she asked Jesse when they were on the street. The bank was only a half block away, so they left the mules and made their way on foot.

"It shouldn't be a problem."

He'd offered her his arm again and she tucked her hand into the crook of his elbow. The June air was warm and she raised her face toward the sun.

"I've written a letter," she said. "It's in the wagon. I'll send it, but I want to wire money this afternoon. And I want to give you your money." She drew in a breath. "I mean you're probably sick of me and never want to see me again. I don't blame you. I promised not to be a bother and I don't think I was anything else."

"I usually spend a few days in town."

She glanced up at him, daring to hope he might want to spend a little time with her. "You'd mentioned that."

He nodded. "The horses need rest and the cowboys like to have some time to themselves. I want to make sure you're all right here in town before I go."

"You don't have to."

"I know. I want to."

He did? Her heart fluttered foolishly in her chest.

"While we're married, I'm responsible for you."

"Oh." The fluttering stopped as quickly as it had begun. "I suppose we have to do something about getting the divorce." Maybe they should have talked to the lawyer while they were in his office.

He steered her around a broken board in the sidewalk, then onto the dusty street. The bank was the next building. "If you're not in a big hurry, we don't have to take care of that today."

"That's fine with me. So we'll, um, be together until you leave for home or I leave for New York?"

"Exactly. I don't think you're ready to be on your own in the city yet. It will take some getting used to."

He might be right. Wichita was very different from Jackson Springs. There was a sense of excitement here that home lacked. Maybe it was because she was so close to realizing her dream.

"Just think," she said as they paused outside the entrance to the bank. "In a few days Honeysuckle will make her stage debut."

Jesse didn't say anything.

"You don't look happy," she told him. "The sooner I'm a success on the stage, the sooner you won't have to worry about me."

"I know, but as I've told you before, I'm going to miss Laura Cannon."

She looked at the bank, then around at the other storefronts. "I might miss her a little, too. I'm excited about starting my new life, but it's not exactly what I thought it would be. I'm not sure why. I've spent so much time imagining this moment, I'm sure I thought everything through." She smiled. "Probably for the first time in my life. Oh, well, there's no going back. When we're done here, I need to see a dressmaker about having my gown made."

"I need to find us a place to stay."

"Where are the cowboys?"

"Somewhere you don't want to be." His eyebrows lifted slightly. "I'm sure Wellington will have stories to tell when he gets home."

"Harry said he would look out for my brother and Bobby, so I'm not concerned. Wherever you think is best is fine with me."

"I'll get us a room."

Her heart took up its foolish fluttering again. She put her hand on her chest and felt the palpitations. A room? Was Jesse finally ready to teach her the secrets between a man and a woman? She hated parting from him without spending the night in his arms.

He raised his arm and touched his index finger to her chin, closing her mouth. "A suite," he said. "With two bedrooms."

She looked away rather than have him read her disappointment. He was going to be a gentleman to the end. Laura tossed her head and drew back her shoulders. If that's the way he wanted it, she wouldn't protest the large suite. But she would use their close proximity to her advantage. After all, there weren't going to be any cattle, cowboys, or locked doors between them.

Jesse leaned back in his chair and lit a cigar. As the smoke curled around him, he raised his feet to the stool. He'd already had a bath and the barber had not only shaved him, but he'd trimmed his hair. The only worrisome thought was that Laura hadn't returned yet. For the fourth time in as many minutes, he glanced at the clock over the fireplace. Not quite five o'clock. He'd left her outside the bank a little after noon. How long did it take to arrange to have a dress made? If she wasn't back by five-thirty, he was going to go looking for her.

He stood up and walked to the window. From there he could see the four saloons, one on each of the corners. Even if Laura wasn't with him, he wouldn't be in one of them. He couldn't stand the crowds, the noise, and the confined space.

He glanced around the spacious parlor. As soon as he'd entered the room he'd pulled back the thick velvet drapes. Sunlight spilled onto the rug. He tried not to think about how many people were in the hotel or how close the walls seemed to him.

He clamped the cigar between his teeth and folded his arms over his chest. If he turned a little, he would be able to see most of the broken sidewalk. He could watch for Laura.

He'd also been busy while she'd been gone. He'd gone back to the cattle pens and gotten the money for his steers. Beef was still at a premium. He'd made more than he'd thought. Even after paying off the cowboys, he had more than enough to see him through a dozen bad years. When he added in the twenty-two hundred dollars Laura had paid him, he was a wealthy man.

Next year he could bring more steers to town. Maybe hire more men and run two herds. Even as the plans formed, he knew he wouldn't take steers north again. He might send someone else, but he didn't want to be on the trail if Laura wasn't with him. It was going to be hard enough to let her go without forcing himself to remember her by reliving their journey together. He knew he would see her at every camp, crossing every river. She would forever be branded on him.

The parlor door opened and Laura swept into the room.

"I'm back," she called. Her arms were filled with boxes. Before he could take them from her, they tumbled to the floor. She laughed. "Oh, Jesse, everything is wonderful in Wichita, isn't it?"

He smiled. Before Laura he'd forgotten what it felt like to smile. "You've been shopping," he said, pointing to the boxes.

She bent down and picked up two, then set them on the low table in front of the settee. "Just for a few things. The trail is harder on clothes than I'd realized." She stood and brushed a strand of hair out of her face.

He walked over to the fireplace and pulled on a

tasseled cord hanging there. While he leaned against the mantel, she showed him blouses and skirts, a ready-made dress. She opened a box of something lacy, blushed and closed it quickly. Heat flared to life low in his belly.

"I saw a dressmaker," she said, settling back into a wing chair in front of the fireplace. "She even has the red satin. The hat and wig will take the most time, but I should have everything in about a week."

He frowned. "Why do you want to cover your hair?"

"Red is more exotic. It will be wonderful, you'll see." She paused and glanced at her lap. "That is, if you're still here."

"I'll be here." Somewhere along the trail he'd decided to stay with her for as long as he could. She'd talked of leaving Wichita and going to New York. Until then, he would be at her side, protecting her as best he could. He grimaced. Who was he trying to fool? He wasn't staying for her; he was staying for himself.

She leaned forward in her chair. "I wired some money to my family, along with a telegram explaining about the inheritance. I mailed my letter, too. I hope they'll understand."

Laura had been working on the letter for nearly a month now. She'd read him parts of it. In it she'd explained why she'd left and what her dreams were. The heartfelt appeal had touched him.

"They'll understand," he said. If they didn't, when he returned to Jackson Springs, he was going to make them understand. Laura missed her family and she needed to know they still cared about her.

"There's one more thing," she said. "I have a job."

"What?"

She smiled broadly. "Isn't it exciting? I was walking to the hotel when I saw a saloon. I didn't dare go inside, but it was called 'The Texas Belle' so I couldn't resist taking a peek in the window. Anyway, the owner, Charles Lewis, saw me and he came outside and spoke with me." She clasped her hands tightly together. "I told him I was a singer and that I'd come here to begin my career. Then he hired me. I start tonight."

Jesse couldn't have been more shocked if she'd started undressing. He'd known about her dream for months, but he hadn't thought it would become a problem so quickly. "You said your costume won't be ready for a week."

"I know. I told him that, but he didn't care. He said to wear something pretty and none of the patrons would mind."

Holy shit. Now what? "Did you sing for him?" he asked cautiously.

"No. That's the odd part. I wanted to but he said it didn't matter. I'm not sure Mr. Lewis is a very experienced employer. Papa always hires people for a trial period in the store. It only makes sense."

Before Jesse could answer, there was a knock on the door. Three young men came in carrying buckets of hot water. By the time they'd filled the tub, Laura had forgotten about their conversation. She'd moved into her room and stepped behind the dressing screen.

The suite had one parlor and two bedrooms. He'd taken the smaller one. The plain furnishings and narrow bed suited him. He'd pulled the drapes back and opened the windows. Laura's room was opulent, with a double bed and elegant furniture. There was a fireplace across from her bed, but like the one in the parlor, it was unlit. June was already warm in Kansas.

He walked to the parlor window and stared out. Laura had left her door open and he could hear the lapping of the water as she stepped into the tub. There was silence after she settled in, then a blissful sigh.

"This is heaven," she called. "You looked all cleaned up so you must have had your bath already."

He had to clear his throat before he could speak. "I did. Do you want me to order something to eat?"

"Yes, please. I'll need to keep my strength up for tonight."

He pulled the bellcord again. When a young girl appeared, he gave her their order. She repeated it back to him, then left.

"I've been trying to decide which song to start with tonight," Laura said. "Do you have a favorite?"

He rubbed the bridge of his nose. "I like them all," he said lamely, not knowing what else to say. The truth would destroy her. She'd come all this way to live out her dream. He didn't have the right to take that away from her. She'd made it clear she wanted more than Jackson Springs or a ranch could offer her. No matter what happened, she wasn't going to come home with him.

With the money he'd made on the cattle drive, the ranch would be prosperous. He could fix up the house, but he knew Laura well enough to know she didn't care about that. If she did, she wouldn't have done so well on the trip north. She wanted adventure, new experiences. She wanted to be famous. He wanted to be invisible, feeling nothing, living out his days in the safety of dull routine.

"I'm so excited," she said. "This is the beginning of everything I've wanted my whole life."

He sat in the wing chair she'd used. Bracing his elbows on his knees, he rested his head in his hands. He didn't know what was going to happen when she opened her mouth, but it was unlikely she would survive the cruelty of the crowd. What was he supposed to tell her? How could he be the one to take everything away from her?

"If the singing doesn't work out, you could still travel and have adventures," he said.

She laughed. "Why wouldn't it work out? Oh, Jesse, it's so sweet of you to worry, but please don't. I'll be fine. I know exactly what's going to happen and it will be wonderful. But I do have one question. What are saloons like? I've never been inside one."

Her complete faith in herself made him feel old and cynical. As if he'd never had the strength of character to believe.

"They're loud," he said. Maybe that would help. Maybe no one would be able to hear her. "There's a bar, and gambling. The stage is at one end."

"Are there a lot of people there?"

"Usually." Too many for him. He couldn't remember the last time he'd been in a saloon.

There was a sloshing sound, as if she'd stood up and stepped out of the tub. At the same time, someone knocked on the door. He let in the girl carrying a tray containing their meal. After she left, he arranged the food on the table by the window.

"The food's here," he said.

"Good. I'll be right out. Then afterwards, I'm going to have to find something to wear tonight. I didn't bring any fancy dresses with me, but I must have something nice enough."

He didn't want to think about her drying off, or slipping into her lacy things. He tried to concentrate on the people walking by on the street, but when that didn't work, he reached for the bottle of whiskey they'd brought up with the meal.

"Jesse, will you come hear me sing tonight?"

He poured three fingers of whiskey in a glass and downed it in two swallows. The fire burned all the way down, where it joined the heat from his arousal.

He didn't want to go. Not because he couldn't bear

to watch her dreams destroyed, but because saloons were crowded and noisy and they made him remember. He couldn't go inside, and he couldn't not go. Laura needed him.

"I'll be there," he said quietly.

"I'm glad." He heard the rustle of clothing, then she sighed. "Jesse, I've got to apologize to you. I'm so embarrassed about the wedding and all. To think we didn't have to get married. Although if we hadn't, my parents wouldn't have let me leave with you, but . . ." She paused. "Now that I know you better, I know what you sacrificed by agreeing. I understand more. Oh, I know I'll never understand everything. Washington once told me a woman can never understand. About the war and all."

Her compassion would be the death of him. Her sweetness filled him and made him want to believe in her world.

She came out of the room. He stepped back from the door jamb, but they were still standing close. Too close. Her hair hung loose over her shoulders. The blond tresses tumbled nearly to her waist. She'd pulled on a robe over her camisole and pantaloons, so she was covered from her neck to her ankles.

Tension and need coiled through him, making his hands tighten into fists. He glanced down and saw her feet were bare, and he was lost.

Desire filled him, making the hardness between his thighs ache more. He wanted to take her in his arms and let his body speak the words his lips could never say. The hell of it was she wouldn't refuse him. Laura had never refused him anything.

"I never meant to take advantage of you," she whispered.

He raised his gaze to her face. Her wide, blue eyes met his unquestioningly. The innocent trust there would save her from him. But what about from the rest of the world?

"You didn't," he said. "I'm glad you came on the cattle drive."

"Really?"

He nodded.

She smiled then, a wide, brilliant smile that made him think of the first time he'd seen her. She was beautiful, perhaps *because* of her imperfections. He might not be worthy of her, but he knew he would do anything for her. As her smile broadened and her fingers brushed his arm, he wondered when he'd first started falling in love with her.

21

Laura had already gone around to the rear entrance of The Texas Belle. Jesse stood in front of the building, gripping the hitching rail as if it were a lifeline and he a drowning man.

He had to go inside. Laura was about to make her stage debut and he had to be there. If he wasn't, God knows what would happen. He still didn't have a plan, but he knew he would come up with something. But first he had to step in the door.

Even from the street he could hear the noise. Without trying, he could imagine the press of the crowds. It was all familiar, all too much like his nightmares.

In the back of his mind a voice whispered. *Ignore the sons of bitches and go ahead. Just get it over with.* David's voice. David's advice. Nothing matters but getting through. At one time the words had made sense, but not anymore.

Jesse had tried to follow his friend's wisdom, but

he'd been an imperfect pupil. David had taken the words to heart, had lived that credo. He'd gotten through, seemingly untouched by the horrors around him. But at what price? In the end he'd been forced to face what had happened. He couldn't continue to ignore the truth and put it behind him. In the end, the horror had won.

That's what Jesse feared most. That once he let himself care completely, once he gave himself to someone else and released the barriers inside, that the oncoming rush of memories would rip away his sanity. He lived and breathed the fear that he would reach for David's escape.

The saloon door slapped against the wall as it was pushed open by a drunk. Jesse swore under his breath. Not tonight. Even as the past threatened, he ignored the fear and the desperation clawing at him. Laura needed him to be there, and he would be. No matter the price. Somehow he had to prevent her from singing. Somehow he had to keep the truth from her.

He walked inside. The saloon was brighter than he'd imagined, with ornate chandeliers hanging from the beams in the ceiling. The room was crowded, with round tables pushed closely together. To the right was the long, scarred bar, to the left sat the gamblers. And in the center, larger than the bar, was the stage. Right now several dancing girls twirled and kicked to a wildly applauding audience.

The press of the crowd made him break out in a sweat. His chest tightened and he couldn't catch his breath. But he didn't leave. Instead, he started to force his way toward the stage, as if being closer to her would help him find an answer. What the hell was he supposed to do?

Noise surrounded him. The calls for players to put their money on the wheel, the conversation of drunken cowboys, the music from the tinny piano by the stage. Maybe they wouldn't hear her. Maybe—

Someone grabbed his arm. Without thinking, Jesse drew back his fist. Before the blow connected, he realized the man holding him was Harry.

"We got trouble," the old man said, his mouth pulled straight with worry. "Wellington and Bobby gave me the slip. I've been lookin' for them for the better part of two hours, but I ain't havin' any luck."

"Damn." Jesse glanced around the room. It had to be close to time for Laura to sing, but he couldn't leave the boys to roam on their own. "Have they got money?"

"Nearly all their wages. I wanted to keep it for 'em, but they insisted. If they're flashing them bills, they're gonna get jumped and robbed."

Being beaten might teach them a lesson, but it could also kill them. "We've got to find them."

Harry glared at him. "Hell and tarnation, why'd you think I came lookin' for you in the first place?"

He hesitated. "Laura's singing here tonight."

"What?" Harry glanced at the stage. "She-it." He sucked air in through his teeth. "If them boys are lookin' for whores, they could get themselves in a mess of trouble. There's some bad places around here. I know her singin' is gonna be awful, but nobody's gonna kill her fer it. The boys might not be so lucky."

Jesse nodded. "Let's go."

They left the saloon and started down the narrow streets, stopping at every brothel, asking about the two teenagers. At first, they didn't get any information, but coins slid across lacquered tables soon loosened tongues.

At the fifth place they tried, a well-dressed, older woman smiled at his questions. Her black hair gleamed in the lamplight. "I know exactly who you're talking about. I suspected it was their first time, so I gave them to one of the younger girls. She's taking care of them both." The woman laughed. "They're boys. It won't take long. If you gentlemen would care to wait, there's room at the bar. Or perhaps we could find you some other kind of entertainment."

Jesse followed the woman's amused gaze and caught Harry staring at a plump redhead. When Harry looked up at Jesse, he cleared his throat.

"Hell, I've been on the trail as long as you. I can't help it if I've got me an itch."

"Scratch it after we find the boys."

Harry grinned. "According to this lady here, we just did." He pulled a coin out of his pocket and passed it to the lady in black. "Here, ma'am. I think I might take you up on that drink." The scantily dressed redhead crossed the room and smiled at Harry. The cook smiled back.

"I need you to take care of them so I can get back to Laura," Jesse said.

"Hell, I darn near forgot." He gave the redhead a little pinch on her behind. "You wait right here. When I get these boys settled, I'll be back."

"I'll be waiting," she cooed.

Jesse gritted his teeth and started for the stairs.

"Third door on the right," the older woman called helpfully. "They've already paid, so it seems a shame not to let them have their fun."

Laura would have his hide if she knew her brother had visited a brothel. Jesse hoped it went as quickly as the woman had predicted so it would be over before he got there. But if it wasn't, he was still taking both boys with him.

Harry lumbered after him. "Are we gonna pretend to be mad?"

"I don't have to pretend."

He opened the third door on the right without

knocking. A naked blond sat on the bed. Bobby and Wellington stood on either side of her. They both looked as if they'd never seen a naked woman before. They probably hadn't.

When he stepped into the room, they turned toward him. Both their mouths dropped and they blushed.

"We didn't mean nothin'," Bobby started.

Wellington cut to the heart of the matter. "You gonna tell my sister?" he asked.

The blond smiled. "I'm going to have to charge extra if you want to join us."

She wasn't wearing a stitch. Her breasts were well formed, and her nipples the color of peaches. The soft down between her legs beckoned, as did her long pale legs. She was about Laura's age, maybe a little older. Her long hair had been pulled back in a braid. Her eyes were brown, her smile welcoming.

In the past, the sight of her would have been enough to arouse him. He would have taken his pleasure, tipped her and left. But this evening, he couldn't imagine wanting to bed her or any other woman who wasn't Laura. While both boys were in an obviously painful way, he wasn't interested.

"That's very kind of you, ma'am," he said, tipping his hat. "But I'll refuse. These boys are coming with me." He stuck his head out the door. "Harry," he bellowed. "They're right here."

The cook came into the room and motioned for the boys to join him. When they were close enough, he grabbed each of them by the ear. "Don't you go runnin' out on me. We had us a deal. I was willin' to let you have a little fun, but that wasn't enough for you, was it? No, you had go out and pretend you're men."

They yelped in pain as Harry dragged them down the stairs. Jesse followed. The lady in black met them by the door.

"Leaving already?" she asked.

Jesse nodded to the boys. "Their parents trusted them to me, ma'am. No offense meant."

She eyed him up and down. Her skin was smooth and pale as milk. "None taken." She leaned toward the boys. "You two come back next year when you're older. We'll show you a real good time."

"But Jesse, we paid for that woman," Bobby complained. "And we didn't git to do nothing."

"I'll hold your fee on account," the woman said.

"Thank you, ma'am," Wellington said, turning toward her. Harry tugged on his ear. The teenager grunted, then took off his hat and waved it at her. "I'll be back for sure."

Harry started down the street, each boy bent toward him, their long legs tangling together every few feet.

"I'll take care of 'em," Harry called over his shoulder. "You go on and look after Laura."

Laura! Jesse swore. He took off at a run, turned left at the corner and dodged a wagon load of supplies on his way to the saloon.

When he was in front of The Texas Belle, he paused. Bile rose in his throat. The crowd inside was louder now, and probably thicker. He would have sold his soul not to go inside, but he didn't have a choice. Laura needed him. Maybe he could convince her to—hell, he didn't know what he was going to say or do, but he had to do something. He sucked in a breath, then plunged through the door and into the crowd.

Bodies surrounded him. He could feel the heat. Images of the past flashed in front of him. Nausea washed over him as he broke out into a cold sweat. The room seemed to tilt and he didn't know where the hell he was. All he wanted to do was leave; all he could think about was Laura. He had to save her. He took a firm hold on his last bit of courage and made his way to the stage.

Someone was coming out from behind the curtains. He glanced up. It was Laura. She'd put on a pretty blue dress, one that matched her eyes. Her hair was piled high on her head. She was beautiful.

She opened her mouth. She was going to sing and he didn't know how to stop her. He was still too far from the stage for her to see him or hear him if he called out. The room was filled with noise. He hung on to the slender hope that no one would be able to hear her.

She opened her mouth. He sent up a prayer that God would somehow protect her most innocent soul.

"I know a place . . . "

The room grew silent. Everyone turned to stare at her. She smiled and continued. *"Where all things beautiful . . . "*

The crowd erupted into jeers and insulting calls. Jesse tried to move forward, but he was frozen in place. His body locked in one position as he waited for her to learn the truth.

"She sounds like a sick crow."

"No dogs in the bar."

"You call that singing, lady? My goat sings better than you."

Laura stopped singing and stared at the audience. Her confusion was a tangible thing. She opened her mouth to try again, but the yelling drowned her out.

"Get off the stage," someone called. "Go back to your cave and scare the bats."

Laura tilted her head as if she couldn't have heard the man correctly. Color flared on her cheeks. She turned and fled.

Boos followed her. The owner came on stage and apologized, there was some scuffling backstage, then the dancing girls reappeared. Jesse turned and made his way to the bar. From there, he slipped between tables and found his way backstage.

He asked directions from a burly man working the ropes controlling the backdrop. The man pointed into a darkened corner.

"Laura?" he called softly as he crossed the unfinished floor.

"Jesse? Is that you?" She stepped out of the shadows. She held a small valise in one hand and her reticule in the other. She'd thrown a shawl over her shoulders. She raised her chin. "Were you there? Did you see what happened?"

He nodded miserably and took her valise. "I'm sorry. I should have—" He paused, not knowing what to say. He should have told her the truth. It would have been easier to hear it from him, rather than be so publicly humiliated. He'd been a coward, and an arrogant fool. Somehow he'd assumed he would be able to make it all work.

"I shouldn't be surprised," she said, and stepped into the light.

He searched her face, but didn't see any signs of tears. In fact, she didn't even look very upset. "You shouldn't?"

"No." She started for the rear exit. He trailed after her. "I let myself get carried away by the moment. I should have known better." She gave him a smile. "I went up on that stage as plain Laura Cannon. There's nothing special about me. It's not surprising no one was interested in listening to me sing. I should have waited until everything was in place. I need my costume and my wig. I need to be Honeysuckle DeVine. Then it will work. Then they'll applaud me."

"But what about your singing?" he blurted out.

She laughed. "That's the least of my problems. I've always had a fine voice." She shook her head. "It's definitely the costume. You'll see. When I'm Honeysuckle, everything will work out."

He didn't know what to say. He'd never known anyone like her. Her self-belief and determination put his fears to shame. She was the strongest person he'd ever known.

When they neared the hotel, she glanced at him. "Thank you for coming to hear me tonight. I know it was difficult for you to go into that saloon. I felt safe, knowing you were there for me." She stopped walking and faced him. "When I first made my plans, I didn't really think them through." Her smile was rueful. "I suppose you're getting used to that failing of mine."

"It's one of the things I like best about you."

"Really?" She seemed to glow. "I'd thought it would be so easy to be on my own. But I've realized I'm always going to miss my family. I'm used to being part of something. Once we left home, I was part of the cattle drive. When you're gone, I'll truly be on my own. I'm—" She ducked her head, as if she was suddenly shy. "I'm going to miss you."

She walked into the hotel. He followed her up the stairs to their suite. Once inside, she placed her reticule on the table by the fireplace and crossed to the window. She pulled back the drapes and stared out the glass at the night sky.

"Will you miss me a little?" she asked.

"With every breath."

She released the curtain and turned. "Jesse?"

He dropped her valise on the floor and crossed to her. He took her hands in his. "Don't ask me anything else. Don't ask me questions I can't answer right now."

She nodded, although he could tell she didn't understand what he was saying. She stared at their joined fingers. "Did I do all right tonight?" Uncertainty had crept into her voice. "Was I really that bad?"

Here it was—his opportunity to tell her the truth. She raised her gaze to his. Hurt darkened her eyes.

Disappointment tugged at the sweet curve of her mouth. She waited for his pronouncement of her fate. What right did he have to destroy her spirit?

"You were perfect," he said, and knew he told the truth. For him, she was.

Her slow smile caught him like a blow to the belly. She slid her hands up his arms, to his shoulders. She raised herself on tiptoes. He read her intent even before she kissed him. He knew the danger of the moment. They were alone and there would be no interruptions. If he allowed her to touch him, he would be lost. At last she would learn all the secrets between a man and a woman. He would be her first lover. Did he want that responsibility?

Her mouth touched his scar. He felt the whisper of contact through his beard. He'd thought he would be ashamed to have her touch him there, but she had done it before. She seemed to find the scar fascinating. Once she'd told him it was because the scar reminded her he was wounded on the inside.

He'd never known a woman like her. Loving her and letting her go would haunt him for the rest of his days. Not loving her and letting her go would be the death of him. He would rather be haunted by her than forever in the black void of living death. But he still had a question.

"If I bed you, you won't be a virgin." He stared down at her. "Do you know what that means? Once it's been taken away from you, you'll never be the same again."

One side of her mouth curved up. "Being different has always been the point," she whispered, then brushed her lips against his. "Please, Jesse. I want this with you. Only you."

Only you. Pain sliced through him, made all the sweeter by the anticipation filling him.

Her blue eyes darkened with passion. Her mouth parted. "Jesse, I—"

He didn't know what she was going to say, and he didn't want to know. He silenced her words with a kiss. His mouth touched hers gently, carefully, brushing back and forth against her tender skin. That's how he thought of her . . . as something delicate, like a perfect, pale flower. Easily bruised. Yet as Laura raised herself up on tiptoe and pressed her body against his, he knew that image came from imagination and not who she really was.

Laura was as strong as the prairie grasses. She could be bent, trampled, even burned in a fire, but she would come back again, better than before.

She buried her fingers in his hair, urging him closer. His need flared hot and bright. He wanted to thrust his hips against hers, taunting them both with the act to come. But she didn't know all that they would be doing. He was going to teach her. He swore to himself he would make the joining as perfect as he could.

He touched his tongue to her bottom lip, stroking the curve. She sighed softly and opened her mouth. Instead of entering, he teased her, tracing the shape of her lips, then sampling the delicate inner skin.

"Stop it," she whispered, and tugged on his hair.

He raised his head and smiled. "You don't want me to kiss you?" he asked, pretending confusion.

"Jesse! I want you to really kiss me. You know."

He drew back and dropped his hands to his sides. "You want me to put my tongue in your mouth?" He sounded as shocked as she had all that time ago, when they'd discussed what went on between a man and a woman.

"Yes, and you're not cooperating. Now kiss me right."

He bent toward her, more than willing to oblige her request, but this time she was the one to pull away. "I know what's wrong," she said, turning and walking toward her room. "I remember what you told me. We're supposed to be lying down." She paused at the doorway to her room. "I think my bed will be more comfortable."

He swallowed hard. He'd never been with a virgin before, but somehow he'd assumed he would have to coax her through the loving. Jesse shook his head. He should have known better. Laura wasn't like anyone he'd ever met before. She'd been damn direct about everything else in her life, why not this?

He followed her into her bedroom, but caught her hand before she could settle on the bed. He slipped in front of her and sat on the thick mattress. After spreading his legs, he pulled her against him.

He was slightly below her eye-level and her thighs bumped against his groin. His erection surged toward the pressure and he wanted to ask her to rub her leg against him. He didn't. He figured she would want to know why and by the time he got everything explained he would have already perished from frustration.

Instead he took her hands and placed them on his shoulders. "You can say anything to me," he told her. "Touch me anywhere, tell me to keep doing something, or to stop because you don't like it. This is supposed to be—" He paused, not sure of the word.

"For pleasure," she offered, then smiled. "That's what you said before. A man has to teach a woman about pleasure. Is that what you're going to do?"

"Yes." He stared at her face. Her eyes were dark, the pupils already large. Her full lips parted, as if she needed to draw in more air. "What else did I tell you?"

She flushed slightly. The color crept up from the collar of her dress to her cheeks, then clear to her hairline.

"That, ah, a man and woman lie down together and they touch each other all over."

"We'll get to that in a minute. I left out a step."

"What was that?"

"First, they kiss."

22

Jesse tilted his head toward her. Their lips touched. This time he didn't tease her. This time when Laura parted her lips, he plunged his tongue inside.

She was hotter than he remembered, and sweeter. She circled around him, repeating the lessons she'd learned from him before. Even as he tried to arouse her, she brought him to a place of fiery need. She touched him, stroked him, taunted him more.

In self-defense, to keep from exploding, he broke the kiss and drew her lower lip into his mouth. He sucked her skin, then nibbled gently at the fullest part of the curve. She gasped. The hands holding his shoulders went slack. He moved from her mouth to her cheek, then down to her jaw. He traced the bone, then moved to her neck, pressing his tongue to the fluttering point of her pulse.

When he bit her earlobe, she sagged against him, her thighs trembling against his groin. He raised his arms and reached for the pins securing her hair. One by one, he pulled them free. The tip of his tongue explored the shape of her ear. She caught her breath, then giggled as he tickled her.

When the last pin was tossed to the floor and her hair tumbled over them, he wrapped his arms around her waist and lowered himself to the mattress settling her on top of him. Instinctively her hands pressed on the yielding surface. She braced herself on her arms. Her long blond hair fell like a curtain of silk.

"You're so beautiful," he said quietly.

She smiled. "Not me. Augusta's the pretty one."

"I didn't say pretty. You're beautiful." He picked up a strand of hair and rubbed it between his fingers. "So soft."

"You're soft, too." She touched his beard. "I thought it would be prickly, but it isn't at all." She bent close and rubbed her cheek against his. "Nice. I can smell your skin. I think I could find you in the dark."

Her pelvis rested casually on his. No doubt her petticoats and skirt prevented her from feeling his arousal. He couldn't feel much of her, either, but the weight of her was a pleasant torture.

Her body was warm against his. She lay on top of him, fully clothed, and yet he'd never been so intimate with a woman.

Laura traced his features. Her fingers trailed over his nose, then brushed against his eyebrows. She bent down and kissed his neck. When her tongue touched his ear, he felt the fire shoot through him. Involuntarily, he arched upward, as if he could bury himself inside her.

She raised her head and stared at him. "I like your face. Especially this part." She touched her tongue to his mouth, testing the seam. When he didn't part for her, she smiled. "You're teasing me."

"Maybe."

Her smile faded. "Jesse, I feel funny inside. It's all quivering and hot. Everything hurts, but not a bad hurt. I don't know what's happening to me."

"You want the loving. Your body is changing so you can take a man. If I were to touch you between your legs, you'd be wet now."

She stiffened. "I would not."

He was tempted to show her the truth, but there would be time for that later.

For a moment she looked as if she was going to argue with him. Then she lowered her mouth to his. This time he opened for her, allowing her to lead the way. She darted inside with quick, hot forays. She tasted all of him. He brought his hands around her and stroked her back. She arched against him like a cat.

Slowly, he moved lower, until he was cupping her derriere. Before he could roll her on her back, she reached for the buttons of his shirt. One by one she released them. He felt hot puffs of air and was able to prepare himself just in time.

Her kiss was tentative, her mouth virginally pursed, but when she kissed his bare chest, a shudder raced through him. She glanced up.

"Did you like that?" she asked.

He nodded mutely.

She rolled to one side and continued to unbutton his shirt. Finally she slid off him onto the mattress. She sat on one hip and finished unbuttoning his shirt. She stared at it as if unsure what to do now. He pulled it free from his trousers, then raised himself on his elbows and shrugged out of it, one arm at a time. He tossed it out of the way.

"Are you going to take off anything else?" she asked. "I mean, is it time for us to be naked?"

He grinned. "We don't have to do it all at once. Sometimes it's more fun to take it slowly."

"Hmm." She didn't seem sure of that. "This is the part where we touch each other?"

"There aren't rules. I was telling you what generally happens. We can change things around if you'd like."

"Well, don't ask me. I've never done this before. You're the one who's been with the fancy ladies. What did you do with them?"

He sure as hell didn't want to tell her that. Sometimes he hadn't bothered to take off a stitch. But this was different.

He suddenly realized he was going about this all wrong. He was asking Laura to make decisions about something she didn't know anything about. She was probably feeling awkward and unsure of herself. She wanted to do it right, but she didn't know what "it" was.

"I'm sorry," he said.

"For what?" She sounded cross. She sat up. Her loose hair fell over her shoulders, breasts, and back, nearly to her waist. He suddenly wanted to see her that way, but without her clothes. He wanted to touch her all over and hear her cry his name in a moment of total pleasure. He wanted her trembling and weeping, and he wanted to see her smile at him with the wonder of her first release.

"Sweet Laura," he murmured and bent over her.

Before she could say anything else, he lowered her back to the bed and kissed her. There was no teasing this time, no conversation. He tasted her lips, then loved them slowly, thoroughly. He kissed her cheeks, her nose, her closed eyelids, then moved lower to her neck. He suckled her earlobe again, on the other side, this time.

Even as he licked the sensitive spot behind her ear, he reached for the first button of her dress. It opened easily. One by one, he slipped them free. When he'd pulled the fabric apart as far as it would go, he bent down and kissed her breastbone. He moved left and trailed his lips over the curve of her breasts, then up to the already taut nipple. It pushed out against the thin cotton, a dark pink peak of pleasure. He heard her suck in her breath in anticipation.

He pulled the bodice away so her breast was covered only by her chemise. Then he took her in his mouth.

She was sweeter tasting than he remembered. He drew more in and circled his tongue around the tight point. Her chest arched toward him, urging him to do that again. Using the tip of his tongue, he dueled with her nipple, causing it to pucker more. She moaned—an exhalation of breath that was his name.

He brought up his hand and cupped her other breast. He could feel the thundering of her heartbeat as her flesh yielded to him. With his thumb and forefinger, he gently squeezed her taut peak. Her knees came up as did her head. He glanced at her face. She was staring at him, her mouth open, her eyes unfocused.

"Jesse? How do you make me feel like that? It's . . . Oh!" She sagged back against the mattress.

Over and over again, he paid homage to her breasts, moving from side to side, touching her in different ways until her breathing came in gasps and the chemise covering her was transparent from the dampness of his mouth. Only then did he draw her up into a sitting position and pull her dress off her arms.

Her long hair tumbled over her shoulders, half-emphasizing, half-concealing her breasts. The thin cloth clung to her in damp patches. She shook her head. "How do you do that? I've touched there when I've washed or dressed and it's never felt like that."

"Magic," he said, taking her hand and pulling her to her feet.

She stumbled at first, as if she couldn't get her balance. He had her hang onto the bedpost as he moved behind her and undid her petticoats. She was wearing six of them. When they were all hanging loose around her hips, he pushed them and her dress down to her knees, then picked her up in his arms and carried her to the bed.

His injured arm protested the action, but he ignored the dull ache. It was nothing when compared to his need, or Laura's pleasure.

As he set her down, she clung to him, pressing her head into the crook of his neck. He shifted her so she was on his lap, her hipbone pressing into his groin. All day he saw her in long dresses with petticoats concealing her lower half. Now, wearing only a camisole and pantaloons, she seemed smaller, almost slight. Her legs were long and well shaped, her feet tiny. He was about to touch the delicate arch when he felt something hot and wet on his bare skin.

He placed a finger under her chin and forced her to look at him. Tears swam in her eyes.

"What's wrong?" he asked.

She sniffed. "I'm sorry. I'm just afraid because I want this so much. I want to be with you and touch you and I can't help wondering if you're doing this because you feel responsible for me. You had to teach me so much while we were on the trail. I've forced you to do things you don't want to do. About the only time you've ever kissed me or touched me is when I've asked you.

What if you're just doing this for me and not because you want to?"

If she hadn't looked so damn miserable, he would have laughed. Not want her? Son of a bitch. He'd wanted her from the first moment he'd seen her. Their first kiss had nearly knocked him on his ass. He'd had a permanent—

But she wouldn't believe those words. And he didn't want her to doubt.

"Straddle me," he said, taking hold of her waist and shifting her.

She did as he asked, moving so her thighs rested on the outside of his. Her gaze was questioning, but at least she'd stopped crying. He brushed away the remaining tears.

"Do you remember what we talked about before. About our bodies getting ready for each other?"

She nodded.

"I'm going to touch you," he said. "Don't be frightened."

"But—"

"Shh." He touched her lips to silence her. "Then I'm going to show you how much I want you. All right?"

She nodded again.

As her wide eyes held his gaze, he placed his hand on her thigh. Moving slowly, because, damn it, he was determined to make her like this, he slid closer to her center. He could feel the heat of her. Between his legs, his erection throbbed in time with his heartbeat. She was going to be the death of him yet.

When he touched her inner thigh, she jumped. He continued to move slowly, finding the opening in her undergarments. He felt the soft, silky curls that protected her femininity. She raised her hands to his shoulders and took hold, as if preparing for a bumpy ride. He resisted the urge to smile.

Still holding her gaze, watching the uncertainty and apprehension, he touched her. She was wet and hot. He held in a groan. His fingers stroked her carefully, finding the tiny place that would cause her release, then searching out his path to paradise. Her eyes widened. His finger slipped in easily.

"Wet," he murmured. "For me. Hot and wet. If you knew how good that makes me feel."

She bit on her lower lip. "Is that where it goes?" she asked.

He circled his finger around the opening. "Yes. Here."

She blushed, but didn't look away. "It feels nice. Did you, um, change, too?"

She hadn't noticed? But then why would she? She was still innocent. He took her hand and brought it to his groin. Even as he circled his finger around inside of her, he placed her palm against him. When she felt the hard length of him, she sucked in her breath. When she squeezed gently, he was the one who forgot to breathe. Her untutored fingers brought him to the edge of the world, but he clung on. He wouldn't release this way. Not yet.

Before she could drive him mad, he brought her hand back to his shoulder.

"Kiss me," he said.

Laura leaned forward. Kissing she understood. Kissing she could do. It was everything else that had her confused, feeling hot and prickly, as if her skin was suddenly too tight. Jesse's fingers continued to move between her legs. She couldn't believe he was touching her there and she liked it. She liked the feel of him moving in and out of her. Pressure or tension or *something* increased. Her breasts were sensitive, her thighs trembling.

As she pressed her open mouth to his, he moved his hand slightly higher and touched a small spot. Jolts of sensation shot through her. It was like their first kiss, but more intense. She couldn't breathe, she didn't dare move. She wanted him to do it again.

He did. He rubbed that spot creating incredible heat. It was as if someone had set her in a bath of hot water. No, better than that, or different or . . .

She couldn't focus on anything. She strained toward him, concentrating on nothing but the feel of his fingertips rubbing against her. His tongue brushed hers. She closed her lips around him and sucked hard and fast, urging him on. His fingers moved in time with her actions. Her hips rocked back and forth, but she didn't feel that she was controlling them at all. Her breasts flattened against his chest. She was lost and she never wanted to be found again.

The pressure increased. Then it was gone. He'd moved his hand away. She opened her mouth, releasing him, then stared. He'd stopped? Before she could protest, he'd tugged off her chemise. At one time, the thought of being naked with him had frightened her. Now she wanted to be bare before him. She helped him draw off her pantaloons.

He pulled her close, kissing her, touching her everywhere. Just as he'd told her. Their legs tangled. She wove her fingers through his hair, then moved lower to his shoulders. Even as she kneaded his hard muscles, he urged her onto her back. His hand returned between her thighs and she parted for him.

His fingers rubbed the spot again, faster this time. Instantly, she was caught up in the firestorm of need. Her muscles clenched tight, her hips arched toward him. She could feel her own dampness and she didn't care. He raised his head to her breasts, drawing one taut nipple into his mouth. The combination of sensations—his fingers rubbing faster, lighter, over and around, his mouth suckling, drawing more of her in—forced her to a place of heat and desire.

She knew nothing but this moment, nothing but the man and his tender magic. Her breathing quickened, her heart pounded so fast, she wondered if it would leap from her chest. And then she didn't care anymore. All life centered on that tiny place between her legs. She called out his name because she felt herself slipping away. Into a tornado, sucked up through the center. Turning and rising and feeling such pleasure, such incredible pressure with the promise of release of—

She hung suspended, then exploded.

The tornado shot her out into the air. Her muscles convulsed, her hips arched higher. She clutched at his head, holding him in place, begging him not to stop. She'd never known it could be like this.

"Jesse," she murmured.

"I'm here."

He turned and held her close. She felt tears on her cheeks, but didn't understand them. When he kissed them away, she clung to him. As the last shudders rippled through her body, she understood everything. The pleasure, the closeness. The place he'd shown her, the place meant for him, ached to be filled.

"Will it be like that for you?" she asked. "When you're inside me. Will you feel those things?"

"Yeah."

"Then how can you stand waiting?"

He raised his head and stared at her. She saw the fire and knew what he was feeling. The need. How it had consumed her. So, as he fumbled with his trousers, she kissed him. His mouth, the smooth beard over his jaw. She flicked her tongue against his scar, then moved lower, trailing dampness down his throat to his chest.

She remembered how good it had felt to have him touch her everywhere, so she did the same. She slid her fingers through the light dusting of dark hair on his chest, then touched the healing scar on his arm.

Before she could think about following her fingers with her mouth, he'd pushed off his trousers and undergarments and was naked.

She stared at him. His maleness thrust toward her. She supposed if she had any sense she would be frightened, but instead she wondered if he would mind if she touched him there.

She glanced up to ask, but couldn't speak the words. He wanted her. She could see it in the flaring in his eyes and the stiff set of his shoulders. He wanted her as much as she'd wanted him. Happiness filled her, making her heart ache. Jesse wasn't doing this to help her or to teach her about the world. His motivation was more selfish. Their time today wasn't out of pity, but out of need and desire.

Laura didn't know what else to do, so she knelt on the bed and opened her arms to him. He groaned her name and gathered her close. Without quite knowing how he'd done it, he had her on her back and was pressing his maleness against her waiting warmth.

She'd been concerned about touching naked bodies, arms and legs and where everything went. Surprisingly, they slipped together easily. Her legs hugged his, his arms supported his torso. She touched his face, his mouth, then felt him probing her gently.

"This will change you forever," he reminded her.

"I know." She smiled. His mouth came down on hers. As she surged up to meet him, he entered her.

Panic flared for a moment. She could feel herself stretching to accommodate him. Suddenly she felt awkward and unsure. But his kisses were familiar, as was the touch of his hands on her breasts. She closed her eyes and inhaled the scent of him. This was Jesse.

He moved forward slowly, as if testing her ability to

take him. He paused and seemed to tense. Before she could ask what was wrong, he thrust his hips toward her. She felt a resistance, pain, then he was buried deep inside of her.

She shifted to get comfortable. The pain was already fading. Her friends had whispered about it, but she thought it wasn't too bad. She could feel him shaking. The muscles in his back were hard and unyielding to her touch.

He moved in and out. Slowly, agonizingly, if his expression could be believed. She stroked his arms and chest, liking how her touch made him shudder.

A faint vibration began between her legs, as if her body was again stirring to life. She hadn't thought she could feel that wonderful erotic tension again, but it was beginning. As if he could read her mind, Jesse slipped his hand between them and touched her there.

Instantly she was lost. He began to move faster and faster, plunging in deeper, seeking some sacred place that would forever bond them together. She cried out, urging him to keep touching her, to keep slipping in and out of her. With her hips raised toward his, she wrapped her legs around him, pulling him close.

Faster than before, almost without warning, she felt herself straining for the release. Jesse kept time with her, hoarsely calling her name. Her eyelids felt so heavy, yet she wanted to see his face. She watched his muscles grow taut and his eyes darken to the color of night.

His fingers stilled. She nearly sobbed her frustration. She waited—not breathing—then he moved again. Faster and faster. Her body convulsed into paradise. As the ripples broke through her, he plunged into her deeper still, then arched his head back. His muscles bulged with the effort. With his free hand, he held onto her hips. Then she felt the heat of him inside of her and knew his pleasure matched her own. As her eyelids fluttered shut, she heard Jesse whispering her name.

23

Laura bustled happily around the bedroom, picking up the shirt Jesse had worn yesterday. She held the garment to her face and inhaled his scent. She liked taking care of him and his things. Compared with her brothers, he wasn't much work at all, but sometimes he forgot to put away his clothes. She smoothed the fabric, then opened the armoire in the corner and hung it on a hook.

They'd been sharing this room for almost a week. Each day brought new miracles, new feelings and sensations. This was a physical world she knew nothing about. Jesse could do things with his hands or his mouth and she would be soaring through the air like a bird taking flight. When she repeated what he'd done, touching him in the same way, taking him in her mouth, she could bring her strong husband to his knees.

She smiled at the memory of how they'd tangled the sheets just that morning. He slept with her, ate with her, talked with her, shared his hopes and dreams with her. The only time they were apart was when he was seeing to business, or sometimes in the night when his dreams woke him.

Laura sat on the edge of the bed. Twice she had awakened to find him gone. She'd crept into the smaller bedroom and had found him standing by the open window. The night air had seemed to help him. The first time she'd found him alone in the dark, she'd gone up behind him and wrapped her arms around his waist. He'd been naked, but somehow she'd sensed he didn't need her passion. So she'd just held him. At last he'd spoken. Disjointed phrases about events she'd never witnessed. His stories never made sense, but she understood the pain behind the words. At last, when he'd grown silent, she kissed his skin, trying to pass her strength along to him. He turned to her then and took her quickly, gloriously, on the narrow bed he no longer used.

She hadn't known how it could be between a man and a woman. If she had, well, she might have married years ago. How did those famous singers take different lovers to their beds? She only wanted one . . . her husband.

Her smile faded. As much as Jesse turned to her in the night, or in the day for that matter, he never spoke about their joint future. Any plans he mentioned were reserved for the ranch and what he would do when he went home. Alone. She, in turn, talked about traveling. But somehow it wasn't as exciting a prospect as she'd thought it would be.

Without Jesse, nothing was very appealing. But she'd paid him to marry her, then bring her on the cattle drive. The least she could do was keep to her part of the bargain and let him go.

Laura rose to her feet and clutched the bedpost.

When would that be? She'd been afraid to ask, not wanting to hear that it would be soon. She longed to tell him of her feelings, but she didn't want to obligate him. Besides, she'd had her dream for as long as she remembered. She was finally here. She couldn't not try to make it come true. If only there was a way to have both.

In her heart of hearts she was willing to admit if he asked her to go back to the ranch with him, she would. Because she loved him. She was beginning to think she'd loved him from the moment he'd agreed to her ridiculous plan.

For years she'd accused her family of trying to keep her home so she couldn't do what she wanted. What she'd finally realized was that she hadn't been honest with them from the start. She should have explained about her dream. Instead, all her parents knew was that every spring she came up with another scheme to leave. None of the plans had been particularly well thought out. It was no wonder her family kept her close; they wanted her safe and happy.

A knock interrupted her thoughts. She crossed the floor and opened the door to the suite. Mrs. Miller, the dressmaker, stood there holding two large hatboxes. A young boy stood just behind her. The box he carried was nearly as wide as he was tall.

"Everything's ready," Mrs. Miller said as she swept into the room. The tall, imposing woman nodded at her assistant. She looked close to forty, with a large nose and small eyes. But her expression was kind and she'd been willing to make the dress exactly as Laura described. "Bring that box in, Johnny, and set it by that table."

The boy did as she asked, then gave Laura a shy smile before leaving. Mrs. Miller began opening the largest box. Laura hovered nearby, anxious to finally see the fruition of all her imaginings. Would the dress be as beautiful as she'd hoped?

The box contained yards and yards of red satin trimmed in black lace. As the seamstress held up the gown, Laura gasped. It was stunning. The bodice had been tucked and pulled so it would fit tightly. From the narrow waist, fabric draped across the hips. Underneath, the full skirt fell into a ruffled flounce that swept the floor. Tiny sleeves set on a wide neckline would leave most of her arms bare. Black lace edged the sleeves and the lower flounce.

"I had four girls sewing on this for three days," Mrs. Miller said, then smiled. "I think it came out right pretty."

"It's beautiful," Laura breathed. "Better than I imagined." The satin caught the sunlight and shimmered like a dragonfly's wings.

"Let's see if it fits. I had the corset special made, like you wanted," the seamstress said, reaching down in the box again.

Laura started on the buttons of her calico dress. She tossed it over a chair, along with her petticoats. Mrs. Miller carefully placed the dress over the settee, then approached. She settled the corset around Laura's midsection and began to tighten the laces.

"I'll need to hold onto something," Laura said, then panted as the stays drew tightly around her ribs. She could feel the boning pressing the air out of her lungs. She walked to the bedroom doorway and the older woman followed.

"You're going to need them loose enough to be able to sing," Mrs. Miller reminded her. "This will just give you a little shape."

After three months of not wearing corsets, Laura felt confined in the undergarments. Still, she would sacrifice for the dress. After her corset cover was in place,

Mrs. Miller lowered six petticoats over her head and tied them at her waist. The dress came last.

The satin was heavier than she would have thought. It settled over her like a thick cloud, the smooth fabric slipping to the floor and hugging her torso. The red color was rich and dark. In the light of the saloon, it would glow like a ruby.

When the hooks were fastened, Laura stepped into the bedroom and studied herself. The dress did make her look different. A little older and more worldly wise. The corset pushed up her bosom, making her appear larger. Her arms were slender and pale, her waist reduced to nothing. She drew in an experimental breath. She would be able to sing . . . barely.

"Sit down," Mrs. Miller said, drawing a small stool over to the vanity. "I'll get the wig and the hat."

Laura raised her skirts and petticoats, then stood over the stool. When she released the fabric, the stool was under her dress. Then she was able to sit without wrinkling anything.

Mrs. Miller returned with the two hatboxes. From the first she pulled a wig. It was auburn, with fringed bangs and ringlets cascading down the back. The dressmaker swept Laura's hair high on her head and pinned it in place. Then she set the wig on top, covering all traces of blond.

The hat came next, a frilly concoction of black lace with wisps of red satin. Before she could adjust to the stranger in the mirror, the other woman set a pair of high-heeled shoes on the floor. They were made of the same satin as her dress.

Laura didn't know herself. The darker hair of the wig made her face look smaller and her skin appear more pale. Her eyes were huge blue pools. But the hat was stunning, wide and high, with cascading black lace and red satin trim.

She rose and walked to the full-length mirror across from the bed. A stranger stood there. A sophisticated woman with a knowing smile.

Laura clasped her hands together. "Mrs. Miller, this is wonderful. Everything is perfect, exactly as I imagined it."

The seamstress smiled. "I'm glad you're happy, dear. We worked hard to finish the job in time, but it was worth it. You let me know if you want another dress made before you leave for New York."

Laura thanked the woman and walked her to the door, then returned to the bedroom and stared at herself in the mirror. There was nothing in the way now. No excuse not to try for everything she'd always wanted. She had her costume. She could become Honeysuckle DeVine. She was on her way to fame and fortune.

The door to the suite opened. "Laura?" Jesse called.

She rushed out to greet him. "I got my costume. What do you think?"

She paused in the doorway so he could look at her. Slowly he removed his hat and set it on the table in front of the fireplace. His gaze never left her. He studied her hat, then the wig. Finally he took in the dress. She twisted her fingers together nervously, waiting for his judgment. She so wanted him to think she was pretty.

When she thought she might scream from frustration, he crossed the room and took her hand in his. Bringing it to his mouth, he kissed her palm. The soft hairs of his beard tickled. She smiled.

Jesse looked at her, his dark eyes lingering on her mouth. "This must be Miss Honeysuckle DeVine. I'm pleased to finally make your acquaintance."

She pulled her hand free and held out her skirts. After making a quick turn, she laughed. "So you approve? Isn't the dress wonderful? And the wig, it's perfect. I love the hat. Mrs. Miller did an amazing job. Everything is exactly the way I wanted it to be."

"You are beautiful, but while I might admire Miss DeVine, I'm going to miss Laura."

"Jesse, why?"

"I don't know this other person." He smiled sadly. "I suppose she's too fine for the likes of me."

"That's not true," she protested, but he was already moving away.

"I spoke to Mr. Lewis," he said. Mr. Lewis was the owner of The Texas Belle saloon. "He's agreed to give you a second chance. He's put up a notice announcing your debut tomorrow night. As Honeysuckle DeVine, of course."

Nerves fluttered in her stomach. The thought of getting up on that stage again terrified her. But she had to if she wanted her chance. She knew exactly what had gone wrong before. She hadn't been prepared. But she was now. She'd been practicing for several hours a day, and she had her dress.

"I'll be ready," she said.

Jesse smiled at her. "You'll be fine. A great success."

His belief in her made her strong. "Thank you for saying that. Are you going to come to see the show?"

He nodded. "The men will all be there, too. We're going to arrive early and get good seats."

He walked into the bedroom. Laura stared at herself in the mirror above the fireplace. She didn't look the same at all, then she reminded herself that's what she wanted. The whole point of the adventure was to be someone else. Someone other than plain, old Laura Cannon.

She drew in a deep breath, then coughed when it was cut off by the corset. She'd had a wonderful adventure on the trail. There could be more adventures with

Jesse. Different ones than her dreams of fame and fortune, but perhaps just as exciting.

She stared after her husband, watching him as he moved around the room. The only problem was he hadn't asked her to stay with him. Or even hinted that he wanted her to. Maybe he couldn't wait to get rid of her. Maybe he was just being kind. And even if he wasn't, had she really come this far only to walk away without even trying?

She raised her chin slightly and knew, no matter what, she owed it to herself to experience her dream, at least once.

The crowd was as thick as the smoke drifting through the room. Jesse ignored the crawling sensation and the need to bolt. Instead he counted out the money and divided it between Harry, Mike, and Lefty.

"You know the plan," he said. "Fan out in the crowd and start giving away money. All they have to do is act like they're having a good time. Anyone booing has to answer to me outside."

"Maybe she should know the truth," Harry muttered.

"You want to tell her?" Jesse asked.

The old man shook his head.

Jesse shoved his hands in his pockets. "I don't like doing this any more than you do, but I don't see that we have a choice. Laura is determined to have a career on the stage. I don't want her heart broken. So we're going to make sure everyone applauds and acts like she's the best singer to ever visit Wichita."

"What happens when you run out of money?" Mike asked.

Thanks to Laura's inheritance and the ten percent she'd paid him, that wasn't going to be a problem.

"She'll have moved on long before that happens. Now hurry. It's almost time for her show."

He moved toward the door, catching a breath of fresh air and sucking it in greedily. Being in the dark, crowded saloon was hell. But he didn't have a choice. Laura was going to sing here tonight, and she needed him.

Wellington and Bobby were still at the table where he'd left them. Much to their disgust, they weren't being allowed to drink alcohol. As Jesse pulled up a seat, Bobby glared at him.

"It's my money and I earned it. You ain't got no right to keep me from spending it."

Jesse didn't have time for his complaints. He leaned forward and grabbed the kid by the shirtfront. "Listen to me, you little bastard. You're young enough and small enough to get into a mess of trouble in this town. Thanks to you and Wellington, Laura has already been booed off the stage once. I'm going to make sure that doesn't happen again. If you get in my way, I'll take you outside and teach you a lesson myself."

The boy paled. He shrank back as much as he could with Jesse holding onto his shirt. Fear filled his eyes. Jesse released him and felt as slimy as steer shit in a rainstorm.

"We didn't mean nothing by running off," Wellington said. "We worked hard on the cattle drive and we thought we deserved a little fun. You don't tell the other cowboys what to do."

"I'm not responsible for them." He eyed Bobby. "I'm sorry, son. I'm a little nervous about tonight and I'm taking it out on you. That's not right." He motioned to one of the bar girls. A tall brunette in a low-cut dress sauntered over.

He ordered a whiskey for himself and two beers for the boys. "But don't let them have anything else," he instructed the woman, handing her a coin. She smiled.

Judging from Bobby and Wellington's rapt expressions, she must have been pretty, but Jesse didn't care. There was only one woman occupying his thoughts these days and she was about to come on stage.

He turned around and checked on his men. They were making their way through the crowd, handing out money and explaining what the payment was for.

The dancing girls finished performing with a high kick, then left the stage. Jesse swallowed hard. He hoped the money worked, because he couldn't bear to have Laura hurt again. The tinny piano music played the opening bars of her first song. She walked out onto the stage, singing.

The crowd started at the first few off-key notes. Bobby shivered. There were a couple of calls of "What the hell?" but they were quickly silenced. The saloon was as quiet as it could get with cries of "Place your bets on the wheel," and requests for drinks flying around the room.

Jesse exhaled the breath he'd been holding. It was working. Laura was going to get her chance. It was worth every penny, and more.

As he watched, she strolled across the stage and smiled at the audience. A couple of men applauded. This was what she'd wanted. This was where she belonged. As he watched her, he realized this woman was a stranger to him.

He missed the excited young lady who'd had the audacity to hide a dog in her wagon, who sang so horribly she started a stampede. He missed the woman who baked pies in a Dutch oven and fearlessly crossed rivers. He missed the water siren who tempted him beyond reason and the gentle spirit who had listened to the sad story of his life. He missed the loving wife who had sewn up his arm as easily as she had his shirt, and who warmed his soul as well as his bed. Honeysuckle was none of those things. She needed more than he could ever offer.

When she finished, there was a moment of stunned surprise, then loud applause. She began her second song. A few men came in off the streets. They started to call out to her, but they were hushed by others around them. Everyone caught on to the spirit of the charade. Soon there were whistles and yells of praise. Laura flushed with pleasure. By the time she finished her last song, men were standing, hooting and cheering. She laughed happily.

Jesse joined them, applauding loudly. Her gaze searched the room. When she found him, she gave a little curtsey, then disappeared behind the curtain.

They'd agreed to meet backstage. Jesse made his way through the crowd. He was already in the long corridor leading to the back when he realized he'd forgotten to be afraid. He'd been so worried about Laura, he hadn't had time to notice the press of the crowd.

He found Laura's tiny dressing room. She shared it with two other women, both dancers, but they were gone. She sat in front of the small vanity. When he stepped into the room, she looked up at him and smiled. She was all happy brilliance as she rose to her feet and rushed to him.

"Were you there? Of course you were. Then you saw, didn't you? Wasn't it wonderful? I'm so happy. They applauded and cheered. Oh, Jesse, I knew it would be like this."

Her arms came around his neck and she pressed herself against him. He held her close. Her eyes were bright, as if lit by stars.

"Thank you for everything," she said.

For a moment he thought she'd guessed. He didn't know what to say.

"You were there for me, and helped me believe in myself," she continued. "I was afraid, but I wanted to make you proud."

"You did," he told her, relieved she didn't know the truth. She would have to learn it eventually, but not tonight. He didn't want anything to spoil her happiness.

She pressed her lips to his. Instantly fire flared in his groin. He opened his mouth and she swept inside. He kissed her back, silently telling her all the things he couldn't say.

When they were both breathing heavily, he raised his head. "You're on your way," he said.

"I know." She lowered her hands to his chest and pressed her palms flat against him. He could feel her warmth through his coat and shirt. "It's funny, everything went exactly as I hoped it would. I knew having the costume would change me. But . . ." Her mouth pulled straight. "I suppose I'm a little disappointed, too. I thought this would be the adventure of my lifetime. But it's not nearly as exciting as the cattle drive. I suppose it's the difference between wanting something and finally having it."

She smoothed his lapels. With her head bent down, he couldn't see her face. With her red hair and fancy clothes, she was a stranger. But if he closed his eyes, he knew it was her. The scent, the way she touched him, all of it was gloriously familiar.

"I know you have to go back to the ranch soon."

"I told you, I'm staying until you leave Wichita."

She raised her head and looked at him. "Are you sure you want to?"

She'd been nothing but trouble from the moment they'd met, yet he couldn't imagine life without her. "You're not a bother."

She wiggled closer, hugged him and sighed. "This has been the most perfect night. There's only one thing that could make it better." Her breasts pressed against him in invitation.

The heat flared between them. He glanced around the tiny space, but there wasn't room to do anything. "We can't do it here."

She reached one hand between them and stroked his arousal. He'd taught her well and she instantly brought him to mindlessness.

"Stop that," he said, trying to push her hand away. But he didn't really want her to stop. He wanted to be with her, in her. He wanted to brand her with his seed, again and again, because in the end, the memories were all he would have.

He bent over her and kissed her. As her mouth parted and her tongue dueled with his, he reached behind her for the hooks on the back of her dress. When they were unfastened, he pulled down the thick satin to her waist, exposing the corset cover. With a quick tug, he loosened the bow and shoved it down as well.

At the same time, she was reaching for the buttons of his shirt. She popped them open, then stroked his chest. Their arms bumped, but it didn't matter. Frantic need overtook them.

As she pressed her hot mouth to his chest, he fumbled with her camisole. The boned corset held it in place. He contented himself with stroking her breasts and rolling her taut nipples between his thumb and forefinger.

"Jesse," she murmured against him. She bit his skin, then licked the wound. "Jesse, please."

He knew how she felt. Fire raced through him, flaring in time with his rapid heartbeat. He looked around the room again, but except for the small vanity and chair, there was no furniture, save a few hooks for costumes.

He raised his hands to her head and took off the wig. After setting it on the chair, he started pulling up her skirt and petticoats. She unbuttoned his trousers, then reached inside and drew him out. She stroked the length of him. Up and down, slow, then fast. She traced the sensitive tip. Her eyes drifted shut, as if the act gave her supreme pleasure.

He sucked his breath in. "Damn you, Laura."

She giggled. "I want to make you lose control."

"You do."

At last he reached her pantaloons. He found the opening and plunged his fingers inside. Her curls were soft and already damp from her desire. As she'd teased him, he teased her.

She was tight and ready.

"I'm going to lift you up," he said, his voice hoarse with need. "Put your legs around me."

He turned so her back was to the door. The walls of the dressing room were thin. They could hear people in the hallway outside. With one strong boost, he raised her up so her legs could wrap around his waist. His maleness brushed against her center. They both groaned. She shifted and he slid home.

Damp heat surrounded him. He supported her from underneath. She clung to him, her arms wrapped around his neck. As he drove into her, she arched toward him, taking all of him. He trembled from the need and wondered how long he could hold on. She raised her face and he saw her eyes were glazed with passion. Her long hair tumbled free of its pins. Her dress bunched around her waist, her corset pushed her breasts higher. They were in a tiny dressing room, backstage of some saloon and she didn't care.

God, he loved this woman.

He moved his hips faster, finding the rhythm that would make her writhe against him. She urged him on, squirming closer, sending him deeper. She murmured his name. He felt her muscles tense, then they contracted around him. He'd meant to hold on, to enjoy her pleasure before taking his own, but her rippling milked him past the point of control. He buried himself in her and fell into the release.

When they had caught their breath, he lowered her to the floor and helped her smooth her dress back into place. They bumped into each other in the tiny room. He realized being in there should have bothered him as much as the saloon. He didn't like confined places. But he'd never really noticed it until now.

"What are you thinking about?" she asked as she pulled up her bodice and slipped her arms in the sleeves.

"That you've healed me."

"Nonsense. You did that all yourself. It was just time."

It was more than that, he knew. It was Laura. She *had* healed him. Soon he would be well enough to let her go.

24

"Miss DeVine, Miss DeVine!"

Laura turned toward the call. A teenage boy, maybe Wellington's age, ran across the street. He had brown hair and freckles. As he approached, he pulled off his cap and held out a fistful of wildflowers.

"These are for you," he said proudly. "I ain't been able to come hear you sing, ma'am, but my brothers all talk about you. Maybe when I'm old enough I can listen." His grin was engaging.

She smiled back. "Thank you, sir. You're very kind."

The boy blushed, stammered a word or two, then turned and ran back the way he'd come. Laura shook her head in amazement. It happened everywhere she went. Even without the wig and costume, people stopped her and wanted to know if she was really Honeysuckle DeVine. They'd all heard about her. She was famous.

She picked up her skirt and hurried toward the hotel. She needed to collect a few things before making her way to the saloon. She was going in a little early today. As she walked through the lobby, the desk clerk and bellman called out their greetings. She remembered seeing them at last night's show.

Her career couldn't be going better. The crowds were larger and larger each evening. Jesse always came to hear her sing. Afterwards he walked her back to the hotel, and they spent the rest of the night in each other's arms. If she could forget that he would be leaving soon, her life would be perfect.

She opened the door to the suite. Jesse was sitting back in one of the wing chairs, sound asleep.

She closed the door quietly, not wanting to wake him. Despite his claims at being healed, he still didn't sleep very much. More nights than not, she woke up to find him in the other room, staring out the window. She'd grown to understand the darkness of his time at war would never go away. He would never be the man he'd been before. She didn't mind. This Jesse was the only one she knew and he was the man she loved.

She set her reticule on the table in front of the fireplace, then walked to his side so she could watch him. His face was strong and handsome. How she would miss him.

She'd finally figured out he meant what he said. He wouldn't leave her as long as she was in Wichita. So if she really loved him enough to want him to go back to his ranch, she was going to have to be the one to make the plans to go away.

Which was why she'd spoken to the attorney that afternoon, then bought a ticket for New York City. She was leaving at the end of the week.

She knelt on the floor beside him. His hand lay on his thigh. She ached to touch his long fingers, but she didn't want to disturb him. He needed the rest.

She sighed silently and wished there was a way to make it all work. If only he would come with her to New York, or else ask her to stay. While she enjoyed being Honeysuckle DeVine, having people notice and speak to her on the street, she also missed being plain Laura. For whatever reason, Jesse preferred her old self. She would gladly walk away from everything to be with him. But he hadn't asked, and she wouldn't offer. She suspected, in his heart, he wanted to be rid of her.

Oh, but she would miss him.

A single tear slipped down her cheek. Before she could brush it away, Jesse reached out and touched his fingers to her face.

"Why are you crying?" he asked.

"How long have you been awake?"

"Since you opened the door."

"Why didn't you say anything?"

He opened his eyes and smiled. "I was hoping you'd take your clothes off and I could watch."

"All you have to do is ask. I'm happy to take my clothes off for you."

"It's not the same as having you think I'm asleep."

She swatted at his arm. "You're terrible."

"That's not what you said last night."

She flushed at the memory. Last night she'd been especially noisy in his arms. She looked at him. His heavy-lidded gaze told her what he was thinking. Her body began to quiver in anticipation. But instead of moving into his embrace, she stayed kneeling on the floor.

"We have to talk, Jesse. It's time to stop pretending." This was harder than she'd thought. She stared at her hands and wished it wasn't going to hurt so much. "I've bought a ticket for New York. I leave at the end of the week."

"I see." His smile faded and his eyes darkened as if someone had closed a shutter.

"It's for the best," she said. "I'm keeping you from the ranch. And the longer we act as if we're going to be together always, the harder it's going to be when we're apart. At least for me. Now, you'll be able to get on with things without me being in the way."

"And you'll have your adventure."

"Yes," she agreed, but she wasn't happy as she said the word. The plans that had once driven her no longer seemed important. She supposed she would get excited again. When she was able to not think about Jesse all the time, to not imagine him with her and hear his voice wherever she went.

She cleared her throat. "I spoke to Mr. Ackerman this morning. As soon as you're ready, we can go in and discuss the divorce."

His expression didn't change. She had been hoping for a sign of regret or disappointment, but she didn't know what he was thinking. She blinked several times, trying to hold back the tears.

"You don't have to do that for me," he said. "I don't mind if we stay married."

"You don't?" A small flame of hope flared to life inside of her. Maybe he didn't want her to go. "But we'll be apart, won't we?"

He shifted on the seat, sitting straighter. "Being married might offer you a measure of safety," he said. "There are certain types of men who prey on single women. If you're married, you'll be able to mention your husband. Having my last name will be some protection against all that's out there."

The flame flickered, wavered, then died. He was being practical, not romantic. She told herself his concern was something, maybe even enough. At least he cared about her. But a coldness clutched her heart.

She'd wanted more than caring. She'd wanted to know that Jesse felt the same way she did. She wanted to know he loved her and desperately wanted her to stay with him.

The words hovered on the tip of her tongue, but she didn't speak them. This time it was going to be his decision. No matter how much that hurt her.

"But what if you want to marry again?" she asked. She didn't want to think about that possibility, but she forced herself to go on. She hadn't been very proud of herself for a while now, but she was going to change that. "It's sweet of you to want to protect me, but I'll be fine. I've learned a lot from you and the cowboys. I can take care of myself."

He stared at her. His dark eyes, deep as the night, concealed his heart and his soul. She would never forget him.

He leaned forward and placed his hand on her face, cupping her jaw. "I didn't plan on ever marrying, but now that I am, I can't imagine being married to anyone but you."

"Really?" His fingers were gentle on her skin. She wanted to turn her head and press her mouth to his palm. "You might change your mind."

"What about you?" he asked. "You might meet someone else you want to marry. Maybe even have a family."

A family. Babies. She wondered briefly if she could already be with child. "Not while I'm traveling. I think children need to grow up in one place. It would be nice to show them different places by taking trips, but they would need a place to call home. I don't—" Her throat tightened again, but it was from love this time, not pain. "I can't imagine being married to anyone else, either. Maybe you could come visit me in New York."

She bit her lower lip and waited for him to yell at

her. Jesse hated crowds. He would hate that city, not to mention the long train ride east.

But instead of getting angry, he nodded. "I just might do that. So be prepared to explain your husband to all your lovers." His voice was teasing.

She rose to her feet, then bent over him and clutched his shoulders. He drew her down on his lap and held her. She didn't even know she was crying until he wiped the tears from her face.

"Why are you so sad?" he asked.

"I'm not." She sniffed. "I'm happy. I have everything I want. Soon I'll be leaving for New York. Everything is working out exactly as I p-planned." The sob caught her unawares. As Jesse rocked her back and forth, she cried into his shirt. She couldn't seem to stop the tears.

She wanted to go home with Jesse. She wanted to see her family, argue with her sisters, cook with her mother. She wanted to sew curtains for Jesse's house, paper the walls and help him with the record-keeping on the ranch. She wanted to sleep in his bed, love him, touch him, and have his children.

But he wanted her to leave. He wanted her to go to New York, sing on the stage, and take lovers.

"No lovers but you," she mumbled against his shirt. "I don't want anyone else touching me that way."

"That will change," he said. "You'll meet other people, make new friends. You're afraid now, but that will pass. I'd like you to keep my name for a while, but if you ever want to get married again, send me a wire and I'll sign the divorce papers."

He smoothed her hair away from her face. When the tears finally stopped, he kissed her gently, then pushed her from his lap. "You have to get to the saloon early," he reminded her. "You need to give the piano player the new arrangement."

She stood up feeling slightly embarrassed. All that show of emotion and Jesse had never once said he loved her. Maybe he didn't. Maybe he really was going to be glad to see the last of her.

"I'll go wash up," she said, and walked into the bedroom.

Jesse stared after her. He felt as if his heart was being torn from his chest. Holding Laura while she cried had been the most bittersweet moment of his life. It would have been so easy to confess his feelings. She'd practically begged him to ask her to stay. God knows he wanted to. But he couldn't. She deserved more. What did he have to offer anyone?

He was just some rancher with a sorry past. He was scarred, inside and out. He couldn't even sleep through most nights. The dreams haunted him and they probably would forever. Laura needed someone whole. Someone who would face the future with as much optimism as she had. Someone who believed in life and happiness. He didn't believe in anything anymore, except maybe the fact that loving her had been the best thing he'd ever done. He wanted to think that losing her would kill him, but life wasn't that simple. It might stop him for a time. He might feel destroyed. He knew he would never love anyone else. But that was fine with him. Loving Laura had healed him. More than that, loving Laura had reminded him he was still alive.

He'd missed so much pretending to be dead. He was going to live now. Not planning too far ahead, not getting lost in the past, just living.

So he would let her go, because that was her destiny. Maybe in New York she could take a few singing lessons and not be so terrible. He grimaced. She was collecting quite a crowd at the saloon. Many men came out of curiosity, sure she couldn't be as bad as they'd heard. Some were applauding without taking money, although he still sent his men into the crowd every night.

He rose and walked to the window. From here he could see the roof of the saloon. Before she left the city, he was going to have to tell her the truth. He couldn't let her go to New York thinking she could sing. There wouldn't be anyone there to protect her.

He touched the cool glass and wished he didn't have to be the one to destroy her. If only . . . hell, he didn't know what to think. If only she *could* sing. Except if she could, she wouldn't be Laura, and he wouldn't love her as much. It was her faults that made her so beautiful to him. But that was selfish. He would tell her the truth and hope she didn't think he was doing it simply to keep her with him.

For a moment he thought of going with her to New York. He could sell the ranch and travel with her. But that wasn't the life for him. He needed the roots she'd talked about. He needed to belong.

He loved her enough to let her follow her dream. He even loved her enough to risk her hating him forever. She would when he told her the truth. Because he was a coward, he would wait until the last day, stealing every minute he could.

Life without her would be bleak, an endless winter of solitude. But he would survive, because the kindest act of love was letting her go.

Laura walked slowly along the broken sidewalk. It was hotter today. Kansas summers seemed just as bad as those they had back home. A stifling heat made her want to take a nap. She smiled at the thought. If she could have convinced Jesse to curl up with her, she wouldn't have worried about the new musical arrangement.

But when she'd come out of the bedroom, he'd been busy with some papers and hadn't given her more than a quick kiss on the cheek before she left. So she would practice the new song and put it into her show tonight.

She also wanted to speak to Mr. Lewis. She was sure the crowds had gotten larger at the saloon. If she was the reason, well, that would certainly be something to mention when she was looking for a job in New York.

She sighed. The thought of that city had once been enough to set her blood aflame. Now it wouldn't be anything like she'd first imagined. Not without Jesse.

"Stop thinking about him," she told herself. Time enough to mourn when he was gone. For now, she had to worry about her song.

She went into the saloon through the back door. In the early afternoon, there were several patrons sitting around or leaning against the bar. The piano player wasn't there, so she walked back to the tiny dressing room she used. As she approached, she could hear the two dancing girls inside. Although she shared the space with them, they'd never spoken more than a greeting. They went on before her, so she got ready while they were on stage and they were gone when she finished.

"I swear, that ugly hat of hers takes up half this room," one of the girls was saying as Laura approached.

Laura stopped outside the door, hurt by the comment. She knew her costume was bulky, but she tried to keep it out of the way. The second woman, Katie, laughed.

"What can you expect, Rose? She needs something to distract the audience."

Rose, the first dancer, giggled. "I know. It's amazing. According to Mr. Lewis, she doesn't have any idea."

Laura had been ready to announce herself, but now she hesitated to knock on the closed door. What didn't she have an idea about? She frowned.

"You'd think she'd come early and practice a little. Not that it would help."

Laura took a step back. That wasn't fair. She practiced at the hotel.

"It's pretty funny when you think about it," Rose said. "I mean the woman sounds like a dog in heat being tortured when she sings. I've never heard anything so horrible in my life. The only reason she hasn't been booed off the stage is that cowboy of hers is paying off the customers. Why do you think the crowd is so big? It's easy money."

Katie chuckled. "Laura Travers' voice could curdle cream."

"Or break glass."

"Or peel wallpaper."

They both laughed.

Laura gasped. Her mouth grew dry, her palms damp. The pain started low in her chest before spreading. Her stomach turned and twisted. Her cheeks flamed. The humiliation swept over her leaving her dizzy and weak.

She turned and tried to run, but her feet felt heavy and awkward. She forced herself to move forward, nodding automatically as she passed one of the stockboys. When she was out in the sunlight, she leaned against the side of the building and tried not to throw up.

It couldn't be true, she told herself. They were lying. They had to be. It couldn't be true. It couldn't! Could it?

She squeezed her eyes shut, ignoring the crashing sounds as her world fell in around her. Nothing was as it seemed. She wanted to deny the words, but they had a ring of truth she couldn't ignore. Why would the women lie to each other? They didn't know she was there. She'd walked in quietly, so they wouldn't have heard her footsteps.

This was all some hideous mistake, she told herself. Soon Wellington and Bobby would step out from behind the barrels and tell her they were teasing her.

But no one stepped out from behind the barrels next to the back door. She shivered, despite the sun beating down on her. No one appeared at all. She was alone with her broken dreams.

Laura wasn't sure how long she huddled there, clutching her midsection as if to hold in her life's blood. She didn't know if she cried, but she didn't think she had the strength for tears. Not anymore.

She tried to ignore the shame and embarrassment. But pictures flashed through her mind. Small events that had never made sense before. The startled look on Jesse's face the first time she'd sung for him. It had been the first night of the cattle drive. And during her song—

She clapped her hand over her mouth. Had she started the stampede?

She sagged against the building and slowly sank into a crouch. She remembered other times, when the cattle had shied from her, or the cowboys had jumped when she'd sung. She remembered Jesse's carefully worded questions about her plans for her singing career. She remembered being booed off the stage her first night in town.

Her eyes opened wide. *"Go back to your cave and scare the bats,"* someone had yelled at her. At the time she'd dismissed the call as a drunken attempt at humor, but now she knew the truth. She couldn't sing. But no one had told her. Not Wellington, not Harry. Not Jesse.

Jesse! That first night in town he'd disappeared. Later he'd explained about having to find Wellington and Bobby. But he'd been at every performance since. And most of the cowboys had attended as well. Had they really paid people not to boo?

"Laura?" It was as if thinking about him had conjured him. Jesse stood in front of her. "Laura, what's wrong?"

She scrambled to her feet. Her body trembled, but she refused to give in to the weakness. She glared at him. "What are you doing here?"

"You forgot your gloves." He held them out in his hands. "I brought them to you. What's wrong?" he asked again. "Did something happen?"

She tried to laugh, but it came out more like a sob. "Yes, I think you could say something is wrong." Anger flared. She recognized it as the cousin of hurt and knew that her feelings were more about the pain of betrayal. She wanted to be sensible and orderly as she spoke to him, but all she could blurt out was, "Why didn't you tell me I couldn't sing?"

Until that second she hadn't known she was hoping for a miracle. In her heart of hearts she'd thought when she confronted Jesse he would be as confused as she had been. That he would insist she had a perfect voice and convince her those women were simply jealous.

He didn't. For the first time since she'd met him, he wouldn't hold her gaze. His dark eyes glanced away and he shifted awkwardly on his feet.

"How did you find out?" he asked at last.

It was as if someone had stolen the air from her chest. She sagged back against the building and closed her eyes. "It's true then."

"I'm sorry." His low voice offered sympathy. She wasn't interested in that.

"Sorry? For what? For making a fool of me? Why did you do it? Is it because I insisted on coming on the cattle drive, or did you do this to me because I asked that we marry?"

"It wasn't like that."

"What was it like?"

"I wanted to tell you, but I couldn't. I tried, but you had this dream and I couldn't be the one to take that away from you."

"So you let me be publicly humiliated instead? You let me stand there, night after night, in front of all those people? You let me pretend I could sing? You let me think I was successful when all the time I was a ridiculous figure to be pitied?"

She couldn't believe Jesse had betrayed her. Anyone but him. She hadn't thought she could hurt more, but she did.

"I didn't know how to stop you."

She glared at him. "You could have told me the truth. We were on that cattle drive for weeks. Surely there was one time when you could have said 'Laura, your voice makes the cattle stampede and cream c—curdle.'" A sob broke her words. She fought against the tears. Her throat burned. "You should have told me. I thought you cared about me. A friend would have said something."

"I didn't want to hurt you."

"I'm hurt now," she snapped. "Don't you think I'll spend the rest of my life remembering how horrible this is? How am I ever supposed to face anyone again?"

"I'm sorry." He stared at her gloves in his hand. "I—" He drew in a breath. "I wish I could make you understand. I didn't do this on purpose. You wanted to be Honeysuckle DeVine and travel the world. I admired you. You were so alive and determined. Nothing was going to get in your way. I didn't think I had the right to take that away from you. I thought there might be a way for you to be successful."

"Sure. With you paying everyone."

"Maybe that was a mistake."

"Maybe?" Her voice was shrill. "Every night you've let me go up there and be humiliated. All those people laughing at me behind my back. That's the cruelest thing anyone has ever done to me."

"I was trying to be kind."

She turned away, but he grabbed her shoulder and made her face him.

"Listen to me," he said, bending close to her. "I *was* trying to be kind. I only wanted you to be happy."

"By letting me live a lie?"

"By giving you a chance to live out your dream. It doesn't matter that you can't sing. Don't you see that? You wanted something, you believed in yourself and you did it. That's what's important."

He meant what he said. She could read it in his eyes. She wanted to believe him, but how could she? She cringed at the thought of what everyone must be saying about her.

"You wanted to be Honeysuckle DeVine more than anything in the world. I was determined to make that come true."

"I don't understand any of this," she said. His hand felt heavy on her shoulder. She shrugged it off. "I thought I knew you. I believed in you and trusted you and this is what you did to me. It wasn't right, Jesse. It wasn't right at all."

"I know that now," he said hoarsely. "I'm sorry."

She knew her feelings of betrayal were about more than the singing. If he'd cared for her, he wouldn't have treated her this way. That's what hurt the most. That she'd been fooling herself about his feelings. He'd never loved her at all.

The tears fell then, and she couldn't stop them. She felt them roll down her cheeks. He flinched, as if each drop were a deadly blow.

"Were you planning to follow me to New York and pay off audiences there?" she asked.

He shook his head. The pain in his eyes echoed her own. Rarely could she tell what he was thinking. Now that she could, she was sorry. She didn't want to know he was suffering because of her; it didn't change anything.

"I was going to find a way to tell you the truth," he said at last. "I thought maybe if you took some singing lessons . . . "

Her compassion evaporated, burned away by anger. "Singing lessons?" she shrieked. "Isn't it too little too late? How dare you suggest anything to me? You let them laugh at me."

"Never," he said, reaching out to brush away her tears. "No one laughed. Least of all, me."

She took a step away from him. She thought he might have winced but she wasn't sure. She didn't care either, she thought spitefully.

He drew in a breath. Pain twisted his mouth. "I only wanted to love you, Laura. I suppose I did that badly, as well. I know you're hurt. I'm sorry you feel betrayed. I didn't mean for this to happen."

She refused to believe him. She couldn't believe anything anymore. "How dare you tell me you love me? You wanted me to leave Wichita and go to New York."

"I love you enough to let you go follow your dream." He smiled sadly. "You taught me that. I know you don't believe me, but it's still true. I'll always love you."

He was trying to distract her, she told herself. And he was doing a fine job of it. Jesse loved her? No. She no longer believed in good things happening or anything being simple. Nothing was as she thought it would be.

"Laura, I—"

Before he could continue, the back door opened and Mr. Lewis stepped into the alley.

Laura grabbed his sleeve. "Mr. Lewis, I need to speak to you. I can't work in the saloon anymore."

He stopped and stared at her. He wore his hat low over his forehead and kept an unlit cigar clamped in his teeth. "What?"

She dropped her hand to her side. "I can't sing."

"Hell, that never stopped you before."

She shuddered. "Yes, well, it's stopping me now."

"Listen, Mrs. Travers, we have a deal. You perform on my stage and I pay you. You're drawing a big crowd. I don't want to give that up."

Because Jesse was paying people to be there. "But I can't go on again. I can't do that to myself." The tears were starting again.

Mr. Lewis wasn't much taller than her. He took the cigar from his mouth and frowned. "Do the show tonight. I can't get anyone this late in the day. Then you can quit. Fair enough?"

She nodded miserably. He was right, they *did* have a deal. She would have to do one more show. Could she get through it?

"Fine." He tipped his hat to her, nodded at Jesse, then left.

Laura turned toward the door. Jesse touched her arm.

"No," she said. "I don't want to talk to you anymore. I don't want to see you ever again. And I don't want you paying the men in the saloon. I'll take my chances."

"Laura, wait."

She pushed past him and entered the darkened building. She'd created the problem. She would fix it.

Once again she was paying the price for not thinking things through. Not only with the singing, although going on that stage would be about the hardest thing she'd ever done, but also with Jesse. She'd blindly given her heart to him, foolishly trusting him to take care of it. Instead of loving her as he claimed, he'd played her for a fool and made her the object of public humiliation.

As she closed the door behind her, she wondered where she went from here. She had no dreams left. Only a broken heart and tattered wishes for what could have been.

Laura sat in front of the mirror in the small vanity. Slowly she wound her hair into a coil, then held it on top of her head. With her free hand, she reached for the wig. When it was in place, she tucked the few loose strands of her hair under the auburn curls, then stared at herself.

She looked foolish. What had once been pretty and special was simply an ill-fitting masquerade. The color was all wrong. She glanced over her shoulder at the hat hanging on the wall. It was huge. What had she been thinking when she'd ordered it? No doubt the dressmaker had laughed with her friends, telling them all about the silly ideas of a young woman from Texas.

Laura reached for the hat and set it on her head. Just yesterday, sitting on this tiny stool and staring into the same mirror, she'd felt beautiful. Almost like a princess. She'd believed she was filling the saloon with customers, and that while Jesse might not love her, he cared about her. She'd believed everything was possible. Now she had nothing. Not even the illusion of Jesse's affection.

That's what hurt the most, she admitted to herself.

She could have survived the rest of it if she'd been able to believe he cared. Because as much as she'd loved being on the stage and hearing the applause, the place she most felt at home was in his arms. But he couldn't love her. He'd only said that because he felt guilty about what he'd done.

All she'd ever wanted was to be someone special. Had it been wrong to want more? Had the selfish nature of her dream doomed her to failure from the start?

It seemed that way. Here she was, once again, plain Laura Cannon. No, she thought, shaking her head, she was Jesse's wife. That should have given her hope, but it didn't. She'd been willing to turn her back on her plans for the chance of really being his wife. But he never asked, and now she knew why.

She heard the music swell, then there was the thunder of applause. The dancing girls were finished. She rose to her feet and stepped out into the hallway. Rose and Katie were laughing together as they walked toward the dressing room. Laura stepped to the side to let them pass, then raised her chin.

"You won't have to worry about my costume being in the way anymore," she said. "Tonight is my last show."

The women exchanged a knowing glance. It hurt Laura all the more for having heard their earlier conversation. "You must be leaving for New York," Rose said.

"No, I'm going home. I found out I can't sing."

She turned away because she couldn't say anymore. How was she supposed to get through her performance?

"Laura?" Rose called, but Laura kept walking. She didn't want to hear the other woman's words of sympathy. There was no need. They'd only spoken the truth.

"You're next," Mr. Lewis said, motioning her toward the stage.

At the last moment, she took off her hat and tossed it onto the floor. Then she stepped out from behind the curtain and stared at the crowd.

It was bigger than it had been last night. Her heart fluttered wildly in her chest. She didn't know if she could go on. Then she reminded herself it was just one more time. It wasn't as if she was going to sing again.

"Good evening," she said softly.

"Can't hear you," someone called from the back of the room.

She cleared her throat and tried again. "Good evening, I'm Honeysuckle DeVine." There was a round of applause. She wanted to cry. Instead she forced herself to go on. "Some of you are probably wondering why you haven't been paid to sit through a performance tonight."

"Paid, hell, I came here because I wanted to know if you sounded like everyone said." The voice came from the middle of the crowd, but she couldn't see who was speaking.

"You mean if I was really that bad?"

There was a moment of stunned silence. She stared at the upturned faces. A few of the men looked away, obviously uncomfortable.

"It does give folks somethin' to talk about," a man up front said. He grinned. "We ain't been this entertained since the circus came through last summer."

"I'm not going to sing tonight."

"Why not?" an old man midway to the bar asked. "You ain't so bad."

"That's because you're deaf as a post, Bart," someone called.

Bart chuckled. "Maybe, but she's right pretty enough, even without the singing."

Several men murmured in agreement.

"I'm flattered," she said, and found the tears weren't

so close to the surface. "I'm sorry I've been torturing you all this time, but I only found out today I couldn't carry a tune if someone—" She paused, not sure what to say.

"Gave you a horse trough?" a man called from the bar. The crowd laughed and Laura found herself joining in.

"Exactly. Mr. Lewis insisted I come because we had a deal. So here I am." She laced her fingers together in front of her waist. "I'm not sure how everything got so confusing. I only wanted a chance to be someone else. I guess that was wrong." She reached up and pulled off her wig. Her blond hair tumbled over her shoulders. She brushed it back and set the wig on the stage floor. "This isn't really me," she said, motioning to the dress. "I'm not Honeysuckle DeVine. I guess I never was. I'm just Laura Cannon."

"Laura Travers," a man said.

She turned toward the sound. She knew that voice, just as she knew the man stepping out of the shadows. He was close to the stage, on the half-wall that separated the gambling from the rest of the saloon.

"Who said that?" the man in front asked.

"Hush," his neighbor told him.

"Why are you here, Jesse?" she asked.

"You're my wife. Where else would I be?" He moved closer to the stage. There were people all around him, but he didn't seem to notice.

"You did it," he said, reading her thoughts as always. "You healed me, Laura. You took a broken man and made him whole. You helped Bobby and Wellington endure their first cattle drive. You helped Harry with the camp. You made us all your family. You were the best wife a man could have. I think that makes you very special."

She could feel herself softening toward him. She fought to recapture her anger. "You betrayed me."

"I'm sorry," he said. "I wish I could make you understand why I did it. Your dream burned so brightly, it warmed us all. I only wanted you to have everything *you* wanted. A chance to be Honeysuckle. Maybe I did the wrong thing, but my reasons were right."

He moved closer until he was standing in front of the stage. She walked toward him and crouched down. She could see the light in his eyes. For the first time she saw the love there. It was so bright, it was blinding.

"I love you, Laura Travers. I love you enough to let you go off to New York, if that will make you happy."

"I just wanted an adventure," she said, wanting to believe him, but afraid. Terribly afraid. "You should have told me the truth."

He nodded. "I know that now. I'm sorry."

"Hell, Laura, forgive him and get on with the show."

She glanced up, having forgotten her audience. "You want me to sing?"

Several men nodded.

"But I'm terrible."

"We're kinda used to it. 'Sides, Billy here can't play poker for shit, but that don't stop him from losin' money." Billy, a tall, lanky cowboy, punched his friend in the arm.

She stood up slowly. They began to applaud. The piano player touched the keys and she heard the opening bars to her favorite song.

She opened her mouth, then closed it. "You really want me to do this?"

"Sing for me, Laura," Jesse said.

She stared down at him and knew she could deny him nothing. Even though he'd hurt her, she understood why he'd done it. She forgave him because she had no choice. She loved him.

"I know a place, where all things beautiful, bloom in

the sun, bloom in the sun. I know a place, where all things wonderful, live there as one, live there as one. I know a place of miracles, of loving arms and promised love. I know a place where God is smiling, down from above, down from above."

She had to stop because her throat was burning from unshed tears. Jesse stood below her, waiting. All her life she'd wanted an adventure. She'd found it, too. With him. On the cattle drive, here in town, and in his arms. It didn't matter where they were, as long as they were together. She'd only ever wanted to feel special. With him, she did.

The piano player stopped playing. The room was silent. Even the gamblers had paused to listen.

"I've been a fool," she said.

"No, I hurt you. I'm sorry." His dark eyes spoke the truth. He *did* love her. Everything had been for her. From the first moment they'd met.

"I'm sorry, too," she said. "I was selfish. I won't be that way again. I promise. I want to come home with you. I want to live on the ranch and help you. I want to have your children and watch them grow."

"What about seeing the world?" he asked.

"I'd rather see you every day."

"Maybe you can do both. I swear I'll make you happy. We could have children. Maybe a little girl named Honeysuckle after her beautiful mother."

"My name is Laura," she said. "I love you, Jesse."

He held out his arms. She rushed to the edge of the stage and jumped down. He caught her and held her close. As his mouth claimed hers, the saloon exploded into applause. Everyone was talking at once.

"Best show I've ever seen," the man next to her yelled over the noise. "Wonder if they'll do it again tomorrow."

Laura would have told him that tomorrow she and

Jesse would be on the trail heading back to Texas, but her lips were otherwise occupied. It would take weeks to get back to Jackson Springs, but that didn't matter. She'd found her adventure, her lover. She'd found Jesse. And in his arms she was already home.